Age of Assassins

There was only one thing my master valued highly enough to betray everything she had lived and trained for. I did not see it then, but now I am older I see it as clearly as the nails on my fingers.

Me.

It was me.

Merela Karn, the greatest assassin I ever knew, gave up everything for me. Dead gods help me. I should have run.

For both of us.

I should have run.

Age of Assassins

RJ Barker

www.orbitbooks.net

ORBIT

First published in Great Britain in 2017 by Orbit

A CIP catalogue record for this book is available from the British Library.

ISBN 978-0-356-50854-2

Typeset in Apollo MT by Palimpsest Book Production Limited,
Falkirk, Stirlingshire

Printed in Great Britain by Clays Ltd, Elcograf S.p.A.

Papers used by Orbit are from well-managed forests
and other responsible sources.

Orbit
An imprint of
Little, Brown Book Group
Carmelite House
50 Victoria Embankment
London EC4Y 0DZ

An Hachette UK Company
www.hachette.co.uk

www.orbitbooks.net

For Lindy and Rook, who are all my best things

Prologue

Darik the smith was last among the desolate. The Landsman made him kneel with a kick to the back of his knees, forcing his head down so he knelt and stared at the line between the good green grass and the putrid yellow desert of the sourlands. Nothing grew in the sourlands. A sorcerer had taken the life of the land for his own magics many years ago, before Darik's parents were born, and only death was found there now. A foul-smelling wind blew his long brown hair into his face and, ten paces away, the first of the desolate was weeping as she waited for the blade – Kina the herdsgirl, no more than a child and the only other from his village. The voice of the Landsman, huge and strong in his grass-green armour, was surprisingly gentle as he spoke to her, a whisper no louder than the knife leaving its scabbard.

"Shh, child. Soonest done, soonest over," he said, and then the knife bit into her neck and her tears were stilled for ever. Darik glanced between the bars of his hair and saw Kina's body jerking as blood fountained from her neck and made dark, twisting, red patterns on the stinking yellow ground – silhouettes of death and life.

He had hoped to marry Kina when she came of age.

Darik was cold but it was not the wind that made him shiver; he had been cold ever since the sorcerer hunters had come for him. It was the first time in fifteen years of life that the sweat on his skin wasn't because of the fierce heat of the forge. The moisture that had clung to him since was a different sweat, a new sweat, a cold frightened animal sweat that hadn't stopped since they locked the shackles on his wrists. It seemed so long ago now.

The weeks of marching across the Tired Lands had been like a dream but, looking back, the most dreamlike moment of all was that moment when they had called his name. He hadn't been surprised – it was as if he'd sold himself to a hedge spirit long ago and had been waiting for someone to come and collect on the debt his whole life.

"Shh, child. Soonest done, soonest over." The knife does its necessary work on another of the desolate, and a second set of bloody sigils spatters out on the filthy yellow ground. Is there meaning there? Is there some message for him? In this place between life and death, close to embracing the watery darkness that swallowed the dead gods, are they talking to him?

Or is it just blood?

And death.

And fear.

"Shh, child. Soonest done, soonest over." The next one begs for life in the moments before the blade bites. Darik doesn't know that one's name, never asked him, never saw the point because once you're one of the desolate you're dead. There is no way out, no point running. The brand on your forehead shows you for what they think you are – magic user, destroyer, abomination, *sorcerer*. You're only good for bleeding out on the dry dead earth, a sacrifice of blood to heal the land. No one will hide you, no one will pity you when magic has made the dirt so weak people can barely feed their children. There is the sound of choking, fighting, begging as the knife does its work and the thirsty ground drinks the life stolen from it.

Does Darik feel something in that moment of death? Is there a vibration? Is there a twinge that runs from Darik's knees, up his legs through his blood to squirm in his belly? Or is that only fear?

"Shh, child. Soonest done, soonest over."

The slice, the cough, blood on the ground, and this time it is unmistakable – a *something* that shoots up through his body. It sets his teeth on edge, it makes the roots of his hair hurt. Everything starts changing around him: the land is a lens and he is its focus, his mind a bright burning spot of light. What is this feeling? What is it? Were they right?

Are they right?

A hand on his forehead.

Dark worms moving through his flesh.

The hiss of the blade leaving the scabbard.

He sweats, hot as any day at the forge.

His head pulled back, his neck stretched.

Closing his eyes, he sees a world of silvered lines and shadows.

The cold touch of the blade against his neck.

A pause, like the hiss of hot metal in water, like the moment before the geyser of scorching steam hisses out around his hand and the blade is set.

The sting of a sharp edge against his skin.

And the grass is talking, and the land is talking, and the trees are talking, and all in a language he cannot understand but at the same time he knows exactly what is being said. Is this what a hedging lord sounds like?

The creak of leather armour.

"I will save you." Is it the voice of Fitchgrass of the fields?
"No!"

"Only listen . . ." This near the souring is it Coil the yellower?

"Shh, shh, child." The Landsman's voice, soothing, calming. "Soonest done, soonest over."

"I can save you." Too far from the rivers for Blue Watta.

"No." But Darik's word is a whisper drowned in fear of the approaching void. Time slows further as the knife slices though his skin, cutting through layer after layer in search of the black vessels of his life.

"*Let me save you.*" *Or is it the worst of all of them? Is it Dark Ungar speaking?*

"No," he says. But the word is weak and the will to fight is gone.

"*Let us?*"

"Yes!"

An explosion of . . . of?

Something.

Something he doesn't know or understand but he recognises it – it has always been within him. It is something he's fought, denied, run from. A familiar voice from his childhood, the imaginary friend that frightened his mother and she told him to forget so he pushed it away, far away. But now, when he needs it the most, it is there.

The blade is gone from his neck.

He opens his eyes.

The world is out of focus – a haze of yellows – and a high whine fills his ears the way it would when his father clouted him for "dangerous talk". The green grass beneath Darik's knees is gone, replaced by yellow fronds that flake away at his touch like morning ash in the forge. He stares at his hands. They are the same – the same scars, the same half-healed cuts and nicks, the same old burns and calluses.

Around him is perfect half-circle of dead grass, as if the sourlands have taken a bite out of the lush grasslands at their edge

His wrists are no longer bound in cold metal.

Is he lost, gone? Has he made a deal with something terrible? But it doesn't feel like that; it feels like this was something in him, something that has always been in him, just waiting for the right moment.

He can feel the souring like an ache.

There had been four Landsmen to guard the five desolate. Now the guards are blurry smears of torn, angular metal, red flesh and sharp white bone.

Darik rubbed his eyes and forced himself up, staggering like a man waking from too long a sleep. A movement in the corner of his eye pulled at his attention. One of the Landsmen was still alive, on his back and trying to scuttle away on his elbows as Darik approached. The smith knelt by the Landsman and placed his big hands on either side of his head. It would be easy to finish him, just a single twist of his big arms and the Landsman's neck would snap like a charcoaled stick. He willed his arms to move but instead found himself staring at the Landsman. Not much older than he was and scared, so scared. The Landsman's lips were moving and at first the only sound is the high whine of the world, then the words come like the approaching thunder of a mount's feet as it gallops towards him.

"I'msorryI'msorryI'msorryI'msorry . . ."

"It's wrong," Darik said, "this is all wrong," but the Landsman's eyes were far away, lost in fear and past understanding. His mouth moving.

". . . I'msorryI'msorryI'msorry . . ."

Darik stared a little longer, the killing muscles in his arms tensing. Now his vision had cleared he saw beyond the broken bodies of the other Landsmen to the shattered corpses of those who had died beside him. They had been picked up and tossed away on the winds of his fury.

Darik leaned in close to the Landsman.

"This has to stop," he said, and let go of the man's head. The words kept coming.

". . . I'msorryI'msorryI'msorry."

He could see Kina's corpse, dead at the hand of the knights then shredded into a red mess by his magic.

"I forgive you," said Darik through tears. The Landsman slumped to the floor, eyes wide in shock as the smith walked away.

Inside the thick muscles of Darik's arms black veins are screaming.

Chapter 1

We were attempting to enter Castle Maniyadoc through the night soil gate and my master was in the sort of foul mood only an assassin forced to wade through a week's worth of shit can be. I was far more sanguine about our situation. As an assassin's apprentice you become inured to foulness. It is your lot.

"Girton," said Merela Karn. That is my master's true name, though if I were to refer to her as anything other than "Master" I would be swiftly and painfully reprimanded. "Girton," she said, "if one more king, queen or any other member of the blessed classes thinks a night soil gate is the best way to make an unseen entrance to their castle, you are to run them through."

"Really, Master?"

"No, not really," she whispered into the night, her breath a cloud in the cold air. "Of course not really. You are to politely suggest that walking in the main gate dressed as masked priests of the dead gods is less conspicuous. Show me a blessed who doesn't know that the night soil gate is an easy way in for an enemy and I will show you a corpse."

"You have shown me many corpses, Master."

"Be quiet, Girton."

My master is not a lover of humour. Not many assassins are; it is a profession that attracts the miserable and the melancholic. I would never put myself into either of those categories, but I was bought into the profession and did not join by choice.

"Dead gods in their watery graves!" hissed my master into the night. "They have not even opened the grate for us." She swung herself aside whispering, "Move, Girton!" I slipped and slid crabwise on the filthy grass of the slope running from the river below us up to the base of the towering castle walls. Foulness farted out of the grating to join the oozing stream that ran down the motte and joined the river.

A silvery smudge marred the riverbank in the distance; it looked like a giant paint-covered thumb had been placed over it. In the moonlight it was quite beautiful, but we had passed near as we sneaked in, and I knew it was the same livid yellow as the other sourings which scarred the Tired Lands. There was no telling how old this souring was, and I wondered how big it had been originally and how much blood had been spilled to shrink it to its present size. I glanced up at the keep. This side had few windows and I thought the small souring could be new, but that was a silly, childish thought. The blades of the Landsmen kept us safe from sorcerers and the magic which sucked the life from the land. There had been no significant magic used in the Tired Lands since the Black Sorcerer had risen, and he had died before I had been born. No, what I saw was simply one of many sores on the land – a place as dead as the ancient sorcerer who made it. I turned from the souring and did my best to imagine it wasn't there, though I was sure I could smell it, even over the high stink of the night soil drain.

"Someone will pay for arranging this, Girton, I swear," said my master. Her head vanished into the darkness as she bobbed down to examine the grate once more. "This is sealed with a simple five-lever lock." She did not even breathe heavily despite holding her entire weight on one arm and one leg jammed into stonework the black of old wounds. "You can open this, Girton. You need as much practice with locks as you can get."

"Thank you, Master," I said. I did not mean it. It was cold, and a lock is far harder to manipulate when it is cold. And when it is covered in shit.

Unlike my master, I am no great acrobat. I am hampered by a clubbed foot, so I used my weight to hold me tight against the grating even though it meant getting covered in filth. On the stone columns either side of the grate the forlorn remains of minor gods had been almost chipped away. On my right only a pair of intricately carved antlers remained, and on my left a pair of horns and one solemn eye stared out at me. I turned from the eye and brought out my picks, sliding them into the lock with shaking fingers and feeling within using the slim metal rods.

"What if there are dogs, Master?"

"We kill them, Girton."

There is something rewarding in picking a lock. Something very satisfying about the click of the barrels and the pressure vanishing as the lock gives way to skill. It is not quite as rewarding done while a castle's toilets empty themselves over your body, but a happy life is one where you take your pleasures where you can.

"It is open, Master."

"Good. You took too long."

"Thank you, Master." It was difficult to tell in the darkness, but I was sure she smiled before she nodded me forward. I hesitated at the edge of the pitch-dark drain.

"It looks like the sort of place you'd find Dark Ungar, Master."

"The hedgings are just like the gods, Girton – stories to scare the weak-minded. There's nothing in there but stink and filth. You've been through worse. Go."

I slithered through the gate, managing to make sure no part of my skin or clothing remained clean, and into the tunnel that led through the keep's curtain wall. Somewhere beyond I could hear the lumpy splashes of night soil being shovelled into the stream that ran over my feet. The living classes in the villages keep their piss and night soil and sell it to the tanneries and dye makers, but the blessed classes are far too grand for that, and their castles shovel their filth out into the rivers — as if to gift it to the populace. I have crawled through plenty of filth in my fifteen years, from the thankful, the living and the blessed; it all smells equally bad.

Once we had squeezed through the opening we were able to stand, and my master lit a glow-worm lamp, a small wick that burns with a dim light that can be amplified or shut off by a cleverly interlocking set of mirrors. Then she lifted a gloved hand and pointed at her ear.

I listened.

Above the happy gurgle of the stream running down the channel — water cares nothing for the medium it travels through — I heard the voices of men as they worked. We would have to wait for them to move before we could proceed into the castle proper, and whenever we have to wait I count out the seconds the way my master taught me — one, my master. Two, my master. Three, my master — ticking away in my mind like the balls of a water clock as I stand idle, filth swirling round my ankles and my heart beating out a nervous tattoo.

You get used to the smell. That is what people say.

It is not true.

Eight minutes and nineteen seconds passed before we finally heard the men laugh and move on. Another signal from my master and I started to count again. Five minutes this time. Human nature being the way it is you cannot guarantee someone will not leave something and come back for it.

When the five minutes had passed we made our way up the night soil passage until we could see dim light dancing on walls caked with centuries of filth. My own height plus a half above us was the shovelling room. Above us the door creaked and then we heard footsteps, followed by voices.

". . . so now we're done and Alsa's in the heir's guard. Fancy armour and more pay."

"It's a hedging's deal. I'd sooner poke out my own eyes and find magic in my hand than serve the fat bear, he's a right yellower."

"Service is mother though, aye?"

Laughter followed. My master glanced up through the hole, chewing on her lip. She held up two fingers before speaking in the Whisper-That-Flies-to-the-Ear so only I could hear her.

"Guards. You will have to take care of them," she said. I nodded and started to move. "Don't kill them unless you absolutely have to."

"It will be harder."

"I know," she said and leaned over, putting her hands together to make a stirrup. "But I will be here."

I breathe out.

I breathe in.

I placed my foot on her hands and, with a heave, she propelled me up and into the room. I came out of the hole landing with my back to the two men. *Seventeenth iteration: the Drunk's Reversal.* Rolling forward, twisting and coming up facing guards dressed in kilted skirts, leather helms and poorly kept-up boiled-leather chest pieces splashed with red paint. They stared at me dumbly, as if I were the hedging lord Blue Watta appearing from the deeps. Both of them held clubs, though they had stabswords at their sides. I wondered if they were here to guard against rats rather than people.

"Assassin?" said the guard on the left. He was smaller than his friend, though both were bigger than me.

"Aye," said the other, a huge man. "Assassin." His grip shifted on his club.

They should have gone for the door and reinforcements.

My hand was hovering over the throwing knives at my belt in case they did. Instead the smaller man grinned, showing missing teeth and black stumps.

"I imagine there's a good price on the head of an assassin, Joam, even if it's a crippled child." He started forward. The bigger man grinned and followed his friend's lead. They split up to avoid the hole in the centre of the room and I made my move. *Second iteration: the Quicksteps*. Darting forward, I chose the smaller of the two as my first target – the other had not drawn his blade. He swung at me with his club and I stepped backwards, feeling the draught of the hard wood through the air. He thrust with his dagger but was too far away to reach my flesh. When his swipe missed he jumped back, expecting me to counter-attack, but I remained unmoving. All I had wanted was to get an idea of his skill before I closed with him. He did not impress me, his friend impressed me even less; rather than joining the attack he was watching, slack-jawed, as if we put on a show for him.

"Joam," shouted my opponent, "don't be just standing there!" The bigger man trundled forward, though he was in no hurry. I didn't want to be fighting two at the same time if I could help it so decided to finish the smaller man quickly. *First iteration: the Precise Steps*. Forward into the range of his weapons. He thrust with his stabsword. *Ninth iteration: the Bow*. Middle of my body bowing backwards to avoid the blade. With his other hand he swung his club at my head. I ducked. As his arm came over my head I grabbed his elbow and pushed, making him lose his balance, and as he struggled to right himself I found purchase on the rim of his chest piece. *Tenth iteration: the Broom*. Sweeping my leg round I knocked his feet from under him. With a push I sent him flailing into the hole so he cracked his head on the edge of it on his way down.

I turned to his friend, Joam.

Had the dead gods given Joam any sense he would have

seen his friend easily beaten and made for the door. Instead, Joam's face had the same look on it I had seen on a bull as it smashed its head against a wall in a useless attempt to get at a heifer beyond – the look of something too stupid and angry to know it was in a fight it couldn't win.

"I'm a kill you, assassin," he said and lumbered slowly forward, smacking his club against his hand. I had no time to wait for him; the longer we fought the more likely it was that someone would hear us and bring more guards. I jumped over the hole and landed behind Joam. He turned, swinging his club. *Fifteenth Iteration: the Oar.* Bending at the hip and bringing my body down and round so it went under his swing. At the lowest point I punched forward, landing a solid blow between Joam's legs. He screeched, dropping his weapon and doubling over. With a jerk I brought my body up so the back of my skull smashed into his face, sending the big man staggering back, blood streaming from a broken nose. It was a blow that would have felled most, but Joam was a strong man. Though his eyes were bleary and unfocused he still stood. *Eighteenth iteration: the Water Clock.* I ran at him, grabbing his thick belt and using it as a fulcrum to swing myself round and up so I could lock my legs around his throat. Joam's hand grasped blindly for the blade at his hip. I drew it and tossed it away before he reached it. His hands spidered down my body searching for and locking around my throat, but Joam's strength, though great, was fleeing as he choked. I wormed my thumb underneath his fingers and grabbed his little finger and third finger, breaking them. I expected a grunt of pain as he let go of me, but the man was already unconscious and fell back, sliding down the wall to the floor. I squirmed free of his weight and checked he was still breathing. Once I was sure he was alive I rolled his body over to the hole.

"Look out, Master," I whispered. Then pushed the limp body into the hole. I took a moment, a second only, to check and see if I had been heard, then I knelt to pull up my master.

She was not heavy.

For the first time I had a moment to look around, and the room we stood in was a strange one. Small in length and breadth but far higher than it needed to be. I barely had time for that thought to form on the surface of my mind before my master shouted,

"This is wrong, Girton! Back!"

I jumped for the grate, as did she, but before either of us fell back into the midden a hidden gate clanked into place across the hole. Four pikers squeezed into the room, dressed in boiled-leather armour, wide-brimmed helms and skirts sewn with chunks of metal. Below the knee they wore leather greaves with strips of metal cut into the material to protect their shins, and as they brandished their weapons they assaulted us with the smell of unwashed bodies and the rancid fat they used to oil their armour. In such a small room their stink was a more effective weapon than the pikes; they would have been far better bringing long shields and short swords. They would realise quickly enough.

"Hostages," said my master as I reached for the blade on my back.

I let go of the hilt.

And was among the guards. Bare-handed and violent. The unmistakable fleshy crack of a nose being broken followed by a man squealing like a gelded mount came from behind me as my master engaged the pikers. I shoved one pike aside to get in close and drove my elbow into the throat of the man in front of me – not a killing blow but enough to put the man out of action. The second piker, a woman, was off balance, and it was easy enough for me to twist her so she was held in front of me like a shield with my razor-tipped thumbnail at her throat. My master had her piker in a similar embrace. Blood ran down his face and another guard lay unconscious on the floor next to the man I had elbowed in the throat.

"Open the grating," she shouted to the walls. "Let us go or we will kill these guards."

The sound of a man laughing came from above, and the reason for the room's height became clear as murder holes opened in the walls. Each was big enough for a crossbow to be pointed down at the room and eight weapons threatened us with taut bows and stubby little bolts which would pass straight through armour.

"Open the grate. We will leave and your troops will live," shouted my master.

More laughter.

"I think not," came a voice. Male, sure of himself, amused. *One, my master. Two, my master . . .*

The twang of crossbows, echoing through the silence like the sound of rocks falling down a cliff face will echo through a quiet wood. Bolts buried themselves in the unconscious guards on the floor in front of us. Laughter from above.

"Together," hissed my master, and I pulled my guard round so that we hid behind the bodies of our prisoners.

"Let me go, please," said my guard, her voice shivering like her body. "Aydor doesn't care about us guards. He's worse than Dark Ungar and he'll kill us all if he wants yer."

"Quiet!" I said and pushed my razor-edged thumb harder against her neck, making the blood flow. I felt warmth on my thigh as her bladder let go in fear.

"Look at them," came from above. "Cowardly little assassins hiding behind troops brave enough to face death head on like real warriors."

"Coil's piss, no," murmured the guard in my arms.

"Your loyalty will be remembered," came the voice again. "No!"

Crossbows spat out bolts and the woman in my arms stiffened and arched in my embrace. One moment she was alive and then, almost magically, a bolt was vibrating in front of my nose like a conduit for life to flee her body.

"Master?" I said. Her guard was spasming as he died, a bolt sticking out of his neck and blood spattering onto the floor. "They are playing with us, Master."

Laughter from above and the crossbows fired again, thudding bolts into the body in my arms and making me cringe down further behind the corpse. The laughter stopped and a second voice, female, commanding, said something, though I could not make out what it was. Then the woman shouted down to us.

"We only want you, Merela Karn. Lay on the floor and make no move to harm those who come for you or I will have your fellow shot."

Did something cross my master's face at hearing her name spoken by a stranger? Was she surprised? Did her dark skin grey slightly in shock? I had never, in all our years together, seen my master shocked. Though I was sure she was known throughout the Tired Lands — Merela Karn, the best of the assassins — few would know her face or that she was a woman.

"Drop the body, Girton," she said, letting hers fall face down on the tiled and bloody floor. "This is not what it seems."

As always I did as I was told, though I braced every muscle, waiting for the bite of a bolt which never came.

"Lie on the floor, both of you," said the male voice from above.

We did as instructed and the room was suddenly buzzing with guards. I took a few kicks to the ribs, and luckily for the owners of those feet I could not see their faces to mark them for my attention later. We were quickly bound — well enough for amateurs — and hauled to our feet in front of a man as big as any I have seen, though he was as much fat as muscle.

"Shall I take their masks off?" asked a guard to my left.

"No. Take any weapons from them and put them in the cells. Then you can all go and wash their shit off yourselves and forget this ever happened."

"I think it's your shit, actually," I said. My master stared at the floor, shaking her head, and the man backhanded me across the face. It was a poor blow. Children have hurt me more with harsh words.

"You should remember," he said, "we don't need you; we only need her."

Before I could reply bags were put over our heads for a swift, dark and rough trip to the cells. *Five hundred paces against the clock walking across stone. Turn left and twenty paces across thick carpet. Down two sets of spiral stairs into a place that stinks of human misery.*

Dungeons are usually full of the flotsam of humanity, but this one sounded empty of prisoners apart from my master and I. We were placed in filthy cells, still tied though the bonds did not hold me long. Once free I removed the sack from my head and coughed out a wire I had half swallowed and had been holding in my gullet. It was a simple job to get my arm through the barred window of my door and pick the lock. Outside was a surprisingly wide area with a table, chairs and braziers, cold now. I tiptoed to my master's cell door.

"Master, I am out."

"Well done, Girton, but go back to your cell," she said softly. "Be calm. Wait."

I stood before the door of her cell for a moment. An assassin cannot expect much mercy once captured. A blood gibbet or maybe a public dissection. Something drawn out and painful always awaited us if we were caught, unless another assassin got to us first – my master says the loose association that makes up the Open Circle guards its secrets jealously. It would have been easy enough for me to slip into the castle proper and find some servant. I could take his clothes and become anonymous and from there I could escape out into the country. I knew the assassins' scratch language and could find the drop boxes to pick up work. Many would have done that in my situation.

But my master had told me to go back to my cell and wait, so I did. I locked the door behind me and slipped my sack and bonds back on. I imagined a circle filled with air, then let the top quarter of the circle open and breathed the air out. I let go of fear and became nothing but an instrument, a weapon.

I waited.

"One, my master. Two, my master. Three, my master . . ."

Chapter 2

I was at twelve thousand nine hundred my-masters.

The man that came for me did not even glance through the bars to check on me before coming in, which made me sure he must be one of the blessed. Few others in the Tired Lands are so careless, or sure, of their lives.

"So," he said, standing in the door and blocking the meagre light with his bulk, "still here, assassin?" I said nothing. Nothing is always the best way to go. It is especially infuriating for the blessed, who expect the world to jump at their whims. "I asked you a question," he said. I still said nothing and would continue to unless they chose to torture me. Then I would say an awful lot of words while still saying nothing.

The man took another step forward, placing his booted feet carefully to avoid the filth in the cell. I could see a few feet of cross-hatched world through the rough weave of the sacking over my face, and he wore good boots, soft leather uppers and thick soles. My clubbed foot often pains me, and I have become a connoisseur of the cobbler's arts. I am often jealous of good boots.

He was the same man who had ordered our masks kept on while his soldiers kicked me in the ribs. He stared at me then looked me up and down before removing the sack from my head and pulling down the mask that covered my nose and mouth. *When I kill you*, I thought, *I will have your boots*.

"I don't think you are an assassin," he said. "The other one maybe, but you?" He had the breath of the blessed, thick with halitosis after too much good food and high with the scent of clove oil to dull the pain of bad teeth. He spat on the floor by my club foot and leaned in close to whisper theatrically in my ear, "What sort of assassin are you? A crippled child makes a poor killer."

"Maybe you are right," I whispered into his ear. "If I were a true assassin I am sure I could slip my bonds and cut your throat as simply as I could kiss your cheek." I moved my head and let my lips brush against the stubble of his chin. He leaped back like a scalded lizard, and I saw the fear in his eyes and, a moment later, the anger.

He beat me then. He used a small wooden club, and though he was no artist he made up for his lack of skill with enthusiasm. As he beat me I reflected on the fact that although, generally, silence is the better option, sometimes it is good to talk. After the beating he replaced my mask and sacking hood then dragged me through the castle.

To the cell door and out to the left and thirty paces on. Up four tightly spiralling staircases. Along an echoing hall running westward and up two more flights of stairs into a large room where the tramp of my feet on the stone floor echoes from a high ceiling. Up two very short sets of wooden stairs to be placed on some sort of temporary wooden floor that echoes hollowly under my feet – a mirror of the echoes from above a moment ago – and I feel vertigo, as if I am suddenly upside down.

A noose is placed around my neck.

Ice runs in my veins.

A scaffold. I was on a hangman's scaffold and as afraid of Xus the god of death as any of those I had brought his unwelcome gift to.

My hood came off.

A vast meeting hall before me, one that had been built before magic and its sorcerers cursed us with the sourings, in a time when people had plenty and great advances were made. The room was four, maybe five times the height of a man, and the black stone walls had been plastered and painted white. In many places the plaster was flaking and yellowed, and no doubt the huge and colourful tapestries that gently rippled in an errant breeze covered more damage. The weak sun of yearsage streamed in through crystal windows set high in the walls, trapping dust, which drifted slowly in the sunlight like insects caught in honey. I felt like an actor in a theatre.

My master and I often travelled as jesters as they are welcomed by the lowest and the highest of the land. Tradition has it a jester does not speak to those who are their betters, so they are often forgotten about and a jester can move unremarked upon through a castle or village. At the same time a jester is a status symbol, and my master's Death's Jester is famous and she, as a jester rather than an assassin, is highly sought after. I have considerable talent myself. My clubbed foot makes me a second-level jester – a clown of deformity – but despite being one of the mage-bent, my foot twisted by the sickness wrought by sorcerers on the land, I understand wordplay and I tumble almost as well as any other. There are very few things in my life as joyous as bringing joy and my dreams are often of the theatre, of letting go of the hand of Xus, the god of death, and walking out to entertain upon the boards and receive the appreciative hand of the crowd.

But in my dreams I do not wear a noose around my neck or play to a grim-faced audience of two – one my master, bound to a chair. The other a woman of similar age but dressed finely in flowing jerkins and gold-threaded trews who holds my master at swordpoint. Both are illuminated by a shaft of light and utterly still like players before the opening of their performance. I wondered if this had been done on purpose. If so there could be no doubt our captors had a flare for the dramatic.

"Aydor," said the woman, her voice husky as if she were aroused, "make sure the rope is tight around the boy's neck, or Merela may not believe I am serious." The noose around my neck snaked shut and the air in the room thickened. "Good boy," she said.

Aydor's foul breath enveloped me as he whispered in my ear.

"You'll regret that kiss you gave me when you're begging for air, mage-bent. No one treats me like a woman; I'm the king-in-waiting."

The woman turned and tore off my master's mask. "So, Merela Karn —" she walked around my master's chair "— who did you come here to kill?"

There was silence then. A long silence. The sort of silence used to underline the drama in the bad theatre pieces that were performed at Festival, the great travelling trade caravan that toured the Tired Lands. This was a bad thing for me as a cripple. A fast rule of poor Tired Lands drama is that the hero's well-meaning cripple friend dies as early as possible in the first act. This gives the hero a reason to continue; it provides them with some impetus. I had never taken the common hack playwrights' work personally until I stood on a stage with a noose around my neck.

"You know me, Merela," said the woman. "You know you cannot lie about your trade. So spare your apprentice some pain. Tell me who you came to kill."

My master said nothing.

"I am the queen now, Merela. Adran Mennix, queen of the whole of Maniyadoc and the Long Tides. You know that; you helped put me on my throne. Aren't you proud of that?" She walked around my master, who ignored her, staring fixedly forward. "Do we not have some bond, Merela? Does our past not tie us together?" She knelt, putting a hand on my master's leg.

My master said nothing and the queen remained kneeling,

searching her face, then straightened. When she spoke again there was a yearning note in her voice.

"Is there nothing there, Merela? Not even in in your code of murder, that says we are bonded?"

My master said nothing.

"Very well, you were always stubborn. Let's see if we can find something you do care about," said the queen. "Aydor, pull on the rope."

"Wait." My master spoke in nothing more than a whisper but it filled the entire room. It was a skill she had taught me in my tenth year, a way of speaking from the bottom of your stomach rather than your throat that fills your blood with energetic fizzing and a room with sound. The queen, at that moment gesturing towards me, gave an imperious smile and let her hand drop. Aydor, who I had decided must be her son as there was a definite resemblance, gave the rope a spiteful tug that had me standing on my tiptoes to avoid choking. I was desperate to hear what was being said by this woman who called herself a queen. My master had always been tight-lipped about her past, and now it turned out she knew one of the most powerful women in the Tired Lands, Queen Adran Mennix of Maniyadoc. If I was about to die then I would at least try to die with my curiosity sated.

"Very well, Merela, I will wait upon you again," said the queen with a mocking bow. "I hope you understand what an honour that is now."

"We were invited here, Queen Adran," said my master, "invited to meet a contact in the castle, and they would tell us our target."

"You came, to my castle, to kill. Even though we were friends once?"

"Yes, I came because we were friends. Once."

"And do you know who brought you here?"

"We both know that."

"Do we?" said Adran.

"Of course we do. You brought us here."

Once again the dramatic silence. Though I knew my master was right because she is always right. I also knew that I had been the only person in the room in the dark about this as Aydor let the tension on the rope slacken slightly in surprise at being found out.

"And," said the queen quietly, "what makes you think that?"

"A night-soil drain designed as a trap. The insistence on our coming through the night soil gate when we all know the blessed keep them watched. And lastly, and most obviously, that I was asked for by my full name."

"Is that so strange?"

"Yes, the number of people who know my real name and what I do can be counted on the fingers of one hand." She looked up then, a big smile on her face. I do not like that smile. It generally bodes nothing good. "All of them are in this room."

The rope creaked, tightening around my neck as Queen Adran stared at my master. Then the queen laughed. She had a beautiful laugh, a chiming girlish laugh that was full of life and pleasure.

"Sharp as ever, Merela. I knew I was right to bring you here."

"And you, Adran, are as willing to make things needlessly complex as ever. You could have asked to see me."

"You would not have come, Merela. Not for what I want."

"And that is?"

"Your advice. Your help."

"Why?" My master tipped her head to one side. She seemed genuinely confused.

"My son."

"Son?" My master raised an eyebrow. "I thought you only ever wanted daughters?" I felt Aydor's muscles twitch through the tension of the rope.

"What was it you always said, Merela? We work with what we have?" The noose tightened another notch. "Nonetheless, I love my son and someone in the court wishes to assassinate him." She nodded at Aydor, a man with breath only a mother could love.

"Of course they do," said my master, and the rope around my neck tightened again, forcing sweat out of my pores.

"Then you know about this? For sure?" Adran – all angles and worry.

I am an assassin, Adran—"

"Queen Adran," she snapped.

"I am an assassin, Queen Adran –" though she used the title my master did not make it sound respectful "– and your son is the heir to the throne so at least half, if not more, of your court would see profit in his corpse. So if your question is 'Does someone want to see your son dead?' the answer is almost definitely yes." Aydor did not take kindly to this news and I felt his indignation in increments as the noose closed further around my windpipe. "The question you should be asking, Queen Adran, is if anyone has the spine to follow through on their desire."

Adran lowered herself to a crouch so she could look into my master's face.

"Or maybe that is a question that you –" she poked my master in the chest "– you, Merela Karn, should be asking."

"Me?" It is rare I hear my master sound surprised but she was then. "Why would I do that?"

"Who better to stop an assassination than an assassin?"

"Surely the king has a Heartblade for such things?"

I waited for Adran to reply. It is normal for any of the high blessed to have a Heartblade, a man or woman trained to stop assassins.

"He did have. He died protecting Aydor, though the castle thinks he fell down the stairs, drunk. After all, if it was common knowledge an assassin was already here, you would not have come. But now Festival is coming with all its trade and train, they will flood my castle with people, and . . ."

"You have no replacement to watch your son?"

Adran stared at my master, a smile playing about her lips.

"I have someone to watch him, but not to find whoever ordered this. I want you for that."

"Me?" said my master.

Adran turned to me.

"Your boy is quite talented – the way he dealt with those two guards was impressive. I would have preferred he killed them but that is being dealt with." She stared at me then smiled the way a cat smiles before it pounces on a mouse and turned back to my master. "Let us talk in private, Merela. Aydor!" she shouted. "Hoist the boy!"

What was said between them then I missed as I was choking on the rope. I do not know how long they talked, only that it was for less than seven minutes as I did not lose consciousness and that is how long I can survive on one breath. My eyes streamed as they started from my head, and my tongue swelled to fill my mouth while my master and Queen Adran talked.

As darkness started to close around me an agreement was reached between them. Aydor let go of the rope, and I fell to the floor of the scaffold gasping for air while he laughed, calling me a useless cripple as he slit the ropes binding my hands.

"Go talk to your mistress," he said. "Learn your duties."

By the time I had limped over to my master she was also free. She shepherded me away from the queen and her sewer-breathed son.

"We are to find out if there is a conspiracy to assassinate the heir and, if so, we are to stop it." She spoke loudly enough for the queen to hear.

"But the Open Circle . . . The other assassins will . . ." I said, following her lead and keeping my voice audible.

"Don't worry about them. I have given my word to help. We will have to answer for it."

"Why, Master?" My question was genuine. She did not give her word lightly nor, in my experience, ever go back on it.

"The queen says that if I do not do as she wishes she will expose me. Tell people that the great Merela is a woman and that I am a Death's Jester."

"But then—"

"They will wipe every Death's Jester from the Tired Lands, presuming they are all assassins, and an ancient art form will die. I cannot be the cause of that."

"But—"

"I have given my word, Girton." Sharp words meant to cut me off. She would talk no more about a thing once she was decided.

From the theatre we were taken by a slave to a room where two heated tubs of water waited so we could wash off the filth of the day. The slave did not stay. Adran clearly knew my master well enough to trust her word. I itched to know more but knew that questions would be as welcome as a sorcerer at a crop sowing.

The moment she was sure we were alone my master leaned over from her tub of water and said my name in a whisper.

"Listen to me, Girton. Adran wanted to lock you in a cell as surety. Her son has a warrior called Celot to guard him, and now she has me as well. They see no use for you. I have told them I need you to spy for me if I am to achieve their aims but you may walk away from here. Do you understand? I have given only my word and Adran cares nothing for you; she wants me. You may ensure your safety and slip away in the night and, if you do, you will go with my thanks for many good years of service."

"You mean leave you, Master?" I said.

"Yes. Adran did not get to be queen through kind words

and soft hands. She is not someone you wish to be mixed up with if it can be avoided."

"But what would I do without you, Master?"

"Kill people, Girton. It is what you are trained for."

"But I am still an apprentice."

"Do not play the fool," she said, angry. "You are fully ready and have been for long on long. You are twice the assassin of any other I have met."

"Even you, Master?"

"Girton," she said and shook her head, her anger passing as quickly as the warm breezes that bathe the land in years-life. She reached out and ran a cold wet finger down the line of my jaw. "You are always ready with a joke." She smiled then, her real smile, a small, fragile and seldom-seen thing. "Do not stay out of loyalty to me, Girton. We are not loyal; we are death bringers, cold people." Looking into her eyes I felt the same fear that I had felt when Aydor ap Mennix placed the noose around my neck, the same fear I had felt as a scared child when she first took my hand at the slave auctions. She had found me when I was six and been all I had known in the nine years since. She had trained me in weapons, nursed me through sicknesses, held me when I had nightmares of hedgings coming for me and taught me all I needed to pass in the world. "If I do what Adran wants, Girton, the Open Circle will never rest until I am punished for it. They may overlook your actions, at first, but the longer you stay the more they will see you as my accomplice. So if you stay, be sure."

"I am sure, Master."

Those words, spoken so quickly and without thought to anything but my own loss. I often wonder, now I am older and wiser, if I had paused and thought about what she was saying, if I had considered the facts behind the words, then would I have reconsidered? Because what I did not see, through the selfish eyes of my youth, was that Queen Adran

had only one thing she could hold over my master. It was
not her identity as a Death's Jester – a new disguise is ten
a penny to our kind. It was not that an art form would be
lost from the world. That would have saddened her – she
enjoyed the work – but she was always a cold realist.

No. There was only one thing my master valued highly
enough to betray everything she had lived and trained for.
I did not see it then, but now I am older I see it as clearly
as the nails on my fingers.

Me.

It was me.

Merela Karn, the greatest assassin I ever knew, gave up
everything for me. Dead gods help me. I should have run.

For both of us.

I should have run.

Interlude

This is a dream of what was.

He is scared.

He is always scared.

Today he is more scared than he has ever been because today everything changed.

His life, though it is settled and ordered, is not good and it has never been good, but he has never known any other life so he does not know his life is not good. He only exists. Slave-Father is quick with his whip, and the boy fears the whip, but are not all children whipped? And because he is crippled he is always the last to be fed. Always the smallest and hungriest of the slave pack, but is that not right? He is worth the least to Slave-Father so his life is hardest. He will not even make back his investment and maybe they will use him to train the war dogs.

He does not know what an investment is but he knows it is important to be able to make one and that he cannot.

There are other children in the flock, and they share an existence. They play in the same runs, sleep on the same sacks in the same corners. They eat the same meagre food at the same time every day. He is surrounded by people he knows. He knows which ones to avoid and which ones are safe to be around. He knows that if you escape the slavers will let the dogs rip you apart while the other children watch and scream. He even has friends – White-Hair and Blue-Eyes. He is content. There is comfort in routine, comfort in what he knows, comfort in the unchanging cycle of his life and the bars between him and the dogs.

But everything is changing and now he is scared. They are split into boys and girls, and Blue-Eyes cries for him when she is being taken away and loaded into a cart with high wooden sides. He can hear her shouting for him over the excited yapping of the dogs. "Club-Foot! Club-Foot!" Even after Slave-Father screams at her to stop, she carries on until the cart is out of sight.

They never whip the girls or the prettiest boys. He does not know why.

In the boys' cart he sits with White-Hair but they do not talk. They hold hands.

As the crowded cart sways it makes some of the other boys sick and the air is thick with the sweet smell of vomit and that makes more boys sick and by the time the journey is finished they are all covered in each other's sick. Men throw barrels of cold water over them. Big men, strange men who pull them from the cart, strip them and give them sacks, with holes cut for heads and arms to wear. He cannot see Slave-Father, and that makes him feel strange, like a flying lizard is trapped inside him with its wings fluttering against his ribcage. He worries because the flying lizards are delicate and their wings break easily. He does not like to hurt things.

He finds his friend, White-Hair, and they grasp hands so tightly it is hard to believe they will ever be separated.

But they are.

One of the big men tears them apart as if they are nothing but straw dolls. He walks away with White-Hair, pulling the small boy along by the top of his arm in a way that is obviously painful.

"Club-Foot! Club-Foot!" White-Hair can barely say his name for crying but the big man does not care. They are not mean, the men. They are not deliberately cruel. They do not want to hurt them but they do not want to *not* hurt them either. They treat the boys as if they are nothing more than sacks of grain rather than sacks of boy. And one by one they vanish. The children he has grown up with, huddled with in the cold of yearsdeath, starved with in lean times, and fought with constantly for enough to eat. One by one they are gone and he does not know where. He cannot see over the wooden walls.

Maybe they are being eaten. Like the dead are eaten.

Eventually, when the sun is going down and the high walls are throwing a cold shadow over him, it is his turn. A man takes him by the upper arm and drags him along through the dirt. The man smells of sweat. He takes him down a corridor in the high wooden walls. Someone has been sick halfway down it.

From the corridor he is taken out into a place. A place like no other he has ever seen. The low hot sun makes him squint, and he raises a thin arm to shield his eyes. Adults fill his vision, so many adults. More adults than he has fingers and toes. Then he sees the space beyond them. So much space.

He tries to run back to the walls.

The space is huge, impossibly huge. He can see further than he has ever imagined could exist. A never-ending plain of yellow earth and sky the colour of piss. It presses on him, it is a giant hand pushing him to the ground and drowning him in liquid fear, but the man does not care about scared boys, he does not even notice scared boys and he continues to drag him forward. They go up some wooden stairs onto a small platform and he is lifted up onto a small box garlanded with straw dolls. A rope is passed around his middle and they use the rope to hoist him up in the air. That is when he starts to scream, to scream and to kick and to wriggle. A small crowd of people watch as the momentum of his terror causes him to spin round on the rope. He sees that – all around in all directions – the land is flat and dead and like the carcass of an insect left to dry out in the sun. Dust blows in great curling clouds and gets in his eyes so he sees the world through a lens of tears and hurt. Despite the heat all the adults are wrapped in thick woollen cloaks with bright geometric designs on them. A man starts to speak and the words filter through his screaming and shouting.

"Last lot. I know he's a cripple but as you can see he's got plenty of fight in him. Bright too, from what I've heard." An angry wind pushes flapping triangles of blanket away from the bodies of those gathered. Members of the crowd start to drift away in ones and twos. "Ten bits, ten bits for a boy? I'll take ten bits for a boy," the man sings it out in a deep baritone. When there are no replies he drops a tone. "Eight bits for a boy? Five? Five bits for this boy, five bits for this boy, and we can all go home." A pause where the wind begins to howl. Small bits of wood and bones from food cartwheel across the dirt between the few woebegone tents. "Come on. Any less than five bits and I'm better off selling him to the swillers as animal feed." A pause and then the man sings out again: "Three bits. Three bits and I'll break even. No? Then the swillers' pigs will eat well tonight."

"Does he have a name?"

A female voice. He stops squirming and screaming in shock. He did not know girls became adults. And to ask his name? No adult has ever even hinted that they may have a name for him.

"We don't name goods," says the man.

"You want three for him?" she shouts.

"Aye. Three we ask."

"Then five," she says. "I'll pay five bits for him."

That is Merela Karn. Always there at the last minute. Always giving more than expected.

This is a dream of what was.

Chapter 3

I woke from a familiar dream to find I was alone in a strange room.

It took a moment for me to orientate myself. I was not a scared boy at a slave auction, nor was I an assassin's apprentice crossing the land to my next job. I was in a castle room with clean whitewashed walls, lying in the large soft bed I had slept in. A small pallet was also laid out, and my master had taken that as she preferred to sleep near the door. There was no sign she had ever slept on it: the sheets were smooth, the pillow uncreased. I was not surprised or worried at her absence as this was her way – she rarely slept more than a few hours each night. As I wiped sleep from my eyes she appeared at the door with water, bread and a porridge of grains and leftovers that was as filling as it was tasteless.

I think it was that morning, as the weak sun of yearsage shone in through the greased-paper window of our room, that I first realised my master was no longer invincible. Her hair, black and long, had streaks of grey in it and her dark skin, which gave her away as from somewhere outside the Tired Lands, had lines which gathered at the corners of her eyes when she was worried or thinking hard, and they no longer fled when she had made her decisions.

"Eat, Girton," she said. "Eat while I tell you what the day holds." I sat with her and took a bite of the bread. It was still warm. Good.

"How do we go about being Heartblades, Master? How do they train?"

"I suspect it is mostly through skills passed down, Girton. Just like it is with us."

"Do they fight like us?"

"I have never fought one."

"But if you did, Master?"

"The finest warriors are picked to train as Heartblades but, when I trained, my master told me the first Heartblades were picked from the assassins. So they probably do, yes, though you will see no tricks from them."

"Why?"

She stared at the wall, chewing thoughtfully, then spat out a bit of grit from the bread and changed the subject.

"Adran keeps her son's door guarded at all times. The only time he is alone is when he is under training, and even then he is surrounded by squires loyal to him and a warrior called Celot, the Heartblade Adran mentioned."

"Why can't he find who hired an assassin??"

"Celot is an extremely skilled warrior by all accounts, but Adran says he is not an intelligent one, and that is why she wants us." She picked more grit from her bread. "So, Girton, an exercise. If you were going to assassinate Prince Aydor ap Mennix, how would you do it?"

"Gladly," I said, rubbing at the bruises on my throat from the rope.

"Girton," said my master in reprimand.

"Very well." I forced down a spoonful of tasteless porridge, telling myself it was nothing more than fuel for my body and as such did not have to taste good. "Adran is right. I would come in with Festival and keep up whatever cover I had arranged for the length of it. Then I would find some menial job within the castle and work it until I became a familiar face and an opportunity presented itself or the queen relaxed her guard. Then I would act."

My master continued to stare at the wall and nod slowly as she chewed. "That may take a long time. Some would say it was lazy." She said the words quietly and without commitment, as a challenge.

"No, it is not lazy at all. It's common knowledge that Aydor has no children and the queen intends her son to marry the high king's sister. If I am killing to alter the line of succession there is no great pressure on me to act quickly so I wait. Patience is the assassin's greatest ally."

She smiled again, that yearslife shower smile – here and gone. "Patience is the assassin's greatest ally," she said. "That phrase is familiar."

"It is yours, Master."

She nodded and spat out another bit of grit. "So, if there is an assassin here, how do we stop her, my clever boy?"

"Easily." She looked up at me. Raised an eyebrow. "We leave a message in scratch for him to contact us and when he turns up we kill him." She nodded again and picked up her bowl of porridge, lifting a spoonful and then letting some fall, eyeing it warily before she started to eat. She did not look at me. "But we won't do that," I added.

"Why not?" she said, and sprinkled a little salt on her porridge in an attempt to make it taste of something.

"Stopping one assassin is pointless, and they may well not know who pays them anyway. Time is on the side of whoever wants Aydor dead. We stop one assassin and another will come. That one would not answer our scratch messages and will probably bring someone to deal with us."

"So?"

"We must stop the assassin but it is the client we need to find."

"Exactly."

"Good. I do not fancy handing over one of our own. What will Adran think though?"

She was quiet then. For a long time.

"I do not think Queen Adran cares about the assassin, Girton, not really. She would like her for an exhibition, I am sure, but Adran's real concern is in who has betrayed her." We carried on eating in silence for a while before my master spoke again. "For this we must be able to move among the blessed." She reached into her jacket and took out a roll of lambskin vellum. "This is for you."

I took it from her.

"Girton ap Gwynr," I read from the vellum. "I have acquired a family?"

"Yes, and a rather underhand one at that. I am not sure that Adran even knew the Gwynr estate was in her lands until I told her." My master's grasp of the geography of the Tired Lands is often astounding. "The Gwynr are perfect for us. They are a small house that keeps its head down. They live right on the edges of the eastern sourlands so most expect them to be poor, but . . ."

"They are not?"

"No, they are not at all. They breed mounts and own a tract of land which escaped the Black Sorcerer's war and is as fertile as any you'll find. They have not been paying their taxes, which will be unfortunate for them when Adran has finished with us, but for now they suit our purposes."

"They do?"

"Yes. You are to pass as the youngest son of the house and, with your club foot, the least valuable one." The words hurt because they contained the truth. "You have been given as hostage against tax owed to the king. While you are here you will train as a squire. Not a bad advancement for a boy with a bad foot, eh?"

"And you?"

"I am your family's valuable jester, sent as companion to their son in a faraway place and as an apology to King Doran ap Mennix for dodging his taxes."

"So you get to tread the boards while I get to be hit with swords?"

"Yes."

"Thank you, Master," I said.

"Do not sulk, it does not suit you. Besides, it is not all bad. You cannot be a squire without a mount so I have arranged to have Xus brought up for you." Xus was my master's mount and a finer beast you have never seen. "And remember, if Xus comes to harm I will take it out on your hide."

She meant that. She loved that mount but she knew I would hurt myself before I let Xus come to harm. He is the most magnificent of his kind. He stands as tall as a man at his shoulder and under his thick brown and white fur you can feel muscles so strong that the fighting claws on his three-toed feet leave divots in the earth – even when he only walks. His neck is sturdy and his noble head is long and thin, ending in a fuzzy nose and soft-lipped mouth with two well-sized downward-pointing tusks. His small black eyes have thick healthy lashes, and from his forehead sprouts a pair of spreading nine-point antlers, sharp as any knife. There are few things more exhilarating than to ride. The power, freedom and speed is like nothing else, and I was never happier than when my master let me ride Xus. I had begged for a mount of my own but she always said no. I was sure we could easily afford two mounts, but my master said that where one mount attracted comment, two would almost definitely attract the bandits who roamed the Tired Lands.

All in all it was not a bad morning. The priests tell us our world paused when the gods died. That the blessed shall remain blessed, the living shall remain in their trades and the thankful shall be slaves or so poor they starve to death in gutters until the land heals, the curse of magic is purged and the gods are reborn. It is not often that a sheet of vellum allows an ex-slave to defy the holy words of the priesthood and become a blessed squire.

As I walked to the armourer's my master took my arm and pulled me closer to her.

"Remember, your surname is now ap Gwynr. You are the youngest son of a family with a small longhouse; your father breeds mounts and has been shirking his taxes to the king. You are here as surety that this will not happen again."

"Yes, Master. I have read the vellum." She always becomes nervy and detail-obsessed at the start of a campaign.

"And when you are among the squires look to yourself." I knew what she meant. Though I am fifteen I look no more than fourteen at most. I was underfed as a young child as food is more valuable than slaves in the Tired Lands, my small stature and club foot do not make me appear much of a warrior, that is what makes me a good assassin. However, I would not be able to use my skills as too much martial prowess in an unschooled country landowner's son would appear suspicious.

"You mean I should let them beat me, Master?"

"Until it really matters, yes."

"Thank you, Master."

She squeezed my arm. "I must go now. We will not see much of each other. A jester would not be welcome among squires so I will be spending most of my time at court."

"Not with me?" I hated my voice then. It sounded like a childish whine and gave away the fear within. We always worked together. I could not remember a time when I had spent more than an hour without my master. She had always been at my back or I at hers.

"You are growing up, Girton. Soon you will be glad of time alone and some company your own age may do you good." She squeezed my arm again and left to change into her motley while I stood in the wide courtyard between the keep's outer door and the great gatehouse that led into the keepyard. In front of me the water clock, a towering contraption of steel tubes, silver balls, chiming bells and falling water, ticked out the minutes as I bunched my fists and told myself under my breath. "No longer the assassin. Now a lonely boy in a strange and dangerous place."

I walked through the postern door in the wooden gates of the gatehouse and into the keepyard, finding my way to the armourers by asking the servants, who busied themselves around the castle like lizards around a heap. The only people more plentiful than servants were the slaves, who moved with their heads down and tried to be noticed as little as possible. I could not ask them for directions as it would be considered odd for a squire, no matter how lowborn, to do anything but give orders to a slave.

The armourer was a stump of a man. He shared a similarity of face with Aydor, the heir, and a thickness of body, so he was probably one of King Doran ap Mennix's many by-blows. The king was in his fifties now, and sick, but he had been busy in his youth with any who offered. He probably pushed himself on many that did not offer too; it is the way of the blessed and one of the reasons why assassins are often seen as heroes by the poor. As the law stated only a legitimate royal child may inherit a throne, bastards, such as the armourer clearly was, offered no threat and were often taken on as servants, though just as often they were sold off as slaves. When I had been younger and found my training particularly taxing I had fantasised that I was a child of royalty and would be whisked away by royal guards on mounts with loyalty flags flying. Mentioning this was one of the rare things guaranteed to amuse my master.

"Armour?" said the man, rubbing a hand over a head shaved bald. He was no taller than me though he was twice as wide. Bastards clearly ate well here. "And weapons?" he said as if I had asked him to forge them for me there and then.

"Yes."

"Not got your own?"

"I am the youngest son and crippled." I kept my eyes on

the floor, acting the shy child away from home, ashamed of what he must admit. "My father saw no profit in spending money on armour for a cripple. I was bound for the priesthood."

"Your father sounds like a wise man," he said. "How old are you, boy? Thirteen?"

"Fourteen," I said, with the just the right amount of surliness for a boy who finds being considered younger than he is insulting to his manhood. It was not the most difficult part to play.

"Fourteen and small for it," he said, because some people love to labour a point. "I'll struggle to outfit you, child."

"The king has ordered me outfitted."

The armourer let out a sigh.

"Wait here." He vanished into his armoury. I did not follow as it is bad form to follow an armourer into his sanctum; they guard their charges more closely than a nervous mother guards a babe. The man returned with a net of armour which he dropped in front of me. "Should fit you," he grunted. "Try it."

It was very poor armour. Whoever had worn it before had not cared for it particularly well, if at all.

"There's blood and hair in the helmet." The armourer shrugged. "And a bit missing from the chest piece."

He picked up the piece I pointed at. Tired Lands armour is made of hundreds of small overlapping rectangular pieces enamelled in bright colours laid over leather and held together by wire in such a way to protect the wearer. This piece was harlequin armour, its many colours giving away that it had been cobbled together from bits of other armours. It did not hang well and the chest piece was full of gaps. "I can replace those," he said. "You can clean the helmet." I looked over the rest of the armour. The solid shoulder pieces and the fishscale over the leather arm guards were just passable. The leather greaves, inset with iron, and the skirt of canvas and chain were bearable but it was, by any stretch of the imagination, poor armour. I could not say so as the boy I was meant to be would not know enough of armour to know bad from good. In fact, a youngest son with a club foot would probably be over the moon just to receive something as expensive as a full set of armour.

"Gladly," I said and painted on a smile. "How do I clean it?"

The armourer shook his head. "They teach you nothing in the country? Sand and vinegar will remove rust and dirt, and you can get fat from the kitchen to help protect it from rusting further and grease the hard joints at shoulder and elbow. You'll be wanting swords too?"

"Yes."

He looked pained and returned to his room, coming back with two weapons – a longsword and a smaller stabsword, both weapons of very poor quality. "Here, boy, if you can carry them." He dropped them in front of me.

"No," I said. I may let him push his worst armour on me but not a poor blade. A good blade was far more important to me than armour. "I might only be from the country but I looked after my brother's blades. I need good blades, and these –" I nudged the weapons away from me with my foot "– are not good blades."

He gave me a smile that almost reached the corners of his mouth and walked back into his room. He returned with a selection of blades, laying them out on the scarred and chipped wooden table at the side of his workshop.

"Very well, young blessed," he sneered. "As you are such a fine judge of blades you may pick your own."

There were twelve blades set out. Six were not paired, merely orphan swords, and I ignored them immediately. A good smith makes the stabsword and longsword at the same time so they can be weighted against each other for balanced combat. Mismatched blades are better than no blades but it would foolish to choose them when there are other options. In the centre of the remaining six lay a pair of beautiful, shiny, gilded and inlaid weapons. I suspect he thought that, with the thief's eye of the young, I would take those. I hovered over them for a moment, more to build his expectation than anything else, before passing on. They were too weighty and their ornate curves made them easy for an opponent to snag. Of the two pairs left, one set was perfectly serviceable and the other almost completely covered in a patina of rust and dirt.

I realised that the armourer was an oaf. "These ones." I pointed at the rusted blades.

"The rusty ones?" He scratched at his stubbly chin.

"Rust can be removed. With sand and vinegar, I believe you said." I don't know if he was more annoyed at having his words thrown back at him or by not understanding why I had chosen a pair of rusty blades. In either case I would not give him the satisfaction of an explanation. "A bow now?"

"Bows is in the squireyard. Pick one o' them." He reached out for the rusty blades and picked up the shorter stabsword, clearly trying to work out what I saw in it. "There's writing on this," he said.

"Yes," I said, "there is." I held out my hand for the blade and he passed it over, grudgingly.

"These are mine now?"

"Aye, king's gift if you're a squire without." He stared at me suspiciously. "What's it say on 'em?" his brows furrowed, and he looked like a dog that could see food through crystal but did not understand why it hurt its nose every time it lunged for it.

"I cannot make it out," I said, "for the rust." This was a lie. It said Conwy, the name of a bladesmith from before the world soured. I doubted the blade was a real Conwy as they are the blades of kings, but even the copies are held to be excellent weapons. "Shield?"

He shook his head. "In the squireyard."

"Thank you. Send the armour to my room when you've fixed it, my name is Girton ap Gwynr. I'll take the swords with me," I said cheerfully, and left him scratching his head.

Chapter 4

Maniyadoc has stood for a thousand years and squats on a hill dominating the land around it. The main keep is a vast square and in front of it is a courtyard and a gatehouse. The towers standing at each corner are covered in the totems of the dead gods, their faces long ago chipped away. Two similarly decorated and defaced towers stand to either side of the gatehouse a hundred or so paces before the keep and are joined to the main building by walls to create a killing zone which turns the whole construction into a rectangle. The keep and its walls rise for six storeys and have enough room within to house an army and all it needs to keep supplied – smiths, bakers, cooks – though no one in the Tired Lands has an army large enough to fill it. Around the keep is the keepyard, which holds the training grounds, and around the keepyard runs the first wall, the keepyard wall, which is twenty paces thick at the bottom, fifteen at the top and as high as ten men. The outer ten paces are solid; the inner part of it is riddled with rooms and stairs, though many have collapsed through lack of use and care.

Around the keep and its wall is a second and much larger space called the townyard. If you mount the battlements of the gatehouse or the keepyard wall you can look down and see the ghost of the town that once filled it. Brown squares of dead grass trace out buildings of almost unimaginable size. In the first years of the imbalance men had more than they had ever thought possible, but now we know only myths of plenty and live lives full of jealousy for what the long-dead once had.

Beyond the footprints of the ghost town is the second wall, the townwall, designed in a similar fashion to the keepyard wall but thicker. It once had four gates but three had been blocked long ago to make the wall easier to defend and large parts of the townwall had collapsed through disuse. On one side of the remaining gate are the stables where Xus would be and on the other side stood the kennels, from which the discordant yapping of dogs floated through the air.

Small towns spring up around many castles but King Doran ap Mennix long ago razed the shanties that had accreted like barnacles against his walls. Mennix has always been a warrior, and those whose commerce he had a use for were moved within the keep; those who he had no use for were thrown out to join the thankful. It is in the dead ground between the townyard wall and the keepyard wall that Festival will come – a slow, many-wheeled and mounted city, its arrival is as inevitable as the changes of season it follows.

Beyond the wall are many small fortified farms, villages and waycastles. Each is dependent on Maniyadoc for its protection from bandits and outlaws, and in times of need each is as likely to become a predator on their neighbours as the next. The King's Riders patrol the land constantly in a smaller and more martial version of Festival's circular route. The superstitious would tell you hedgings watch them pass from their haunts in the fields, woods and pools.

The yearsage sunlight barely warmed my skin as I walked through the keepyard, but it was welcome nonetheless. Outside the townwall the fruit trees, which grew thick around the castle in ordered rows, would be ripening and the brewers would be getting ready for harvest and to produce the sweet alcohol Maniyadoc was famous for.

"Girton ap Gwynr?" The voice coming from behind me

had the growl and tempering of old age and it took a moment
before I realised it addressed me – I was still new to the skin
of Girton ap Gwynr. I turned to find an old man dressed in
full armour, his shoulder guards stained and scratched in
memories of bright green. Once he must have been a
Landsman, hunting down the sorcerers who'd sucked away
the life of the land and created the sourlands. The Landsmen
were cruel, but it was a necessary cruelty as the destruction
wrought on our lands by sorcerers was far worse than the
pain any man could bring. People feared the Landsmen
appearing in their villages, but not as much as they feared
a new sorcerer rising and destroying what little fertility was
left in the land.

The old man held a flared helmet in one gloved hand,
both helmet and gloves in the same scratched green as his
armour. His white hair and beard had been shaved close to
his skin.

"Yes," I said. "I am Girton ap Gwynr."

Behind him I saw that a number of corpses in various
states of decay and clothed in the uniform of Maniyadoc's
guards hung by their necks from the battlements. Placards
reading TEMPTED BY DARK UNGAR had been tied to
each one. From its size I was sure one of the corpses was
the man Joam, who I had fought at the entrance to the
nightsoil drain. The old man turned when he saw me staring.

"Traitors," he said.

"I thought criminals were sent to join the desolate, to
bleed into the land?"

"The priests say the land will reject the blood of a traitor,
so we hang them or set them on a fool's throne to burn. It
is a waste really."

"They burn them?"

He shrugged.

"Aye, some of them, but a first meeting should not be
clouded by sad tidings." He moved nearer so his body blocked

my view of the corpses. "I was sent to guide you to the squireyard, Girton ap Gwynr. I am Heamus. I use no family name."

"I can find my own way," I said. I was holding my rusty swords awkwardly and one slid out of my hands and on to the ground with a clang.

"Well, maybe I can carry your swords then?" He smiled. He had watery blue eyes that flashed merrily as he bent and picked up the longsword I had dropped. As he straightened up he sniffed the air. A look of confusion passed over his face and then he stared at me strangely. It was as if he no longer saw me and his gaze was transported to some faraway place. He smiled again, shook his head and put out a hand for the stabsword. "Good choice you made in these," he said, letting light dance down the steel between the stipplings of rust on the blade.

"The armourer did not think so," I said, wondering why he had sniffed the air and if I needed to bathe again.

"The armourer is a fool." He shook his head and sighed. "There are plenty of fools in this castle, sometimes I wonder if I am among them." He grunted a little and placed the hand holding the stabsword on the small of his back, leaning into it to stretch his muscles. "I hope you will not add to our fools, Girton ap Gwynr."

"I don't intend to."

"Good. Then follow me, boy. You will not need your blades today."

He led me across the parched ground of the keepyard and around behind the castle where a wall, head high to me, separated off an area. The old Rider unlocked a door and then turned, holding up the key.

"For you. Lose it, and the king will have the cost of replacing it taken out of your hide."

"Yes, Heamus."

He pushed open the door. "After you, squire," he said.

As I passed him he grabbed my arm. "When you introduce yourself, Girton, use your first name only. All the squires who attend training at the keep are of rich or powerful families. We do not use surnames or titles. In memory of the Queen of Balance all are to be treated equally."

"So there is no favouritism?"

"Well –" he smirked "– that is the idea, and you should at least pretend it is the case."

"Yes, Blessed," I said. Something crossed his face then, something between regret and amusement.

"I am no blessed, Girton. Call me Heamus only, that will do." He opened the door. "And, boy, do not be too disheartened by your first day of training. It can be hard." He ushered me through into the training ground, where the squires waited.

There are rules to soldiery and squiredom in the Tired Lands. Any man or woman, as long as they are not of the thankful, may take up arms and pledge to spill their enemies', and often their own, blood upon the ground for their blessed. However, if you wish to have the great honour of dying on the back of a warmount then you must be a man and you must be blessed. My master says it was not always so and in some places women still wear armour and still fight on mountback, but it is rare now. One of the King's Riders, looming over me from his mount, once told me it is because women lack the strength to control a mount, but my master rides Xus, who is always wilful, and she has no trouble handling him at all.

I'd expected there to be more boys waiting, and it was a slight disappointment to see only two small groups gathered. A castle as big as Maniyadoc should have more squires than the twenty or so before me; maybe the others were out with their blessed.

As Heamus had intimated, the idea that keeping our surnames from one another would ensure equality was a fanciful one. Looking at the armour of the sullen boys waiting for me gave me a quick idea of the hierarchy. At the top, and surrounded by a bunch of boys who seemed upset by my appearance, was Aydor, the heir. He was dressed in armour thick with ornate gilding and bright enamelling, making it pointlessly heavy. I reassessed my opinion of Aydor a little. He may have looked overweight but he carried his armour carelessly which spoke of enormous strength in his thick body. An elaborately cast twisting snake crowned his flared helmet.

The squiremaster stepped forward as I stared. He was another stumpy man who looked to be a bastard offshoot of the Mennix bloodline.

"Girton?" he said. He made a face like he had stood in manure.

"Yes."

"Yes, Squiremaster!" he barked back at me.

"Yes, Squiremaster," I replied obediently, head bowed.

"Look at me, boy! You are a warrior, not a mouse." I raised my head to meet his eye. He had the look of a carnivorous flying lizard and I recognised a killer. He was not a man I would ever want to face in serious combat, and if I had been tasked to finish him it would have been done with poison or a blade in his back. "Better," he said with a nod. "I am Nywulf but you will call me squiremaster. What skills do you possess, Girton?" He turned my name into a sneer, the standard approach of squiremasters the Tired Lands over.

"I can ride a mount and shoot a bow, Squiremaster," I said.

"Swordplay?"

"A little, Squiremaster." It would be easier to feign a lack of skill than pretend some moderate skill where a slip-up was far more likely. The squiremaster felt the muscles of my arms and legs, running his hands along me the way one would when buying a mount. His hands were like spades and he made sure to hurt me with his examination.

"Scrawny," he said. I heard laughter from the other boys. The squiremaster silenced them with a glance but I could feel the eyes of the other squires on me. It was a peculiar pressure, like an acid heat on the back of my neck that melted away my confidence, slowly stripping back Girton the assassin and leaving behind something lesser: Girton ap Gwynr, a scared and lonely boy. "You'll need more brawn on you than you have to swing a longsword, boy." He was right. That was why I preferred knives. "And you'll need some weight on you if you want to put a spear through an armoured man from the back of a mount." I would give him that too. He turned from me to Heamus, who had been waiting in the doorway to the training yard, watching. "Heamus, you can leave us now. Take his blades back to his room."

The old man nodded and I thought how odd that was. Here was a man who had once been a Landsmen, one of the greatest powers in the Tired Lands, being treated like a member of the thankful classes by a lowly squiremaster.

"Thank you for bringing the boy," said the squiremaster, making it an obvious dismissal. Heamus nodded again, retreating back through the gate in the wall. "Right, boy," said the squiremaster. "Run for me."

"What?"

He cuffed me with a rough hand and I heard Aydor laugh. "Don't ask questions, boy. Do as you're told. Run for me. Around the wall. Keep going until you can't."

I wondered if he had chosen this exercise because of my club foot. Girton the assassin's apprentice could have hobbled around all day, but Girton the country boy would not have my stamina. As I started my uncomfortable-looking rolling jog it was the oppressive stares of the gathered squires that became the real drain on my energy. The squiremaster set them to practise swordplay, but they took every opportunity to throw suspicious, unfriendly glances in my direction.

As I jogged I watched their swordplay. They were all bigger than me and a talented enough bunch, but I saw something that made me realise how wary I would need to be among them. As two squires fenced, a huge, broad-boned boy and a smaller boy in ill-fitting armour, their fight took them near another pair, one with a damaged face and the other with a blind eye. I saw what was about to happen to the smaller boy before it took place. A look passed between his opponent and the pair of boys behind. A second later one of the pair, the one with the blind eye, disengaged and turned to deliver a vicious swipe with his wooden sword to the smaller boy's arm. There was no way he could have blocked it, he was completely blindsided. When he turned to find out who had hit him his opponent stepped in with his wooden blade, cracking him so hard on the helmet it drove him to his knees. It was a well rehearsed bit of bullying, and from the grins on the faces of the three boys involved it was something they enjoyed doing.

I gave it six rounds of the walls before I started to flag. The fencing practice stopped and the weight of the boy's eyes on me grew. I caught glimpses of their faces: some sneering, some smiling, some laughing quietly and a few simply avoiding looking at me as if I carried some curse. At eight laps I started to stumble, and on my tenth lap, despite being screamed at by the squiremaster, I slowed to a walk. Eventually, the man called me back to him.

"Pathetic," he said, and a ripple of laughter echoed around the walls. "Stand there." He pointed at a spot before him on the scrubby ground. I found myself staring at, not only the squiremaster, but at a wall of hostile boys lounging lazily behind him amid the training equipment. I stood, panting harder than I needed to, and casually studying the squires. They existed in two separate groups and everything about their body language told me they loathed one another. Aydor ap Mennix led the larger group, twelve in all including the three bullies and their victim. The heir's group wore armour of bright colours and differing degrees of elaborateness. Only the tallest of them was dressed differently: he wore plain armour and stared out into the world as if barely seeing it. He also wore real blades and I presumed he must be Celot, the Heartblade tasked to protect Aydor.

The second group consisted of eight squires, all wearing armour that was dented, its enamelling scratched and dull. This was a division of attitude not riches as for all its dings and welts it was still expensive armour. This group laughed and joked with one another, they seemed to possess an easy camaraderie and I wondered what it would be like to share such a bond.

Whatever the differences between the two groups, neither of them looked particularly kindly on me, and I continued to feel a strange withering within. I had tried a few tentative smiles as I had run around the squireyard but had only been met with stony glares or averted eyes. The boy who had been bullied, he seemed as uncomfortable in his skin as he was in his poorly fitted armour, had given me a crooked smile, and I could not decide if he was mocking me or not. Now, while I stood panting, sweating and pretending to favour my bad leg, they fixed me with dead eyes, and I knew any ideas I had of sliding easily into their ranks to uncover plots of murder were the fantasies of a child. I felt very lonely and small. Digging my fingers into the palms of my hands I started to whisper to myself, "I am not Girton ap Gwynr."

"Right, boys," said the squiremaster, "while young Girton gets his breath back you can introduce yourselves."

They started to rattle off their names in a way that made it difficult for me to hear. Some mumbled and some said their names so quickly I could not catch them.

"I am Tomas." I caught this one's name, and he meant me to. He was one of the boys in the beaten armour and looked older than the others – eighteen, nineteen maybe. Old for a squire. Beneath a mop of black hair his face was heavily bruised, though this didn't seem to dent his confidence any. Rather than letting the squires closest to him speak, he introduced them to me. "This is Boros –" he pointed at another tall boy, who wore his blond hair long, as if he had made a vow "– and this is Barin." His angular face and long blond hair were a mirror of Boros' – twins. From the way Tomas acted as spokesman, and the way Aydor sneered at him as he spoke – the heir clearly detested him – I guessed he was the leader of this group.

Aydor stepped forward.

"I am Aydor ap Mennix, and I am your—"

"Aydor!" shouted the squiremaster. "Rules of the ground!" Aydor stared at the squiremaster as if trying to make the man back down, but it was the heir who ended up lowering his eyes.

"These are my men, Kyril, Hallin and Borniya." They were the three who had bullied the other boy. "You'll get to know them. The tall stupid one is Celot." He did not bother pointing out who was who in the rest of his group. Kyril sneered at me. He was a boy nearly as big as Aydor with a pinched, mean face. Borniya, by him, was just as big and stared at me, naked aggression radiating from the piggy eyes in his round, fleshy face. He must have fallen from a mount or been kicked by one as one of his cheekbones had been caved in, giving his face a lopsided look. Hallin was smaller, darker and sharper-featured, he lounged behind his friends, smiling as he peeled an apple with a small knife. A scar ran over his brow, across a milky white blind eye and down his cheek. Not one of them showed any sign of friendship towards me. Aydor glanced over at the other group and then added, "Oh, and we have Rufra as well." He pointed at the smaller boy, the one who had been attacked and whose badly fitted armour made him look uncomfortable and strangely wide. Hallin spat on the ground near Rufra, who, rather than smiling at me, was grimacing. I wondered if he also held some grudge against me.

"Right," said the squiremaster. He walked over to me, wooden blades under his arm. "Longsword," he said, holding up the larger blade. "Goes in your right hand." He grabbed my hand and forced the sword into it. "This is used primarily to keep your opponent at a distance and for lunging. It is sharp on the point and at the edge." He took a few paces away from me and then turned, throwing me the smaller blade. I missed the catch, deliberately, and he shook his head. "That is your stabsword. Does what it says. Used for close work and defence. You'll learn how to use it with a shield later, but for today we'll see how you do in dual-blade work."

"Dual blade?" I asked. It can never hurt to appear stupid. Then your enemies will underestimate you.

"Aye, both blades at once. Longsword in the right, stabsword in the left is usual. But do what feels right for you at the moment."

I almost betrayed myself. I preferred close work and was about to reverse the stabsword so it pointed backwards and use the longsword only to feint and twist, but that was a highly skilled form of swordsmanship. Instead I followed the squiremaster's instructions, taking a few clumsy practice swings at the air with the longsword.

"Celot," said the squiremaster, "test Girton's skills in the circle. Don't kill him."

The Heartblade took up a pair of wooden swords from a rack and went to stand in a chalk circle, where I joined him. Then he advanced with the longsword extended and the stabsword trailing. I stood, looking confused. Celot's eyes barely focused on me as he went into position two and I realised I had seen his like before, but as fools rather than swordsmen. Men and women whose minds were mage-bent which locked them in their own world, though they were often capable of prodigious feats of concentration. A coldness settled on me. In battle he would be completely unreadable, which made him incredibly dangerous. Celot paused then looked from his own feet to mine. He did it again and again until I, clumsily, tried to copy his stance. Then he tested my guard, gently batting my sword aside to create an opening and making a slow thrust with his longsword. I tried to block it with my stabsword and failed; he let his sword prod me. It was hard enough to hurt but not to bruise.

"Celot is holding back, Squiremaster," shouted Aydor.

Celot and I danced a little longer. All the time he gave me subtle hints on how to use my blades, and when I failed he punished me with blows hard enough that I did not want him to do it again, but he was not cruel with it. While Celot and I fenced Aydor and his group taunted us, claiming we were both cowards. I am not sure Celot was aware of the abuse; if he was it didn't touch him, though I felt it as the sapping heat of an overly humid day. Eventually, the squiremaster tired of Aydor's carping.

"Would you like to demonstrate bladework, Aydor?" roared the squiremaster.

"Yes," he said. He stepped forward with a triumphant smile on his face, from the expression on the squiremaster's face it was clearly rare for Aydor to volunteer to step into the circle. Unlike the squiremaster I understood why the heir was so eager to step forward — Aydor knew I had to lose. He knew he was free to punish me however he wanted and I could not fight back without breaking my cover.

Aydor was a good swordsman if not a brilliant one. He was exceedingly strong and preferred to use brute force rather than skill. If I had not been playing a part I would have cut him down in a moment, but I was, and he was a far better swordsman than poor Girton ap Gwynr so he punished me sorely. He held back no blows and only cleverly feigned clumsiness saved me from broken fingers. He clearly intended to cripple me if he could, though it was short-sighted on his part as his life could depend on my health. I feigned tiredness, stepping back and calling "Mercy!" but Aydor still advanced on me. Even when the squiremaster called out "Halt!" he did not stop. Aydor swept his blade low as I dropped my guard, catching me on my shin, and following up with a shoulder barge, sending me sprawling on the ground. He raised his wooden blade to bring down in a heavy strike to my head, and only the squiremaster pushing between us stopped him bringing the strike home.

"I'll not have this," hissed Nywulf. "Understand me, Aydor? I'll not have this on my ground. Cripple a hostage and I have to answer to the king."

Aydor took a step back and dropped his wooden blades onto the dirt.

"The hostage is already crippled," he said, "and before long you'll have to answer to a new king, Nywulf. You should keep that in mind." There was no mistaking the threat nor the disrespect. The two stared at each other like grand boars in the swiller's yard until Aydor walked away holding his arms in the air as if in triumph. *You are weak*, I thought. *Weak, cruel and desperate to appear strong, which makes you dangerous and easily manipulated.*

"You're all dismissed for today," said the squiremaster quietly. "Be here early in the morning. Girton, you should see a healer for your bruises."

I stood and watched as the other boys replaced their wooden weapons and then bustled out through the door past racks of bows and shields.

"You did not see me shoot," I said forlornly.

"You said you could," replied the squiremaster as he picked

up Aydor's wooden blades and replaced them. "I'll not call you a liar."

"Thank you," I said, turning away.

"Boy," said the squiremaster. I stopped, turned back. "I will not say it will get easier, as training is as much a test of will as anything else. But today was a hard day for you. It might be best if you stayed away from the other squires." He nodded his head to the door. "Now get off."

Chapter 5

Heamus waited for me outside the door.

"Ah, Girton, I am glad I caught you. Your mount has arrived, and I thought you may want to see him stabled." He noticed how I was limping on my good leg and favouring my left arm. "But it does not matter if you are hurt – our stablehands are good at what they do. They will see to your beast."

"No," I said quickly. "I am only bruised."

"Would you see a healer?"

"For bruises? No. I am not hurt that badly." Anwith, the god of healing, had been unable to save the gods, and to cross the path of his healer-priests was generally considered bad luck. "I will walk the bruises to stop my limbs stiffening."

"Good lad," said Heamus, clapping me on the back with an armour-clad hand and adding another bruise to my collection. "That's exactly what I learned from my first years of swordplay."

"I learned it falling from mounts," I said.

"Well a bruise is a bruise is a bruise however it is earned. Come." He put out an arm for me to lean on. "Did you enjoy the sword work?"

"I'm not sure enjoy is the right word."

"They were hard on you, but fair, I assume? They are good boys really, for the most part."

"I practised with Aydor," I said. Heamus stared up into the cold blue sky as we walked.

"Ah," he said after a while. "He can be cruel, can the

king-in-waiting, but cruelty is the prerogative of kings. His father was the same, back when . . . back when . . ." His voice faded away as if his mind was visiting a time when he had been young and his life less full of aches. "It is not easy to be a king, see, Girton. They are not like us. Just like the blessed must endeavour to see the living classes as tools and not feel pity at the plight of the thankful, so must a king be cruel and learn to see people as a means to an end and not as lives."

"You are friends with the king?"

"Friends? Oh no. I don't think anyone is ever truly friends with a king, but when I was a young man Doran ap Mennix and I were, well, as close as one can be with a king."

"But you went away?" I nodded at the faded green of his armour, and the smile that had been a constant feature on his face since I met him faded away. I cursed myself. So far this old man was the only person who had showed me any kindness and I did not wish to offend him. "I am sorry, Heamus, I did not mean to pry."

"Not at all. It is a well known story and best you hear it from my mouth than a gossip's flapping lips." He smiled again, but it was as weak as the watery yearsage sunlight. "There was a girl. No one important, a serving girl is all, but I liked her and she liked me. Doran did what kings do with pretty servants."

"You were angry?"

"Dead gods, yes, I was angry." A flash in the eye, a brief glimpse of the steel beneath the smiling old man he presented to the world. "But you cannot challenge a king to combat. So I left rather than commit treason."

"And now you are back," I said to the air.

"Aye, I am back. Age has a way of dimming the pain of the past and the girl is bonded to a smith. They have two children. No doubt a night with the king is something she looks back on fondly now, aye?"

I nodded but I did not agree. My master and I have met many who are haunted by such actions of the blessed. Our blades have helped them sleep a little easier. I did not believe that this woman would look back fondly on her night with the king, and from the look on Heamus's face, neither did he.

We walked through the keepyard gate and across the wide townyard in silence. Festival was already beginning to gather, and its vanguard was setting up, a growing caravan city in the centre of the ghostly one that only existed from above. The caravans were huge – drawn by draymounts, a small and squat breed of mount with curling horns rather than antlers and long hair that fell in matted ropes to trail along the ground. The draymounts were all muscle, and it took six of the powerful beasts to draw the gaudy two-storey caravans that were the homes of the Festival Lords. The Tired Lands may be home to kings, queens and blessed, but, second only to the high king and his Landsmen at Cealdon, the Festival Lords were the only other real power. Festival controlled the majority of trade across the Tired Lands, and the Festival Lords controlled Festival. They travelled in a constant circle, two and a half thousand miles around, stopping at towns and castles to trade and put on shows. The castles and towns relied on Festival as much, and probably more in most cases, as Festival relied on them. From Maniyadoc, which was the centre of the Tidal Flats, they would pick up dried fish, fruit, sweet alcoholic perry, livestock and stock up for crossing the western sourlands. Last time I had seen the Festival caravan it had been five miles long and strewn out in such a way it took two days to pass. It was not only traders and entertainers; Festival had its own guards, Riders, rules, and if you were running from someone it was said you could find sanctuary there and start again – if the Lords had some use for your skills. Festival made itself open to all – faces of every colour and the clothes of every tribe could be found here – but at the same time it was secretive; few saw past the outside of its gaudy tents and caravans. Many were distrustful of it and talked of it being a hiding place for hedgings. Their distrust was heightened as Festival was by far the biggest and richest town in the Tired Lands; it just happened to be one on wheels and mountback.

This distrust did not stretch to stopping anyone coming to it, of course.

We passed Tomas and his group of squires playing some game with a ball and stick. I wondered what the game was, if I would be good at it and if they would let me join them. Their laughter echoed around the townyard, coming closer then receding. It made me think of the story of Eyol who chased eternal happiness: he found it elusive, often within his reach but never staying still.

"Here we are," said Heamus after we had passed the massive caravans. "I have seen your mount – Xus, he's called?" I nodded. "A fine beast, a war beast."

"Not my Xus, he is only for riding. Though he is a fine animal," I said. "My father breeds mounts."

"Strange to name a mount bred for pleasure after the god of death."

He seemed to be reaching for something.

"Not so strange, Heamus. Xus is a contrary and evil-tempered animal on occasion. Most of our stablehands feared him like they feared death so we named him for Xus the unseen." It was not so far from the truth, though his name was actually a joke. Xus was my master's mount and brought death wherever he went.

"That makes sense, I suppose." Did Heamus look a little disappointed? "Anyway, go to your mount – no doubt it will be glad to see you." Shouting came from the stable block. "As will our stablehands, from the sound of it."

The stable block ran along the townyard wall and was

built of the same black stone as the rest of the castle and
the kennels opposite, from which came the faint yapping of
hounds. Snaking columns, scarred where stone faces had
been excised from them, rose to the stables' high roof. It
was tall of necessity as mounts are far taller than a man,
even taller when you take their antlers into consideration.

In the stable block I was surprised by how light it was.
The roof had been built of crystal so the mounts could enjoy
basking in light. On either side of a wide aisle were stalls,
about thirty a side, though only the stalls on one side were
occupied. In the centre of the building two stablehands were
fighting to control Xus as he reared and hissed, striking out
with his clawed feet. They used ropes around his antlers to
stop him goring them but were failing to get him into a
stall.

"Xus," I said, using the Whisper-that-Flies-to-the-Ear. He
stopped his struggling and pawed at the floor with a front
foot. The taller of the two stablehands looked from Xus to
me and then threw his rope to the ground and walked out
in disgust.

"Don't mind Leiss," said the other stablehand, a girl. "He
considers himself an expert when it comes to mounts, and
this beast was defying him." She shook her head. "Is he
your mount?" I nodded. "How did you do that, make him
quieten? You are upwind of him and their eyesight is not
good – he would see you only as a blur from where you
are – but he stopped struggling almost as soon as you
entered."

"Yes," said Heamus, studying both me and the girl with
an odd look in his eye. "That was a good trick, Girton, one
I would like to learn myself."

I had made a mistake, using assassin skills in full view of
strangers when I was not even meant to use them around
other assassins.

"There was no trick, I am afraid. It is simply that Xus is

unusually perceptive for a mount." I walked up to the huge animal, not looking at the girl or Heamus in case they could see the lie in my eye. I reached out to scratch the mount's long muzzle. "Aren't you, Xus?" He cooed gently through his long downward-pointing front tusks.

"Will you introduce me to him?" asked the girl.

"Sorry?" She was pretty, her red hair cut short in a way that showed off high cheekbones. Her slim face was a shade darker than the usual tan of one who habitually spent their days outside, something startling in a castle where so many people seemed like mirror images of each other. She must have come from far outside the castle, maybe even from outside Maniyadoc and the Long Tides.

"Introduce me to him." She pointed at Xus while keeping a respectful distance. "Often when a mount has a strong connection with its owner it is best for them to introduce the animal to a new stablehand. You have stabled your mount with others before and done this, yes?" She smiled and took a step forward. Xus let out a distrustful snort and tossed his head.

"Of course," I said, though I had not. My master was always the one to stable the mount. "What is your name?"

"Drusl," she said.

"Xus," I said, feeling foolish, "this is Drusl." The girl laughed, clapping her hands and shaking her head. "You are funny, Blessed."

"I'm no blessed."

"You are still funny." She walked forward. "Take my hand, like this." She placed my open palm on the back of her hand, and it was like a fire went through me. No woman had ever touched me so candidly before. "And now you place your hand on his muzzle, as you would normally but with my hand between your skin and his fur." I did as she asked. No doubt this was something totally innocent on her part but my heart was hammering fit to burst. Xus rolled his eyes

and snorted through his nostrils, opening and closing them
to take in this new scent mixed with mine. For a moment I
thought he would rear but he let out a final snort and nodded
his head, calmed. "See, now he will accept me," she said. I
was suddenly uncomfortably aware of the warmth of her
body against mine. I stepped away and when I opened my
mouth to speak I found my voice stifled by some unknown
force. I was saved from making a further fool of myself by
the stablemaster, Leiss.

"Country tricks are no way to work for a real stablehand.
That beast needs a whip taken to it," he said from behind
me. He had the same squat body and unappealing features
as so many others in Maniyadoc.

"Take a whip to Xus, Leiss," I said, "and I will take that
same whip to you, do you understand?"

"It'll never learn otherwise." His voice was sullen but his
face full of challenge.

"Xus seems to learn well enough." I pointed at Drusl, who
was leading a calm Xus into his stall. "See?"

"Won't last. Seen it before. Soon as you're gone that beast'll
be back to its evil ways." As he walked into the light I saw
he was scarred about the face. At some point a mount had
gored him, leaving a thick line of scar tissue across his cheek,
jaw and forehead. My master always said a scarred stablehand
should never be trusted alone with your mount, and I was
inclined to agree with her. Leiss had an ugly cast to his eye
that was nothing to do with his disfigurement. He looked
at me like I was his enemy.

"You are to let Drusl care for Xus," I told him. "I don't
want you to go near my mount."

"Pleased to," he said, and turned from me to walk into
an empty stall where he started clattering around with
shovels. Drusl gave me a nervous smile and shrugged her
shoulders as if to say, "what can you do?" and went into
Xus's stall.

"I have some business in the stables, Girton," said Heamus. "Can you make your own way back?"

"Of course," I said.

Walking back to the keep alone gave me the first time to think since we had been given our task. I did not realise how much I had missed thinking time; generally I had plenty while I plodded along behind my master and Xus. Deep in thought I passed strangely dressed women with squalling babes and gaggles of children who stared out suspiciously from the spoked wheels of the Festival Lords' caravans. The task given to us seemed impossible. How to find who had requested an assassin? I tried to turn my mind to it but instead thought of the warmth of a hand under mine as I introduced a pretty red-headed stablehand to Xus.

That warmth fled as I entered the courtyard in front of the keep. To one side of the door stood a small group of people. Nywulf the squiremaster was there, as was a priest of Heissal in his white porcelain mask and hooded orange robes. They were having a quiet, if clearly heated, conversation. With them stood, Tomas, Aydor, Kyril, Borniya and Hallin, but it was not the people that made me catch my breath, it was the war dogs Borniya held on leashes. They were the same beasts used throughout the Tired Lands, huge animals with short sleek fur that showed off their thick muscles. They barked in excitement at anyone who passed, exposing teeth that could rip a man apart. Without thinking I changed direction and walked the long way around the water clock so my path would not cross that of the dogs. Borniya stared at me, a look of puzzlement on his face, and then he glanced from me to the dogs and back to me again, and a cruel smile spread across his bent face. He nudged Aydor and whispered something to him, behind them Tomas looked on thoughtfully while Nywulf and the priest simply watched.

I cursed myself as a fool. Never show weakness. How

many times had that been drummed into me? But to change direction again would make me look foolish. I had made a decision and I must live with it.

Chapter 6

"Why do I have to wear a kilt?"

It seemed a fair question to ask. Kilts are vile pieces of clothing, too warm where you would be cool and too cool where you would be warm. Not to mention how the ridiculous fashion of swathing the upper body in material restricts movement. Worse, the kilt showed the bruises on my arms and legs that my master had covered in white salve, so I looked like the victim of some strange skin disease.

"You wear a kilt because you are of the blessed and it is expected of you at the feast to welcome the Festival Lords."

"I could be a rebellious blessed set upon starting a new fashion."

"And what new fashion –" she pulled a comb through my long brown hair "– would that be?"

"Not a kilt. Ow!" She loosened a knot by pulling out a tangle of hair at the root.

"No beauty without pain, rebellious young Girton," she said and ripped out another chunk of hair

"Ow!" I dropped back into the Whisper-that-Flies-to-the-Ear. "How will we do this, Master?"

"Do what?"

"Catch an assassin's client, how can we do this? I have been tumbling it through my mind and cannot find my feet."

"Do not worry about that; I have set in motion the capture of our assassin already. You go through your days, watch and note everything and tell me it all at the end of each day."

"And what will you do, while I do that?"

"The same, for now."

"And we share what we learn?"

She looked at the floor and shook her head. "I do not want to pollute what you see." She smiled up at me. "I will formulate my own theories, and you yours."

"But we will not share them?" I was suddenly angry. "I stayed here with you when——"

"Yes, you did –" her words were quiet but forceful "– and you are free to leave at any moment, but if we are going to do this together we must do this my way. Do you understand?" I bit my lip but did not reply. Instead I nodded. "Good. Now, this evening I will present the story Why Xus the Unseen No Longer Shows his Face."

"But that's——"

"Ill omened, I am aware. The Festival Lords are important so the entire court will be there, and afterwards Adran will be meeting with the Festival Lords. We will be there too."

"We will?" My bad mood sloughed away. "I have only ever seen them from afar and always wondered what they are like to talk to, or if they are even human under their——"

"Don't be ridiculous, of course they are human! Sadly for you we shall not see them, as we will be hiding while the queen talks to them."

I leaned in close to whisper, "Does she suspect them?"

"She suspects everyone. But as we are talking of suspicions, did any of the squires seem suspicious?"

"They all seemed suspicious. But only of me."

"Who are they?"

"They do not use family names. So, Aydor apart, I do not know who they are, and they are mostly a nondescript lot. There is one called Tomas, a leader. Some twins called Boros and Barin. Aydor has some cronies, boys named Kyril, Borniya and Hallin. There's a boy named Rufra, who they bully and I do not like the look of – he slinks about like a thief. And they are split into two very distinct groups, which struck me as odd."

"Sometimes I think I have kept you too sheltered." She put a hand on my shoulder and stared into my eyes. "That is normal for boys your age, and men, to split into groups."

"It is? They do not want friends?"

"They want the right friends, Girton."

"I would take any at the moment." She smiled at me and shook her head, then became very serious.

"Bad friends are worse than no friends, believe me. Do your best to join a group and I will quiz the servants about the squires. Before tomorrow we will have some information on them." She took her hand from my shoulder. "Tell me of the others."

"The squiremaster, he is a hard man, though a good one, I think. The armourer I met was a fool." The feeling of discomfort fled and I brightened, realising I had forgotten to tell my master something important. "My blades, Master, you should see my blades. Reach behind you."

She paused in straightening my hair and retrieved the swords.

"Rusty." She placed the stabsword on the bed and ran her eyes over the long sword before picking it up and feeling its weight. "But very well balanced and . . . Oh. Conwy blades? And he just gave them to you?"

"I do not think he knew what they were. They are copies of course."

"Are they?" Her eyes shone like she had discovered something magical. "These are a king's weapons, if anyone sees . . ." She reached down to her pack and took out a roll of bandages. Binding the bottom of the blade was traditional for squires, to make sure they were not mistaken for Riders. It also covered the name on the blade.

"I also met an old man called Heamus, after I picked up the blades."

"Heamus Galdin," she said.

"You know him?"

"He was famous once." She put down the bound longsword and began to bind the stabsword.

"He may have reason to want the king's son dead."

"Really?"

"Aye. When he and the king were young they fought over a girl. He is still angry. He says he is not —" I stared at the floor "— but he is."

"You like him." It was not a question.

"He was kind to me."

"The Scourge, they called him as a Landsman. Maybe you would not like him so much if you had seen him locking village wise-women in blood gibbets or leading the sick, the mage-bent and the miserable to join the desolate's journey to the sourlands, where he bled them into the dead ground."

"I . . ."

"Secrets and false faces," she said. "It is the same in all these places, Girton. I would tear them all down if I could." She stood. "I must change my motley now, and you must make your way to the banquet room. I will meet you there."

She left while I finished hanging my kilt. It took me another half-hour because a kilt is a truly stupid garment and I question the sanity of any man who would wear one voluntarily.

The castle was busy and the kilt's shoulder pieces kept sliding off as I walked. Although almost everyone of status was wearing similar clothing — a parade of rainbow colours — I felt more conspicuous than ever. The bright blue material shouted, "look at me!" For someone who had spent their life in drab browns hiding in the shadows it was an uncomfortable feeling. Walking the corridors, sandals padding on thick carpet, I felt as if all eyes were on me. Slaves dressed in little more than liveried sacks, and unaware I should really be one of them, stepped to one side and stared at the floor nervously as I passed. More than once I caught a flicker as I was looked up and down when they thought I was not looking. Servants were a different matter, and each one that I passed politely moved aside for someone they saw as their social better, but I could feel their judgment. Whether it was because I was new and they recognised me as an outsider or simply because I wore my kilt badly I'm not sure, but their gaze made the back of my head itch and sweat. Any of them, if not all, could have been reporting on me.

I passed more and more of the blessed in their ragged finery, kilts mostly. They were gathered in little groups having whispered conversations and slinging filthy looks at each other. As I walked by they would cease their muttering and stare openly at me as if I was some sort of curiosity brought in to entertain them. More of the blessed started to fill the corridors, streaming up through the castle and I let myself become part of them. A twig drifting along on powerful currents. I was drawn up stairs and down corridors and felt more comfortable as I became lost in the mass of people. I was about to climb a staircase when a man I had never seen before grabbed my arm. My instinct was to hurt him but I held myself in check.

"Aydor or Tomas?" he whispered urgently. The man had ears of corn plaited into his hair and his nose and cheeks were red from too much alcohol.

"Sorry?"

"You're new here. Who do your family support? Ap Mennix or ap Dhyrrin?" there was something almost desperate about the way he spoke.

"I . . ."

He shook his head and looked me up and down. "Another stupid country boy," he hissed. "You people have no idea what matters. You should make your mind up quickly if you value your life." He let go of my arm in disgust and melted back into the mass of people, leaving me shocked and confused.

We passed through huge open double doors. An arch had been woven from twigs and boughs cut from the fruit trees which grew around the castle – an enormous expense. If cutting the trees back so severely killed them there was no guarantee new ones would grow: the Tired Lands were sick. Even outside the sourlands the land was sick, but tonight I and all these people would feast and pretend that everything was plentiful. Outside the walls of Maniyadoc, Xus the unseen stalked while starvation did its slow work.

A servant with the same stumpy body and blocky features stamped on so many in the castle led me to a place of honour on a bench at the first row of tables. On the raised stage the scaffold I had been hoisted on was gone, replaced by a long trestle table covered with white cloth. Behind it were two thrones, and several high-backed seats had been set out on either side of them. Straw hobby dolls, bright with warding rags, had been strung across the stage to keep hedgings away from the feast. Behind me were more tables and benches, which would be filled by people of lesser and lesser importance as they neared the back of the hall. Adran had clearly decided to put on a show of riches for the Festival Lords as slowly dying branches had been tied to all the columns to hide the excised faces of dead gods. I ran my hand across the bottom of the ancient wooden table before me and found I sat at an old assassin's contact point, where I could read a history in scratch writing. To any other it would have felt like simple scoring and weathering of the wood, but to me it was a tale of decline. The older marks, now mostly rubbed away, were thick on the wood but unreadable. As they became newer they became clearer, and I could read them – this one begging for the death of a blessed who treated his slaves badly, that one asking for the death of a guard or King's Rider – but the newer the marks the fewer had replies saying the job had been done, and as more time passed fewer and fewer names were scratched in the wood. I took my hand away, placing it on top of the table, and sat there feeling out of place as the room filled with kilted men and women and the air grew thick with the scent of people.

A cloaked figure sat beside me, and I wondered if I would get another quizzing about taking sides. "This seat is taken," I snapped.

"By me, Girton," said my master. She wore a thick cloak, cowled like a priest, the better to keep her motley and made-up face secret. "Let me tell you about your squires while we wait for the top table to grace us with their presence. You are right about them being split into two groups. There is little love lost between them."

"You said that was normal."

"Normal enough, but blood has been spilled more than once. The squiremaster, Nywulf, is new. The old squiremaster had an accident."

"Fatal?"

"No, but he will not be back for a good while. Servants' rumour puts the blame on Kyril, Borniya and Hallin. They are rough and not well liked. Kyril appears to lead that little group, but it is Borniya and Hallin who the servants really fear. The current squiremaster should be careful."

"I think he can handle boys; Nywulf has the look and movements of an exceptional warrior. I thought it strange such a man was training squires. Could he be the assassin?"

My master tapped a finger on the wood of the table.

"I doubt it, but remember it is who hired the assassin that matters so keep your eye on that blade. Now, the squires, as you have seen, fall into two camps: Aydor's lot and Tomas's. Aydor's group is bigger."

"Only by a couple."

"No, there are more. Two are out visiting the waycastles and one is laid up hurt. Tomas's group are the least interesting to us at first glance. They are all the sons of the blessed but not of any of the true lines."

"So if they cannot inherit the throne they are unlikely to be our quarry."

"Not exactly. They are all loyal to Tomas, and Tomas is an ap Dhyrrin."

"And?"

"Clearly I have neglected your history as well as your social skills, pupil. The ap Dhyrrin ruled Maniyadoc before the ap Mennix and some would say they have a better claim. Tomas is the last of his line. His mother, Aytir Mennix, was sister to the king, and his father was Dolan ap Dhyrrin, eldest and only son of the house. They both fell victim to accidents."

"Our type of accident?"

"Most likely," she said. "Tomas survives as he has the protection of his great-grandfather, Daana ap Dhyrrin, who we shall see soon enough when he comes to the top table. He is an old friend of the king and acts as his chief adviser."

"So Tomas has reason to want Aydor dead."

"Yes, but so do his friends. If Tomas becomes king they will do well from it."

"But they are just boys . . ."

"As are you, Girton, and you are more than capable of planning a death. Aye?" I nodded and stared at the table, deep in thought. "Now, Aydor's group are at the same time more and less interesting. They are all of old families, but to inherit they would need to kill both Aydor, Tomas and whoever else in their little group stood before them in line."

"Were this a normal day we could become rich."

The flash of a grin beneath her cowl, the merest hint of a laugh.

"If Aydor falls there will be ample opportunity for us to catch our coin, Girton, if we can escape alive."

"There will be blood whatever; the heir and his boys enjoy cruelty."

"Such is the way of the blessed." I could not see my master's face but I could hear the distaste in her voice. "It is unlikely that one of Aydor's group would kill him. They all stand to do well when he comes into his inheritance. Most of them anyway."

"Men are ever greedy though."

"True, so you must watch them all, just in case. Try and insinuate yourself into one of the groups."

"That had not occurred to me, jester," I said, and then yelped as my master gave me a playful kick under the table. "I will try for Tomas's group. I am sure Aydor would not have me. He would rather I was in a cell, and Tomas's group seem to be more about martial skills. Maybe I can impress them with my bow work. I—"

"Quiet now and pay attention. The high table comes." She nodded at the stage.

First came the Festival Lords. There were four of them, each clad from head to foot in blankets covered in bright geometric designs. Meshes made of straw covered their faces, and ears of wheat stuck out from either side of their conical hats. They kept their arms within their blankets, turning them into strange pyramidal beings, like fertility gods long cut from folk memory. They sat in pairs on either side of the thrones, and their triangular shapes made the top table look oddly architectural. They had no serving places set out, the Festival Lords were governed by an arcane set of rules which dictated their behaviour and they would not eat with us until Festival was set up.

Heamus came next, together with another old Rider who wore the yellow tabard of Castle Maniyadoc.

"Heamus Galdin you know, the other is Bryan ap Mennix, cousin to the king and commander of his armies," whispered my master. "An idiot, though plenty of idiots have worn crowns. But he is an unlikely suspect – he has no heir and prefers the company of men."

The two knights bowed to the empty thrones and sat at opposite ends of the table, quietly joined by two women.

"The women?"

"Next to Heamus is the king's aunt, who is of little interest. The other is her maid."

Next came priests, cowled in the colours of their deities: orange for Heissal, the god of the day, purple for Lessiah, the goddess of night, red for Hayel, the goddess of fertility, and black for Xus, the god of death. All had their faces hidden by white masks bent into the sadness of mourning – except the priest of Xus, whose mask showed something that could have been hilarity or mania. Curiously, the priest of Xus did not sit; instead he chose to stand, almost lost in the shadows behind the thrones.

"Pay attention to the priest of Heissal. He is called Neander, and a squire called Rufra is his illegitimate son. They pass him off as a cousin." She shook her head. "And they are ap Vthyrs."

"Didn't we . . ."

"Kill one? Yes. They caused a lot of trouble because it was said they were not truly blessed, but now they have a new leader and pay tribute to the Mennixes. King Doran allows them to rule their lands as they wish and has titled them blessed rather than start another fight."

"But if you are not born blessed . . ."

"Then some convenient bloodline can be found to raise you, if needed."

"No wonder they bully him."

"They may have cause. In killing their old leader the king may have made a hedging's deal and swapped a bull mount for a poisonous lizard. The new ap Vthyr blessed are ambitious and looking beyond their lands. They may have settled for the title of blessed under Doran ap Mennix or they may be biding their time before they make a play for real power – and I would bet on the latter before the former. They are an old family with a lot of grudges. They are shedding their old ways but keeping the grudges. You should watch this Rufra boy."

"Is there anyone I shouldn't watch?"

Candlelight reflected from her eyes as she glanced at me. "No."

Next onto the stage came the oldest man I had ever seen. His face was as wrinkled as dried fruit and his beard reached down to his golden belt. All of his clothing was gold, but the most striking thing about him was not his great age or the golden clothes he wore but the lizard cages — one on each shoulder, one worn as a hat — that were part of his clothing. It looked impossible that someone so old and frail could support such an elaborate castle of wires and cloth. Each cage contained a small fire-lizard — they do not actually breathe fire, only idiots believe that, but they do spit a kind of venom that burns the skin.

"That is Daana ap Dhyrrin, great-grandfather of Tomas and son of the last ap Dhyrrin king. He is adviser to the king and the king's father before him, and I would think that if he were going to make a play for power he would have done it years ago." I glanced along our table and saw Tomas at the end, he seemed transfixed by the old man. Daana ap Dhyrrin gave the boy a wink. My master noticed this as well. "Maybe what Daana ap Dhyrrin would never take for himself he would like to gift to another." She went quiet while she thought about that, then added. "Do you remember, you used to be quite sure that fire-lizards breathed actual fire?"

Chapter 7

The king and queen appeared next. It was common knowledge throughout the Tired Lands that King Doran ap
Mennix, one of the greatest kings of our age, was sick and
dying of some wasting disease. It is testimony to my naivety
that I had believed it.

King Doran ap Mennix was being poisoned with nightsmilk.
I could see it in the yellow bags beneath his eyes and the
unmistakable way his veins throbbed against his papery skin.
If I could see it then I bet almost every other person in the
hall could see it too. I felt like turning to the man sat next to
me and saying, "He's being poisoned!" but as we hadn't been
asked to protect him I guessed his poisoner sat next to him
– Queen Adran ap Mennix. "As ambitious as she is beautiful"
was what people said about her. Though she wasn't beautiful,
not really. Her eyes were too small for her nose, and her mouth
was a hard red line. Adran wore green, a tight-fitting top and
trousers that flared out into skirts sewn with thousands of
lizard scales which shimmered in the candlelight. Her face was
painted with rouge and dark colours to accentuate her bone
structure, and her hair was lifted into an elaborate construction,
strands of thick black hair woven in and out of antlers of hard
bread, the ultimate show of wealth – food for nothing but
decoration. All in all she looked like some magical and haughty
forest creature, but we could all have been wearing sacks and
a blind man would have known she was a queen.

She was definitely attractive, I'll give her that, but it came
from her sense of assurance not her face or her fine clothes.

Once it had been believed Adran Mennix would be high queen and Doran ap Mennix high king. Twenty years ago High King Darsese had been unsteady on his throne and it had been expected that Doran ap Mennix would take his place. Darsese was a weak king, and the Tired Lands were on fire with minor resource wars. The Landsmen, protectors of the high king's order, were more concerned with their eternal hunt for sorcerers. Doran ap Mennix, young, strong and loved, rode his army right up to the walls of Ceadoc, the capital. All expected him to be crowned high king within the week.

But he was not.

Every village know-it-all has a pet theory about why, but I have always believed the answer is obvious. Doran ap Mennix was a man of action; the high king is a man tied to a throne. To be high king is to be little more than a figurehead. Doran ap Mennix was not the sort of far-seeing king who would think of change over time; he was the sort of man who thought of now and so he walked away, into a land where he could see the changes his blade wrought. He became the attack dog of High King Darsese, and he was happy.

Rumour has it his wife was not. It is an odd coincidence that Doran ap Mennix, despite having a castle full of by-blows proving his fertility, has only one legitimate child. And that child is nineteen years old, which would mean he was conceived just before Doran ap Mennix walked away from the palace of the high king.

It does not do to disappoint the ambitious.

When the king and queen were sat the food came out and my master, with a brief touch on my arm, vanished from the table. Plate after metal plate of pork, cooked in a myriad different ways, and bread so gleaming white I was unsure if it was real until I saw someone tear it apart. With the food came pots of cider and perry which were slurped up eagerly by everyone around me. I only sipped at mine as I watched the men and women at the top table.

They did not talk much. Occasionally, Daana ap Dhyrrin leaned over to say something to the ailing king, but Doran ap Mennix only stared ahead into the hall, as if lost in a world very far away from this one.

The one thing the king paid attention to was his jester, Gusteffa the dwarf, a mage-bent jester of the second order like me. The little man was extremely skilled, tumbling, twisting and performing a set of elaborate tricks in the space between the stage and the table where I sat. The court were clearly used to him and ignored his antics, but I watched rapt as he went through the classic iterations without putting any real effort or thought in. Such ease is the mark of a master. He did not deserve to be ignored, and when he finished I clapped him enthusiastically. He gave me a smile, though no doubt those around me thought I was a gauche country boy who was easily impressed.

The room had slowly become thicker with noise and the scent of people. The stink of urine floated through the air and the blessed's love of kilts was explained. Men and women staggered to the edge of the room to piss in the rushes; waiting slaves would run in and gather up the fouled reeds for disposal. As the light died more slaves appeared, candles were lit, bathing the room in a warm glow, and their smoke mixed with incense to create a thick fug in the air.

Amid the hubbub my master appeared on the floor in front of the stage. She had used a trick, the Simple Invisibility, in which she melted in with the people around her before throwing off her cloak so it seemed she suddenly appeared from nowhere. She was knelt, knees bent, one slim hand on the floor and the other arm pointing up to the ceiling with her fingers extended as if she strived to touch the candelabra far above. Few noticed at first – they were too caught up in conversation and drink – but people slowly realised something was happening and silence settled on the room like snow. My master did not move while she waited for absolute quiet. Gusteffa, in a piece of excellent comic timing, pretended to take a jealous kick at my master and missed, falling on his back and causing a burst of uproarious laughter. The dwarf got up and stalked away as if disgusted at this interloper but he shot me another smile and a wink.

Slowly the laughter died away until there was only the fuzzy hum of whispered conversation.

My master did not move.

It was as if she were frozen, and from her an icy cold spread discomfort across the room: people stopped talking, stopped eating, stopped drinking. Servants and slaves ceased their constant to and fro. When the room was utterly silent my master rose from her position of introduction so all could see her. She wore a single, loose-fitting garment of shiny black slit along the arms, legs and chest to show flashes of the white material beneath. On her head she wore a hat – black, soft and sewn into a long tapering point that fell down her back to end in a small bell which tinkled softly as she moved her head. Her face was painted black, highlighted with white around the orbits of her eyes, her nose, mouth and the line of her jaw. As she surveyed the room with wide eyes she looked like an animated skeleton, causing an excited intake of breath throughout the room.

She jinked, bringing her arms up and bending her left leg so she almost fell to the side, catching herself at the last minute and freezing in an odd, lopsided, position. The room exploded into chatter, "Death's Jester!" repeated again and again. My master stayed statue-still until silence ruled the room again. Then she went through a set of the iterations, the same tumbles, steps and jumps Gusteffa had been doing earlier but the alchemy of her talent transformed them from something merely amazing into something truly spectacular. The room filled with applause. Clapping hardest of all were Gusteffa and myself because there is a great joy in seeing something you love done well.

When the noise died down my master assumed the posture of the teller: feet together, hands held palms together in front of her chest with her elbows sticking out.

"Gentlefolk, fear no horror or hedging, for I am Death's Jester." Her voice filled the room though she spoke quietly. "I am brought here to honour the Festival Lords and the coming of Festival to this ancient castle." She jinked again, one leg bending and her hands coming up to either side of her face, framing an exaggerated look of surprise. Somewhere behind me a woman squeaked. "To honour them I will dance a story, and the one I have chosen is as ancient and venerable as this castle. I will dance for you. I will dance, Why Xus the Unseen No Longer Shows his Face."

Another collective intake of breath followed by a burst of noisy chattering. My master stayed still until the room was silent again, though it took far longer this time. This dance was rarely performed as it was seen as ill-omened. While waiting for the noise to die down I watched the faces of those on the top table. None looked happy; Queen Adran looked ready to rip my master's head from her body, but the king?

The king was smiling.

Why Xus the Unseen No Longer Shows his Face

Before there was imbalance and sourings there was balance and happiness and the gods were as familiar to men as misery is now. The Queen of the Gods, Adallada, held the land in her hands and her consort, Dallad, held the scales that kept the land in balance. Each year the harvest was enough to feed all without surplus or waste. For each drop of rain there was a beam of sunlight. For each hour of darkness there was an hour of light. For each tear there was a smile. For each fortune a misfortune. For every death a birth.

Torelc, the god of time, moved forward but never made any

progress. There was the same merry-go-round of seasons: yearsbirth, yearslife, yearsage and yearsdeath going around and around and around. Torelc longed and planned and schemed for change. He saw the magic beneath the land and the power it had, but whenever it seemed like the Adallada would free enough magic to make a real difference she would check her consort's scales and stop the magic flowing.

So Torelc spoke to Xus, the god of death, who was his brother and friend. He said, "Xus, are you happy?"

"Yes," said Xus.

"I would have thought you would be lonely," said Torelc.

"Lonely?" said Xus. "I am never lonely. I am surrounded by people."

"Yes," said Torelc, "I suppose you are. But they are never happy to see you."

"No," said Xus "they are not. They are always surprised to see me, and sometimes I am unwelcome, but, with time, they understand."

"But then they leave you and return to the world," said Torelc.

Now, as time passed, Xus could not stop thinking about what his brother had said. Whenever he turned up to take a life back to his dark palace he saw their misery and he saw the misery of those around them. This hurt him. It was the first time he had felt pain and he did not like it. He could not understand how the mortals coped. With Xus's understanding of loss came an ache, and Xus, the god of death, sought out Torelc.

"Do you know," said Xus to Torelc, "how I can stop this ache?"

"I do," said Torelc. "It is simple. If some people stayed with you then you would no longer ache. It would only require the balance to be off by the smallest, smallest amount."

"Torelc," said Xus, "how can I change the balance by the smallest, smallest amount?"

Torelc smiled a secret smile to himself and whispered a plan into the ear of Xus, the god of death.

Torelc told Xus to gather together his creatures who flew. So he did.

"I ache," said Xus. "Take your kind and fly up to the scales of balance and perch upon the dark arm of the scales. Make it move, just a little, so that I may no longer ache."

And Xus's creatures, who loved him, were happy to help. As they left Xus's dark palace they met Torelc, the god of time, who was waiting for them.

"Where are you going?" said Torelc.

"Xus aches," they said, "and we shall perch upon the dark arm of the scales and move them just a little so he may no longer ache."

"Oh," said Torelc. "Why should you move it only a little? What will you do if that is not enough?"

Xus's creatures said, "We do not know."

"I know," said Torelc, and he smiled a secret smile to himself and whispered a plan into the ear of Xus's flying creatures.

And Xus's flying creatures heard Torelc's plan and gathered together all of the animals who relied upon Xus for their lives. They gathered all the beasts that brought death and all the beasts that fed on corpses and said, "This is what we must do to stop Xus aching." Then the gathered creatures flew or crawled or ran or climbed onto the scales, and each found a place to sit or perch or squat or lie on the dark arm of scales.

The scales did not move a little bit.

The scales did not bend a little bit.

The scales snapped.

The Queen of the Gods saw her consort's scales break and she lifted her hands from the land to cover her face. Without her hands to contain it the magic became free and wild. No longer would each deed be repaid strike for strike, and no longer would men and women be free of hunger and disease. Torelc clapped with happiness as he felt himself change from a shadowy, willowy thing to something muscular, powerful and creative.

This will serve me well, he thought.

But of all the gods only Xus was to be well served by Torelc's actions.

With the scales broken, the land soured. People warred, and war spread like fire until even the gods took sides.

Only Xus did not fight – war gave him no time – but he saw.

Xus saw the Consort Dallad slay his son, Torelc. Xus saw the queen, Adallada, slay her Consort, Dallad. Xus saw the queen, mad with grief, take her own life, and he watched the bodies of the gods sink deep down to the bottom of the sea where Xus could not go. Xus was shamed by his part and ashamed of surviving when all the other gods had not.

And that is why Xus, the god of death, no longer shows his face.

Though his creatures still love him.

She finished frozen in the position of Xus's black bird and a susurrus of conversation filled the room. Three of the priests at the high table stood and walked out. There is little that priests like less than to be reminded their gods are dead and just as foolish and fallable as any human. Only the priest of Xus remained, stood behind the king, and when my master turned to bow to the high table he gave her a small nod.

Queen Adran stood. "I am sure you are all as thankful as I am to have seen something as rare as a performance by Death's Jester." She looked as if saying those words was as pleasurable to her as chewing on rocks. "And it is always good to be reminded of the folly of the past which has led us to the position we find ourselves in. Now, let us look to the present and be thankful of the peace we have. I ask you to raise your pots and drink to our king, Doran ap Mennix, who has given us so many years of peace." With a shout of, "Aye!" the room toasted the king.

"And raise your pots again to his heir, Aydor ap Mennix,

who will give us many more years of peace." Another cheer, though this one I felt was a little less enthusiastic and I noticed quite a few who looked around, as if noting who was most fervent for the heir.

The queen continued to talk of all the wonderful things her husband had done and the wonderful things her son would do for the people when I felt a tug on my kilt. Gusteffa, the jester, stood by me.

"Blessed ap Gwynr, the queen wants you to follow me," he rasped. I wondered how he knew as the queen was currently waxing lyrical from the stage. "You should come now." He tugged at my kilt again, making me worry he might accidentally undo all my earlier hard work and leave me naked. "Come," he said again, "before the uproar."

"Uproar?" I stood and followed Gusteffa as he pushed his way along the benches. "What uproar?"

"Come," he said again. As we reached the exit from the sweaty smoky room I heard the queen's voice.

". . . and as I know you are all as appalled as King Doran and I at the threat to the heir, I am sure you will take the news I have with good grace. Once the full Festival is here, the keep and the gates to the keepyard will be shut. No one will leave or come in through them without the king's say-so."

The room erupted into shouts of dismay.

Ah, I thought, that uproar.

Gusteffa led me to the highest floor of the castle where the king, queen and Aydor lived, then opened a door and motioned me in. As I walked through I felt a gentle tug on my kilt and turned.

"Death's Jester," he said, "She came with you?"

"Yes," I said. "My father sent her to keep me company."

"And she leaves with you?"

"Yes." I nodded, suddenly realising how he must feel and how worried he must be that he was about to lose his livelihood.

"You are sure?"

"Yes, no matter what she was offered she would not stay, Gusteffa. She would not see another jester lose their place."

"She is an artist," he mumbled. "I have never seen the like."

"Gusteffa, I watched you perform tonight, though many didn't. You are an artist yourself. Even if you were to be pushed from your place here many would be glad to have you."

"Thank you, Blessed," he said with a small bow. I watched him hobble away and thought how perilous life was for most people. I had commented in the past to my master on how worn out everyone looked in the Tired Lands but had never really understood why.

"Girton?" I turned to find my master, motleyed and painted, standing by my shoulder. "You are a million miles away."

"Sorry, Master. Life is hard for people, isn't it?"

"Yes, Girton, it is."

"It is not fair."

"No, it is not." She pulled me into a sumptuously outfitted room. Padded wooden chairs sat in front of a roaring fire and a fantastically expensive desk, made of the slow-growing darkwoods found only in the north, dominated one corner of the room while richly embroidered tapestries covered the shuttered window and plastered walls behind it. My master pulled aside a tapestry to reveal a small alcove. "In here, Girton. Any minute now the Festival Lords will appear to try and strong-arm Adran into leaving the keep and the gates to the keepyard open. It is a perfect time for us to observe the Festival Lords – well, listen to them," she said as she let the tapestry fall back and shut out the light. "As there's little to be learnt from staring at the back of some embroidery."

I counted three hundred my-masters before the Festival

Lords shuffled into the room. From behind the tapestry I heard them settle into position and wondered how they coped, wrapped in thick blankets in all weathers.

"This is not acceptable," said one. I was surprised to hear it was a woman.

"A woman? I thought they were all men," I said in the Whisper-that-Flies-to-the-Ear.

"Why?" My master said. I did not reply as there was no good answer. "Now be quiet and listen."

"You are right, it is not acceptable." This speaker was a man.

"We shall not stand for this." Another man. "It is imprisonment."

"No, Festival cannot be controlled, it must not be." The woman spoke again.

"Quiet," a second woman said. "It is more than likely we are listened to. These dead buildings are riddled with tunnels and passages."

My master smiled at me when the woman said that. Then whispered, "The Festival Lords follow the old ways — they balance. Two men, two women."

"Lords." Queen Adran's voice, confident as ever.

"You cannot imprison Festival," said one of the male Festival Lords.

"I have no intention of imprisoning Festival," said Adran "You said the gates would be closed."

"Yes, but not the townyard gate. Your caravans and your suppliers will still be able to get to you and come and go as they wish."

I leaned to one side so I could look through a tear in the tapestry. I could see two of the Festival Lords and the back of Adran as she paced back and forth. The Festival Lords did not move at all. Swathed in blankets, their faces covered by corn stalk masks, it was easy to understand why people thought them inhuman.

"And how will our tumblers and entertainers make their living, Queen Adran? They pass through the castle and get paid by your blessed."

"Did you fail to understand what I said in the theatre hall? My son is—"

"Your son is not our concern."

"The death of the heir should be everyone's concern." There was steel in Adran's voice.

When the Festival Lord replied his voice was low, almost threatening. "Do you accuse us of this?"

"No," said Adran, "of course not. I would never intimate such a thing. But Festival is huge and it is possible an assassin could use it to slip into the castle."

Silence for five counts of my-master.

"To shut us out is not done," said a male Festival Lord. "It has never been done. It is not the way of things."

"Well, change is often unstoppable," said Adran coldly.

"If you had listened to your jester you would know change is not always a good thing," one of the women said.

"That was not my jester," said Adran. "And besides, the blessed of the castle will still visit Festival, only in groups so no intruders may slip in."

"If you force this on us, you may find that Festival stops elsewhere next year and your fruit and fish are left to rot."

Another silence. Ten "my-masters".

"Listen to me," hissed Adran. "I had hoped to avoid this, but you leave me no choice. Let us be plain: you need Castle Maniyadoc as a stop. There is nowhere else before the western sourlands that can provide enough fodder and water for your animals, and I know the sort of profit you make on our produce – more than enough to put up with a little inconvenience."

I heard a rustle of material that I presumed was one, or all, of the Festival Lords standing.

"Profit is not everything, Queen Adran. Leave the gates

open as tradition dictates or we will find some way to avoid your castle next year."

"No," said Adran. As she spoke her voice dropped further and further, becoming quieter and quieter which only served to underline the threat she made. "You should keep in mind, before you threaten me, that the marriage of my son and the high king's sister is only a matter of time. The high king has no heir. Aydor will be next high king and I will stand behind him. He will be no figurehead when he's on the high throne; he will be a power. I, and he, will remember who was his friend, Festival Lords. My reach will be long and if you do not accept the closure of the keepyard I will make sure you pay. Taxes on Festival will increase; the Landsmen will be less respectful of your autonomy, check you for sorcerers more thoroughly and be slower to come to your defence if you are troubled. So choose wisely, Festival Lords, for you hold your future in your hands."

I waited, not knowing what would happen. I had never been in the same room as powerful people when they chose to bump heads and the air almost throbbed with tension.

"You dream, Queen Adran."

"Do I?"

She did not sound like she dreamed and the ensuing silence lasted ten my-masters.

"Close your gates then, Queen," said one of the female Festival Lords quietly. "You need not throw the traditional leaving banquet for us though; we will not be attending."

The rustle of clothes and then the closing of the door.

"Merela, come out," said Adran, and we squeezed out of our hiding place. "Well, what do you think? Are they likely to want my son dead?"

"They may now," said my master. "But they would not have before. You should not have pushed them so hard."

Adran sat heavily on one of the overstuffed chairs. "And what else could I do?" When she looked up there were tears in her eyes. "What else could I do, Merela? He is my son and I love him." She stood and gathered herself, straightening her green jerkin. "Of course, I should not expect you to understand a mother's love. Go, it is late," she pointed at the door. "Leave me!"

We walked to our room in silence. When I was huddled in my bed and my master had blown out the candle I gave voice to a question that had been burning within me: "What did she mean?"

"Who?" said my master.

"Adran, when she spoke of you . . ." I was suddenly awkward, having to think of my master as a woman. "Well, you know. Not understanding a mother's love?"

"It doesn't matter, Girton. Go to sleep."

Five my-masters.

"How well do you know Adran?"

"I said you should sleep."

Ten my-masters.

"You would think your past was gold, Master, the way you hoard it."

She replied quickly, angrily: "And you would think your words were piss, Girton, the way you strew them about so carelessly." I heard her turn away on the small truckle bed.

"Why do you always treat me like a child?" and as I said it I heard the whine in my voice.

When she spoke again she sounded tired. "Go to sleep. Tomorrow will no doubt be another long day."

Interlude

This is a dream of what was.

He doesn't understand what she is doing.

He doesn't understand what he has done wrong.

They have stopped outside a small village, no more than a couple of falling-down huts built on a rare bit of solid land in a place where the trees and grasses grow out of stinking water and sucking mud. It is easy to imagine hedgings in the wood, in the water. Has she bought him for them?

She has a thin rope, the type that can be used as a lash. She is looping it in her hands. The rope scares him. When she walks over to him he steps back. She says, "No," and he is more scared than ever. What did Slave-Father always say? "Running only makes it worse." She kneels down so she is at his height and looking into his eyes. "I am not going to hurt you." She stretches out a hand, but even that gentle movement makes him flinch. She looks at the ground. He is sure he has made her angry. She drops the rope in the dirt, walking away into one of the tumbledown houses.

Low voices murmur.

The skies whisper out an infinity.

It never occurs to him to run away.

When she comes back she has a whip. The whip is the type he knows the sting of. A thin wooden handle that can be used for striking. Attached to that are four knotted leather strands that will cut the skin and rip the flesh. A whip hurts far more than a rope. *Running only makes it worse.* She strides over to him with the whip gathered in one hand, holding it out so he can see it clearly.

She is tall, she is dark, she is frightening.

"You know what this is?"

He nods, trying so very hard not to cry because crying only makes it worse as well.

"I will never," she says and she grabs the whip by each end of the handle. "Never —" the word as hard any whip-crack and she brings the whip down on her knee, breaking it in half."— Never —" she throws the broken whip into the filthy water and the ripples go on and on and on. "— Never use something like that on you, boy. Do you understand? Never."

In the way she says "never" there is a vehemence that, even as a six-year-old, he hears as a promise. He recognises it as a promise given utterly and totally and for ever and he nods, scarcely able to believe it.

"Good." She smiles at him and uses the same gentle voice she uses to coax the giant warmount, Xus, into doing her bidding. She holds out her hand. "Now, I can't call you boy. I shall call you Girton, it is a good name." She puts out her hand. "Come, Girton."

He takes her hand and she lifts him onto the saddle of the mount.

It feels like flying.

This is a dream of what was.

Chapter 8

I woke to find my master sitting cross-legged on the floor with a tray of bread and pork in her lap. She was ignoring the food and reapplying her make-up with thick sticks of animal grease impregnated with pigment.

"What will you do today, Girton?" she said, smearing on black grease.

Rubbing sleep from my eyes I avoided her gaze, feeling foolish for my outburst last night – though she knows everything about me where I know almost nothing about her. "Go to training, collect more bruises." I smiled at her. My way of letting her know I was not angry with her any longer. My master never carries grudges and her anger is like the rain – sudden, furious and gone as quickly as it comes.

"I am glad you are not sulking, Girton."

"I never sulk, Master." This was not entirely true. "Will Aydor really be high king?"

"Why do you ask?

"I do not think he would make a good king, never mind a good high king."

"You are probably right, but kings are chosen by accidents of birth, not suitability." She put down the black panstick. "It surprised me. Adran said it to be truthful." She picked up the white panstick. "It was a dangerous bluff to play if it was not true and the high king's sister is no more interested in men than our high king is in women."

"Queen Adran seemed very sure of herself."

"Yes. She did."

"Maybe the high king wants to secure the succession?"

"Possibly. But he has cousins to inherit."

"Do you think Adran plans war?" I asked quietly.

My master glanced around our small room as if looking for spies. Then she lowered her voice. "She would be a fool to go to war. The Landsmen would destroy any army she could bring to the field. Doran ap Mennix had the support of all his blessed when he warred, but you have seen him now. He is not about to head an army and the blessed do not like or trust Adran." She shrugged and started to smear white onto her face. "But the future succession at Ceadoc does not concern us. Who wants Aydor dead does, and with that in mind I have managed to set up some meetings for you. You are popular at the moment, Girton. Important people always want to meet a new hostage in case there is something in it for them. I want to hear what you think of them, and I want you to familiarise yourself with their rooms, you will no doubt be going back uninvited at some point."

"Oh," I said.

"Do you have other things to do?"

"I was hoping to check on Xus, is all."

She paused in applying her make-up

"You think the stablehands will not look after him properly?"

"The stablemaster, Leiss, I do not trust with our mount at all. The girl though, Drusl, she seems to know her job." My master stared at me for a moment and then shook her head.

"I have never known you to be interested in stabling before, Girton." I could feel my face reddening as my master, clearly amused, stood up. "I am sure you will be able to find a moment to check on Xus," she said, brushing dust from her black trews.

I grabbed a piece of bread from the plate.

"Have you found the assassin yet, Master?"

"It is in hand, do not worry about that."

"Good." I stuffed bread into my mouth and almost choked trying to speak through it. "I should get to the training yard, Master. I do not want to be late and make any more of a bad impression. They already think me unable to hold a sword without falling over it."

I ran from our room and through Maniyadoc. Even early the castle was busy with slaves and servants rushing backwards and forwards. My passage through the corridors disturbed the usual course of their day and I felt resentful eyes on my back as I passed. My run slowed to a jog, and my jog slowed to a fast walk, which slowed to a stately saunter. As I walked down the cold stone of the main staircase I felt myself wilting under the imperious gaze of the chief household servants, who guarded propriety like attack dogs. Even away from them it felt like everyone I passed watched me with suspicious eyes.

Aydor arrived at the squireyard just before I did, amid a tightly knit formation of guards with armour and weapons far more ornate then any others I had seen. After seeing him safely into the yard they turned smartly and marched past me. Their captain, a man with a short beard and missing front tooth, hissed, "Mage-bent," and spat at the ground by my club foot as I watched them walk past.

Squires were already lining up to take bows from a rack as I entered. Targets made from large bales of hay with white circles painted on them had been set up at the far end of the yard.

"Take a bow, Girton," said the squiremaster. "Today we shoot."

"You may shoot," said Aydor, walking away from the rack. "I will not. A bow is a thankful's weapon."

"And one you will need to master if you wish to become a Rider," said the squiremaster.

"Kings have no need to pass skills tests," said Aydor, and

a few of his group smiled, though I noticed they still picked up bows. I walked to the rack, trying to watch the confrontation between Aydor and the squiremaster without obviously staring.

"You are not a king yet, Aydor, so I am still your master on this field. Pick up a bow."

"Aydor does not want to shoot because his eyes are bad." The whisper came from by my elbow. It was Rufra, the squire my master said was the child of Neander from the vicious ap Vthyr family. His eyes were constantly darting around the yard and he immediately struck me as shifty, running to tell tales. I nodded uncomfortably and went back to studying the bows.

Aydor walked over to the rack, pushed me out of the way and picked up the first bow his hand touched. I wondered again if the squiremaster was the assassin – if not he was a brave man to talk to Aydor the way he had. The heir would one day hold the squiremaster's life in his hand.

"There," said Aydor, "I have a bow."

"Well done," said Nywulf. "And you, Girton? Will you hold us up further?" He stared at me and I finished looking over the bows. They were a poor lot but I picked the best of them. "Right, who will shoot first?"

"I will," said Aydor. An offer which surprised everyone.

"Very well," said Nywulf. "Take your mark."

Aydor stepped forward to a line Nywulf had marked in the sand with a stick. Arrows had been stuck in the ground along it.

"Draw," said Nywulf.

The heir's armour creaked as he nocked an arrow and brought the bow up, pulling the string taut so it rested against his cheek and holding the bow like that for far longer than was needed for him to aim. It was bravado, a display of strength that would do nothing for his ability to hit a target. Then he spun on the spot and a little cloud of dirt rose around his feet. He pointed the arrow at the squire-master. Nywulf did not flinch. He stared straight down the shaft of the arrow into Aydor's eyes.

"And loose," said Nywulf.

Sweat stood out on the heir's brow.

He let the arrow fly.

"No!" The boy by me, Rufra, shouted the word, articulating what everyone on the field was thinking. Even Kyril, Borniya and Hallin, Aydor's little clique, looked shocked.

With a sound like cloth ripping the arrow shot across the training yard, flying past Nywulf's head in a blur and burying itself in the wooden wall.

A silence settled over the training yard. Nywulf did not move. He stared at Aydor.

"You missed," he said.

Aydor spat on the ground. "It seems I have no skill with these thankful weapons." He dropped the bow in the dirt.

"I doubt anyone else will shoot so poorly, Squire Aydor," said Nywulf. It seemed inhuman that his voice did not waver or crack. "So you have placed last. You may leave now."

Aydor seemed at a loss for a moment, his thunder stolen from him by the steel core that ran through Nywulf. Then he turned and walked out the gate watched by everyone on the field, Celot jogging after him like a loyal dog.

"Right," shouted Nywulf, so loud it made me jump. "Who's next?"

"Me," said Tomas. He walked to the line, drew and loosed at the target in one fluid motion. He hit it dead centre. One by one the other squires followed. All were reasonably skilled – in that none missed the target – but some were better than others. Each archer had five arrows and those who scored lowest in each round of shooting were out. After five rounds it came down to Tomas, Rufra, Boros and myself – though only Tomas and I could win. The others shot for third place, which Boros won. Then Tomas and I stepped up. Tomas shot first. Both he and I had been shooting straight centres right through the competition. I was a little ahead as Tomas's second shot had gone into the painted line of the centre rather than the actual centre.

Tomas took his last shot – a centre again.

I nocked an arrow to my bow and drew. I would not miss – we were far nearer the target than I generally practised at and it should be an easy win – but I was not here to win, even though I wanted to. I let the bow waver as if my strength was going and when I loosed the arrow it flew straight and true into the second circle, giving Tomas victory.

His small group of friends let out a roar of approval and ran over to clap him on the back. I shook my head and stared at the ground as if ashamed.

"You shoot well." I looked up – it was Rufra again. "And you look surprised that I am talking to you." He glanced around. His nervousness was contagious and I had to stop myself flinching as if in expectation of a blow. "We are not all like the heir." He put out his hand to grasp. I was confused and annoyed. I had expected Tomas to talk to me not this nervous boy. After a near-run match it was normal for the winner to compliment the loser. I glanced over at Tomas. He smiled at me but it was a cold, aloof smile, and any friendship that may have been in it swiftly died when he saw I was talking to Rufra.

"Thank you," I said to Rufra without taking his hand. There was an aura of barely suppressed frustration around the boy, as if he were a coiled spring ready to burst into violent action. When he smiled it seemed as much a mask as that of any priest.

"You are a hostage, I heard?" he said, letting his offered hand fall.

"Yes," I replied, trying to work out why he was talking to me. Evidently the rest of Aydor's clique were wondering the same as they watched us with interest. Hallin, the boy with the blinded eye, was running his thumb along the back of his knife. "My father was lax in his tributes so I am here as surety."

"My family is not trusted either." Rufra gave me an unconvincing smile and then glanced over his shoulder. "They are old country and still follow some of those ways. My aunt even rides a warmount and commands men." His face lit up at the mention of his aunt but I did not return his smile. "She taught me to shoot a bow."

"I thought women could not become Riders?"

"It is not common now," said Rufra, and then his words came out in a jumbled rush, "but Aunt Cearis says it was not always the way. My uncle hates it and his wife says Cearis is not a proper lady. I know you may have heard bad things about my family, but it seems we are both held here under the sword, Girton." He gave me another smile then added, "Do you think women should be allowed to become Riders?"

I could not think of a reply. Certainly my master had no trouble mastering a warmount but to say openly that I thought women should fight as cavalry would mark me out as unusual, and I wanted to fit in. Nywulf saved me from further uncomfortable conversation, calling us to go through a series of sword-work exercises, which I bungled expertly. Despite Nywulf splitting us up Rufra managed to find his way back to me again and again. I could feel any chance of getting near Tomas ebbing away. He clearly loathed Rufra and now I was tainted by association. Often the boy gave me tips on how I could improve my defensive work or make a certain move in a way that would tax my strength less. He was well meaning but I found his words increasingly irritating. What infuriated me the most was that he was often right.

It was hard not to compare Rufra to Tomas: Rufra, small and dark in ill-fitting armour, and Tomas who, although bruised, looked every inch the warrior from the tales we told as jesters. His sword moves were elegant, where Rufra looked like he was chopping wood, though there was a lethal, workmanlike efficiency in the way he went about it. And if Tomas was occasionally a little high-handed with his followers then that was only to be expected of a boy who should be a king — and he so clearly should have been. He was no cruel, overweight, tyrant-in-the-making like Aydor.

When training ended I was first out, keeping my armour on despite the discomfort. It squeaked where it needed more grease and pinched me painfully in places. My wrapped swords banged against my bruised legs as I limped quickly away.

"Girton!" My name echoed over the keepyard but I did not turn — I recognised Rufra's voice. "Girton ap Gwynr!" This time his shout was followed by the sound of running steps. I knew I could not outrun him, not with my armour on and my club foot.

"Rufra," I said, turning to meet him.

"Aye." He smiled. Without his armour he looked taller, though everyone was taller than me, but he cut an altogether unremarkable figure, not handsome but not ugly. He had long unruly dull-brown hair that he was constantly having to scrape away from his face. Away from the other squires his eyes no longer jumped as if he expected to find a threat in every corner. "I missed you leaving, Girton. You did not stay to take off your armour."

"No," I said, keeping my voice dead. "No, I did not." His smile faltered and when he spoke I could barely hear him.

"I am always hungry after training; you must be too. I wondered if you would like to come with me to the kitchens? Cook was making honey buns this morning."

"I cannot," I said, and watched him become more and more uncomfortable. "I must see to my mount."

"Oh, of course." He looked away, the smile falling from

his face. "You must think, as I was with Aydor when you came, that . . ." He let the words tail off. "He hates me, you know, Aydor. And you must have insulted him somehow as he does not like you either." He smiled again, as if this should form some bond between us. "Aydor cannot stand to be insulted," he added quietly.

"I hope you enjoy the honey buns, Rufra," I said. Something hopeful that had been in his eyes slowly faded. He nodded, pushing his hair behind his ears and bowing his head.

"I understand. I had just thought that you are an outsider and I . . ." he glanced at my club foot ". . . and I am also. I thought that maybe we could be . . ." He shook his head. "It was presumptive of me. I am sorry." He walked away and I should have let him go. Alienating Rufra would put me in better standing with both Tomas and Aydor. My master would have watched him walk away but I am not as cold as she is, besides, I was curious about something.

"Rufra," I said. He turned. "If Aydor hates you, why are you not in Tomas's group?"

He laughed, though there was no humour in it. "Simple really. Aydor hates me, but Tomas hates me more. That is the only reason Aydor wanted me with him. He is kingly though, is he not – Tomas?" He kicked a stone along the ground. "It is all right, Girton. I understand that Tomas would make a better friend than I. I'll not hold it against you or stand in your way." He turned once more, but before I could walk away or call him back my name was barked out. Nywulf was stumping towards me from the squireyard, a huge filthy bucket in one hand.

"I have a job for you, boy. You can feed and clean out the dogs." He handed me the foul-smelling bucket full of meat scraps and slops.

"The dogs?" I knew it was one of the squires' tasks but had not expected it to come to me so soon. My insides shivered at the thought of sharp red teeth and hard muscled flesh.

"Are you questioning me, boy?" His bald head reddened in anger.

"No, Squiremaster." I bowed my head and walked away with my filthy bucket, feeling his gaze all the way. I passed Aydor, surrounded by his guards, and he shouted after me, "Found your level, have you, country boy?" I ignored him. Tomas passed me soon after but said nothing, only stared at me as I struggled with the bucket. I tried to think of anything but dogs as I walked. I was distracted for a moment when I passed the stables and saw Drusl, but she was with Leiss and could not stop to talk. Seeing her with Leiss made me angry and I stamped along, spilling some of the slop on my skirts, which made me even more cross.

The kennels had little of the stables' glory; they were a long low windowless building made from stone that had fallen from the walls, and if the builder's intention was a construction that looked constantly on the edge of collapse then he had been entirely successful. I promised myself that once I had finished my reward would be a visit to Drusl, but that didn't make me feel much better; the kennels continued to grow ominously in both size and stink as I approached. When I stood at the door, my heart racing, the animals inside sensed my presence and filled the air with angry noise. By the kennel door was a flaking wooden handle used to open the cages inside. I checked it was down and the animals locked up before I considered entering.

The kennel door opened onto darkness full of barking, shrieking animals that sounded as hungry and terrifying as any hedging. War dogs are huge creatures and I counted four pairs of eyes glowing in the darkness. Each animal was fed by way of a funnel which delivered food directly into a trough in an empty cage next to its own. The food would coax the animal out so its home cage could be cleaned. I took a step into the building and stood – *Breathe out, no room for fear. Breathe in, I am the instrument* – forcing my eyes wide open as I concentrated on the exercise of the False Lantern. Slowly, my eyes became unnaturally wide and the darkness changed. The kennel took on a curious look, becoming a collection of sketchy silhouettes outlined in shivering white against absolute black. Some lines were still: the edges of the cages, the handles which pulled up the inner gates to funnel the fierce animals from one cage to another. Other, more terrifying shapes bounced and snarled as they snapped furious teeth in my direction, eager to be at this stranger who stepped forward, stinking of fear.

I reached the first empty cage, and as I lifted the heavy bucket the huge animal next door threw itself against the mesh. I recoiled, spilling more of the filthy slop on my clothes. The three other dogs joined in with the noise, filling the stifling room with barking, growling and the clash of rattling cages. I forced myself back to the cage and emptied out a portion of food but the gelid slop of animal innards, old porridge and bones sliding into the empty cage did nothing to distract the huge animal next door. It seemed intent only on me. As I walked to the next cage it followed me down the length of its own. I put food into the remaining troughs but the other dogs were also more interested in my throat than the food. Then I walked to the handle which would lift the inner gates so the dogs would move to their eating cages.

As I touched the handle I thought I heard something above the dogs – a stifled laugh that turned the blood in my veins to ice. No one should be here. I turned. A silhouette filled the doorway, identity hidden by the glare from outside. In slow motion I saw an arm reach out for the edge of the door and before I could shout, "No!" the door was slammed shut and I heard the bar fall on the other side.

Panic flooded through me.

This was a prank, a cruel and stupid prank by some squire. No doubt to them this was little more than a game or a way of currying favour with Aydor or Tomas.

Breathe! Breathe out, breathe out.

With a screech of complaining metal, the shining lines of the outer gates on the cages began to move. Someone was pulling on the handle outside.

No.

Breathe in, breathe in.

I was frozen to the floor.

No room. No room for fear or . . . Breathe! Breathe.

I was moving, my body reacting while my mind remained clouded and chilled. I ran for the back of the room – *Not away from the door, not away from the door* – and grabbed the spade used to shovel dirt from the cages. The beasts scrabbled at the ground beneath their gates with huge luminous paws, clods of filthy hay flying as they dug and whined in their desperation to get at me. The space beneath the gates slowly grew. Glimpses in silver: a paw, a muzzle, an ear.

No time for fear no room for fear breathe out – fear – breathe in. I am an – breathe – instrument. I am – breathe – a weapon. Breathe!

The gate creaked up a little further.

Breathe!

Dead gods, whoever was doing this was taunting me. They were enjoying it.

Don't scream for help.

The cages inched open further and one of the dogs, the biggest, managed to get its jaws underneath the gate, snapping out lines of phosphorescent saliva.

Everything in me wanted to run for the door. This was no prank; this was an attempt on my life and I'd take a hedging's deal before I'd give them the satisfaction of hearing me banging on the door, screaming to be let out.

My tormentor became bored of the game and the gates

opened with a screech. The first dog came at me, a huge beast of shimmering white ropes. Its mouth yawing open impossibly far as it jumped for my throat. I brought round my spade, smashing the blade into its head. The war dog yelped as it hit the floor but got straight back up, circling round to join the pack. I knew I was finished.

. . . *if you escape the slavers will let the dogs rip you apart*. . .

With a blade I'd be hard pressed to protect myself when the four animals attacked together, without one there was no way I would be able to hold them off.

Three dogs waited at bay, growling, while the dog I had hit gathered itself to lead their attack. I could almost feel the gathering tension in their muscles as they prepared to leap.

The dogs growled, deep and hungry, and then there was a pause in the moment − an unexpected strangeness. An unreality where the air was honey-yellow and the filthy stink of the kennel was banished by something other, some exotic and spicy scent. It confused the dogs. Growls turned into whines, jaws closed, tails went between legs and the dark kennel was suffused with unworldly light. In my fear I felt as though another stood in the room with me, willing my escape.

I threw myself sideways and squeezed under a gate, making it into the cage that had housed the biggest dog just as the strange light vanished and the dogs rediscovered their fury. The gate was attached to its lifting mechanism by a piece of twisted old rope and I swung the shovel, cutting the ratty length and bringing the gate clattering down. Denied their prey the dogs descended into a form of insanity and my life became nothing but sharp teeth, angry barking and paws scrabbling at wire mesh that looked far too delicate to hold them back.

Breathe.

Time ceased to have meaning.

Can't breathe.

All was teeth and claws and noise. I closed my eyes and let time flow over me.

A change in the timbre of the barking snapped me out of my terror. The dogs, instead of barking, were letting out low growls. I opened my eyes to see they had turned from me towards the door. It creaked open. I could just make out a figure. At first, as the dogs did not bark, I thought it must be someone they knew, but as my eyes became more used to the glare I recognised the slim form of my master in her motley. She stepped forward, slowly and carefully, placing her feet like she was doing a knife dance. She had one hand outstretched and the nearer she got to the dogs the more the growling subsided until I could hear her speaking in a whisper, repeating the same set of nonsense words again and again as she inched forward. The biggest dog took four stiff-legged steps towards her and stopped to sniff her outstretched hand. It let out a whimper and turned twice on the spot before lying down with its head on its big paws. Then its fellows did the same. My master was using the Wild Gaze to calm the beasts, a skill I had never managed to learn.

"Come out, Girton," she said in a low voice. "Step around the animals, if you move slowly and calmly they will not harm you."

I pushed up the gate which had kept me safe and squeezed out through the opening, letting it down gently behind me so it did not bang and startle the hounds. Then I made my way between the dogs, slow-dancing a path that kept me as far from the animals as possible. When I was near her my master took my hand and led me out. After she had shut the door behind us she reached out, putting her hand on my cheek.

"You are safe now."

"They would have killed me, Master. Someone wanted me dead."

"They would not have killed you, Girton. Those are

manhunters, trained to hold down a capture, not kill it. You would have recognised the breed if you had stopped to think."

"Then someone wanted me scared." I realised I was shaking.

"And they succeeded." She put her hands on my shoulders and we stood like that until I had control of myself again. "Do you know who did this?"

"No." I turned away. Slumped by the door was the body of a guard. "They set a guard? You killed him?"

"Of course not. You think I would announce our presence to the whole castle? I used the Tired Forgetting and sprinkled wine on him. He'll wake with a terrible headache and not want anyone to know about it."

I knelt by the man.

"What are you doing, Girton?"

"Remembering his face, Master. Someone must have set him to guard me and when he wakes I intend to find out who." I stared at the man, committing his pocked face to memory. "How did you know to come for me?"

"I came to find you after training. When I could not I found one of the squires, Rufra. He said you were sent to feed the dogs."

"Literally."

"Don't be so dramatic, Girton. Go and change your clothes. You are filthy and it will do you good to be rid of the smell of dogs."

"I know," I said sullenly and made my way back to the castle to change. Once that was done I decided to make good on my promise to myself and visit the stables.

In the stables I was greeted by the familiar smell of mounts – dung and warm fur, it was a comforting sop to my earlier fear. Drusl was running a brush down the centre aisle, pushing a stream of acrid mount piss down the intricate floor mosaic of a half-naked woman on mountback.

"Blessed," she said, keeping her eyes downcast like a slave.

"Drusl, please. Call me Girton. I am the youngest and least important son of my family." The lies slipped so easily from my mouth. "I am hardly a blessed; there is no need to avert your eyes."

"I cannot call you by your name. If Leiss hears he will think . . . Well, he will be jealous."

"Oh." Something within me died a little. "You and him are . . ."

"Dead gods no," she said and looked up. It was the strangest thing. If you had asked me at that moment I would have said there was some connection between us, something past the simple attraction I felt. It was like her presence created a physical pull that was centred on my chest. "Leiss would like me to be with him." The sense of being linked vanished, leaving me thinking I had imagined it. Her voice became very quiet. "Though sometimes I think he hates me." She shrugged and changed the subject. "Have you come to see your mount?" she asked, walking towards Xus's stall. "He is well cared for; you do not need to come and check on him."

"Oh," I said. Something within me fluttered. "You do not want me to come?"

"No, not at all." She shook her head and a shy smile crept across her face. "I welcome your visits. Too few of the blessed of the castle take a real interest in their mounts." We slipped into Xus's stall and the great beast huffed at me. "He is a gentle creature once you know him, isn't he?" she said.

There are many words I could use to describe Xus but "gentle" has never been one of them. Maybe Drusl would change her mind if she ever saw a corpse skewered on the mount's antlers.

"Yes," I said, and ran my hand along the animal's flanks.

Drusl looked up at me. She seemed so small and delicate, her eyes huge.

"He is a very fine beast," she said, but she was not looking at Xus. Then she put out her hand and rubbed the animal's velvety muzzle. I put out my hand and laid it on top of hers as I had to introduce her to Xus. It felt like the bravest thing I had ever done, to make the presumption that this pretty girl could possibly have an interest in me, Girton the club-footed minor son of a faraway house. Girton the liar.

Drusl did not move her hand, and again, it was as if an invisible link existed that joined us in some way I could not understand but it felt as real as the mount stood by us.

"Drusl?" Leiss shouted her name into the stable, breaking the spell. Our hands shot back to our sides.

"I am with Xus and his master," she shouted. "He wished to check the animal was stabled correctly."

"Of course he is," said Leiss. "We look after 'em. Even an evil-tempered beast like that one."

I disliked Leiss, but I recognised more of the Xus I knew in his description of the mount.

"Good," I said, stepping out of the stall and attempting to appear imperious and blessed. "He seems in good condition. I am pleased."

Leiss stared at me. "Good," he said slowly.

"I think you mean, good, Blessed," I said. Behind him I saw Drusl hide a smile.

"Good, Blessed," said Leiss through gritted teeth.

"Thank you. I will return tomorrow," I said, turning and walking away as Drusl let out a stifled giggle.

"Those stalls need mucking out, girl," shouted Leiss. I heard Drusl say, "Yes, Leiss," and had to fight not to look back. The strangest thing was that the further I went from the stables the less sure I became of what had happened in there. With Drusl I had felt sure she liked me, that she didn't care about me having a club foot, saw past that and found some worth in who I was. But as I walked through the swiftly growing tent city of Festival I started to doubt. What had seemed an obvious connection, me putting my hand on hers, became a simple act between rider and groom. She had shown me before how to introduce her to Xus, was that all it was? All that had happened? And when she had said, "He is a very fine beast," I had felt sure that was meant for me. But Xus really was a fine beast. Maybe she only talked of Xus; maybe my ears heard what they wanted to hear rather than what had been said. I had left the stables feeling like I could take to the air but by the time I re-entered the keepyard gate I was firmly attached to the ground. The world once again became a dark and impossible place in which I was a very small part.

Chapter 9

I spent the afternoon with priests.

There are many ways to spend an afternoon, and plenty of them are unpleasant, but few are worse than spending time with priests. I find the priests of the dead gods unsettling – their porcelain masks hide their faces and they are trained to keep their voices free of any emotion or tone. When the gods lived, their priests were immortal; now we make our priests interchangeable so we can pretend they never die.

There were four priests in Maniyadoc. Although our celestial graveyard has a dead god for every occasion people are choosy about which they pay tribute to. Different blessed prefer different gods and some are only worshipped in specific areas of the Tired Lands, for the sake of tradition. The priests of Adallada, queen of the dead gods, and her consort Dallad, for instance, are only ever found at the high king's palace in Ceadoc and at Festival, because power is jealous of power. Even when your gods are dead it is best to keep the strongest ones close.

Maniyadoc's priests were the most common ones. I had already had two interminable meetings with the priest of Lessiah, the goddess of night, and the priest of Mayel, the goddess of fertility. The conversations had gone the way conversations with priests always go.

"I have not seen you at the signing sermons in my buried chapel. Do you not worry about the hedgings? What if you fell upon hard times, and Fitchgrass – or worse, Dark Ungar – made you an offer? You are far too young to recognise that a hedging's offer can take many forms; only the dead gods can provide that wisdom. Have you signed the book of the god today?" The books of the gods and fear of the hedgings were the reasons the priesthoods still existed. Though all our gods, apart from Xus, had perished in the wars of balance and now we lived a lonely life without their guidance. The priests promised that one day the sourlands would be healed and then the gods would return. However, remnants of the gods' power remained, and these remnants, lost and broken, had become the hedgings which haunted field, wood and pool, hungering for the lives of men and women. Until the rebirth we were told only the priesthood's books and knowledge could keep people safe from the hunger of the hedgings. They said that when the gods returned from their graves in the sea those who had remained loyal would be rewarded. So the pious attended worship every morning in the buried chapels and signed their names in the books of the gods.

But that was my afternoon. Two earnest lectures on why I should attend worship and sign my name in the book. The priest of fertility, who I saw second, was heavily pregnant. Unlike the other priests she was not expected to be celibate; quite the opposite. It was expected that she be almost constantly pregnant and even hidden behind a mask and under thick red robes she could not hide how tired she was. Her room smelled of spoilt milk and was filled with nothing but the book of names and toys for the gaggle of children running around. An unseen child screamed in the back of her small room and two more hung on grimly to her robes. I had spent the previous two hours resisting the entreaties of the priest of Lessiah, out of sheer pig-headedness, but when the priest of Mayel asked me to sign her book I did just so she could get rid of me. She seemed happy for me to go, which suited us both.

Outside her room my master waited.

"So?" Her voice out of that alien black and white face. It

was always strange when she was Death's Jester. It obliterated her – everything about her changed. Her mannerisms were more thought out and exaggerated, and it became as if every step she took and every tilt of her head was part of an elaborate dance. She carried herself more lightly and even her voice was different – more mocking. I had to consciously remind myself it was all part of an act.

"She is as pious as the other, jester, you were right in that."

"Next we shall see Neander, the priest of Heissal. I expect he will be less pious."

"He is Rufra's father?"

"Aye, so rumour has it. You should be alert around him. You need to concentrate."

"I have been concentrating."

I had not.

"You have not," she snapped as we walked down the corridor past bowing slaves. "You have been mooning around like a stunned pig."

I had.

I could not concentrate for thoughts of Drusl. One moment elation, the next I was despondent. I had thought of love before but could not imagine anyone looking at me that way – a small-for-his-age skinny boy with a club foot. Coupled with the fact we rarely stayed anywhere for more than a couple of days, and when we did stay longer my cover was usually among the thankful in the lowest places, doing the most unpleasant jobs. I became the people no one wanted to look at, or a jester, and rarely had to interact with people. So this feeling was entirely new to me. Is this what it was to love?

No wonder my master has chosen to avoid it.

"Gusteffa spoke to me last night," I said, in an attempt to deflect the conversation. It was worth mentioning because a jester is meant to be silent unless acting on the orders of their blessed. "He asked if you would replace him."

"Understandable, I suppose. Doran ap Mennix has had the jester for ten years," she said. "Gusteffa is probably used to being spoiled."

It was true. Sometimes I wondered why my master was so committed to the art of murder when she could make twice the living as a jester.

"But still, it was unusual, and you said to look out for—"

"Ten years is a long time for someone to stay in cover, Blessed ap Gwynr," she said. "Gusteffa is not the assassin."

"How do you know?"

"Because I do." She did not add anything, and when the silence had become strong between us I spoke again.

"Rufra wants to be my friend."

"Oh?" she said.

"I've put him off," and I felt bad about it. "He said Tomas hated him. There's no way I could become part of his group if I was friends with Rufra. Not that Tomas shows any sign of wanting me in his group."

"Poor, lonely, you."

"You know —" I changed to the Whisper-That-Flies-to-the-Ear "— the more I think of this, Master, the more I think our task is hopeless. How can we prove someone has hired an assassin? It is not like they would be foolish enough to keep a note of it or put it in a diary."

"People are often foolish." She flipped herself up into a handstand and walked on her hands along the corridor, "they do foolish things."

"And if they are not foolish? What then."

She flipped herself back onto her feet and leaned in close to me as we walked. "Then, my pupil, we find the most likely suspect and we *make* it appear as if they have been foolish."

"You mean set them up? But they'll be killed."

"And that worries you why? Have you forgotten what we are?"

"No, but . . . you have always said we kill for justice."

"When we can, Girton." She refused to meet my eye. "You cannot cling to childish ideas for ever. What use are high ideals if we end up feeding the pigs? What good can we do then?" I had never heard her so vehement before. When she spoke again her voice was calm and as dead as any priest's. "So, as well as looking for an actual suspect you should keep an eye out for a likely one. This Rufra for instance. It's easier if you don't like them." Before I could think about what that implied she gave me a dazzling smile. "Next door on the right," she said, walking away. As I was about to knock on the door she reappeared at my side, as if she had materialised out of thin air.

"Remember, you're an innocent from the country. Play that part."

"I am doing."

"You were, Girton. But now when you're not mooning about you have a strut in your step like a boar fresh to the rut. I don't begrudge you any joy, but it's not in keeping with what people will expect."

I turned, ready to tell her she was imagining things, but the corridor was empty apart from the priest of Xus standing at the far end. He gave me a small bow of his head and walked out of sight.

My master was right: Neander ap Vthyr, the priest of Heissal, was not as pious as his fellows. He was not wearing a mask for a start, and had pushed his bright orange hood back off his head. He had a face like the sourlands, his features sculpted from hollows, ridges and the shadows which grew between. Tiny wisps of orange material stuck to the stubble on his skull and waved in the breeze squeezing in past a loose pane in the windows of his untidy room. He glanced up and smiled.

"Well, you must be Girton ap Gwynr," he said, lifting the open cover of a book with one finger. He raised the cover to the point where it was balancing and then pushed it with his fingertip, letting it fall closed with a bang. "I am pleased you chose to see me." He offered me his palm to kiss, which was the traditional greeting of a high priest to a supplicant, and I was unsure how to act as he was not a high priest. I kissed his palm. It was dry and when I licked my lips I could taste salt and something sweet. "Sit, Girton ap Gwynr." His smile barely reached the corners of his mouth and failed to change the barren landscape of his face. I perched on the dusty stool he pointed at.

"Priest of Heissal," I began.

He tried to smile again.

"Please, call me by my name, Girton. We have no need to be formal."

"Thank you," I said, and waited. He had not given me his name and he let the silence drag on.

"Of course! I have not told you my name; I just presumed you would know of me." I did, but I didn't want him to know that or to appear too knowledgeable. "I am Neander, Neander, once an ap Vthyr. Of course, I gave up such loyalties when I took up my calling." He raised a hand, "I know, the ap Vthyr name has some dark stories attached to it but I am not like the rest of my family. I am only a man in search of spiritual truth." He took a small knife from his desk and started to clean under his fingernails with it. "I do not believe we have had an ap Gwynr in the castle before. You are from far to the west, yes?"

"The east," I said.

"Of course, of course. The east, how foolish of me. I am an old man and I often make mistakes." He leaned in close to me and sniffed the air, taking two great lungfuls of breath through his hatchet-shaped nose. "You have a curious perfume, Girton ap Gwynr. Has anyone ever told you that?"

I sniffed under my arms. "I have been training, Neander. It was hot."

"Of course," he said slowly, "of course. I have never been under force of arms but it looks exceedingly strenuous." He put his knife down. "Tell me, did Heamus bring you to us?"

"No, my father judged me to be the least useful of his children —" I looked down at my club foot in case he had not noticed "— so I was sent as hostage until he can raise the money the king wants."

"Your family are rich, I hear."

"My father breeds mounts."

"I have seen your creature. He appears to be a fine animal."

"He is." It was difficult to hide my enthusiasm for Xus.

"I expect he is a fine animal in a fight."

"Yes," I said, before catching myself. "Well, Xus himself has never fought but his bloodline has proved fearsome under my brothers."

"Fearsome," he said quietly. "With money, good mounts and such privacy your father could build an army and no one would know." He leaned in close to whisper to me. He smelt of old vellum and ink. "It is hard, to be far away and without your family. Should you need a friend feel free to come to me." He sat back again. "Are you ambitious, young Girton? Castle Maniyadoc is a fine place for an ambitious boy to advance." He laughed then, but it was not the laugh of someone amused. It was the laugh of someone trying to set another at ease. Had I been the innocent I was pretending to be it may have worked — but false humour and smiles did not come easily enough to the priest for him to fool me into liking him, or seeing him as a surrogate father. All it did was make me uncomfortable.

"Do you want me to sign your book?" I said, to fill the gap in our conversation.

"Book?" he said.

"Your book of names."

He remained silent for a moment. Staring at me with eyes the green of grass. "Of course, of course. When Heissall

awakens and the day is of equal lengths with the night –"
he stood and started sorting through the books on his desk
"– then Heisall will look in the book and find your name.
Should a hedging curse you with hunger –" he moved aside
a bottle of alcohol "– then think of your name written here
and be sated." He moved another book and picked up the
book underneath. A bottle had left a ring on its cover. "Here
we are."

He lay the book down and opened it at the day's page.
There were very few names, which I thought odd. Heissall,
the god of the day, is one of the more popular gods. I signed
the book and left Neander's messy room. As I walked back
to our rooms my master materialised out of the darkness by
my side, making me jump.

"I wish you would not do that."

"I am Death's Jester. It is expected."

"It was not expected by me."

"Did Neander give up anything?"

"He sniffed me. Then complimented me on my smell, said
I had a curious perfume." My master's eyes flashed in the
dim light of the corridor.

"He did?" she said thoughtfully, letting her words die
away. I had no idea why she thought it important.

"He makes my skin crawl."

"Well, that is unpleasant but not a motive, Girton. Was
there anything we can use?"

"He, not so subtly, tried to pump me for information about
my family. Then hinted at how my father's land could be
used to raise armies and told me if I needed a friend to go
to him."

"He openly asked about raising armies? Did he mention
treason?"

"No, but that was the subtext."

"So you think him suspicious."

"Yes."

She nodded but said nothing else.

That night I lay awake thinking about the day's events, the people I had met and the feel of Drusl's hand under mine. In the stillness of the night I heard my master rise from her bed and leave the room. Curious, I counted out twenty my-masters and then I followed her. The castle was quieter in the night. Thankful moved through the corridors like ghosts; they did not acknowledge me or I them as I was drawn in the wake of my master, drifting along behind her on the lingering, spicy smell of the greasepaint she used to paint her face. Around the castle we went, around and down, past the kitchens and the steep tunnels which led to the buried chapels. Twice I saw figures in the shadows and twice, thinking it was my master, I nearly let an excuse leap out of my mouth, but it was only thankful, grabbing a quick sleep upright against the wall and, in one case, a couple of blessed having an illicit liaison in an alcove.

Her route took her out of the castle and I could no longer follow her scent – a quick breeze stole it from the air – so instead I followed the damp outlines of her feet on the scrubby grass, and when she left the grass I followed the subtle disturbances of the sandy ground left by her tread. Eventually, I found myself in a courtyard that I had not known existed – it was at the back of the castle, reached through an archway that had once been a door. A pair of stone eyes looked out angrily from the top, as if annoyed at my intrusion. Above the door was a window, shadowed by the bulk of the castle. I climbed the wall and hid in the empty window so I could look down into the courtyard. Plainly, it had been inside once and where there had been a grand corridor was now a pile of rubble, thick with dead vines, brown and starved crisp by yearsage.

From a doorway opposite a woman emerged, dressed like a slave. I do not know where she had come from, or how she had got there because, like everyone, I barely paid attention to slaves. Slaves are simply another part of a cruel world, much as hunger and sourings are. I could have walked past this woman a hundred times in the castle and not seen her, she had a face so unremarkable I would have struggled to recognise her if I saw her again the next day. The woman moved long hair from her face, some accident or violence had taken half her hand – the little and third finger were missing.

She was not a slave, of course, as no slave carried a long-sword and stabsword, or walked like a maned lizard. I knew what she must be – assassin. She gave my master a nod and my master returned it.

"You are Merela, the Barren?" My master nodded.

And you are Sayda, the Halfhand?" The woman nodded. They drew their blades.

"Let us see who stays then," said the woman.

Sayda Halfhand attacked first, a slicing pass at neck height that my master ducked, swatting away the stabsword thrust that followed. I watched, rapt. I had never met another assassin, never seen another work. I knew that they existed and were few and far between but had always taken for granted that they were like us, used our methods and styles, but this woman showed me I was mistaken. Where we were about speed and attack she was about solidity and defence; she stood like a rampart, barely moving from the spot she occupied as she cut and thrust with her blades.

My master was a whirlwind, her opponent a mountain, and for the first time ever it occurred to me my master could lose. I drew my blade. As I did, a movement caught my eye. Hidden in an arch, high up the broken wall on the other side, was Sayda's apprentice. Little more than a shadow, but I could make out the bow that she drew and aimed at me. And the shake of her head she gave me. I returned my blade to its scabbard and the bow was lowered.

Below us my master's blade worked, only to be batted

away by a longsword. A return thrust to her midriff and she let herself fall out of the way, *the Drunk's Tumble*. She turned the fall into a roll which she continued, forward and round, forward and round, her blade flashing and glinting as she struck out and each time she found her blade met. Very quickly, my master ceased to use the iterations I had grown up learning and the fight became an interpretation of our style through pure reaction, a blade quick thing. On occasion I saw the route of a move. This move used a stance from the Carter's Surprise, that move a version of the Quick Steps, but it was far removed from what I knew, not once did my master use any of her tricks, or Sayda Halfhand use any either.

The strangest, eeriest, thing was that this fight took place in almost complete silence. There was no talking, no grunts of effort or exhaustion, and although I had thought my master's opposite's style was dull, together she and my master were a symphony of blades, a quickstep of cutting edges and chinking parries. Her way was not my master's and my master's was not hers, but neither was one method inferior to the other or one opponent less skilled. I had thought my master had no equal, but here she was.

And then the killing blow was struck.

I saw the space in Sayda Halfhand's defence, saw the dummy thrown by my master and saw her opponent take it. As my master's blade rushed to the kill I felt sad, sad that this quiet and skilled woman would die here so that we could protect Aydor.

But she did not die. The blade never so much as touched her skin, only paused a hair's breadth from the woman's throat. The dance went on: twice, three, four times I saw moments when my master could have finished her opponent. I became more used to this new style as I watched – deconstructing it, considering how I could add it to my own repertoire. I saw times when Sayda Halfhand could have ended the fight but did not, and I realised this was not the duel to the death of Riders, out to seek revenge in blood for an insult. This was a competition of equals. A bloodless decision was being made as to who had precedence here.

Abruptly, and without warning, the two combatants parted. Sayda Halfhand smiled, sheathed her sword and bared her throat to my master, who put her blade to her opponent's throat but did not cut, only whispered something into her ear which made the other assassin's smile widen slightly. As she did, I caught a movement in a broken doorway opposite and I found my double once more, little more than the gleam of a pair of eyes in the dark, but she, or he, was there. Somehow she had come down from the arch without me seeing, and she watched me as I watched her.

"Two weeks," said Sayda Halfhand. "And if it is not done I will presume you have failed and return."

"Very well," said my master.

The woman walked away and my master remained standing in the middle of the clearing.

"Girton," she said quietly, "you can come out now."

"Oh." I jumped down from the window, rolling to absorb the impact and so as not to pain my club foot too much. "You knew I was there?"

"Of course."

"Why didn't you kill her?"

"Why would I?"

"Well . . ." I had no good answer. "It is what we do."

"When there is reason, and there was no reason for Sayda Halfhand to die, or for me. Now I have bought us time, Girton, we must use it well or it may be our names that are scratched on a wall."

"She fought −" I glanced back over my shoulder "− differently to you."

"Yes, she fought as Aseela's Mount, strong and steady. We fight as Xus's Bird, quick and light."

"Where did she learn that?"

"From her master, as you learn from yours."

"I thought everyone—"

"Fought like us? No, and even those who fight as the bird will fight differently to us. Each sorrowing has their own way."

"I thought the Open Circle had rules and told us what to do. I thought we were all . . ." I stopped; I did not know what I thought we were.

"Companions?" I nodded. "We are, Girton, but it is a silent companionship and there are few of us left."

I thought on that for a while as we walked back.

"She was good," I said.

"Yes. She very nearly beat me." I stopped, shocked at her words.

"But you are the greatest assassin of our age," I said.

"As you keep saying," she said and she smiled, but it was the smile of an adult indulging a child. "Come, Girton," she said. 'It is cold and I am tired." She led me back to our room, where she slept the sleep of the exhausted while I thought on how much I did, and did not, know.

Interlude

This is a dream of what was.

She squats behind him, her warmth against his back, and if she can feel him shivering in fear she says nothing about it. She picks up the loose end of the rope tied to the tree and puts it in his hand. Together, they start the rope moving through the air where it traces out a giant oval. "Good," she says, "don't stop." She walks around and looks at the rope spinning through the air and then steps into it. He is so surprised he drops the rope.

"Sorry, Master," he says.

"Do not worry." She comes back and shows him how to spin the rope again. "Do not stop this time," she says. "No matter what I do."

"Yes, Master."

"Girton, my name is Merela. You may call me that."

"Yes, Master," he says. He always will.

This time when she steps into the rope he does not drop it. He expects it to hit her but she jumps over it without even looking. She is watching him and smiling and jumping. Then she starts to hop from one foot to another. It makes him laugh because she pulls funny faces when she does it, but she never lets the rope touch her. She pretends to fall, catching herself at the last moment and making him giggle. She lands on her hands and then flips from her hands to her feet and her movements get more and more complex, and always the rope goes round and round and round until she is tumbling and leaping and cartwheeling in and out of the steadily spinning rope. Then, with one last twirling spring that flips her out of the rope's reach, she finishes. She stands with her legs slightly apart and her hands held loosely at her side. She is barely even breathing hard.

"This is how we stand when we are finished, Girton." He nods. "Now it is your turn." She sees panic starting on his face. "Don't worry. All you have to do is jump over the rope, nothing more. The rest will come with time."

"I can't."

"Yes, you can."

"I have a bad foot."

"Girton." She walks over to him, lowering herself to his level. "Among the blessed of the Tired Lands there is a belief that a woman is good for nothing but sitting in a parlour sewing and giving birth to children. Do you believe that of me?"

"No, Master." He really, honestly, completely believes that she can do anything.

"Good. And I do not believe you will let a bad foot hold you back. Now, jump the rope. Breathe out when you jump, breathe in when you land. It will help, and if you cannot do it then you cannot. But you must try."

"Yes, Master."

He tries, he fails. And he fails and he fails again. His club foot hurts but she never gets angry. Never stops smiling. Never stops coaxing him on and saying that, maybe next time he'll do it. Even though he is sure it is beyond him.

Then he jumps the rope.

And again.

And again and again and the rope gets faster and he is laughing with the joy of it as the rope whips through the air. Eventually, it stops, and she stares at him like he's forgotten something and he remembers her words – *This is how we stand when we are finished*. He does his best to copy how she had stood and is rewarded with a smile.

"Not bad for a boy with a bad foot, eh?" she says.

And she always will.

He skips the rope, hops the rope, leaps the rope. Years pass as he works through the acrobatics until there are two trees and two ropes and they spin so fast they make a sound like the wind roaring in his ears when Xus runs and he can flip and spin between them without ever being touched. Always when he is finished she will say, "Not bad for a boy with a bad foot," and smile at him.

And the ripples in the water go on and on and on and the skies whisper out an infinity.

This is a dream of what was.

Chapter 10

My mood was not good the next morning. I had wanted to ask my master's advice about Drusl but instead we had argued, though I did not know why. I questioned what we did – how we could be putting ourselves in jeopardy and throwing away our futures as assassins for people like Queen Adran and her odious son. My master had listened patiently while I ranted. She seldom removed her Death's Jester make-up once it was on, and her brown eyes stared out of a face alien and distorted by sleep-smeared make-up. She had waited until my anger had run out of words and then risen. She was smaller than I was now. I wondered when that had happened.

"Girton," she said, "you may leave whenever you wish."

I had no answer. Instead I acted like a child – I walked out, slamming the door behind me. Storming out may have been dramatic but it accomplished little as I left my armour and blades in our room. I could not bring myself to go back and get them even though I had an hour to waste before I was due at the squireyard. After I had skulked about in the corridors of the castle for a while I decided to do something constructive. I would try and track down the guard who had been outside the kennels when I was locked in. Few people know the ins and outs of a castle like its jester, and if I wanted to find someone then Gusteffa, the king's dwarf, was probably my best chance.

The water clock was tolling seven as I made my way into the depths of the castle. At seven the signing sermons began in the buried chapels, the processions of devout in the morning and evening were ripe times for gossip – no decent castle jester would miss them. On the floor above the buried chapels were the common kitchens, Gusteffa would probably wait there for people to leave the signing sermon so that was where I headed.

In the kitchens the vaulted ceilings were lit by the cooking fires and the place was uncomfortably hot and moist. A cook worked at a spit, sweating as he turned a whole pig, and behind him pot girls were washing pans. The long wooden preparation table in the centre of the room was empty apart from a one-armed man sharpening a carving knife.

"Ain't no place here for you," he said. "Ain't no place for a blessed boy among the living. You come here to spy on us?" The knife in his hand glinted and the way he held it made me wonder if he had been a soldier once.

"I'm looking for Gusteffa," I stammered.

"To tease 'er?" said a potgirl.

"Her?" I said. I had thought Gusteffa a man.

"Is it hedging's hunger that makes you squires so cruel? You should go sign a book and think on what you are about."

"No," I said. "I wanted to—"

"She said you should go." The one-armed man stood, threat in his eyes. I took a step backwards. "Go." He pointed his knife at me then at the door.

"Peace, Dirif." Gusteffa appeared from behind a teetering stack of pots. "Girton means me no harm." Even this early she wore her make-up, a white face with red dots on the cheeks. She motioned at the one-armed man to sit, her tiny hand looking like a paw.

"I wanted to ask a favour, Gusteffa. I can pay, I have –" I dug in my pocket "– half a bit."

The dwarf shook her head.

"Keep your money, boy. If I can I will grant your favour." She passed her hand before her face, turning her smile into a serious mask. "But if I do you will owe me a favour, you understand?" I nodded. She passed the hand again so she smiled once more. "Ask then, Girton Club-Foot."

I stood near so we could speak more privately.

"Yesterday," I whispered, "a guard may have been found outside the kennels, asleep and drunk. I want to know who he is and where I can find him."

Gusteffa stared at me. I tried to think of a reason to give her when the inevitable "Why" came, but she seemed uninterested, only nodding her head thoughtfully.

"You mean the man found drunk outside the kennels when you were locked in?" I blushed and nodded. "I heard it had happened but not who the guard was. I shall do my best to find out for you."

"Thank you, Gusteffa," I said.

I left the kitchens to find the corridors full of people leaving the buried chapels, moving in little cliques and giving each other shifty-eyed looks. I saw more than one surreptitious elbow dig a fellow hard in the ribs, and the odd "accidental" kick to the shins. The castle guards' attitudes varied markedly depending on who approached them. For some people they moved slowly, in what was clearly a calculated piece of disrespect, and for others they would jump to their task. The more I walked among the blessed the more aware I became that the corridors of the castle were crawling with old rivalries brought to the surface by the turbulence of Doran ap Mennix's impending death. These were currents so deep and complex I had no idea how to navigate them.

Nywulf, the squiremaster, was not pleased when I entered the squireyard as I was both late and improperly dressed. He took one look at me as I tried to slip in through the door and shouted, "Swordplay!" I ached with the foreknowledge of bruises.

The other squires stood in their groups. Aydor was surrounded by his cronies and Tomas by his. I looked around for Rufra. He was standing with his back to me and seemed smaller than he had the day before. I was glad he was not looking at me; I did not want to see that wounded look in his eyes again.

I glanced over at Tomas. He had a haughtiness that befitted a king, and when I caught his eye he gave me a small nod, the way a king would a subject. Aydor sneered at him. I saw in the heir and his squires a group bound through privilege and riches, which held no appeal for me, but in Tomas and his boys I saw a small group of warriors – a brotherhood – a group of friends bound through force of arms, and I realised I wanted to be part of it. I saw in Tomas and his group the opposite of Aydor – a group committed to right where Aydor was committed only to himself.

But I was not a fool. I knew I had painted Tomas and his friends dented armour with storybook knights from our jester's tales, and my master had always told me to judge by actions not by imaginings. Apart from disliking the heir what had they done to be worthy of a story?

Rufra stood alone. No longer welcome even on the outskirts of Aydor's group, and that was probably because he had spoken to me.

It is difficult to describe the powerful draw of a band of brothers to a boy who has never had companions. It washed over me in a tide of longing as I watched Tomas laugh about something with Boros and Barin. Rufra could not offer me that. His nervousness made me uncomfortable and he was an ap Vthyr – reviled throughout Maniyadoc. He probably deserved to be set up as the assassin's client; his family had done terrible things and I did not owe him anything. Also, my master wanted me to find a way in with Tomas . . .

But Rufra had walked away from boys who had, however grudgingly, accepted him, and he had done that because he thought he saw a kindred spirit in me.

"Dead gods paint my face for a fool," I whispered to myself

and went to stand by Rufra at the sword rack. I started sorting through the practice swords. "I have forgotten my armour, Rufra," I said, "so please do not take too much advantage of me when we fence."

He turned, making a puzzled face that turned a startlingly plain visage into an ugly one. "I do not want your pity, Girton," he said and turned away. I grabbed his arm, turning him back.

"Outsiders, you said, Rufra. I thought on that all night so do not think it pity that I recognise a kindred spirit." He smiled at me then, a curious reaction to my anger. "You are amused, Rufra?" Words that would cut him waited in the back of my throat but he spoke before I could launch them.

"Sorry, Girton. I let my hurt pride speak. I am thankful that you have chosen me as a friend. Truly I am." He laughed. "But Nywulf said I am not trying hard enough and should tax myself more in sword work. I am glad of the offer of your friendship but I am worried he will think I am being lazy, choosing you as a partner."

For a second I was insulted, and then the truth of what he said struck me. I started to laugh. He knew me only as Girton ap Gwynr, who was more of a danger to himself than anyone else with a blade. Rufra joined me in laughter, and his laugh was an infectious thing that made me laugh more. Soon we were helpless, no longer warriors in training but only two boys doubled up in hysterics while tears of laughter streamed from our eyes. We laughed so much we could not look at one another and were too young to recognise we laughed from a sudden break in the tension between us.

"Something funny, boys?" said Nywulf, his ire drawn by our amusement.

"No, Squiremaster," we said together, though the words were barely discernible as we had to hold our breath not to laugh.

"Well, Rufra," he said, "you may think your new friend

means an easy ride for you, but it is not the case. You can spar with me today." The smile fell from Rufra's face.

"Yes, Nywulf," he said and then the squiremaster turned to me.

"You have other business – the castle calls," he said and passed me a square of paper. It was sealed with the queen's symbol, though the paper was cheap.

"Thank you, Squiremaster," I said, but he had already turned away to choose a practice sword.

Outside the squireyard I opened my note. It was from Gusteffa. It gave me no name, only a time and a place to be if I wanted to intercept my guard, and I wondered at how she had got the information so quickly. From the height of the sun I didn't have long to act so made my way around the wall and to the barracks at a run.

I had barely waited ten minutes before the guard who had been outside the kennels left to take up his duty at the keep. I checked I had my small eating knife on me and followed him, watching for the right moment to act. He stopped to chat amiably with the men and women on the gate. I loitered, pretending to be interested in the ruined carvings on the walls, until he moved on. The further into the keep he got the more nervous he became. It was like the man was a puppet controlled by an increasingly shaky puppetmaster: his body spasmed and tensed, his hands clenched and his breathing became staccato. Twice, he almost physically jumped when other guards appeared around the corner. All this made following him more difficult as he would stop to peer around and I would have to hide to avoid being seen. I trailed him to the higher floors of the keep where the corridors ran in a square with rooms off either side. As the guard reached the top of the stairs he turned left. I followed, almost walking into him at the top of the stairs as he had turned on his heel and was hurrying back the way he had come. Curious about what had made him retreat, I carried on walking and came across a group of guards with splotches of red on their armour. They watched in silence as I sauntered past and then their whispered conversation resumed behind me.

When I turned the far corner I saw my guard stationed outside a room. He was nervous, holding his pike tightly and constantly glancing up and down the corridor. When he looked away I inched my way along the wall using the door recesses to hide in. When I was near enough to make a dash for the man I slipped my eating knife from its sheath. A shudder ran through me and for a second I was back in the kennels, white teeth flashing, the scent of dog shit thick in my nostrils as one of the brutes launched itself at me.

Breathe out.

I was going to find out who had locked me in there and I was going to make them pay.

Breathe in.

I took a step forward and a hand closed around my knife, pulling me back into the alcove. A voice whispered into my ear and the smell of facepaint filled my nostrils.

"What are you intending to do with that, apprentice?"

Muscles, tensed for combat a second ago, relaxed, though only a little.

"Find out who locked me in the kennel, Master."

"You think he'll tell you?"

"I think I'll make him."

She laughed quietly.

"How?" Her hand tightened around the knife. "Cut him? Has anger driven everything I ever taught you from your mind?" She cuffed me around the back of the head, hard enough to hurt. I wanted, more than anything, to lash out at her.

"They locked me in with war dogs," I said through gritted teeth.

"And he likely knows nothing more than he was set to

guard a door. One shout from him will bring every guard in Maniyadoc running. Unlike you, Gusteffa is only a fool in name and told me what you were about. I will get you your information. Stay here, stay quiet. Watch what I do."

She let go of me and walked out into the centre of the corridor. The guard turned, looked her up and down and then ignored her. A jester was no threat to him. My master cartwheeled up the corridor, stopping in front of the guard and leaning forward until her face was right in front of his. She brought her hands up, pulling at the corners of her mouth and sticking out her tongue.

"Piss off or I'll gut you," said the guard.

She acted hurt, miming tears, and I saw her palm a small mirror on a string from her pocket and knew what she intended, the Careless Gossip, a way of causing someone to talk and forget all about it afterwards. Like the Wild Gaze it was a skill I lacked the patience for. As the guard opened his mouth to say something my master brought up the mirror. It dangled from her finger and she set it spinning with her thumb, then placed her other hand on the back of the guard's head. He stiffened at the unexpected touch and she leaned further forward, whispering to him in the Voice of Sleep. He shook in her hands, frozen in place, and my master slipped the spinning mirror back into her pocket and continued to whisper to him. She gently removed his pike from a limp hand and leaned it against the wall. The she placed a hand on the top of his head and with a gentle push he fell to his knees, looking up at her like a quill holder at a priest on signing day.

"Girton," she said quietly, "ask him your questions now and then think about how much easier tasks are when tackled with the right tools."

I bristled at the implied criticism and placed myself between my master and the guard. He was drooling and his eyes were unfocused.

"What is your name?" I asked.

"Anjohn."

"Anjohn, recently you were set to guard the kennels, is this true?"

"Yes."

"Who set you to it?"

"Captain Dollis."

"And who commanded him?"

"I do not know."

"Don't lie," I barked, drawing back my hand to slap the man, but my master grabbed my wrist.

"He cannot lie, Girton, you know that. He will remember nothing of this, but if you give him a bruise his mind will wander back along this track to find the cause. Is that what you want?"

"No, Master."

"Ask then."

"What were your orders, Anjohn?"

"Guard the kennel. Wait to be relieved."

"Who relieved you?"

"Dollis came, beat me for being drunk though I swear I never touched a drop."

"There has to be more," I hissed, looking back at my master.

"Doubtful – he is only a guard," said my master calmly and then leaned in close to Anjohn. "Wake at the next waterclock bell, Anjohn. Remember nothing of this." My hand itched for the knife my master had taken from me, even though I knew it would be pointless to hurt the man; he knew nothing and had not been responsible for locking me in with the dogs. My master took my arm and pulled me away. "Come. Best we are not discovered here."

"Who is Dollis?"

"Aydor's man. Captain of his dayguard."

"The heir. I should have known." I remembered the man with the missing tooth and how he'd sneered at me.

She pulled me to a stop in the corridor, staring into my eyes as she spoke.

"Girton, I think you are best to forget this whole business. I am sure it is little more than a prank that went too far and we have far more pressing concerns."

I remained silently staring back at her and she shook her head before walking away. Part of me wanted to go after her but pride made me walk in the opposite direction. I wandered downstairs deep in thought and, as if of their own accord, my feet took me out of the keep and towards the stables.

When I passed the squireyard I saw Rufra, sitting alone outside.

"Rufra," I shouted, giving him a wave. "I need to go and check on my mount. Do you have an animal in the stables?"

"Two," he said. "They are called Balance and Imbalance."

"Would you show your animals to me?"

"Aye," he said. A smile lit up his face and almost tilted the scales of his looks into handsome.

We made our way around Festival. Huge wooden walls, painted with capering horned and leafed hedgings, had been raised around the central caravans and the air was filled with the stink of animals. I had the uncomfortable feeling we were being watched and twice I thought I caught a figure in the corner of my eye, but Rufra was oblivious to my worry. He chattered happily, telling me Festival was still setting up and would be for a few days and until it was fully set up no one would be allowed to enter. As we came around Festival he slowed his walk.

"Girton," he said quietly, "I must warn you not to go alone at night in the townyard, keepyard or anywhere that is quiet during the day. Slights are not forgiven easily here."

"Slights?"

"Tomas prides himself on his martial skill, and you came close to making him look a fool with your bow."

"That is not the way Riders are meant to act, Rufra," I said.

"Girton —" he put a hand on my arm and brought me to a stop "— we are not Riders. We are boys. You should remember that." Even then Rufra had a knack for seeing the truth of a thing.

"They are squires, don't their Riders keep them under control?"

Rufra looked at me as if I was a fool.

"Girton, do you walk around with your head in the clouds? How many Riders have you seen in this castle?"

As soon as he said that I felt like a fool for not noticing, Heamus was the only Rider I had seen.

"Why are there no Riders here, Rufra?"

He kicked a stone across the ground. "The same reason some of us are still squires when we could easily pass for Riders. Aydor."

"He sent them away?"

"Not him, his mother. When the Landsmen came and set up the trials Aydor did not pass for Rider so no one else was allowed to try. His mother could not have the heir shown up and, gradually, she has sent away all of the king's Riders. Worse, no squire may take the trials until Aydor has passed, and he will never pass the trials. Partly because he is lazy and partly because his eyes are so bad he could not hit the keep with an arrow. I feel sorry for him sometimes."

"A king does not need to pass for Rider; it is bestowed on him with the crown," I said, more to myself than Rufra.

"Aye," said Rufra. "For some the old king cannot die soon enough. We wrote to Daana ap Dhyrrin asking for Aydor to be removed from training, but nothing came of it."

"Talking of Aydor," I added, "do you know the captain of his dayguard?"

"Dollis?" His eyes widened and he looked away. "No more than I have to. He's a nasty piece of work, hates anyone he thinks is better than him."

"Does he do Aydor's dirty work?"

"Aydor's and anyone else who can pay. Why?"

"Just curious. Our paths crossed."

"Then I'd uncross them as quick as you can."

When we entered the stables Drusl was leading out a stinking cart drawn by a heavily muscled draymount.

"Girton!"

"Drusl, you are leaving?" I could hear disappointment in my voice and hoped Rufra did not notice.

"Leiss is sending me to get fodder for the mounts and drop this pressed dung off for the farmers, but I will be back . . ." Her voice tailed off as she saw Rufra. "Blessed –" she gave a small bow "– forgive me. I did not see you there." She seemed a different person when she noticed Rufra: smaller, meeker, the humour gone from her to be replaced with worry. It was almost as if she were trying to disappear into the ground.

"You are friends with Girton?" said Rufra.

"I only look after his mount, Blessed," she said. She did not look at him.

"Well," he said, and took her hand in his. "I think you are his friend then, and any friend of Girton's can count themselves a friend of mine." He executed a perfect court-style bow and the ridiculous formality of such a thing – a sweaty squire bowing to a stable girl in charge of a cartload of dung – was not lost on her. She let out a giggle. For a moment I hated Rufra.

"I cannot stay, Girton. Leiss will be angry if I dally but I will see you later? If you can come by?" Any dislike for Rufra vanished as her attention came back to me. She led the draymount and cart away and I noticed Rufra staring at me with a huge grin on his face. The heat of a blush rushed onto my cheeks.

"What?" He only grinned in reply and I hurried past him into the stable to see Xus. The mount was skittish, baring his tusks and snorting as if he picked up on my embarrassment. "Shh, Xus, shhh." I said and stroked his thin muzzle. The animal calmed under my touch.

". . . is beautiful," Rufra said from behind me.

"Yes," I said, "and he is fast too."

"Fool," laughed Rufra and gave my arm a push. "I was not talking about your animal, though he is a beauty. I was talking of Drusl. No wonder you were desperate to get down here yesterday."

"We are only friends."

"Really? Well, I suspect she hopes for a little more." I tried to hide my blushing face but my heart leaped.

"What would she see in me?" I couldn't look at him. I was afraid he would see how desperate I was to hear something good.

"Hmm," he said, "what would penniless stable girl Drusl see in Girton, a blessed?" He realised his arrow had hit closer and harder than he had meant and quickly added, "A jest, Girton, that is all. Drusl is very pretty and if it was only privilege she wanted she would have accepted one of the other squires when he tilted his lance at her."

"But she hasn't?"

"No." Then he whispered conspiratorially, "If you can imagine it, Girton, I suspect she would even turn me down." He put his arm on my shoulder. He was slightly taller than me and I felt a little uncomfortable. "She could have her pick of the castle and yet she has chosen to be alone. We had all thought her and Leiss were together. You are lucky, and as the youngest son you may even get to marry for love rather than duty."

"Yes," I said, but my happiness fled. I would not get to marry at all. What was I doing? As soon as my master and I were finished here we would be gone and I would never see Drusl again. "Show me your mounts, Rufra," I said glumly.

"I will," he said, and either he was so excited by his

animals, Balance, a huge white mount with eight-point antlers, and Imbalance, a slightly smaller black mount with one antler shorter than the other, or he was too polite to comment on the dampening of the fire which had burned in me only a moment before. We spent well over an hour in the stables. Talking of mounts and the other squires, laughing together and finding more common ground than I had ever imagined could exist between an assassin and a blessed. Every so often he would steer the conversation back to Drusl and I would steer it away to more comfortable ground.

"How did you meet her?" asked Rufra again, and before I could find a new a way of politely avoiding talking about Drusl the waterclock chimed one.

"One already? I said. "I must run, Rufra. I am meant to meet General ap Mennix and Daana ap Dhyrrin so they can try and work out what use I can be to their courtly intrigues."

"Then you should run as fast as you can, Girton." He smiled. "Bryan ap Mennix has been known to lecture on lateness for over an hour."

I left Rufra and ran up to the castle, noticing two new corpses hanging from the battlements. I was forced to detour by a guard who told me the main hall was off limits to "filthy squires and cripples". He pointed at the back corridors and, not having time to argue, I followed his instructions. Three squires in the ap Mennix livery of yellow and purple, a writhing snake embroidered in a diagonal across the torso, blocked my way. Kyril headed them. Like the heir he was a big boy with little skill in anything but bullying others. Behind him stood Borniya. Close up he was even bigger than Kyril. Behind them stood Hallin. Though he wasn't as big as Borniya or Kyril Rufra had told me to watch him most closely. He was the mind behind some of the trio's more vicious acts. The guard must have been placed to funnel me to here, where Kyril and and his friends were waiting.

"Girton ap Gwynr," said Kyril.

"Kyril." I gave him a short bow of respect and tried to go around him. He blocked my way.

"This is the cripple who thinks he can be a Rider, Borniya," he said.

"I've no wish to be a Rider; I was forced to—"

"I've heard your father breeds mounts." He pushed my shoulder.

"That must be why you smell like a thankful born in a stable," said Hallin. The others laughed and I tried to join in.

"Aye, I've been seeing to my animal. Now I have a meeting so I must wash."

"I heard you didn't like animals much, dogs anyway," said Borniya. He grinned at me, the old wound on his face twisted his words and his mouth into strange shapes.

"Been hobbling down to see that stable girl you like?" said Kyril. I bit down on my tongue before I answered.

"I really must get on, Kyril," I said and tried once more to pass. Again he stepped in front of me.

"We've all had her, you know. Me, Aydor, Borniya, Hallin, everyone. She loves it, bit of a tussle with a blessed boy. I didn't know she had a thing for cripples though." He was baiting me and I knew it, but anger, like a heavy black liquid, rose within me at the mention of Drusl. "Or maybe she thinks cripples are disgusting and pathetic, just like we do, but she needs to do you to complete the set. So she can say she's bedded all the squires. She'll probably throw up afterwards." I bunched my fists, digging my nails into the palms of my hands.

"She's even had that filthy upstart little friend of yours," said Hallin. "I heard she likes it Ruf-ra." He and his friends laughed again. I concentrated on breathing – *out, in* – and trying to still the swelling fury within me before it spilled over and something happened I would regret. I did not know what it would be, but I knew Kyril and his friends would not survive. The more he spoke the more it felt fated to happen.

At the moment I was about to act I was distracted by a movement at the far end of the corridor.

The priest of Xus, a shadowed black robe, a flash of white mask, appeared, and a trick of perspective made it seem as if he stood on Kyril's shoulder. I stared as the priest tilted his head until it was almost entirely on its side.

Kyril hit me.

It was more of a shove really, a hard, open-palmed, shove in the centre of my chest that sent me sprawling. I was so surprised I didn't react and only stared up at the bigger boy as he towered above me. "I said, cripples should look at their betters when they speak to them," he shouted.

But the distraction caused by the priest of Xus had been enough to poor some oil on the waves of darkness within me. Kyril's violence had also brought me back to my senses. I was trained for violence and I found violence far easier to cope with than cruel words. Violence sharpened my mind and my reactions and steeled me for pain. *I am the instrument.* This boy was determined to hurt me, and either I would have to let him or I would have to kill him and his two friends, then somehow hide all the bodies if I wanted to keep my cover.

I stared up at Kyril.

"You are right," I said. "Cripples should look at their betters when they talk to them." I let out a long breath and then made an ostentatious show of staring at the wall. "I will make sure I always do that in future."

"Oh," said Kyril, the muscles of his arms bunching as he stepped forward, "you're a mouthy little mage-bent yellower. We're going to enjoy this."

"Kyril!" The voice was parade-ground loud and used to being obeyed. "What are you doing?"

I looked up to see Heamus striding down the corridor.

"Just a game, Heamus," said Kyril meekly.

"Girton," said Heamus, "was it just a game?"

"Yes, Heamus," I said.

"Well —" he glanced from boy to boy "— I am sure you all have duties to attend to and do not have time for any more games. Girton, I am come to take you to meet the general, and you need to wash. I can smell you from here. The rest of you, go find something useful to do before I bring Nywulf's wrath down on you, and stay away from the stables." Heamus and I watched as Kyril and his two friends walked down the corridor with the stiff walk of boys who knew they had been caught misbehaving. Heamus helped me up. "Did he hurt you?" asked the old Landsman.

"No, Heamus."

"They are not bad lads, only a little boisterous. Perhaps they are a little too fond of throwing their weight around," he said. "You should fight one of them. There is nothing more likely to seal a friendship among boys than a bit of a fight."

"I will think on it, Heamus," I said.

"Good, good." He took a sniff of air and looked puzzled. I wondered whether he had reached the age where his wits were leaving him. "Now, go wash yourself and put on a tabard. It does not do to be late to meet Bryan ap Mennix."

Chapter 11

I followed Heamus up the freezing servants' stairs wishing I'd worn more than a thin jerkin, skirts and a tabard. When I left the stairs and entered the blessed floors, where fires roared and carpets absorbed my steps, I moved from one world to another.

"What do you know about General Bryan, Girton?" said Heamus.

"He is the king's chief military adviser –" Heamus nodded "– his cousin and commander of his armies."

"Good. Remember those things when you meet him." He ruffled my hair like a friendly uncle. "Truthfully though," he said in a conspiratorial whisper, "Bryan is a fool but Doran needed his side of the family's money and loyalty so do not take anything Bryan says too seriously. I also hope you brought a couple of small twigs."

"Twigs?" I replied, puzzled.

"Aye." He grinned and used his fingers to widen his eyes. "To keep your eyelids open. If Bryan ap Mennix ever won a victory it was by boring his enemies to death." He laughed, a wheezing laugh full of mischief. It was difficult to imagine him strapping someone into a blood gibbet or leading the desolate into the sourlands to bleed their lives away for a few paces more of fertile land. "Well," he added, "you'd best be on your way. Soonest done, soonest over." I wondered how often those words had been followed by the bite of a blade into a neck.

"Yes." I started to walk away.

"Oh, Girton." The way he called my name was almost too casual. It was often the way when people had an important question to ask but did not want you to know it was important to them. They would bring it up last, as if it was only an afterthought.

"Yes, Heamus?"

"You have become friends with Drusl?"

"Yes." I almost stuttered over the word and felt the warmth of blood rising to my cheeks.

"Good, good," he said. "Be kind to her, Girton. She is one of mine."

"Yours?" My smile started to fall away. Did this old man have some sort of harem?

He laughed again, but this time the humour was forced and the twinkle in his eyes was missing. "Not in that way, boy. Every twicemonth I do the rounds of the waycastles that guard our roads. And well . . . you know how it is out there. Life is hard and there are many orphans. Those I can take off the roads and find work for in the castle, I do." A hedging's touch crossed his face, a shadow of pain. "To redress the balance, see."

"I will be kind to her," I said. I meant it with every part of me.

"Good, good. Well —" he ushered me away with a hand "— don't be late. I'll make sure that Kyril and his friends are kept busy for the rest of the afternoon."

Regretfully, Heamus was right. Bryan ap Mennix was dull. His quarters were more like a meeting room for troops or a museum than a place someone lived in. I entered to find him standing at parade rest with his back to me while he stared out the window at the keepyard wall. He made me wait three hundred my-masters before he turned. When he did he had the florid face and walnut nose of a drunk. Dead gods, the man loved the sound of his own voice. He lectured me interminably. First, and at great length and in unneeded detail, he lectured me on the responsibilities of my wholly imaginary father. Then he lectured me on being late and the importance of good timekeeping in young men. Next he lectured me on military tactics – about which he knew very little. And finally he lectured me on etiquette – about which he knew very much.

If he was only acting the part of a know-nothing blowhard then he was the best actor I had ever met.

Daana ap Dhyrrin, Tomas' grandfather and my next meeting, was another beast entirely. The king's adviser was so old his body had started to betray him and he burned scented logs in his fire, to try and cover the smell of sickness and age which clung to the soft furnishings filling his room. He sat in a chair, sumptuously stuffed and covered in thick red fabric that looked like flesh, and stared into the fire. When he stood to welcome me I saw some disease of the bones had bent his back so he had to fight to look forward rather than at the floor.

In a corner of the room stood his golden cloak with the fire-lizard cages built in and the accompanying conical hat. It was constructed around a clever framework which ran on wheels and had a bar inside for him to lean on – or maybe he used it to straighten himself, as I was sure he had been taller at the feast. I imagine that the pain of forcing his spine straight must be excruciating and made a mental note that, although his body may be frail, it held a mind that must be as determined and strong as any in the castle. Maybe more so.

"Admiring my cloak of office, eh?" He stood, then coughed, which bent him double. "Throw more logs on the fire for me, Girton ap Gwynr. The lizards like the heat." The animals squawked when he gestured to them. "And I. Yes, my dears, I like the heat too." His face had been fleshy once and now skin hung from his bones and wobbled when he moved, looking like the wattles on a fighting lizard. I wondered if he had the disease that ate away a body from inside. If so he hid the pain well. "The cloak is impressive but it is an unwieldy thing. Doran likes me to wear it, but that will not matter much longer." His eyes clouded over but whether he looked into the future or the past I do not know. "I suspect the new king will have little time for such uncomfortable formalities as my cloak." He opened a cage and fed a tidbit to one of the squawking lizards

"Aydor does not like the traditions?"

"Aydor." An uncomfortable silence grew as he stared into the fire. "Aye, I am sure King Aydor will let many traditions fail, given the chance."

"Change is inevitable."

"Change is the curse of time, boy." He suddenly sounded stronger, angrier. "And yet sometimes it need not be a curse." He let the air out from his lungs in one long sigh, as if expelling the anger that had suddenly filled him, then he became still, like an animal waiting in ambush. I waited for his next breath and, when it did not come immediately, worried he had died and if he had how would I explain it to Queen Adran? Then his shoulders heaved and he turned to me, his watery eyes searching my face. "What do you think of Aydor?"

"I have not talked with him much."

"Ha!" His laugh was a whipcrack that made me flinch. "'Not talked with him much'. Very diplomatic young man. Very diplomatic indeed. I am not diplomatic. I am too old for diplomacy. I can see through you, boy." Fear ran through me. "You do not like him. You need not lie about it. No one likes him. He is a deeply unpleasant young man – spoilt. A pig of a boy."

I breathed again.

"You do not need to be liked to be a king," I said.

The old man nodded. "No, you need not. You need to be

respected to be a king or, even better, you need to be feared."
He moved nearer to the open cage and the fire-lizard hopped
out to sit on his stooped shoulder.

"Is Aydor feared?" I asked.

"Is. Aydor. Feared." The old man stared into the fire. "In
the way of a brute he is. Feared the way you fear a wild
animal. His mother though?" He chuckled. "If she'd been a
man we'd all be in trouble."

"What about the king?"

"Feared and respected, once. But now he is dying, and
dying men scare no one. They do nothing."

"But he is still king."

"For now." He fed the lizard another bit of meat. "I hear
your family are rich, young Girton, that they own growing
lands and breed fine mounts like the beast you ride." I
nodded. "Then think on this, boy. When Doran ap Mennix
dies, Aydor will take the throne. He will not answer to his
mother's rein then, no matter what she thinks. His father
was hard but he knew there were lines not to be crossed.
Aydor will not see those lines, and when he pushes too hard
the people will push back."

"Why are you telling me this?"

He ignored me.

"There was a rising during Doran's time – over food." He
fed another scrap to his lizard. "It always starts over food.
Some blessed saw their chance and allied themselves with
thankful rebels to try and take the crown. If kings are not
clever and feared and respected such risings are an excellent
time for castles and crowns to change hands."

"And your family has a claim to the throne."

"Aye, we do. My father was king but he passed the
throne to his sister's husband, Ostir ap Mennix, to punish
my mother for an imagined infidelity." The old man's eyes
were grey, like flecks of stone. "I watched her burn on a
fool's throne."

"But you did not try and take the crown back?"

"No. I had watched Doran grow into a king, and a good one, though that is not the reason we sided with him."

"What was?"

"I'd seen Doran fight." Another bit of meat to the lizard. "With triple his numbers it would have been a struggle to beat him, and there were rumours about a sorcerer having risen in the south."

"The Black Sorcerer?" I said. We all knew the story of the last sorcerer. He had promised to heal the land, bringing about balance and the rebirth of the gods. Instead he had maimed the land afresh and would have done worse if Doran ap Mennix had not cut him down.

"Yes, the Black Sorcerer. So the ap Dhyrrin sided with Doran ap Mennix against the rebels, and even though I lost my eldest son I am sure we did right. But if there is another rising, Girton? What then? Is Aydor a genius? Is there some threat that would make us look past our own ambitions?" He fed more meat to the lizard. "I think there is not."

"This is treason," I whispered. "Talk like this will get us both a pyre and a fool's throne, like your mother."

"You've gone moonwhite, boy." He let out a quiet chuckle, almost a growl. "Don't worry, boy. Adran knows I speak like this –" he raised his voice "– and if her spies are at my door then they can tell their mistress to teach her boy some control before it is too late." He sat down with a sigh. "We all want Maniyadoc and the Long Tides to be stable, Girton. It is good for trade, and that is good for us all. Adran will not move against me and I will not move against her, we know too much about one another. If Aydor becomes high king all is solved anyway. Adran has already agreed Maniyadoc will come to Tomas, and we will part as allies."

"But I have heard the high king's sister has little interest in men."

He shrugged.

"Adran has ways of getting what she wants. If these were the old times, and queens could rule, then she'd be formidable."

"Why are you telling me this?"

He leaned forward so he could whisper to me. His breath smelled like old books.

"The heir already dislikes you, Girton. You should choose your friends wisely and with an eye to the future, give some thought to rebuilding bridges you have broken. Do not make a hedgings deal." He lifted a finger gnarled with arthritis. "Sometimes, Girton ap Gwynr, when we are young we do not realise the way the decisions we make will weigh upon us as adults. Look at me, Girton, bent over by choices made in youth. Make choices now that will help you stand tall as a man, do you understand?"

I did not reply, I did not think the youngest son of a country blessed would know how to reply to what Daana ap Dhyrrin said.

"I have made you uncomfortable," he said with a false smile. "I apologise, but politics is an uncomfortable business, young Girton. Think on what I have said. Even when Aydor becomes high king strife is coming, boy, and you have made choices likely to leave you lonely when it does. Think of what best benefits your family if you cannot think of yourself." He sat back in his well padded chair. "I tire now." He held out his hand and the lizard jumped from his shoulder to it. "If you could place my lizard back in its cage I would be obliged."

I took the lizard from him and its tiny claws dug into my skin as I took it to its cage. It jumped in and then hissed at me. When I turned, Daana ap Dhyrrin was asleep, so I snuck out of his room and made my way back to my own. My master waited there, curled up on her truckle bed and covered only by a thin blanket. She looked very small and tired.

"Girton," she said quietly, her voice as dead-sounding as her make-up made her look.

"I have had my meetings with Bryan ap Mennix and Daana ap Dhyrrin."

She pulled herself up to sit cross-legged. "And?"

"I do not think Bryan ap Mennix has the wit to plan an assassination, but Daana ap Dhyrrin talks quite openly of treason."

"Aye," she said, pushing back her hood and starting to undo the plait in her hair, which had become tangled and knotted. I felt a little crestfallen. What I had said was clearly not new information to her. "And do you think him capable of planning a killing?"

"Undoubtedly." I sat by her and pushed her hand aside, then started to untangle her plait. "But he is clever and believes Aydor, if he does not become high king, will be the architect of his own destruction by turning the people against him."

"I have heard him say as much."

"One thing, Master. He said, 'when Aydor becomes high king', though he does not seem to think Aydor will marry the high king's sister."

"A slip of the tongue?"

"Maybe, but he sounded very sure of it, and he seemed like a very precise man so it struck me as odd. He talked as if Aydor would be high king, marriage or not. But he is old. Maybe his mind wandered."

"Do you think him a likely assassin?"

I tried to put myself in the old man's shoes.

"No. I think he would kill if the opportunity presented itself and he was in a position to get away with it. But if Aydor makes himself unpopular then Tomas could ride in as a hero to the people, dead gods know he looks the part. Daana seems to think he only has to wait."

She nodded. "But remember that Daana is old and passed

over the throne once. He may feel the hand of Xus pressing upon him. The proximity of death can make even the wisest men foolish." She winced as I pulled at a particularly tricky knot in her hair. "We should not write Daana off completely, Girton."

"No." I let a beat pass. "The assassin, master . . ."

"That is done with."

"But I know so little."

"You know more than many others. It is done with."

I wanted to ask more, but the words would not come. I could not understand why she was always so secretive, and eventually I decided it was best to move on rather than frustrate myself asking questions that would never be answered.

"Did you know that Aydor failed his Riders trial?"

"I did not," she said as I ran the comb through her hair. "Is that important?"

"It could be. No other squire is allowed to take the trials until Aydor is crowned, for fear of showing him up."

"That must have ruffled a few feathers."

"Indeed."

"So we have more suspects, not less, for our days investigating." She sounded tired beyond bearing.

"Yes, and another thing I discovered. Did you know the old Landsman, Heamus, brings in waifs and strays?"

"He does?" Her hand came up and stilled the hand holding the comb.

"Yes, I met him, and he, well . . ." I did not really want to discuss Drusl with my master now, although it appeared everyone in the castle knew about her. "He told me it was his attempt to redress the balance."

She nodded and then stood.

"Something haunts that man, Girton. It can be seen in his eyes, though I see no profit in Aydor's death for him. We should watch him anyway." She rolled her head on her shoulders, easing kinked muscles. "Girton, you look like you have a question."

I did, though I was unsure how to approach it, and when I opened my mouth I found myself asking something different. "What do you do all day, Master? You look so tired in the evening."

She put her head in her hands, squeezing her fingers together, making strands of her hair curl into loops. "What do you think I do all day?"

"You act as Heartblade for the queen, protecting her."

"When I am not keeping you safe I am Heartblade in a way, yes. I protect the queen, and Aydor too, but that is because they are together most of the time. It is long hours and I do not sleep well for trying to fit together puzzle pieces in my mind. Is that really what you wanted to ask?"

"Master," I stood. "You knew Adran had asked you here and yet you still came. What is between you and the queen?"

"We knew each other. When we were young."

"But what—"

She stood and turned, placing a finger on my lips to quiet me.

"Sshh, Girton. There are old wounds here with much pain in them. I would rather they were not reopened."

She took her finger from my lips.. "I am tied to the queen and the heir. I am rarely able to carry on my own investigation which makes finding who may have ordered an assassin doubly difficult – and it is an almost impossible task to start with." She placed her hands on either side of my head so she could stare into my eyes. "I need you to be my eyes, Girton, be my eyes and ears and watch everything and everyone."

There was worry etched into every tired line of her face, and if I had not known her better I would have thought her about to cry.

"I will, Master," I said.

"Good," she said, and gave me a tired smile. "You don't do badly for a boy with a bad foot."

Chapter 12

It may seem strange, considering that both my own and my master's lives hung in the balance, but I had some of the happiest days of my life at Castle Maniyadoc. In the midst of the castle's turmoil I had found a friend, something I had never had before, and away from the training yard, where he was always awaiting a surreptitious blow or cruel word from the other squires, Rufra was a different person. He was funny and had a rare wit and a glad hand with people. Old servant women would suddenly find an apple for us, or a slave would stand near and whisper that the other squires were searching for us and where they were. Little could spoil those days: not the almost constant feeling I was being followed, or that I could never quite find an opportunity to talk to Captain Dollis about the incident with the dogs.

Often Rufra and I would end up running from Kyril, Borniya and Hallin, who acted as Aydor's enforcers, or Tomas and a bunch of his cronies. It became a game, albeit one that could have a painful end if we lost. Rufra showed me a long scar on his leg that Hallin had given him the year before I came. He said Hallin enjoyed others' pain, and had cut him slowly while Borniya held him down, but as they were Aydor's friends he could not strike back. There was something very bleak in his voice when he spoke of Hallin.

When I wasn't with Rufra I was with Drusl, and if I was too shy to act on my feelings I felt more and more sure a bond was growing between us. Rufra often joined us, and though I hated myself for the lie I was forced to live, I was mostly happy.

In the few moments I had spare I explored Maniyadoc, and it was on one of these trips that I saw my master at work and started to wonder if I knew her at all.

I had found a place in the rafters above the stage where Aydor had been disappointed not to hang me. It was a good place to hide from Kyril, Borniya and Hallin, and watch the world go by. Below me people went to and fro on castle business; at one point I saw a small boy sit upon the king's throne before being shooed off by his mother. After I had been there about an hour a small group of guards entered through the door onto the stage and spread through the hall, closing doors and moving people out. Most were happy to go, but I noticed one man waited until the guards were distracted and slipped behind one of the tapestries. Once the hall appeared empty the door at the back of the stage opened again and my master walked through, glanced around and then gave a small nod to the figure behind her, Queen Adran, who passed her and walked over to the throne. She scanned the hall as if enjoying the recognition of an invisible crowd and then turned to her guards.

"Leave us," she said, and she and my master stood in silence while they waited for the guards to exit.

"Why have you brought me here, Adran?" said my master.

The queen ran a hand over the back of the throne.

"Have you given any thought to what I said, Merela? To staying?"

There was a ripple in the tapestries as the man I had seen moved further up the room. He had not been carrying a bow and did not look near enough to hurt them so I presumed he was eavesdropping. If it was more than that then I had no doubt my master would stop him, nonetheless, I loosened one of the throwing knives I kept up my sleeve.

"Girton and I will leave when we have uncovered who wants your son dead. Then I will consider any debt I owe you paid."

"Do you forget I dragged you, half dead, through a forest?" My master's reply was quick, vehement.

"Do you forget I didn't want to live?"

Adran paused, looked almost hurt by my master's words.

"We worked well together, once, you know," said Adran. There was none of the haughtiness in her voice I was used to hearing.

"Once," said my master, and the tapestry rippled again, drawing her eye. She tipped her head, watching for more movement.

"The king will not last much longer, Merela. Together, you and I could make changes, bring back the old ways."

"You talk of a better world we dreamed of but you will give the throne to your son." She sounded dismissive and took a step towards the tapestry where the man hid.

"Aydor is not as bad as he seems and he is weak. I can control him." Adran moved a straw hobby doll from the throne, threw it to the floor, and sat.

"So you have abandoned dreams of the old ways and will slip in another king. Aydor is an animal, like those from our youth, and he will only draw more like him. They will push you aside eventually," said my master quietly.

"And your boy?"

"He is different."

"Not like those from our youth, then?"

"No."

Adran gave a snort.

"Make up your mind — you cannot have it both ways." Then she sat forward, her voice heavy with threat. "And watch how you speak of my son. For all his faults I do love him. He is my blood."

"An end to cruelty, Adran, remember?"

"We are not girls any more, and life is not so simple. To rule, Merela, some cruelty is necessary and—"

My master pointed at the tapestry and silenced Adran with a cut of her hand. A good thing as I had leaned over so far to listen to their conversation that I may have fallen from the rafters if they had continued to speak. I watched my master and wondered what she meant about "the old ways". In some of the stories, the ones seldom asked for by the blessed, women and men ruled together and sometimes women ruled alone. I was distracted from my thoughts as my master approached the tapestry. She reached for it, but before she could touch it the hanging was ripped away to reveal the man I had seen earlier. His hand rested on his blade hilt, though he looked quite calm. He had the look of a mercenary, a rough man of the type common throughout the Tired Lands. I raised my throwing knife in readiness.

"No need to be frightened, ladies," he said. "I was only having a piss behind the hanging and got stuck in here, is all."

"I doubt that is true," said Adran. He looked at her and his smile fell away.

"I am simply a man paid to hear things. I am leaving," he said. "I heard nothing of any great import, so you just let me walk away, ladies, before someone gets hurt." Adran laughed at him. "You laugh, but you sent away your guards, Queen Adran,"

"I have my jester."

"Hardly a threat." He drew his blade. "I've never killed a jester though, first time for everything."

"I think I'd like to see this," said Adran. "Merela, do your job." Adran stood, walking down the steps from the stage to stand by my master. "And take him alive so I can have him questioned."

For a moment the man looked confused, then he lunged at my master. He was good, well practised and he looked

like he had fought many times before. My master did not
even bother drawing her blade or taking up the position of
readiness. She simply stepped out of the way of his thrust
and, using her empty hand, struck him in the throat with
stiffened fingers. I knew what she had delivered was a killing
strike that crushed the windpipe, there was little to do but
watch as the man choked to death on the wooden floor.
When he stopped moving Adran walked over to where my
master stood by the corpse.

"I wanted him alive."

"I made a mistake."

"You don't make that sort of mistake."

"You would have tortured him." She turned to the queen,
and I saw Adran's face twisting as though my master was
some sort of strange creature she had never seen before and
could not understand.

"You used to call me the soft one, do you remember?"

"It was a long time ago."

There was a silence, a long one while Adran stared into
the face of my master and she stared back. Eventually, Adran
turned from her to the corpse on the floor.

"Was he an assassin, do you think?" She turned the man
over with her foot.

"You know better than that."

"Just another spy then. Sometimes I think they outnumber
the lice in the castle beds." She walked up the stairs to the
throne and laid a hand on it. "It seems this place has nothing
to offer you, Merela. Let us return to my rooms."

When they were gone I tried to understand what was
between them but could not, and I could not ask my master
without revealing I had listened in. So despite what I had
heard she remained as much a mystery as ever, maybe more
so.

Despite this one, puzzling, event, on occasion I would
forget completely that I was Girton Club-Foot, the assassin's

boy, and would only be Girton ap Gwynr playing with his friends in the weak sunshine of yearsage. Those moments were the happiest of all.

It was not to last. Xus the unseen, god of death, waited in the wings, and his call to enter came far too quickly.

"Girton!" The voice was urgent but sounded very far away. "Girton!" It came again, an echo from far above while I glided along through the black sea of sleep. "Girton, wake up!"

I sat bolt upright and my master's skull face swam into focus before me.

"What? What is it? Is it training? Am I late?"

"No, you have barely fallen asleep. Queen Adran wants to see us."

"Why?

"There's been a death. One of the squires."

Immediately, any remaining tiredness was swept away. I feared for Rufra.

"Who?"

"A boy named Kyril."

"Kyril?" I shook my head to rid it of sleep. "Then I can't say I'm sorry."

"Don't speak like that in front of Adran, Girton."

"Why? It's no secret that we were hardly friends."

"Kyril's body doesn't have a mark on it."

It took a moment for that to sink in.

"He was assassinated?"

"Maybe. Kyril's family are influential and are yet to commit their support to Aydor. So Adran will be looking for a scapegoat to blame the death of their boy on."

"A scapegoat." I paused as I pulled on my jerkin. "You mean me?"

"Girton," she said, holding my head in her hands so I stared into her eyes, "did you kill him?" It felt like a kick to the stomach that she'd even ask.

"Of course not," I said. "I would have liked to but if it were me I would have made it look like an accident."

"Good," she said, and then put her hand gently on my shoulder. "I had to ask that, you understand? Adran will ask and she will want it to be you because it will be easier for her. Do not worry. I will not let her force the blame on to you. When she questions you say little and let me answer."

I nodded. My throat was too dry with fear to speak. I had seen how swiftly traitors were dealt with here, and this was a timely reminder of the danger we lived in, danger I had almost managed to forget.

Adran's rooms were on the top floor of the keep. A suite of three: a reception room, a dressing room and a bedroom hidden behind them. She waited in the reception room, one of the most beautiful rooms I had ever seen, full of heavy pre-imbalance furniture and hung with thick tapestries to absorb the constant draughts of the castle. Adran paced backwards and forwards, barely looking up as we entered. Behind her stood Aydor, Neander the priest in his bright orange garb and white mask, Daana ap Dhyrrin in his finery of gold and squawking lizards and Nywulf the squiremaster.

A chill ran through me. My master would not be able to protect me now. In front of Adran she could be Merela Karn, assassin, but in front of these witnesses she could only be a jester, and jesters were forbidden to speak in company. Adran intended me to take the blame and did not want my master getting in the way. The queen slowed her pacing and came to a stop before me, straightening her back so she could look down on me.

"Did you do it, boy?" she said gently. "No one would blame you. Tempers among the young can become frayed and Kyril could be impetuous. We know you and he have had run-ins, that you did not get on."

"Has something happened to Kyril?" I said. Her hand

flashed out and slapped me across the face, leaving stinging heat on my cheek.

"Don't use that glib tongue on me, child." Her face was inches from mine. "Kyril is dead, and you know it because you killed him. Maybe a bit of rough and tumble was too much for you, or maybe you thought he was sniffing around that doe-eyed stablegirl you keep chasing after." She stepped back. "I don't really care why you did it. But you did kill him. Admit it to me now in front of these witnesses and it will go far easier for you than if I need to have the truth pulled from your bones." I could barely speak and, absurdly, my embarrassment at hearing Drusl named was greater than my fear. "Are you shocked that I know about your little infatuation, boy?" she said. "You shouldn't be. I know everything that happens in this castle because it is my castle." She lowered her voice. "That is how I know you killed Kyril."

"I did not kill Kyril, Queen Adran."

"Who did then?" She screamed the words into my face. "Who else would want him dead?"

"I don't know. But I did not kill Kyril, Queen Adran."

"If the young blessed says he did not do this thing, my queen," said my master, "then he did not."

"Be quiet, jester," hissed Adran. "You have no right to speak here."

"My queen," said Daana ap Dhyrrin. "Death's Jester may speak out of turn, but she is right. Girton may not have liked Kyril but he does not possess the martial skills to best him."

Adran had not been as clever as she thought in inviting witnesses here. She may have stopped my master from speaking in my defence but it also meant she could not reveal that I was quite capable of killing Kyril without leaving a mark on him. If she did she would expose who I was, and that she had lied to her court and put an assassin among the squires. No blessed would support her if they thought she was considering the murder of their children – which is how it would appear. These men gathered in the room saw me only as a clumsy boy. The idea I was a killer must seem ludicrous to them.

"What about Rufra then, Nywulf," said Adran. "Rufra is skilled and he is friends with Girton. Where was Rufra this night? Out in the darkness acting from a misplaced sense of honour?" I saw alarm cross Nywulf's face, but it was only there for the briefest second before it was gone, replaced by a mask as blank as that of the priest standing next to him.

"Rufra was with me, Queen Adran," he said slowly and deliberately. "He was revising tactics until late and then he was locked in with the rest of the squires as you have ordered."

"And yet Kyril wasn't?"

"Kyril has special dispensation from your son to leave the barracks when he wishes."

Adran's fists were bunched in frustration.

"So what then, he just dropped dead?"

"People do," said Nywulf. "Even the heart of the strongest may burst without warning."

"Not the sons of the powerful!" she shouted. "Not in my castle and not under my care!" She walked over so she was close to me. "Maybe I should send you to Kyril's family anyway." I moved so the queen's shoulder blocked my mouth from the sight of the others, though I could still see them.

"I am an assassin, Queen Adran," I said in the Whisper-that-Flies-to-the-Ear. "I would kill your guards and escape. I would make you look weak." She stared into my face and for a moment I thought she was going to hit me again. Behind her I could see Neander, his expressionless mask fixed on me.

"Daana, Nywulf, you may go," she said. Her intent stare did not waver from me, and it felt like she was reading my spirit. "Send Heamus to me."

"Yes, my queen," said Nywulf. Daana ap Dhyrrin said nothing as he left, but his lizards squawked noisily as if amused by the drama around them.

Once they had left Queen Adran turned to Neander.

"Your opinion, Neander?"

The priest pushed up his white mask and wiped his face with his sleeve. "I doubt this boy did it." He nodded at me, and it was as if I ceased to exist for Adran. "Daana is right: from what I've heard he can barely hold a sword." There was something in his tone that was wrong, as if he knew this was a lie, and I wondered if Queen Adran confided in the priest. "Kyril's family will not be pleased by their son's death but they have other sons, and maybe if their boy died a hero that would ease their grief a little? It may even tie them to you, depending on the circumstances."

Adran brought her thumb to her mouth and chewed on the nail as she paced backwards and forwards again, her gown swishing and sparkling in the candlelight. She stopped and turned to her son.

"Aydor."

"Yes, Mother?"

"Where is the slave who found Kyril's body?

"Heamus put it in the dungeon, Mother. He did not think you would want others to know about Kyril's death." She nodded, and the door creaked as Heamus came in and bowed low.

"Heamus," said Adran before he could speak, "talk to the captain of my nightguard and tell him to find three guards whose loyalty he doubts. Find well muscled ones if possible. I want them removed from the barracks, quietly mind. Then bind them, gag them and put them in a cart."

"You need them alive, my queen?" The old Landsman sounded tired, beaten.

"It doesn't matter as long as no one knows we have taken them. Tell him to take the slave that found the body and the

corpse of the boy and put them in the cart also. A covered
cart, mind. Then he should drive the cart out to Barnew's
Wood. Early this morning I want you to put on Kyril's armour
– you are a similar size – and ride out to the wood with
Aydor. I want everyone to see you leave, but you will keep
the visor of your helmet down. Neander will make sure
Daana ap Dhyrrin and Nywulf know not to mention Kyril's
death to anyone."

"Very well, my queen," he said and left the room followed
by the orange-clad priest.

"We're not going to hurt Girton?" said Aydor. Plainly, he
was disappointed in my continued existence.

"No, Aydor, we are not going to hurt Girton any more
today," said his mother. "Neander was right. Kyril's family
may feel some obligation to us if their son dies a hero in
our cause. You and Heamus, posing as Kyril, will ride out
to Barnew's Wood. When you get there, if the slave and
those guards still live, cut them down. If they are already
dead slash the bodies with your blades, but it must look
like they died in a fight. Then you will put Kyril's body
back in his armour and drive a sword through him." She
stared out of the crystal window. "Do it more than once.
A few survivable wounds and a lethal one. It should seem
to any that see him that he went down fighting hard. Then,
Aydor, you will bring his body back over his mount – scar
the animal too. Heamus will come back with the cart and
my captain. I will send a messenger later to Kyril's family
and tell them he gave his life to protect his beloved heir
from bandits."

"Very well, Mother." He bowed and I could see a smile
on his face. The idea of cutting down a few defenceless men
appealed to him.

"My son, come here." Queen Adran put out her arms as
if to hold her son. He let her hold him, briefly. Then she
leaned back and touched his face with her hand. "My

beautiful boy," she said gently, "I am afraid it cannot look like you simply walked away from this."

"What do you mean—" he began and his mother's other hand flashed up, slashing him across the face with a dagger. "Dead gods, you mad bitch!" he shouted as his hand came up to the wound. Blood ran freely down his face.

"A scar will look good on you," hissed his mother, "and when, one day, you meet Kyril's family and take their oath of loyalty you can truthfully say you got that scar when their boy died."

"It hurts," he said.

"Be a man, not a child, Aydor. If you think becoming high king will be pain free you are a fool. This is only the start. Now leave us. You have work to do."

He slammed the door as he left and Queen Adran stared at the wood as if the whorls of the grain would spell out her next move. "Merela," she said eventually, "come and look at Kyril's body with me before they take it. I dislike a mystery and you know more of death than most. You can bring your boy if you must."

We followed Queen Adran through the veins of the castle – like most old keeps it was riddled with secret passages so the powerful could go unseen. Kyril's body was on the dungeon level in a clean room where statues of age-of-balance kings had been carved into the wall. Most had lost their stone hands, feet and noses, and rather than looking like kings now looked like criminals, mockingly crowned and fresh from punishment. A granite block made a table in the centre and was covered by the yellow and purple Mennix flag; Underneath the flag the contours of a body rose and fell; the yellow parts reminding me of the sourlands, the purple of night. Adran pulled the flag away and I watched in silence as the slight material of the flag drifted slowly to the floor to reveal Kyril. He looked smaller in death.

"Kyril," I said.

The queen turned her stare on me. "Did I ask you to speak?"

"No." I stared at the floor like a slave.

"No, Queen Adran," she reminded me.

"No, Queen Adran."

"Good. This is poor Kyril, Merela. Once a friend to Aydor and now a problem to me." She stepped over to the table, placing her hands on the stone at either side of the boy's head and staring down into his face. "He was an unpleasant character and given to leering at anything with a bust, but he would have been useful." She turned her gaze from the body to my master. "I have not asked as it was not convenient before: did you do this, Merela?"

"What do you think?" My master brought her hands up, palms outwards, fingers spread in the gesture used to show surprise when storytelling. The movement involved enough of a pause to make her next words obviously disrespectful. "Queen Adran."

Adran stayed where she was and stared at my master. "You look ridiculous in that costume."

"To some. But others find it distressing, and it pleases Xus the god of death, which is fitting, considering the moment."

"I am sure, Merela, you no more believe fairy tales about gods than I do." She touched Kyril's still face. "Is Nywulf right – did this boy's heart really burst? Death is your domain."

"Is it really?"

"Don't!" Adran slapped her hand on the stone slab, the noise echoed around the mortuary room. "I am not in the mood for silly jester games, Merela. Tell me how this boy died."

My master stepped closer to the corpse. In my mind's eye I had built Kyril up into something monstrous and huge, but dead he was just a boy and a boy who looked younger than his sixteen years.

"Girton," said my master, "take your knife and strip him."

"No." The queen held up a hand. "Undress him if you must but don't cut his clothes off. His family may want them returned and I want the only cuts in them to be from the sword that kills him."

"Very well." My master smiled at Adran's choice of words as she started to unbutton the boy's jacket. "Girton, some help, please."

Though I have been the cause of many corpses I have been close to remarkably few of them for long and I was surprised by how heavy and cold Kyril was. His unwieldiness made getting his clothes off a struggle, when we finally had him undressed my master called for more light. I held a torch while she looked over the body. First she manipulated the neck to check for breaks and then she used the span of her hand as a measure to methodically check every part of the pale, almost blue, skin of his body for puncture wounds. The flickering torch made the shadow of her hand jump, spider-like, across the corpse. She found nothing on his front but a bruise over his heart, though it was a yellow that made me think it was days old. She sniffed at it, but the dancing torchlight hid her face and she did not seem to come to any conclusion, only bit her lower lip and glanced at me. Then we turned him and she checked his back using her hand as a measure again. Lastly, she had me turn him back onto his front and put her nose close to his mouth while I pushed, first on his stomach and then on his chest.

"No assassin did this, Adran."

"How can you be sure?" Queen Adran spoke almost absent-mindedly. She seemed transfixed by the body, utterly unable to take her eyes from boy's limp form. She was so fascinated she forgot to correct my master for not calling her Queen.

"There are no puncture wounds, no broken neck or

bruising of the nerve points and no scent of poison on his breath."

"Then how did the boy die?"

"His heart probably burst, as Nywulf said. It can happen even to the young and healthy."

"Are you suggesting Coil the Yellower or Fitchgrass jumped out of a hedge and frightened the boy to death?" My master ignored the sarcasm and rested a finger on Kyril's chest.

"See the bruise, here, over his heart?"

"It is old."

"Yes, it is." Something in my master's voice – did she lie? "He may have been kicked by a mount or hurt in training. Such things can cause a heart to burst days later."

"You are sure?"

"There is only one way to be sure," said my master. "Girton, I will need your knife. And a saw to get through his ribs."

"No!" Adran moved in front of my master. "I believe you. We'll not cut him open." She stared at the body again. "It is sobering, is it not, Merela? We could be struck down at any moment with no warning. It makes a mockery of all our struggles."

"But does not stop us struggling."

"No, nothing stops us." She took a final look at Kyril, leaning in close to his face. "Nothing but death." She turned to my master. "Merela, you and your boy will not talk to anyone about the bruise. We will tell the family he died a hero saving the future king. I will have Neander conduct the ceremony of leaving tonight."

We left the laying-out room and returned to our own small bedroom. The first thing I did was change out of my clothes as I felt like the smell of Kyril's corpse was clinging to me. My master was distracted, pulling aside the greased paper cover so she could stare out of the window.

"Girton, you really had nothing to do with Kyril's death?"

"No." Again that sense of betrayal that she thought so little of me. "I hated him, but I have more self-control than to go about murdering people I don't like. Why don't you believe me?"

"I do. It is just that if it was not you then our lives are more complex than I thought."

"What do you mean? Did you lie to Adran? Was Kyril murdered then?"

"Yes, he was murdered. Someone used the Black Hammer to kill him. That was the cause of the bruise over his heart."

I went cold. My flesh seemed to freeze and my skin to be punctured by painful spines. "Magic? Are you saying there's a sorcerer loose in the castle? How can you be sure?"

"I could smell it on him."

"Smell it?"

"Aye, magic leaves a scent like pepper and honey. It is faint but recognisable if you know to look out for it. That is how the Landsmen find sorcerers, though it only works for those unable to control themselves."

A vivid image came to me: of Heamus sniffing the air around me, of Neander doing the same. Something dark, cold and slow moved within me and it sucked the moisture from my mouth and the feeling from my fingers and toes.

. . . *if it was not you then our lives are more complex than I thought.*

The world seemed to spin, as if the earth moved beneath me while I stayed still.

"If it was not me?" I said, the words small and confused. "What do you mean, if it was not me?"

At first she looked puzzled. Then surprised. Then a terrible sadness came over her, almost fear. She sat on the bed, unable to look at me.

"Oh Girton," she whispered, "what we do? The Whisper-that-Flies-to-the-Ear? The Simple Invisibility?" I stared at her. It seemed she had suddenly become something alien, and though I understood her words they made as much sense to me as the lowing of a draymount.

"Magic, Master? Magic in me? That cannot be."

"Girton —" she lifted a hand as if to reach for me and then let it fall "— you have always been so clever, my clever boy, so very clever. I thought you knew. When I said tell no one our secrets, not even other assassins, I thought you knew. I thought that you had realised this long ago." She looked up. "Sometimes I forget you are a child still. That I have always been able to ask anything of you and you do it — your trust in me has always been total. I should have thought harder on that. Why would you question our abilities when I told you they were only tricks?"

"No," I said, and felt the world around me folding in, becoming pale. Its angles ceased to make sense and our room became both impossibly large and impossibly small at the same time. My skin burned with a cold fire and the air became thick and soupy. "It cannot be," I said again. "I am not a monster." She reached out for me and I pulled my arm away. "What we do is only tricks, Master. Tricks." My heart beat, thready and quick like a small animal desperate to escape a cage.

"Some yes. The Careless Gossip, the Wild Gaze, these are techniques that, given time, anyone can—"

"I cannot do those things."

"Not yet, but you can do other things and . . ."

"Magic."

"It is not what you think."

"I am a sorcerer?" It was as if my life stretched before me along a path of desiccated yellow lined with the corpses of the innocent, at its end was a swinging blood gibbet, door open, waiting for me — and it was as if I had always known this. Now she had said it I could not deny it.

"Yes, We are sorcerers, Girton, if you must use that word." She sounded so reasonable, as if she had not pronounced a death sentence on me. "And it is not the curse others would have you believe."

I took a step back, meeting the wall and sliding down it until I sat on the floor.

"Have I ruined you?" said my master. "Leaving this so late? You must try and understand, Girton." She slid from the bed and went to her knees, taking my hands in hers. "This does not change you. You are no more a monster than I am."

"Why doesn't the land die beneath my feet?" My voice was as brittle as a tree in the sourlands. "When I whisper why doesn't it affect anyone?"

"Because it is a very small magic —" she sat back on the bed "— and we pay the land back with our blades. We follow an older way."

"You have trained me to be a . . ." my voice rising.

"No," she said softly. "There is no training. You were born with a gift. Your mother had it and you inherited it."

"You knew what sort of creature I am." I breathed. "You knew all this time and you didn't say."

"Yes, Girton," she said gently. I took my hand from hers. "I knew. We are the same. Why do you think slavers raised you in the sourlands? It was because they feared you. They knew so little about magic they thought little boys could tap into the life of the land."

"We were all sorcerers there? All of us?" The information like body blows.

"No, not all. Only you had the gift in any strength that day, Girton, but you were all the children of magic users or relatives of those with the gift."

"But how?" I felt like I was shouting but was unable to raise my voice above a hoarse whisper. "How can that be? The children and family of sorcerers all join the desolate. They all die, they all bleed into the land."

"No, Girton. The Landsmen are as corrupt as any other

power in the Tired Lands. They find some harmless wise
woman eking out her power to heal wounds or ease childbirth and lock her in a blood gibbet." There was a quiet but
forceful anger in my master's voice. "Then they take all the
adult relatives to join the desolate, but they sell the children
off to slavers and line their own pockets. They send them
far away and think that is enough to stop it ever coming
back to haunt them."

"I thought you chose me for who I am —" I could feel my
words turning into a sneer "— but you chose me for what I
am."

"No!" She sounded desperate. Tried to grab my hand again
but I pulled it free. "I was not there to recruit." I stared into
her face looking for a lie but found only pain and fear. "I
chose you, Girton. I chose you. I saw a life about to be wasted
and I could not bear it. I chose you."

I lifted my hands and stared at them. I half-expected them
to burst into flames or leak poisonous black liquid. "I don't
want to suck the life out of the land, Master. I don't want
to be like the Black Sorcerer."

"Girton," she said, holding my head in her hands and
making me meet her gaze, "every day we are lied to. Magic
is part of nature and it is no more evil than an angry mount
or a hailstorm. It is a tool to use and those who misuse it
do so because they lack discipline. You have discipline, you
have been trained and trained well. You are no danger to
yourself or the land. Nothing has changed, Girton." She let
a heartbeat pass. "You have not changed."

I could see how desperate she was for me to understand,
but all I felt was betrayal. Everything I knew had been
turned on its head. I was something terrible, and she had
always known. She could have told me at any time but she
had not. If not for Kyril's death, would she ever have told
me? Or would she have waited until I ripped a new souring
into the land?.

"I'm tired," I said. The words came out parched of emotion. My master nodded.

"I understand." She stood away from me, glanced back and then blew out the candle. In the darkness I curled up into a ball and, wrapping myself around a centre of anger and betrayal, tried to ignore the sound of my master quietly sobbing until she fell asleep. Far beneath, the world carried on. In the townyard the fires of Festival sparkled like a mirror of the cold stars in the night sky above. All indifferent to me, Girton Club-Foot.

Girton the mage-bent.

Interlude

This is a dream.

They are running. In the distance he sees Rufra. Following Rufra is his master. Following his master is Drusl.

They run through the loose dirt of the sourlands and for every ten steps run they only make one step forward. They run hard but the land is against them. The stink of it is thick in their nostrils. On the horizon the sky is gold as if a huge fire burns beyond it.

There are dogs behind them. Big dogs, small dogs, medium dogs, black dogs, white dogs, tan dogs and brindle dogs. All snarling. All barking. A roiling wave of sharp teeth and dripping saliva, eager to catch them.

They are running. Not speaking, not able to speak. Only able to run. Only able to lift their legs and pump their arms but the ground gives way beneath their feet and the golden sky never comes any closer.

He's scared. Even though he knows this is a dream, knows it completely.

Wake me.

This. Is. A. Dream.

Wake me, Master.

He wakes. The room is pitch-black and his master is not there. He gets out of bed. Drusl is there but she doesn't talk to him. She turns away. In front of her the corridor of white-washed stone elongates and he feels like he's falling. Rufra appears further up the corridor and from behind Rufra comes his master.

The barking starts.

This is a dream.

Rufra runs, then his master and then Drusl. They don't speak to him and he doesn't speak to them. He wants to shout and tell them to run harder but the words are held in his mind the way the dry, dead earth of the sourlands holds his feet. For every ten steps he runs he only makes one step forward.

Wake me.

Teeth shine in golden light.

Wake. Me.

Snapping mouths splash saliva against his legs.

Please, Master, wake me.

He wakes. He is in the warm absolute black of the rafters of the castle. He reaches out but there is no one there. A torch bursts into life, golden light that shows Drusl, Rufra and his master. He is naked but he feels no shame. He looks over his shoulder and sees the dogs, a wall of dogs coming on impossibly quickly. He runs. The loose, warm, dead earth of the sourlands is trying to hold on to his feet. For every ten steps he runs he only takes one step forward.

He realises he cannot escape.

They're not real! Wake! Wake!

He stops. Turns. Spreads his arms as if to embrace another.

Wake. Me.

The dogs.

A snapping, stinking, yapping, barking wave of furious animals. But there is no pain. There are no bites, no ripping or tearing or crushing. Instead he is lifted by them, buoyed up on a tide of heavily muscled canine flesh. The wave rises and breaks. He becomes dogs, and dogs become him. His arms end in sharp mouths. He sees through hundreds of glowing eyes. His body is a hunched, muscled mass of brindle fur. His legs are powerful and clawed. He is fast and dangerous and out of control.

He shouts, but his voice is a hideous un-symphony of barks.

Drusl is first.

Jaw-hands rip into her under the golden light of the sourlands sun. She doesn't scream, but he sees the agony in her eyes as he tears her apart. The sourlands sop up her blood. His master next. For all her arts and training she can no more avoid the dog beast than Drusl – the sourlands soak her up as if she had never been. Then Rufra, who turns and stares as he bears down on him. In his hands he holds a flaming silver sword.

Wake me.

He is unstoppable.

Wake me.

This is a dream.

Chapter 13

I woke alone and scared. The idea I could somehow harness magic was ludicrous, I was Girton, born a slave boy. Had I dreamed the whole thing?

It felt like it.

A note written in scratch was pinned to the door.

Girton,
Kyril's body was found round the back of the stables, and you have a legitimate excuse to be seen down there. I want you to examine the whole area for anything strange.

A souring, that was what she meant, but she was not foolish enough to put it in writing in case anyone found it.

Thoughts of magic drifted into my mind like the bad smell that came when the winds blew from the sourlands. I pushed them aside but no thought can ever be truly banished. Like mice they always find some hole through which to creep back into your mind. I was glad when the bell of the water-clock tolled out time for training. I needed something to occupy me and hoped training would be the cat to chase away mice-thoughts of magic, but it was a morose affair that morning. News of Kyril's death had left even those squires who disliked him subdued. When Aydor turned up, proudly showing off his scar, there was such a rush to hear his story that Nywulf called the session to an end early.

"Come on," said Rufra. "My desire to hear about the fight

isn't as strong as my desire to get away from Aydor. Let's go to the stables." Following Rufra, I glanced behind and saw Aydor talking to Borniya and Hallin and pointing in our direction.

We had to detour around Festival. The tent city was now surrounded by miles of zigzag fences making enclosures for the livestock which would start flowing in from the surrounding countryside, not only the ubiquitous pigs but also sheep, goats and rare and expensive animals like cows. At its centre was a walled city of brightly coloured tents and caravans, and in the middle of that the two-storey Festival Lords' caravans. Around them, like skeletons of dead mounts rising above a colourful grassland, were the frames for rides which would swing you up and out and round in terrifying circles.

"Are you all right, Girton?" asked Rufra as we jumped over fences.

"Me?"

"Yes, you seem out of sorts."

"Sorry," I said, and tried to force a smile onto my face.

"Is it Kyril's death?"

"I didn't like him," I said quickly.

"Who did?" He shrugged and we walked in silence for a while. "Is it the first time you have been close to death?"

"Yes," I lied to my friend, and he put an arm around my shoulder.

"The first person I knew who died was a servant called Danyl. He was a beast of a man – all the hall's children were terrified of him. One day he fell over a loose cobble and broke his neck. I was nine and it unsettled me for days but not because I liked him – I didn't – it was because it made me realise I could die. But you cannot change the way life is, Girton. You must carry on and do the best you can."

We jumped the last fence, finding ourselves on a well worn path thick with those about their daily business.

"I suppose," I said, and although it was magic not death

that was my problem I realised he spoke the truth. Not that it helped much; I still felt like a sewer ran through me.

"You should come to First of Festival with me tonight, Girton. That would take your mind off death."

"I am sleeping in the castle, Rufra, and the gates are kept shut to anyone who doesn't have a pass."

"Do you have any money?"

"Money?"

"Yes. Look out for guards who wear something red. Most of them would rather Tomas was the heir. Aydor has not made himself popular. The captains hide it well – trouble-makers are put into more loyal units or moved to a later shift where they are not seen – but they are there, and their numbers grow. So if you see a guard with a splash of red somewhere on them they will probably take a bribe."

The more I learned about Maniyadoc the more it seemed like a castle on the edge of tearing itself apart.

"I do not know if I can afford a bribe, Rufra. I have money doled out to me and little of it."

He stopped and took hold of my arm, steering me into the shadow of the townwall and away from the steady stream of servants, slaves and Festival staff.

"Here." He put some coins in my hand. "That should be enough."

"Rufra, this is four bits, I cannot—"

"You are my friend and the money is my uncle's. It is a pleasure to give it away as he hates charity." Rufra grinned at me, slipping into almost-handsome. "I will be to the right of the keepyard gate at nine. If you cannot get out you cannot. I will wait for half an hour."

"Thank you, Rufra."

"You need not thank me, but it would be nice if you could attempt a smile."

I tried but my mood would not lift. My mind could find a thousand worries but, curiously, not one was magic. Either it had some power of its own that would not let me examine how I felt or it was simply too enormous and frightening for me to confront.

When we arrived at the stables Drusl was sitting on the ground outside, soaking up what little of the cold yearsage sun remained. She smiled as we approached and my mood lifted a little.

"Is it true?" she said.

"Is what true?" I asked.

"Oh come on. The whole castle is talking about it. Kyril and Aydor were set upon by a hundred bandits and both have been hacked into pieces." She was very grave, as if the whole idea left her puzzled and sad.

"If only that were true," said Rufra.

"Kyril is dead," I said. "The heir was hurt but not badly, and it was not a hundred bandits, merely a handful." I tried to look past her into the stable. "Is Leiss here?"

"No," said Drusl and tried to smile. "He will not be back for an hour or so yet. He has gone to collect more fodder for the mounts before the stockers bring in their animals and the prices shoot up."

Rufra made an elaborate show of looking into the sky at the sun.

"Oh, it is later than I thought. Nywulf will have more interminable lessons on tactics for me. I should be gone."

"You need not," I said. I did not want him to feel unwelcome, though I wished, more than anything, to be alone with Drusl.

"Oh, I think I need to," said Rufra with a grin. "Nywulf has been in a strange mood recently and I don't want to upset him any more by being late. You two have fun."

I sat on the ground by Drusl, leaving enough room between us so that another could have sat. The ground and the wall of the stables were acting as a sun trap, and though the air had a cold nip the ground was warm to the touch. We did not speak straight away, and for the first time that day my mind seemed to settle rather than constantly slipping and sliding around the idea of magic.

"Did you know him well?" she said. "The boy that died, Kyril?"

"Yes, well enough," I said. I noticed she sat with her hands by her thighs, palms up in a slightly unnatural posture. I moved so my hands were by my side, palms on the warm ground.

"He was fond of the whip," she said. There was only four palm-widths between my hand and hers. "I often treated his mount for cuts, though it was a gentle animal and did not deserve them."

"He was that type." I moved my hand, only a fraction, making it look like an accidental move, but it left me nearer to touching her hand. "He and his friends liked to throw their weight around. He once pushed me over in the castle just because he could." My hand crept a little closer to hers, inching across the ground.

"Be glad you're not what he saw as attractive; his type often try more than a push." My hand froze.

"You?"

"He tried, but Leiss intervened and said he would tell Nywulf." My hand relaxed. "Kyril and his awful friends Borniya and Hallin came back. I hid in the loft while they gave Leiss a beating, which he seems to think should be the key to my kilts." We sat quietly until she spoke again. "He threatened to find me alone one day."

"Leiss?"

"No, Kyril. That does not mean I wanted him dead," she added quickly. Drusl looked so miserable that I wanted to sweep her up in my arms and hold her close, but I was too cowardly. "Leiss is not as bad as he seems, you know," she said. "He can be kind and I think he presumes that he and I will one day . . ."

"But you and he will not?"

I let my hand inch a little closer.

"No. He thinks I will come round to him but . . ."

My hand a little closer.

"But?"

"I'm different to him," she said. "He says I can be content with him, but I want to be happy, Girton, not content." She looked right at me. "However impossible that seems."

"Drusl . . ."

"Why aren't you working?" Leiss towered over us and the sun at his back turned him into a looming dark figure – it was as if Xus the unseen had suddenly appeared.

"I was taking a rest, Leiss," said Drusl, getting up.

"With him?" He pointed at me.

"He has a mount here, Leiss," said Drusl. "He is allowed to be here."

"Aye, but that doesn't mean he can stop you working. Those mounts need cleaning out." He turned to me. "You might be blessed, but it don't mean you can stop us doing our jobs just 'cos you 'as nothing to do. Now get off with you or I'll 'ave Nywulf find you some real work."

I stood with my fists balled. I wanted to beat Leiss down in front of Drusl, but that was Girton the assassin's wish. Girton ap Gwynr would never have done that, so I walked away listening to snippets of Drusl and Leiss arguing: "Boy's a yellower, he'll only make you unhappy . . . Gods don't allow our sort to rise . . . Spoilt blessed's get . . . I'd be far better for you, Drusl." Her replying: "Never. You can be my friend but nothing else . . .You're not like me, Leiss . . . I need someone like me . . ." I wondered what she meant. With a sinking heart I realised it was unlikely she spoke of me; what did a stable girl and a crippled blessed have in common?

I headed back to my room, sinking into self-pity, but was stopped by a slave in the keepyard.

"Blessed." She bowed low. "The guard captain, Dollis, is drinking alone at a hole tavern in the townwall. We know you looked for him."

"Thank you," I said and dug in my pocket, taking out one of the bits Rufra had given me, a fortune for a slave. "Here."

She bowed her head and made the coin vanish with all the skill of a Festival trickster.

I ran for the townyard wall and started checking the wallroom taverns, finding most full of raucous guards and Festival staff. As I searched for the guard captain I could almost hear my master advising me to stop – to think and not hurry into the encounter – but until then it had been impossible to find Dollis alone and I was worried I would lose the opportunity if I dallied. Time is ever man's enemy.

I found him in the fifth wall room, one strangely muted and empty compared to the others. He was drinking alone and looked up as I entered, his hand going under the table to his blade, then he stared at me and a calculating smile crossed his face.

"Well, if it i'nt the queen's favourite cripple." He took a swig of his perry as I sat opposite him. "Dangerous places for cripples, these drinking holes." It sounded like a threat.

"Then it's fortunate you're here to protect me, eh Captain Dollis?"

He stared at me. His missing front tooth had broken off just above the gum making it look like a new, angular, predator's tooth was growing down to replace the lost human one. He leaned forward, squinting his eyes to see me better in the gloom.

"I don't like blessed. Like smart-mouthed blessed even less," he growled.

"What about Aydor?"

"The fat bear pays my wages but the yellower couldn't win my respect if his prick depended on it." Someone came into the hole and Dollis's eyes flicked up. I wondered if he was worried Aydor was likely to walk in and hear the way his guard captain talked of him.

"Did the heir put you up to locking me in the kennels?"

He stared at me, weighing me up.

"What makes you think I was involved in that?"

"People talk."

"Anjohn," he hissed under his breath. "Well, it don't matter. I was only obeying orders, weren't I? Nothing wrong in obeying your betters, eh?" He cackled to himself

"Aydor's orders?"

"Wouldn't you like to know." He took another drink and his eyes slid to the door hole.

"Yes. I would like to know."

His glance strayed back from the doorhole to me. A strange grin spread across his face, one that I could not place the emotion behind.

"It weren't the fat bear asked it, though 'im and his friend's 'ad a good laugh about it."

"Who then?"

He leaned forward.

"If I tell you, mage-bent, I'll upset important people. Very dangerous people. So you'll need to make it worth my while. Youse family are rich I 'ear."

"I have three bits."

"Three bits!" he burst out, laughing. "I wouldn't piss on you for three bits, cripple. Fifteen is what I need to make it worthwhile."

"Fifteen? You could outfit a troop for that." Anger bubbled up and I leaned over the table, speaking in a whisper. "I think you need to lower your price, Captain Dollis. How would the queen feel if she knew the man in charge of her son's guard was taking jobs on the side?"

Dollis's hand shot out and grabbed my jerkin, pulling me off balance and forward to hold me in front of his face. It was all I could do not to go for my knife and slash the tendons in his wrist.

"You threaten me, boy?" he growled. "I should slit you from ear to ear for that." He loosened his grip and pushed me back into my seat as if disgusted with me. "Adran knows I work on the side and as long as it doesn't affect her or the boy she don't care." He picked at his teeth using his dirty thumbnail. "But I don't like upstart little blesseds trying to blackmail me, and it's going to cost you. Twenty bits is my price now."

"I can't possibly find—"

"The extra is for the insult, and be glad I don't take it out your flesh. I still might. Feel good to scar a blessed . . ."

"But I can't afford—"

"Then you should piss off, boy." He stared into his drink and waved me away. "I've got my own problems to sort and I don't like the mage-bent. You're hedge-cursed and you sour the drink." I stood, at a loss for what to say. "I said piss off," he growled and drove his knife into the table. I backed away and out through the doorhole, sure I could hear Dollis chuckling to himself.

Angry for not thinking the encounter through properly I returned to our room. I was unlocking the door when my master appeared, as if from nowhere, at my side and pushed me in.

"Girton, Heamus is busy with Adran and Aydor this evening between eight and nine. It would be a perfect time to search his room. Spend this afternoon familiarising yourself with the servants and slaves' shifts around his quarters." Her words were cold and to the point.

"Break into his room? But he is my—"

"Have you forgotten why we are here?" she hissed. "It is not to make friends."

"No, Master, I have not forgotten," I said, then added, "Leiss may have killed Kyril."

"The stablemaster?"

"Yes, Kyril had threatened Drusl. Leiss and he had almost come to blows and Kyril came back with his friends later and they beat Leiss."

"The stablemaster strikes me as an unlikely sorcerer, Girton. Did you find any signs of magic in the stables?"

"Nothing." I had not looked. I had been too busy enjoying being nothing but a boy for a few moments. I do not know what possessed me to lie about it as my master can read a lie the way a general reads land or a swordsman reads the movement of an opponent's feet.

"Nothing," she repeated. "And how hard did you look? Or were you distracted by your friends?"

"I . . ."

"Don't lie to me again, Girton. If you have not done something tell me so."

"I'm sorry, Master."

"Don't be sorry, do better." She sat on the bed. "I understand this may be hard for you, Girton, I do. You have never had the opportunities most boys your age have and you have had some –" she searched the air for the right word "– difficult news. But our lives are in danger. Queen Adran could lose patience with us at any moment."

"I am sorry, Master. I will look properly tomorrow, I swear it." Resentment bubbled within me.

"Good, now will you search Heamus's room?"

"Yes, but—"

"What?"

"May I attend the First of Festival with Rufra this evening?" My words were so quiet I was surprised my master could hear them. She, in her turn, was quiet for a long time.

"If I say no, will you obey me?"

I stayed silent, frightened that if I spoke the simmering anger I had felt since she had told me about the magic within us would burst out. Meeting Rufra for First of Festival seemed like the most important thing in the world, even though I knew it was a small thing. Then she was in front of me, moving across the room with the Speed that Defies the Eye. Her skull face was all I could see, huge and unreal. Her eyes searched my face.

"I will not stop you, Girton," she hissed, "but you would do well to remember that these people who think themselves your friends do not know you. They are friends with a fiction and you need to keep in mind what you really are."

Then she was gone.

I remained in our room, in a black mood, and must have spent at least half an hour pacing backwards and forwards talking to myself about how unfair life was, and it was. Eventually I realised that if there was a rogue sorcerer loose in the castle then we were all in danger, including the people I said were my friends – Rufra and Drusl. What this could have to do with a plot to assassinate Aydor I had no idea, but my master clearly thought the two were linked. Also, and whether this is a failing or not I have never been sure, I have always struggled to sustain a dark mood and my master has drilled into me that the best way to banish darkness is to occupy yourself. With that in mind I left our room, proceeded to Heamus's room and set about memorising the paths of the servants and slaves in the corridors around it.

Heamus lived on the second floor of the castle in an inner room. It was a quiet area with little traffic, though annoyingly what traffic there was seemed completely random. I walked past Heamus's door a few times, and each time I took a moment to examine the lock and listen at the door. Someone was at home. I could hear the scratching of bootnails on the floor. Once I had done as much as I could, and knowing I had time to spare, I decided to visit the kitchens and see if I could find something to eat.

On my way down the tight spiral staircase I heard the echo of tears. This was not an unusual thing to hear in the castle – not a day passed without some slave being beaten, some servant being reprimanded or a blessed lady being caught in a web of romantic intrigue – but there was something haunting in the sound. I found myself drawn to it, winding my way down the stair and through a stiff and seldom-used door. Behind the door I entered a disused part of the castle. Dust lay thick on the floor and rose in gauzy clouds as my feet disturbed it. Dim light struggled in through layers of cobweb and illuminated a smudgy, but well-used, path through the dust. I followed the path and the sound of sobbing through grey rooms. Old tapestries wept loose thread into mouldering piles; chairs and tables were being slowly digested by woodworm. The sound of tears faded and grew as I walked, making it difficult to follow and leaving me wondering if it was real at all. Maybe this was some hedging, luring me to it in hope of a deal for my life. In such a quiet and decrepit part of the castle hedge spirits were much easier to believe in.

I rounded a corner and walked straight into Neander, the priest of Heissal. I did not immediately recognise him as he had covered his flowing orange gown with a nondescript brown cloak, waxed against wind and moisture, but there was no disguising the harsh landscapes of his face.

"Girton!" he barked. He was clearly as surprised to come across me as I was to come across him. "What are you doing here?" The raptor claw of his hand darted out and closed around my wrist as tightly as an iron cuff.

"I . . . I was running an errand for Nywulf and I got lost. Then I heard crying." Running an errand for Nywulf was a good excuse, and one commonly used by squires who were not where they should be.

He looked me up and down, and it felt as if his blue eyes drilled into my mind in search of lies, though if he had the power to do such a thing I am sure he would quickly find himself lost among the web of untruths I had woven.

"Did you think the crying was your young lady?"

"No." A blush rising to my face. "I have no young lady. Why would I think that?"

He examined my face, looking for a lie.

"In my experience young men are often unable to think of anything but young ladies." He tried a smile. "I was much the same in my youth." His grip tightened a little and he cocked his head to one side. "What is this errand you are running for our squiremaster?"

"He wanted me to find Rufra," I said.

"Well, Girton —" Neander's grip was cutting off my circulation and I could feel my hand beating in time with my pulse "— you will not find your friend here. He has many faults but is more sensible than to come into the disused areas of the castle. It is not safe here, a lot of the stonework is loose." Another tightening of his grip. "There have been deaths, Girton, deaths." I nodded, and I think he saw the question I was about to ask in my eyes. "You wonder why I am here if it is dangerous?" I nodded again. "I am here because of the tears you hear. A servant girl has got herself into trouble with a squire and wanted my counsel. The servants believe they will get more privacy in these disused areas of the castle, and as their priest I must go where they wish, even when it puts my life in danger." The words slid out of his mouth so smoothly it was either true or a very well practised lie. He looked down at his hand, as if only now becoming aware of how tightly he held my wrist. "Am I hurting you, Girton?" He stared into my eyes. "Sometimes I am overcome with fervour for my vocation and forget myself." He let go of my wrist only when he had finished speaking. His grip had left a ring of red skin on my wrist and pins and needles fizzed across my hand.

"No, it did not hurt, Blessed," I replied.

"Blessed." He laughed. "I am no blessed man of power, Girton. I am only a simple priest and that is my lot. I dream of no more."

"Of course," I said, but his laugh was false and there was a look in his eye that left me sure he did dream of more, of much more.

"Now, you be on your way back to the castle proper and stay out of this place, boy. Go, get on." He tried to smile again. "I have no doubt Nywulf's errand is far more important than gossiping with this lonely old soul." As I walked away he stood staring after me and I could feel his gaze as an itch at the nape of my neck. It was odd that he had referred to Rufra as "your friend" rather than calling him "my nephew", which was the fiction he wished to sell to the castle. A little shiver ran down my spine and I rubbed at my wrist. Something about the priest, possibly his naked ambition, set me on edge.

After my detour I visited the kitchens then returned to the corridor with a view of Heamus's room. I settled into a shadowed alcove to wait in a state of half sleep until Heamus left his room. It was a long wait.

When the water clock struck eight I was itching for Heamus to leave, but he did not. At half past eight I was cursing him under my breath, and by nine, when he finally left, I had become sure my master had known he was leaving later than she said and had lied to keep me from First of Festival with Rufra. I waited five minutes, counting out the my-masters faster than I should have, and then ambled over to Heamus's door. I had tied my picks inside the sleeve of my jerkin and dropped them into my hand with a twitch of my shoulders. Standing with my back to the door so I could see both ways down the corridor I worked the lock behind me. Usually this was a frustrating way to work but the lock on Heamus's door was so simple it clicked open almost immediately. With a quick glance around I let myself in.

Inside was nothing of the man. No personal mementos, no trophies of battle, no ornaments or reading material. It was like the cell of a hermit. A thin hard bed with one blanket sat against one wall and opposite stood a sturdy set of drawers which came to my knee. On top of the drawers was a washbasin, a rag and a candle. The dim light in the room came from a skylight above the door that let in reflected light from the corridor, but like most inner rooms in the keep it was a gloomy little place. I had brought a stub of candle with me – nothing surer to give you away than using the candles already in the room – and lit it. I used the light to check under the bed – nothing. Then I checked through the drawers. Clothes mostly. In the bottom drawer I found a tidily curled five-tailed whip and an oddly shaped knife. Something about the drawer bothered me, so I removed the whip and the knife. Beneath them was a badly fitted false bottom and beneath that two packages of notes. One was slim, no more than one sheet, and the other fatter and tied with ribbon. I slid out a note from the tied package. It was an old and faded love letter. The rest of the package was more letters, all in the same handwriting until I came to the final letter which had clearly been written by someone else and read simply, "I am sorry, Heamus, but Mathilda died in childbirth. The baby also."

I sat back. "Oh, poor Heamus," I said to myself, remembering the look on his face when he had told me he had loved a girl once. I could only imagine these letters were from her. Why had he lied and told me she still lived? Maybe it was easier for him that way. Like the magic roiling within me, maybe his lover's death was something he could only cope with if he hid it from himself. Making sure I put the letters back in the correct order I replaced them and opened the second package.

I dropped it immediately.

It was a single piece of vellum. Written on it were symbols. The lines and curls made no sense to me, but they writhed and moaned in my mind and left a taste in my mouth like I had been forcing down rotting meat. I tried to commit them to memory but, as with the magic, my mind slid off them. I couldn't understand why. My memory was prodigious. I had practised and practised and could commit to memory whole pages after only a glance. But these symbols defied me, and it soon became clear that if I continued to stare at them my stomach would rebel and I would end up leaving undeniable proof someone had been here. Touching the paper to pick it up felt like handling hot irons. I tidied it away as best I could and replaced the false bottom, put the whip and the knife in the drawer and left.

As I made my way to our rooms I heard the water clock strike half past nine and cursed. Rufra would not be waiting for me any longer, but it was important I tell my master what I had found. Something about those symbols would not leave me.

My master sprang up from her cot the minute I entered. "Girton?"

"Yes, Master. I have found something in Heamus's room."

"Good," she said, and pushed herself up. Where she had been lying down her black hair was mussed and sticking out at odd angles. "But before you tell me I must speak to you."

"Yes?" I wondered whether she was about to tell me off again.

"What I said earlier, about your friendships . . ." She ran a hand through her hair, as she often did when worried. "I cannot apologise for the truth in my words, Girton, but I apologise for speaking in haste and anger."

"I understand, Master." I had never heard her sound so sad and it melted away the anger in me like the sun melts snow. "I have things to tell you."

"You will be late for First of Festival."

"Not if I am quick. I have two things and then a question."

"Well, speak, Girton."

"First, I came across Neander in a disused part of the castle."

"Why was he there?"

"Ministering to his flock, he said, but I have seen how empty his book of names is and do not believe him."

"Good work, Girton. It does sound odd. Since we have been here I don't think Neander has been near his buried chapel."

"There is more. In Heamus's room I found a five-tailed whip and a strangely shaped knife."

"Did the knife have a kink a third of a way along the edge, so it curled in on itself?"

"Yes. But that is not all. I found a vellum covered in symbols that made me feel . . ."

"Ill?" she asked, and I nodded. "The Landsman's Leash." She looked like she wanted to spit. "Little wonder you found it unpleasant; it is a filthy thing. The Landsmen use the knife to carve the symbols into the flesh of magic users." I shuddered at the thought. "It stops a magician accessing their power. Other parts of it cause pain or fear, but little is known as the Landsmen guard their secrets as fiercely as we guard ours. If Heamus has a copy it may be he has not left the Landsmen at all. On the other hand, they could be souvenirs and mean nothing. He was a Landsman for a long time."

"But that is not all, Master." I told her about the letters and Heamus's love affair as a young man.

"That is interesting," she said. "If these letters were all from the same women it gives him a motive, for revenge against the king at least."

"Maybe he assists Adran in poisoning the king?"

"Possibly. Though she needs no help on that count."

"But he lost a child too." I felt guilty about throwing suspicion on a man I liked, but when I thought about the symbols and how it must feel to have them carved on your flesh a large part of my guilt vanished. "A child for a child. The death of Aydor would not be a huge leap to take for a vengeful man."

She nodded slowly and chewed on her thumbnail. "You are right, Girton, absolutely right. It seems Heamus is another we must keep a close eye on." She gathered her blanket around herself. "But our suspicions are for tomorrow, Girton." A little light entered her voice and she took a slip of vellum from inside her black jerkin and gave it to me. It was a signed letter from the queen allowing me to go through the keepyard gate that night. "Go and meet your friend. Leave what you are here for tonight. Go to First of Festival without burden. Be nothing but a boy. Do nothing but enjoy yourself."

Chapter 14

A long snaking queue of well dressed men, women and children destroyed any chance I may have had of meeting Rufra. When I got near the front I interrupted an argument the guard on the keepyard gate was having with a well dressed woman and showed him my letter from the queen. He looked it over and then looked me over and, grudgingly, let me through before returning to his argument. Traditionally, First of Festival is a holiday and everyone in the castles and towns Festival visits, guards included, but not tonight. Adran had decreed the castle guards would be on duty to protect the heir, and as I walked away it sounded like the guard was enjoying ruining First of Festival for others as it had been ruined for him.

Festival was arranged as concentric circles of tents and caravans with a wooden wall enclosing the centre and gateways into the greater Festival at each compass point. That afternoon the first livestock had come in, and in the outer circles the smell of animal droppings mingled with woodsmoke. I had seen Festival before but only from afar; this was the first time I had ever visited it and I don't think I had ever been anywhere as busy or unfamiliar.

Outside the gate there was no sign of Rufra, but the night was thick with the smell of woodsmoke and the sound of music and excited people. Inside Festival's wooden walls, huge fires had been lit to keep the chill at bay, and the tents and caravans threw capering shadows. I searched around the Festival gate for any sign of Rufra in case he had waited inside, but it was half past the hour of ten, and I had not really expected him to have waited so long for me, so I headed into Festival alone hoping to run into him. It was strange to move through the night without my master and without having to worry about being seen. Clouds had come in to block the stars and moon and where the light of the fires did not reach, the darkness was absolute. I understood why Festival worried Queen Adran now. It was a perfect place for an assassin, and I imagine the queen had made sure Aydor was locked up tight in his room. People loomed out of the night: a thankful wrapped in sacking, a Festival guard in black and red, groups of blessed from the castle in their ragged finery.

Meat was being roasted, and soups full of spices bubbled away in huge cauldrons, the scents mixing with the fragrant smoke of fires sprinkled with herbs that made them burn with strangely coloured flames, blue, green and red. A huge bonfire in the centre of Festival attempted to scorch the sky. It had been fenced off to stop drunk people falling into it and was surrounded by a ring of stalls and entertainments. The Festival Lords' huge caravans loomed over the people; black and red flags hung limp in the still air, the palisade walls had been painted with the symbols of Adallada, queen of the dead gods, on one side of the huge gate, and of Dallad, her consort and the god of balance, on the other. Outside the high king's palace these symbols were seldom seen and were a silent reminder of the Festival Lords' power. Hedgings, some horned, some made of twists of branch and grass, danced around the feet of the gods, in supplication to the masters they had served before the wars of balance.

I continued to search for Rufra, but in the heaving mass of people I had little chance of finding him. Stilt walkers moved through the crowd handing out drinks, and fire breathers shot huge plumes of flame into the air. Hucksters shouted their wares; cymbal bands played loudly to scare away hedgings; singers wailed along with them, and together with the roar of the bonfire it was almost impossible to hear anything. Whichever part of me faced the huge fire was always too hot, while whichever side faced away was too cold. All together Festival was as exciting as it was uncomfortable.

I bought a stick of spiced meat from a Meredari trader with bone-white skin, and a cup of alcohol to replace the one I had just finished then wandered aimlessly among the stalls looking at things I had no money for: bright materials, small statues of the Festival Lords in traditional dress, dolls made from corn stalks and so many different types of food it made my head spin.

Another drink.

Was this what it was like to be normal? To not have a care?

My face sweated and the world became a whirl of colours.

I would never be normal.

The dark mouths of alleys between tents and caravans gaped, and in each one I saw an opportunity. I saw thieves working the crowds and lifting purses. When one tried to ply her trade on me I could not resist using the Shy Maid, a double sidestep, to send her sprawling in the mud. The longer I stayed and the more I drank the more being surrounded by so many people made me feel like I was being followed, even if I thought it for no other reason than I knew how easy it would be. I started to become sure that every person who passed stared at me. I no longer saw bodies and people, I only saw eyes because that was where any threat began. If I was to be attacked I would see it there just as I had seen that thief mark me as an easy target in a glance she gave as I passed a stall filled with teetering piles of clay pots and plates.

A stilt walker, so dark-complexioned he seemed made of night, handed me another drink and I knocked it back. I considered heading for the stables but knew it was more likely Drusl would be here. Among the people.

All the people.

The need to get out came upon me in a rushing wave of fear and nausea. Maybe it would have been different if Rufra or Drusl had been there to distract me. Maybe it was the effect of the alcohol, which was sickly sweet and easy to drink. I was not used to alcohol and it fuddled all my senses, making me feel more vulnerable than I ever had before. Whatever it was, the urge to escape became overwhelming. I turned my back on Festival, on the food and the entertainments and, in a stumbling run, made my back towards the keepyard gate.

My sense of direction, which was usually so good, now betrayed me, and I cursed every drink I had taken. My night vision had been ruined by the fires, and once in the dark I saw only amorphous blobs of colour which spun slowly and added to my nausea. I knew I was heading away from the centre of Festival, because the noise was slowly dying away behind me to be replaced by the grunting of pigs, but I couldn't tell in which direction I went. I left through a different gate to the one I had entered through and ended up on the far side of Festival in an alley between caravans and the townyard wall. The stink there was as loud as the noise of the hogs and I rubbed my eyes, trying to rid them of the after-images of the fires. I turned from the pigs; figures crowded the other end of the alley. Five, maybe six people, but it was hard to tell in the dark smoky air and with my mind fogged by alcohol. I heard laughter and muttering and felt sure they wanted nothing good. I fell into the position of readiness. In hand-to-hand combat I should be able to escape five brigands easily enough. Surprise would be my ally; they would not expect a boy to be so well trained in martial skills.

Wisps of alcoholic fog blew from my mind. What if these

were not brigands? Rufra had warned me that events in the squireyard had consequences outside it. If these were squires coming to administer a punishment beating then fighting back was not an option if I wanted to keep up the fiction of Girton ap Gwynr.

Why had I been such a fool? Rufra had warned me not to walk about alone.

Or had Rufra lured me here? It had been his idea for me to come to First of Festival. What if he had never been by the keepyard gate? Never been my friend at all?

And if they were brigands and I did not defend myself? My life could end here with a quick blade between my ribs and my body pitched in with the pigs. There would be nothing left of me in the morning.

"Lost, boy?"

The voice was almost recognisable behind the muffling effect of a cloth mask. Did I know it?

"Who asks?" I said into the darkness, and words were said in return. What words? I could not hear them properly. It could have been "It's him," or it could have been "Get him."

Breathe . . .

No time.

Brigands or squires?

Death or the shame of giving myself away?

With a roar I ran at the figures, my arms windmilling just as a boy with no idea how to defend himself would do. I heard laughter and as I approached the nearest figure side-stepped, leaving a foot in my way and sending me sprawling onto the filthy ground. Then the kicking began. I curled myself into a ball and did my best to roll with each kick to minimise the damage done. The beating seemed to go on for a long time but there were too many of them and they got in each other's way, that and my rolling protected me from the worst of it. Once they had tired themselves they stood back and I heard the scratch of a flint. A torch flared into life.

Six men. Two hung back – they could have been squires as they were a little smaller in build, but it was hard to tell as they were behind the light of the torch. The other four were definitely not squires – too big. My bet would have been on guards but they could also be hired ruffians. Plenty in the Tired Lands would happily take coin to hurt another.

"Show me his face." Rough hands on my body, pulling me to my knees, and then my hair pulled so my face was in the torchlight. "This definitely him?"

"Yes." Whoever spoke did so quietly, too quietly for me to decide if I knew them.

"Girton ap Gwynr, I have a message for you, country boy –" I knew the voice, I was sure of it "– a message about knowing your place among your betters. Ain'tn't you in the right place now, eh? In the pig shit!" A round of laughter. "You understand, cripple?" I tried to nod but was held too tightly to move. "In future you shoot your bow like a fool from the country and learn to respect your betters." The hand holding my hair let go. "Wait," said the speaker. I could not see his face for the torch but the voice, I knew the voice. "I have my own score to settle with this boy." A knife glinted in the torchlight, an invisible hand gripped my stomach. Dollis. That was the voice. It was Dollis, the man who had locked me in with the dogs. I tried to kick out but I was too well held. "I can think of a way to ensure that he never outshoots anyone again, and to settle a score of me own." He laughed and then growled out, "Hold him still." I struggled but it was in vain. The men who held me were strong. "Told you in that drinking hole, didn't I, boy? Always fancied scarring a blessed. So, you favour your left eye or your right eye?"

"No," said one of the figures in the background. "That was not what you were told to do." I was sure it was one of the blond twins, Boros or Barin, who spoke.

"Quiet or I'll do you too!" roared Dollis "The cripple insulted me – this is between me and him." He pulled down his cloth mask so I could see the grin on his face and the gleam in his eye. "I might even go down as low as ten bits for your information after this, boy, if you survive. He cackled, and the point of the blade grew huge and silver in my vision.

I threw up, hot vomit spewing from my mouth. Dollis laughed.

"Scared of a bit of pain?" He grabbed my hair, bending my head back and starting to bring the point of his knife down. "Not feeling so blessed now, are you?"

His fun was interrupted by a single, quietly spoken, word. "Enough."

Dollis turned. His grip on my hair loosened so I could turn my head to see a stocky figure standing between the two shadows who I thought were the twins.

"This is castle business," said Dollis. "Who are you to tell me enough?"

"You know who I am. The boy's learned his lesson; now leave him be and we'll agree never to speak of this or each other again." I knew the voice of the speaker but alcohol and panic had left me confused.

"Nywulf," said Dollis. "Ain't no need for you to interfere here." He walked away from me and towards Nywulf. As he came within arm's reach of the squiremaster he began to speak again, "You should walk away unless you want me to t—"

Nywulf's arm shot out, and Dollis's sentence ended in a scream. He fell to his knees in the filth, clutching his face and sobbing in agony.

"Anyone else?" shouted Nywulf. "Anyone else want to argue with me?" No one answered. "Then go." The remaining five men and boys streamed past Nywulf while Dollis remained kneeling in the mud moaning with his hands clasped to his face. Nywulf stalked over to me. "Did they hurt you, boy?" he said surprisingly gently.

"No worse than after sword practice."

He pulled me up and helped me walk to the end of the alley between the caravans. Lying in the mud in front of Dollis was his eye. Nywulf had plucked it out. "One moment, Girton," he said and walked back to Dollis. He placed one hand on the man's chin and one on the back of his neck. "Are you ready, Captain?" he asked. Before Dollis had time to reply Nywulf broke the man's neck with a vicious twist of his upper body. Then he picked up Dollis's limp corpse and threw it over a fence. The excited squealing of hungry pigs filled the air and I realised, with dismay, I would never find out who had ordered me locked in with the dogs. "No remembrance parade for him," said Nywulf. "No great loss either. Come on, boy."

"Thank you, Nywulf," I said, staring at the heaving mass of animals. "How did you . . ."

"I saw you at Festival and then I saw Dollis signal to his friends and follow you. He's up to no good, I thought."

"I think the other squires—"

"Will be sorted out if they had anything to do with this. But that is for me to do, so no reason to mention what happened tonight to anyone else, you understand?"

I nodded. Nywulf saw me up to the castle, and I did my best to sneak into our room without waking my master. I may as well have been trying to grow corn in the sourlands.

"Girton?" she said, and sat straight up. "What happened to you? You stink and are covered in filth. Are you all right? Let me see to you."

"I am fine, Master. I was set upon is all – some of the other squires trying to settle a score – but I am only bruised, nothing more."

"I have salves." She reached for the bag she had hidden under my bed. "You saw who did this?"

"No, they were masked."

"And you let them beat you? They could have been brigands, Girton."

"I did not want to risk giving myself away." I peeled off my shirt with a grunt. "And I had been drinking. I wasn't sure—"

"Child," she said softly, "what a world this is I have forced you into. I am glad you suffer no worse than bruises. This is not the first beating you have taken, eh?" She rubbed salve into the bruises on my arms.

"No, but you were always there before, Master. This time . . ." The image of the knife descending sent a shiver through me. I may as well have written a letter to my master saying I had not told her everything.

"What else happened, Girton? Was this Rufra boy part of this?"

"No, I do not think so. From what was said it was Tomas. He hired the captain of Aydor's dayguard, Dollis, who beat me."

"The same who was involved in locking you in the kennels?" I nodded. "You defended yourself though? Escaped?"

"No, Nywulf, the squiremaster, turned up. He saved me. Dollis feeds the pigs now." My master helped me remove my boots and then rubbed salve into my clubbed foot. My clothes were caked in mud and pig shit. I had got it on the bed but could not bring myself to care.

"You should stay away from alcohol, Girton. You are not used to it and it is not good for —" a gap in her words "— people like us." I stared at her as her hands worked over my twisted foot and it all seemed too much — the beatings, the magic, the fear and the lies.

"He wanted to take my eye." The words leaked out of my mouth as if they were ashamed of being heard.

"Your eye?" Her hands paused in their movement.

"He was going to blind me, Master." A dam broke. Tears came in great shudders and my master put her arms around me, not caring that I was filthy with pigshit, holding me the way she had done when I was a child woken by yapping nightmares. "What use is a blinded assassin, Master? Who would want me then?"

"I would, Girton," she said and she kept repeating it, "I would."

Interlude

This is a dream of what was.

He is ten. He knows what his master does but he has never seen her kill. He is not sure he wants to, but there is foreknowing in the dark clouds of the horizon, in the brown crisp leaves whipped up by the wind biting through his woollen clothes, in the whispering bare tops of the stunted trees.

Today he will witness death.

"Master, are they people or hedgescares?" he says as he trots along behind Xus. His master raises her hand to cover her eyes and stares into the distance. The long golden grasses with heavy seed heads hiss in the wind.

"People," she says. "Come." She puts down a hand and lifts him up onto Xus's saddle. "Shade your eyes, Girton. Tell me what you see."

He does as he is told. It is hard to tell the difference between rag-wrapped people and the rag-wrapped statues believed to scare away the hedge spirits of field, forest, pool and souring.

"Mounts, Master. Three mounts and a blood gibbet."

"Yes," she says. Her words are no more than breath on the wind. "Down, Xus," she says, and the mount hunkers down into the grasses. She does not want to be seen by the people. He does not need to ask why so he stays quiet and counts as he has been taught. "One my master. Two my master." He loses count at two hundred and twelve and, eventually, the people leave and Xus rises.

They make their way to the blood gibbet. It has been erected on the line where the grasses abruptly stop and the yellow land of the souring begins. Below the gibbet is a black mark where blood has been spilled on the ground. Green shoots are pushing their tips through it.

In the gibbet is an old woman and she terrifies him. She is a sorcerer and people like her caused the sourings. Maybe she will curse him or suck his blood to replace what she has lost.

She doesn't look evil, not when he looks closely. She looks old and pained. With a squeak the breeze spins the windvane which lifts the brake on the slow-weight with a click that makes him jump. The old woman grunts as dirty blades are spun to reopen half-healed wounds on her arm and let out a slow trickle of blood.

"Barbaric," he hears his master hiss.

"But the magic has to be reclaimed by the land," he says. He heard a Landsman, looking fine in bright green armour, say as much in a village a year ago.

"Maybe, but there's no reason it should be strung out so. Blood is blood, life is life."

"But why do they do it this way then, Master?"

"Girton, when I buy you a bag of crispy pigskin, do you eat it all at once or do you save it and make it last?"

"Make it last." He doesn't understand what crispy pigskin has to do with anything. He would like some crispy pigskin though, it is his favourite.

"Does that change the taste?"

"No, but it lasts longer. I want to savour it."

"Well, that is why those green Riders do this." She points at the old woman across the road from them and then slides down from Xus. "Keep watch, Girton," she says. Then he is climbing into Xus' saddle and she is climbing the blood gibbet.

"Don't hurt me." The woman's voice is little more than a croak as his master hangs by her on the metal frame. When his master puts her hand through the cage the old woman flinches.

"I won't hurt you." She caresses the old woman's cheek.

"I'm not a sorcerer," says the old woman.

"There's no need to lie, wise mother," says his master in the Whisper All Should Hear. He does not know why his master uses it, but the old woman's eyes become wide.

"Free me, daughter," she says.

"I will, but I cannot let you out. You understand wise mother?"

The old woman stares at his master and a tear tracks down her face, flowing along the banks of her many wrinkles. Then she nods her head slightly. "You are right, daughter. Where could I run to? I am old and will only endanger those I love."

"I am sorry, wise mother."

"Thank you for your kindness, daughter," says the old woman, and then her eyes become wide as his master applies the Touch of Sleep. Once the woman's eyes close his master climbs further down the blood gibbet, stopping to slash the woman's wrists so her blood spatters into the dirt.

He has been so transfixed by the horror of what is happening that he has quite forgotten to keep watch.

"What are you doing?" A man's voice. When he turns he freezes. A Landsman, huge on his hissing warmount and surrounded by the stink of rancid fat and rust coming off his grass-green armour.

A mount is far more dangerous than a man, Girton. Never face one if you don't have to.

Beneath him he feels Xus, desperate to act, to rear, to bite and scratch and fight, waiting for the command he is too frozen with fear to give.

"A kindness, Blessed," says his master, but she does not sound like herself. She sounds meek and scared.

"It's not a kindness to interfere with a blood gibbet, woman. It is treason. What are you, a sorcerer yourself?"

"No, Blessed. Only I knew the old lady from my village and she was kind. I—"

"No excuse," he barks as his mount saunters past Xus and the two animals bare their tusks at each other.

"Please, Blessed, please do not hurt us or me boy. My mount, you can have him." His master sounds panicked, and it freezes him to the saddle of Xus. He has never thought his master could be scared of anything. "Please don't hurt me. Please."

But the Landsman keeps on coming.

"I'll have the mount anyway."

"Blessed, I am not unattractive." She starts to unbutton the top of her jerkin but she does not take her eyes from the ground.

"I'll not touch a sorcerer —" he draws a club "— but you'll live long enough to water the land in the old woman's place."

When the Landsman nears her it looks like his master falls, as if she faints with terror, but the fall turns into a roll and she comes to her feet below the Landsman's mount with her twinned stabswords in her hands. She cuts the girth of the Landsman's saddle and disembowels his beast in one slash. The creature falls, letting out a jumble of wet and red intestines and the most hideous scream he has ever heard. The Landsman falls with the beast, but he has been trained well and jumps from his dying mount, clearing the creature, which rolls onto its back kicking its spurred feet in the air and screaming until the Landsman silences it with a slash of his longsword.

"You'll pay for that, woman," he growls. "I loved that animal." He comes forward with his longsword held loosely in one hand and his stabsword in the other. His master stands drenched in blood and with a stabsword in each hand. Her hair is black ropes, sluggish in the lazy wind. Mount blood moulds her kilt to her body and drips down from its hem to define the muscles of her calves in gore. She is black and red and so still she could be a hedgescare statue standing against the hissing wheat. The Landsman towers over her, his breath comes in gasps like the snorts of an angry mount. He brings his longsword round in an arcing horizontal sweep sure to cut his master in half. The boy is so scared he cannot even scream a warning.

She moves.

She dances.

What is she doing?

He wants to scream at her, "Defend yourself! Don't die!" but instead he is silent as she goes through the iterations. He wants to shout, "The iterations are not for fighting!" They are dances for entertaining drunks outside village drink holes and gathering a few pennies. They are not for facing huge armoured men!

She laughs as she teaches him. "Oh, Girton, won't you impress the fine ladies!"

If he could move he would cover his face.

The Landsman is dangerous, intent on death. Fury is in his eye and he grunts with effort. His blades move smooth as water. They trail streamers of light. His master goes into the fifth iteration, the Boatgirl's Dip, something he knows so well – *She holds his hand and twirls him under her arm* – she takes his part. The Landsman lifts his longsword and his master goes under the Landsman's arm. She spins around him, deflecting a thrust from his stabsword as she twirls, and then she is standing behind him at the iteration's end point. She is still, legs slightly apart, hands at her side, and she is holding only one blade. The Landsman, that huge creature of green and metal, slowly falls forward, as much a corpse as any felled tree. His master's left stabsword hilt protrudes from the unarmoured place beneath the Landsman's arm. She takes the blade out of the man.

Schluup-skish.

Then his master is running. She vaults up into Xus's saddle

behind him. She stinks of blood as she shouts, "Ha! Xus, Ha!" And the mount runs, it runs like he has never known the animal could. It runs so fast it seems impossible he can breathe and the tears running from his eyes flow horizontally into his hair and the world becomes lines of colour and streaks of speed and, eventually? A blur.

The world becomes a blur.

This is a dream of what was.

Chapter 15

I ached the next morning.

I ached in body from my beating and in my head from the drink.

My master had laid out clean clothes, and between the jerkin and the trousers was a note in scratch.

Find climbing rope. Stout nails. A grappling hook if possible. Tell no one.

Take care.

M

The room stank of pig shit.

Once I was dressed I put on my harlequin armour. In my spare moments I had been scouring it with sand and fat and although it didn't, and would never, shine it was at least useable and would not shame me.

By the time I arrived at the squireyard I was aware of every kick that had been gifted to me the night before.

Rufra's eyes widened when he saw my bruises as we lined up to choose wooden practice swords. I glanced around the yard, busily plotting how I could accidentally manage to give Tomas or one of the twins a bruise or two in return for mine without giving myself away.

"Girton," whispered Rufra, "your bruises, are they my fault?"

"How could they be your fault?"

"I was not there to meet you. I was called up to the castle by Neander."

"Neander?"

"Well, his letter called me away, but Borniya and Hallin were waiting for me."

"They hurt you?"

"Hallin threatened me with his knife but they didn't manage to catch me." A shudder ran through him. "He scares me, you know."

"Borniya or Hallin?"

"Hallin. Borniya I could beat in a fair fight, but Hallin . . ." He was rubbing his leg where Hallin had scarred him. "He's as sneaky as a hedging, the sort likely to stab you in the back."

"But you would beat him in a fair fight too, Rufra."

"Hallin can be fast, if he wants to be. He has some of the quickest reactions in the squireyard."

"You are quicker. Don't let him get in your head."

He looked down to where he was rubbing his scarred leg and jerked his hand away.

"Nywulf says that's where a fight is won or lost — in your head." He transferred his concentration to the wooden swords, picking one up, studying it until he noticed a crack and letting it drop back in the rack. When he spoke he did not look at me. "Sometimes, when I close my eyes, I see Hallin's knife opening my skin." A shudder ran through me at the thought of knives. "I sent a message with a guard —" he looked up from the rack "— telling you not to come as I had been called away."

"It never arrived," I said, and he looked dismayed. "I was delayed and thought I had missed you but I should have heeded your warning about not going alone at night. They jumped me in an alleyway."

"Who?"

"Thugs, thieves probably."

He shoved the next wooden sword back into the rack with more force than was needed.

"They hurt you, and it is my fault."

"No, and besides it is only bruises." Again a shudder ran through me, and this time Rufra noticed.

"Girton?"

"I am fine."

"No, you are not. And that you think it was thieves only shows how little you know of this castle." He leaned in close, his face a mask. "What did they do?"

"One of them, he threatened to take my eye."

Rufra cursed to the dead gods and grabbed the next wooden sword without paying any attention to its quality.

"It is time I stopped being so meek and taught some of those here manners."

I grabbed him before he could walk away.

"No!"

The whole yard turned at my shout. Tomas smirked at Rufra and I felt the muscles of his arm tense under his jerkin. "Rufra, you are not even wearing armour, and besides, I do not think that was part of the orders given. I think one of the thugs overstepped his mark and he has paid the price for it."

"What do you mean?"

"Nywulf stopped them." I leaned in and used the Whisper-that-Flies-to-the-Ear: "He broke the neck of the man who would have blinded me and threw his body to the pigs." With a sudden mix of revulsion and fear I realised I was using magic and glanced down at my feet, expecting to see a circle of dead grass – but there was nothing.

"Well," said Rufra, "that at least is good to know, but it doesn't change my mind. Lessons need to be taught, for me and you. I shall start by tutoring Tomas."

"It will do me no favours if they think I cannot fight my own battles."

"It is not just for you, Girton, and besides, if you face one of them you'll only get more bruises. It is perfectly

acceptable for a Rider to fight on behalf of a weaker friend."
He saw the sting of his words on my face. "I did not mean
that how it sounded. Only that I have trained longer —" he
kicked a stone along the ground "— and I am sick of holding
back so I don't offend Tomas or Aydor's egos." He removed
my hand and stormed across the squireyard. Tomas stood
waiting with a half-smile on his handsome face and his
wooden sword held loosely in his hand.

I was about to go after Rufra when I was grabbed from
behind and spun round.

Borniya's bent face staring into mine. He spun me again,
holding me by looping his hands behind my elbows and
pulling me against him so I could not move. I heard Rufra
and Tomas shouting. More of Aydor's squires moved in,
shielding me from the rest of the squireyard with a wall of
rainbow armour and I could not see what happened between
Rufra and Tomas.

"Where is he?" Aydor's foul breath around me in a cloud.
His scabbed face staring out from under a white-enamelled
helm etched with blue curlicues and flying lizards.

"Where is who?"

"Dollis, captain of my dayguard. Where is he?"

In a gap between two boys I saw Rufra pointing his practice sword at Tomas, who, with a lazy smile on his face,
ignored the challenge as if Rufra was beneath him.

Something cold against my waist. Hallin stood at my side,
grinning at me. He had the tip of his small dagger pushed
through one of the gaps in my armour. He made an exaggerated sad face and applied pressure so that his blade nicked
the skin of my stomach, drawing blood.

"What do you mean, Aydor?"

"Heir!" he hissed. "You give me my title when you speak
to me, country boy, and when I ask where my man is you
tell me."

"I don't know what you're talking about."

I saw Rufra take a step towards Tomas.

Borniya pulled my arms tighter, pushing my stomach against Hallin's blade. Aydor glared at me, and I wondered if behind his blue eyes his mind was frantically trying to work out how much he could say without betraying me. Or maybe he was considering betraying me and whether it was worth his mother's wrath. That he called me "country boy" made me hopeful he wasn't about to denounce me as an assassin.

"I did not arrange any beating, cripple," he hissed, "but my man lets me know what extra work he takes on, and I asked him to give you a reminder of me. Just a kiss, mind." So, all this hate was simply because I had made fun of him when I had been in the dungeon. What a poor king he would make. Aydor leaned in very close and it was all I could do not to recoil from his breath. He spoke so quietly I had to strain to hear, though his lips were practically touching my ear. "I warned him you were more dangerous than you seemed. That's two I owe you, assassin, Dollis and Kyril. It was you, wasn't it?"

I moved my head so I could whisper into his ear. "You will never know," I said. Then I let my lips brush against his ear and he jumped back like a scalded lizard, knocking Hallin away. If we had not been interrupted at that moment I am sure Aydor would have attacked me with a naked blade. Instead Nywulf distracted us, his voice loud enough to make my ears ring.

"Do as I say, boy!"

Borniya let go of me and the squires around me scattered, all sure Nywulf had been speaking to them.

But he was not.

Rufra lay on the ground in front of the squiremaster, his wooden swords in Nywulf's hands and the trainer's ball of a head was red with fury. Behind him Tomas watched, a wide grin on his face. 'All of you," Nywulf shouted, "stop standing around like thankful at a giving. Form line. Do it now! You too!" He pointed at Rufra. "Now!" His voice filled the squireyard, and we reacted like animals to his anger, scurrying into our lines. Rufra stood next to me and stared at the ground, his anger showing in every taut muscle of his body.

"Rufra," I hissed, but he would not look at me. His chest rose and fell as he took deep breaths. A tear fell from the end of his nose.

"Last night," said Nywulf, his voice had returned to a conversational level, "Girton ap Gwynr was attacked when leaving First of Festival." He paced up and down the line of squires, pausing at the blond twins, Barin and Boros, whose faces were shiny with sweat though they had done nothing to earn it. "I would like to remind you, all of you, that Festival can be dangerous and brigands always follow it." He took another step so he was in front of Tomas. He had to look up at the boy. "I do not want any more of my squires getting hurt," he growled. Tomas met Nywulf's stare as if the boy was equal with the warrior. "Do you understand me?" he said to Tomas and then added, louder, "All of you?"

"Yes, Squiremaster," we mumbled. Tomas did not speak.

"Louder," he said. He did not break eye contact with Tomas.

"Yes, Squiremaster," we shouted.

Still Tomas did not speak. Nywulf gave him a grim smile.

"Good," he said. He walked away and then turned back to us when he was ten paces away from the line. "Today we will spar. However –" he gave us the cold smile of a venomous lizard about to strike "– it has come to my attention that some of us believe they deserve better than the squireyard. Is that true, Tomas?"

Tomas looked up into the sky but did not answer. As we waited for Tomas to reply, the silence in the squireyard felt like a weight on my shoulders.

"I asked, Tomas," continued Nywulf, and he sounded friendly though I cannot imagine anyone was fooled, "if you believe yourself past my training? If you think you are more skilled than anyone else?" Tomas continued to stare at the sky where the pale disc of the moon was still visible. "Or, Tomas ap Dhyrrin, are you afraid to answer my question?"

"I am better than any other here." The words escaped from his mouth like angry dogs breaking their leash. A ripple of offence went up and down the line of squires.

"Better," said Nywulf with a smile and shake of his head. "It is my job, blessed boys, to train you. And an important lesson for any warrior to learn is that there is always someone better than you are. That is why you need men you trust around you."

"No one here can best me with a blade," said Tomas quietly. Nywulf stared at him.

"Care to prove that, Tomas?" he said. "Care to prove you are better than everyone here, even me?"

"Real blades," said Tomas, a smile growing on his handsome face at the shocked reaction his words drew from the squires. "And after I beat you, Squiremaster, if you survive, then you will stand down and we will find another squiremaster." He glanced at Rufra when he spoke. "A real one."

"Very well," said Nywulf. "And if I win?" He met the eye of every boy there, looking from one end of the line of squires to the other, pausing at Aydor before he let his gaze run back. "If I win, no more cliques and no one is punished outside the yard for what happens within it. And you will all give me your oaths on that, do you understand?"

"Yes, Squiremaster," we said.

"Again," shouted the trainer.

"Yes, Squiremaster!" we shouted, though I noticed Aydor did not join in.

Tomas went to the gear he left by the gate and drew his longsword and stabsword then made his way to the sparring circle. Nywulf followed him but he wore no armour and still carried only the wooden practice swords he had taken from Rufra. We followed him and stood around the edges of the circle. My blood fizzed with a mixture of excitement and worry and I felt like I needed to run or piss.

"I will enjoy this," whispered Rufra to me. There was a bruise on his cheek.

"Did Nywulf hit you?"

"Only once. Tomas is about to suffer much worse."

Tomas and Nywulf stood opposite one another in the circle, a ring drawn in white on the sparsely grassed ground.

"I said real blades," said Tomas.

"And you have them," replied Nywulf.

"Very well," said Tomas with a grin. He did not fall into the familiar "At Ready" position which traditionally started a fight; he attacked without warning by bringing his long-sword over followed by his stabsword in a movement called the Wheel, a showy move of little value in a real fight. Nywulf simply moved out of the way, and as the weight of Tomas's swords carried him past, the squiremaster swatted him on the backside with his stabsword. Tomas spun on the spot, his eyes bright with anger, and brought his blades up into a defensive cross, but Nywulf did not attack; instead he walked around Tomas.

"Come at me then, boy," he said.

Tomas did, three thrusting attacks with the stabsword he held in his left hand followed by a slash of his longsword at head height then one at hip height. Nywulf simply backed away, occasionally swaying left and right to avoid the blades. There was no hurry in the squiremaster's movements; they were all very deliberate. He knew exactly how far Tomas's swords would reach and where he needed to be to avoid them. When Tomas paused, Nywulf stepped forward and delivered a blow to Tomas's leg that landed with an audible smacking sound and made the squire fall to one knee.

Tomas got back up. Anger in his eyes

Most of the squires cheered for Tomas. I thought them fools. It should have been clear to anyone with the slightest knowledge of swordplay that Nywulf was a master. Rather than cheering on Tomas they should be watching Nywulf work and learning from him.

Tomas lunged again. This time he tried to dummy Nywulf into coming in close. It seemed to work. When the squire-master was within range, Tomas thrust forward with his stabsword, a rage-filled grimace of triumph on his face. But Nywulf simply dropped his stabsword and used stiffened fingers to hit Tomas's wrist, making the boy's hand convulse and the short blade fall to the ground. Then, as Tomas was bringing his longsword back to strike, Nywulf hit him in the chest with the palm of his hand, sending the squire sprawling into the dirt with a crash of armour.

If I give the impression Tomas was without skill, then that is only a mark of how good Nywulf was: he made Tomas look like a child with his first blade

"Get up," said Nywulf. He kicked the stabsword across to Tomas but did not bother picking up his own wooden blade. "We are not finished yet."

I do not know how long they fought for. It seemed like hours though it was probably only minutes, and by the end there was not a handspan of armour on Tomas without a dent or bit of missing enamel, or a place on his flesh that did not show a bruise. Tomas could barely walk back to his place in the line when Nywulf finally let him go. Once he was there, Nywulf brought forward the twins and gave them the option of real blades, which they turned down, and then made them fight him. He did not punish them the way he had Tomas. He told them both to fight him at once and then casually knocked them on their behinds.

Celot stepped forward with an aimless smile on his face but Nywulf shook his head.

"Not you, Celot," he said gently, leaving the boy looking disappointed. "We are done for today." Despite his exertions Nywulf was not even breathing heavily. "The petty squabbles of this place —" he hit the ground with his wooden blade bringing up little puffs of dust "— are nothing, you understand? You do not need to like each other. I do not ask that. But you must know each other's strengths and be able to trust one another in battle." He paced up and down the line. "That is how a Rider works. We are heavy cavalry. We charge together. You are all the cavalry this castle has at the moment, and if any organised force attacked and you were called on to defend us they would cut you apart. Ask yourselves if boyish pride is worth death at the hands of the living and the thankful you deride. If it is, then carry on as you are, but know this: if there is another beating then whoever —" he stopped at Aydor, and glanced either side of him at Borniya and Hallin "— whoever arranges it will duel me and then I will use real blades." He walked away and sat on a bench by the wall, removing his gloves and throwing them at the ground. "Now go," he said without looking at us. "Go before you make me sick."

Chapter 16

I waited outside the squireyard for Rufra, but when he appeared he was with Nywulf. My greeting died in my mouth.

"Rufra has his studies to attend to, Girton," said Nywulf. "You will have to find another playmate for today." Nywulf placed his hand on the back of Rufra's neck and walked him away from me, not letting him look back. There was clearly more going on there than the relationship between master and student. Could Rufra be involved in the plot to kill Aydor? He hated him but did not strike me as the type to skulk about, neither did Nywulf.

This suspicion of my friend felt wrong, like a betrayal, and I put it aside. My master's note was in my pocket so I decided to attend to her list of items sooner rather than later. Rope should be easy to find at Festival but the drovers were bringing herds of goats into the circles, and their hooves filled the air with choking dust and cloying stink. There must have been every goat for twenty miles around streaming through the townyard gate and into Festival. I found they made a surprisingly effective wall.

"You won't get in to Festival today, boy. Better come back at night." I turned to find a drover swathed in rags with only her eyes showing. "Be worse tomorrow when the cows come in. The guards'll be jumpy too, lot of money in a cow. Someone always tries to steal a few."

I nodded, watching the animals. "I didn't know there were this many beasts in the Tired Lands."

The drover nodded as she chewed on a stick of miyl.

"Goats, sheep, pigs – plenty of 'em as they'll eat anything. Cows, less of 'em so they cost more money. Still, you boys will be looking forward to a jaunt tomorrow, I imagine."

"Sorry?"

"You're a squire ain'tn't you?" She spat.

"Yes."

"Well tomorrow's cow day. Usually the Riders'd be out protecting the cows, but as there's few Riders here, I reckon you boys'll be out."

"Yes," I said, "of course. I should check over my mount then."

"Be wise." The drover nodded then spotted something among her herds and walked away shouting, "Vinor! Vinor! Yon goats are running all away!"

I made my way to the stables, my stomach fizzing at the thought of meeting Drusl. If I was to ride Xus tomorrow he would need to be exercised, after being cooped up he was always skittish and slow to obey the rein. In the stables the comfortable warm smell of mounts filled my nostrils and I found Drusl cleaning out the stalls, throwing the muck and hay into a barrow to be taken to the presses or the orchards.

"Girton!" Her smile was as warm as the air in the building. "I am so glad you are here." She ran over to me and took my hand. "Leiss has gone to fetch another barrow. Come with me," she whispered, pulling me into Xus's stall. The huge animal whuffled gently when he sensed me and I scratched his velvety nose. He snorted loudly and lowered his head so I could scratch between his antlers.

"You care a lot for him, don't you?" It was part statement, part question.

"Yes, that is one reason why I came, Tomorrow we—"

"Ride out. I know." Xus moved and forced her against me. She looked up into my eyes, smiling. "Xus will be exercised, do not worry, but I need to talk to you about something else."

"What?" My voice sounded heavy and I was overly aware of my body and the warmth of Drusl against me. She stood on her tiptoes so she could whisper to me.

"I need you to get a message to Rufra."

I stepped back and the stables suddenly seemed a chill place full of unwelcome stink.

"Rufra?"

"Yes, it's about Leiss."

"Leiss?"

"Aye." She moved to the entrance to the stall and looked out into the stables.

"Leiss considers this a job not a calling. He does not love the animals the way I do and he is not as slow with a whip as I think a mountmaster should be." I started checking over Xus, running my hands down his legs and checking his flesh for whip marks. "Xus is fine, Girton," said Drusl. "Leiss is too scared of him to come in here."

"Rufra's mounts?"

"There is nothing you can see." She stood closer to me again and held up a rounded wooden implement. "This is a paddle. It's meant to hold the mounts' feet when we put the razor spurs on, but if you hit a mount right with it then it won't leave a mark on the skin the way a whip will. It still hurts them though, and Leiss often beats the animals." She stared into my eyes. Seeing the condemnation of the man she worked with there she put a hand on my arm. "Leiss isn't a bad person, Girton; he's cruel sometimes because he's scared of the mounts. If I told the other squires what he did they would kill him."

"You don't think Rufra will?"

"He's your friend, Girton. I thought if you could persuade him to scare Leiss a little then it may stop Leiss hurting the mounts. I dislike the way Leiss treats the animals, but I don't want him dead because of me." She closed her eyes as if suddenly overwhelmed by emotion. "I don't want anyone dead because of me."

"I'll do my best, Drusl, but you must do something for me."

"Yes?" She looked up into my face. The moisture in her eyes gave them an unreal shine and her voice was husky.

"I need rope."

"Rope?" She stepped back.

"Yes, a lot of it. As strong and thin as possible, but I don't want anyone to know I have it." She furrowed her brow. "And nails, if you have them?" I added.

"What for?"

"I can't say."

"Oh." She seemed disappointed. I ran my fingers through Xus's thick fur and felt a sudden need to fill the silence.

"Last night, a few squires jumped me at First of Festival."

"I thought you had new bruises but didn't want to say anything." She reached up and gently touched my cheek. "They hurt you?"

"Bruises only." *A point of sparkling metal descending toward my eye.* My fists clenched and I swallowed, coughing to clear my throat. "More my pride that was wounded. I would like to teach them a lesson."

She laughed. "Boys! There is rope in the back of the stables with the presses. And nails. Leiss takes poor care of the stores so it will not be missed." There was a crash of wood on stone as the main door was thrown open. "He is back. Go. I will distract him while you sneak in the back. And remember to tell Rufra about the paddles."

"I will."

"And Girton?"

"Yes?"

"Thank you." She pulled herself up using the collar of my armour and kissed me on the lips, her tongue darted, quicksilver-quick, into my mouth. Then she was gone. I was so surprised that although my heart leaped I did not have time to enjoy the sensation of the kiss.

"What were you doing in there?" I heard Leiss grumble at her.

"Readying Xus for exercise. Unless you would rather do it?"

"Have you cleaned them all out?"

"Yes, Leiss."

"Good. Then help me take Tomas's mounts to the pasture. You can take Gliyo – dead gods but that beast's vicious."

I waited until they had taken Tomas's mounts from the stable and then, before I slipped into the back room, quickly checked the empty stalls for anything that could be linked to Kyril's death, but found nothing. I considered checking the other stalls but decided against it. Most mounts were gentle enough but these would be war trained, like Xus, and there was no telling how they may react to a stranger.

I heard Drusl and Leiss return and slipped into the back to find a room almost as big that was dominated by the astringent smell of mount urine and the earthier smell of dung. Two huge wooden presses filled the far end, giant devices used to crush dirty bedding and dung to remove urine for use by the tanners – the compressed dry dung and hay was used for fires and fertilising gardens. One press was open at the top and a movable ramp led up to it, a barrow half full of hay and dung perched precariously at the end. The second press was screwed about halfway down and a steady dribble of brown liquid ran from the spout at the bottom into a wooden cask.

This part of the stables was new, and it could be seen in the poor quality of the stonework around the open window holes above the presses. Patches of dead grass marred the floor and for a moment I felt the paralysing hand of fear – *sourings from sorcery?* – before realising my own foolishness. Mount urine was acidic and killed grass, that was all.

An untidy stack of badly wound bundles of rope lay in a corner, and by them was a bucket full of rusting nails that looked strong enough. I found a feed bag to carry the rope and nails in and added a small hammer to my haul for good measure. Drusl and Leiss were bickering about something, and when I heard a stall door open and Xus snort I touched my lips where she had kissed me. With a smile I climbed the ramp and clambered out through a window hole, making my way down some convenient steps of hay bales on the other side.

At the keepyard gate the guards waved me and my heavy bag through. They were meant to be on high alert, but either I have a trustworthy face or they were still out of sorts about being on duty during First of Festival. The rope and nails I hid under my bed and, as it was still daylight and my master was out protecting unworthy royals, I made my way up to the battlements.

The only use for ropes and nails I could think of was for climbing. My master must have decided that listening to conversations, subtle questioning and hoping something may happen was not working quickly enough. As breaking into Heamus's room seemed to have reaped rewards, a more direct method was to be used on the others – burglary. With that in mind it was a good idea for me to inspect the lie of the land, and the walls.

The castle keep was a rough oblong – the keep a square joined by walls and towers to its gatehouse. Between the gatehouse and the keep was a killing ground; arrow loops looked down from the two round towers of the gatehouse and the two towers and angled front of the keep. Around the edges of the killing ground were stalls, and in the middle stood the water clock, an ornate mechanism powered by water brought up by a clever system of wells and pipes from the river the keep backed on to. The stairs I used brought me out above the gatehouse, from where I watched people below move backwards and forwards, some purposefully and some aimlessly. I could have sat all day learning their habits; I enjoyed watching people and seeing into their secret lives.

A well dressed woman in felt trousers sewn with silver thread wandered across the inner courtyard looking at the few stalls Queen Adran had allowed to be set up as a sop to the Festival Lords. She feigned an interest in the goods of a silversmith, who I knew was weighting his scales with clay. Occasionally the woman would look over her shoulder at the keep gate. A woman appeared there and gave her a subtle nod, and both vanished through different doors to some prearranged liaison.

A castle guard, no red splash betraying his allegiance, spoke to the silversmith, putting out his hand as he did. The silversmith shook his head until the guard pointed at the scales and then he passed over a handful of coins. From the look on both men's faces each thought he had got the better part of the deal.

Across from the smith sat a woman selling grain and flour. Twice, when she thought no one looking, she opened a flour sack and poured in sand. When someone dressed in the triangular coverings of the Festival hierarchy bought flour from her I noticed she took it from a different bag, the unadulterated one.

The guards in the courtyard would have been a disappointment to Adran if she expected them to be committed to their jobs. In fact, the more I watched the more clear it became that Rufra was right about a schism running through the castle. When backs were turned there were sneers, shakes of the head and weapons slightly drawn from scabbards in mock threat. I saw a confrontation happen in one of the rooms cut into the walls. One of the guards with a red rag around his wrist slipped into the room, which held a water butt, and was swiftly followed by two others who grabbed him and pushed his head under the water. They pulled him out, and had I been nearer I could have read lips and

discovered what threats were being made, but instead I just
watched as they repeatedly held him under the water, almost
drowning him. When the guards left, their victim's red rag
remained on the floor of the room.

The whole atmosphere of this castle was like a bowstring
held taut, pregnant with violence.

The gatehouse tower I watched from could be seen from
the window of our room. We were on the third floor, and
it was not hard to find us, right in a centre of the wall
between two of the towers. It was pointless for me to try
and guess where my master – or more likely I – would be
climbing to, but from the top of one of the huge corner
towers I would be able to check the walls and at least ensure
my nails and rope would be up to the job. The tower on my
left had an added attraction – it was the highest place for
miles around and I fancied it would feel like being one of
Xus's birds to stand on top of it.

Wind bit into me as I walked around the wall, and I was
thankful for the small shelter provided by the tower's inner
stairs. It always amazed me that at ground level the world
could be still, but at height the wind could be roaring.
Sometimes I imagined the wind as a beast flying above the
land looking for an opportunity to swoop down and cause
havoc. I leaned over the tower's battlements looking at the
surface of the inner wall, which was ill kept and full of holes,
perfect for climbing.

Further round the tower I stared out between two cren-
ellations and marvelled at how far I could see. The weak
yearsage sun brushed the land with tentative fingers and the
orchards below wore the variegated reds and browns of a
coat of leaves about to fall. At the edges of the orchards trees
were already bare, a reminder of all the land lost to the
sourings. To the south, the Festival roads ran through squares
of fields and past small houses oozing smoke, it rose in gauzy
columns until it hit the wind and was whipped away. Streaks

of flattened smoke were smudged across the landscape as the road vanished into copses of pines, which grew quickly and were our main building material – the stinging scent of pine sap infused almost all of our furniture. To the north were more fields and eventually the capital city of Ceadoc, where the high king sat and the Landsmen pretended they had an answer to the sourings in the blood of criminals, sorcerers, or those too poor or ill to feed themselves. Half a mile to the west of the castle the fields stopped abruptly in a line of yellow, marking the edge of the western souring which had been created by the final battle with the Black Sorcerer. I shivered at the sight of the sourlands where magic had sapped the land of all life, ripping open a crevasse thirty miles long and a mile wide.

"There was a forest once." A weak and almost inaudible voice spoke over the hollow whisper of the gusting wind. I turned and immediately fell to one knee.

"Sire," I said, "I did not see you there."

King Doran ap Mennix sat in a curious wooden chair, one that had wheels on it. He was wrapped in thick blankets and nothing but his head showed from within. His beard was still dark and thick, but scabrous pink patches marred the tanned skin under his hair, which had been treated with some sort of dark paint to make it appear thicker – if only from a distance. The skin around his watery eyes sagged and showed the wet red flesh beneath the yellowing mask of his face. He was far more wrinkled than was normal for a man of fifty-five and looked constantly pained, as though the effort of existing was an agony, and his rasping breath did nothing to dispel that impression. He took short, audible breaths, letting them out out in a wheezing sigh almost three times the length of the intake.

"Rise, boy," he said. "My time left is too short to waste on formalities. You were looking to the west, eh?" I nodded. "Wheel me over," he said. I stood and went to his chair, pushing it to where I had stood. "It was forest once. I hunted there with Heamus and my other friends. Dead now. Mostly . . ." His words faded away as memory overwhelmed him. "Do you know how we made it? That souring?"

"No, sire." I did of course. But it is a fool who tells a king not to speak, even if that king is dying.

"The Black Sorcerer they called him, boy. They like such names, and it was apt in its way. See the hill?" He raised a hand from within his nest of blankets. His fingers were swollen and bent, incapable of holding a blade but use enough to point out a rise in the yellow of the western sourlands. "From the crest of that hill running south all the way to the pine copses lay my forest, she was thick with boar and wild mounts. The Black Sorcerer set himself up at the forest edge; him, four hundred pikemen and thirty Riders, all marked with shields that had his signs of safety on them." His hand moved slightly northwards. "Fields and grasslands it was there, all of it. In yearsbirth it would be mottled red and blue with flowers, and in yearslife it would turn golden with ripening corn." He turned his head to me. It seemed to be a tremendous effort. "Even in that year, when the Birthstorm had not come and we were stricken with drought, the land was gold, boy. It was a golden land, not the bile-yellow it is now." Breath wheezed in and out of him. "My army stood looking up at the sorcerer from the valley. Five thousand they were. The largest army the Tired Lands had seen since the gods died. Eight kings and one hundred and fifty free knights. Two hundred Landsmen stood with us and four hundred men-at-arms, all mounted and armoured. With them were two thousand soldiers with pike, blade and shield. The rest were free men and women — the living, the thankful come of their own will and with whatever they had at hand as a weapon. And we even armed the slaves — can you imagine? We were that desperate. People left their families and travelled from all over the

Tired Lands, so strong was the horror at another sorcerer having risen."

I tried to imagine so many people in one place. They must have filled the valley, and yet it had almost not been enough. What must it have been like to know you faced the old horror again? I fought down a shudder.

"They say, boy, I led the charge." King Doran ap Mennix coughed. A racking cough that twisted him in his chair. His breath smelled of mint. "It is a lie, boy. So many lies. If I had led the charge I would be dead." Breath wheezing in and out of his lungs. "Have you ever been in a battle, boy?"

"No, sire."

"It is frightening. If you meet a man who says it is not he is a liar or a fool. It is exhilarating too, I will not lie –" his voice, which had risen, fell again "– but mostly it is frightening. The men and women waiting down there were brave beyond imagining. They should be celebrated, not me." He let out another long breath. "I realised that too late." Doran ap Mennix went quiet and I thought he had fallen asleep, but the king was only gathering strength to speak again. "I was in the forest behind the Black Sorcerer with my fifty best. The Landsmen had copied the sorcerer's filthy protections onto as many shields as they could, it was hurried work and we did not know if it would be successful in protecting us. I watched my army charge. I watched my army die. The first thousand came at him accompanied by a hundred Riders. The Black Sorcerer turned to the man by him, a Rider named Dyrun. I had known him, trained with him. I heard Dyrun say, 'Not yet.' I was near enough to see that the sorcerer was shaking. I put it down to his power but maybe he was as frightened as we all were. Then our second thousand committed and the valley was full of dust thrown up by feet and claws. It was a hot day and a beautiful day. Until he cast."

"You saw it?" I was so intrigued by his story I forgot to say "sire".

"Yes. It was not like they say. He made no grand gestures; there was no feeling of building power. He raised his hands and then threw them forward with a great shout. A battle cry, I suppose. It had no words. It was as though the world took a breath, and then . . . and then the colour of the land was gone. There was no gradual leeching away of life, no wave of death spreading around him. The grass simply died." His voice, already quiet, was barely audible, and his eyes no longer looked into the world I shared with him. "In the Landsmen's hurry to draw the sigils, mistakes were made. Not all were properly protected. Ten of the men around me died without a sound. The trees around us melted. They sucked in their leaves and stalks and branches, leaving only bare trunks pointing at a yellow sky that stretched away as far as I could see. The Black Sorcerer took all the life he had stolen and he threw it at my army. He ripped the land apart, ended five thousand lives and created a souring thirty miles long. When the land stopped shaking we were all stunned by it – the suddenness, the death. Even the sorcerer stood there with his hands still raised as if unable to believe what he'd done. My men and I were no longer hidden – the trees were gone. If any one of the Black Sorcerer's group had turned we would have been seen, but they were all mesmerised by the crevasse in the land where there had been an army only moments before. We hit them then. From behind, and they never had a chance. Didn't notice us until we were among them. I cut down the Black Sorcerer myself. He was young, terrified. Not only of the death I was bringing but of what he had done. Three years before he'd been a black-smith forced into the desolate because the Landsmen believed there was magic in his grandmother. Now here he was, the destroyer of lands, about to die at the hand of a king."

"What of his Riders?"

"Most dropped their blades and gave up, horrified by

what they had been a part of. They were idealists, you see. They thought that sorcerers were persecuted."

"The same way murderers are persecuted," I said and I tried not to shake, tried not to let him see that he could be talking about me.

The king shook his head.

"I am old now. I have become softer, mellowed maybe. Do you know what I have realised?"

"No, sire."

"They were right. In a way we created the Black Sorcerer, but my pity changes nothing. If the sorcerers were welcome among us they would still sour the land. If they did not believe joining the desolate an easier way of dying than the blood gibbets and we let them be free then one would come, one who saw the opportunity for power." He looked me in the eye. "I mourn for those afflicted with magic, boy, and I am saddened by what must be done." I saw the ghost of what the king must once have been under his worn-out flesh. Something hard and unforgiving. "But it must still be done," he whispered, sounding scourged. Then he screwed up his face and beckoned me closer. "You are one of my squires?" he said. I nodded, and he reached out bent fingers to take gentle hold of my jerkin and pull me closer "I do not recognise you. You must be new. What is your name?"

"Girton, sire."

"Girton what?"

"Girton ap Gwynr, sire."

"Girton ap Gwynr," he said to himself. "Girton ap Gwynr." A focusing of his eyes. A hardening of his mouth. "I know the ap Gwynr, Girton ap Gwynr," he said, "and they have only daughters." The wind suddenly bit far more deeply into my skin as he continued to stare at me. "So you must be my assassin," he said quietly and pulled me even closer. "Girton ap Gwynr —" he raised his head to expose his throat "— make it quick. Do that one thing for me."

I was about to tell him that I was not here for him when my name was called.

"Girton." The king let go of my jerkin, and I turned to find Rufra standing in the door that led to the spiral staircase. "I saw you from below and— sire!" He fell to one knee.

The king waved us away.

"Go, boys, go. And Girton –" he gave me a sad smile "– until later."

Chapter 17

"You are not going to be popular with the squires," said Rufra as he made his way down the tightly twisting staircase. His voice echoed oddly around me and in the flickering torchlight I had the oddest feeling we were the only people in the castle.

"That's why you tracked me down, Rufra? To tell me something I already know?"

"No, I tracked you down because you were not at the meeting we have just had."

"Meeting?"

"Yes, to make up for the guards having to work on First of Festival the queen is having a feast for them tonight. The squires are to stand guard in their place."

"And that's my fault?"

"No, but you are invited to the feast because the queen heard about the beating you got. Wasn't that what the king meant when he said he would see you later?"

"It must have been," I said, but I sensed the hand of my master at work. From the way Rufra turned and lifted a quizzical eyebrow he knew there was something off about this arrangement. "Is it true we will ride out tomorrow, Rufra?"

"Oh yes!" His eyes lit up with excitement. "We ride to protect the cows. I did it last year with a Rider named Stenna. The stink and dust are unbelievable, but it is still exciting." He grinned at me. "Try not to drink too much tonight."

"I do not think I will ever drink again."

"Everyone says that, Girton, but we always do. Just don't do it tonight as Nywulf takes a perverse joy in punishing the hungover."

"Is it safe, Rufra?"

"There are likely to be bandits. The cows are valuable, and if they know only squires are guarding them this year they may think they stand a better chance of making off with a beast. But they will not stand against mounted cavalry, even if we are only squires."

"I don't mean that," I said. "I mean we will be out alone with real weapons and a bunch of boys who hate us."

He stopped and turned to me. His face furrowed in concern, and the poor lighting on the staircase took him past ugly and into something almost bestial. "Nywulf will be with us, and besides, it would be too suspicious if you died from a sword in the back so soon after your beating. Tomas has been humiliated enough. I would be more worried about being late for the queen's feast. It is due at the striking of the eighth bell and you have not even put on your kilt."

"Oh dead gods, my kilt."

"Well, if you would rather stand in the cold all night then I can affect a limp and rub mount dung on myself. I am sure I could pass for you. . .."

"I do not smell of mount dung." I punched him on the arm and he feigned a look of hurt.

"I meant it as a compliment to your farmyard heritage. If you feel insulted must we duel?"

He looked so serious I couldn't help but laugh.

"I will survive the insult, Rufra."

"Should I get myself some dung?"

"I would not want to rob you of a night in the cold, Rufra. It would feel cruel."

He gave me a smile.

"Try and smuggle out some pork for me. I am sick of porridge and scraps."

"I did not know it was possible to become sick of porridge," I replied with a laugh, and we parted – him to get ready for guard duty and me to prepare for the feast and the struggle with my kilt.

My master waited in our room. She sat cross-legged and so still she could have been one of the gruesome statues outside the empty temples of the capital city. Her skull face had been reapplied and it glistened in the candlelight. In her lap was the rope I had brought. She was rubbing soot into it and had laid out a black nightsuit on my bed.

"Girton, how has your day been?"

"Good." A memory of Drusl's kiss returned and a thrill ran through me. "I checked the stables for anything odd but could find nothing." She nodded slowly. "And I met the king. He told me of the battle with the Black Sorcerer."

"It haunts him, I think. Battle often haunts those who survive." She shifted the rope from her lap. "Do not be fooled by the weakness of his body, Girton. His mind is alert even though he is infirm. I think Adran still fears him."

"He thought I was an assassin come for him."

"So would you if your wife was poisoning you."

"Will he send guards for us?"

"No, Adran will not allow it. She controls his troops now. All Doran ap Mennix has left to order about is the jester."

"What is going on in this castle, Master?"

"The king is dying, Girton, and not everyone thinks Aydor is the best choice to take the throne."

"Me included."

"I know." She smiled. "But you for more personal reasons. Some support Aydor because a young and inexperienced king is traditionally an easy way to advance; the blessed who do not favour Aydor believe he will always be controlled by his mother. Their upset is passed on to the guards, all of whom have familial allegiances."

"So who would these blessed prefer?

"Tomas ap Dhyrrin, I suspect. Though few are foolish enough to voice it. His great-grandfather would rule him, at first, but Daana is very old and they see opportunity there."

"So any blessed who favours Tomas is a suspect?"

"Yes, but . . ."

"But?"

She stood and walked to the door, leaning her head against it. "I have been among them all for days now. They all spy on each other but they are generally a small and timid lot. I have not yet met one I think would risk voicing an opinion Adran may disagree with, never mind one who would plot against her." She turned to me, her make-up leaving a smear of black on the honey-coloured pine of the door. "Doran ap Mennix picked his sycophants well, mostly. Which brings me to tonight."

"I see you have put out a nightsuit," I gestured at the black clothing on the bed.

"Yes, hastily stitched but it should hold together. I hope you have not grown too much since the last time I made you clothes." She stepped towards me and placed her hand gently on the side of my head. "You are nearly a man now, Girton. Sometimes I forget."

"I do not feel grown up, Master."

She shook herself out of her reverie and took her hand away from my face. "Tonight Adran throws a feast for the guards. I will perform Death's Count."

"That is a children's rhyme, Master."

"I know. Stay long enough to be seen, in case any ask where you were, but after I perform there will be uproar and Adran will command me to dance again. I will do something less patronising. Her ministers at the top table will have to stay but you can use the uproar to sneak out. No one will be paying attention to a squire. Return here, blacken your hands and face and put on the nightsuit. Two floors up and three across is the room of Neander the priest. Search it. One floor down from there and one across you will find the room of Daana ap Dhyrrin. Search that too. Find me something, Girton – anything." She sounded almost desperate but her face remained an unreadable deathmask. "Now get ready," she said.

"A kilt?"

"You are spared that; tonight is to be informal."

"Well, small mercies are all one can expect of dead gods."

"Have you suddenly become religious, Girton?"

"When I must climb the sheer face of a castle in full view of anyone below? Yes." I knew I sounded moody, but she laughed, short and sharp, before leaving the room to make her way to the main hall. Soon after, I followed.

Soldiers filled the benches, the noise of their drunken chatter like a wall, and even unarmoured the cloying smell of rancid fat and sweat clung to them. A whole bench across the centre of the room was unoccupied. About two thirds of the guards sat before it, while the rest, with occasional splashes of red, were behind. Every so often food would be thrown from one set of tables at the other, but it was good-natured and the room was filled with laughter. As I fought through to my place on the front bench I saw why. Gusteffa, the king's jester, was staging a mock fight with a tame bear. She wore a skirt of red which had been cut and shaped to move like the legs of a mount, two twigs in a crown served as antlers. I took great joy in Gusteffa's performance, but while I laughed at her I also listened to those around me. I sat among the larger group of guards, loyalists, and quickly learned they were not loyal to Aydor; it was his mother they respected. Now I understood at least a little of why Daana ap Dhyrrin had felt able to talk so freely of treason. His son would outlive Queen Adran and, unless she worked a miracle, Aydor would find little loyalty in his own castle.

Gusteffa finished her act with the bear, the end of which seemed needlessly cruel. At the last she produced a spear and slashed the bear's throat with it, leaving a pool of blood and a smear of red across the floor as servants dragged the animal's corpse out. I wondered whether this had been done to inconvenience my master, but it did not bother her. She walked into the area before the top table, approached the pool of bear blood and bent down and dipped her fingers in it. Then she smeared her cheeks with red like a warrior of old and assumed the start position while waiting for the guards to quieten.

When they did she went through a set of acrobatic manoeuvres that earned a huge cheer and then fell into the posture of the teller.

And then the dance really began.

Death's Count

One is for Xus, the god left after strife,
I am Xus the unseen the god who takes life.
Two is for sorcerers who ravage the land,
I am Xus the unseen, all come to my hand.
Three is for blood, drip, drip life is bidden,
I am Xus the unseen, always there, always hidden.
Four for the living who make and they mend,
I am Xus the unseen, I bring them their end.
Five for the thankful to whom life is a gift,
I am Xus the unseen, see them oft on my list.
Six is for blessed whose hands guide us all,
I am Xus the unseen, see them rise see them fall.
Seven is for priests with masks and with books,
I am Xus the unseen, leave the priests as they're loved.
Eight is for sourings where nothing exists,
I am Xus the unseen, blame yourselves for those gifts.

Nine is for mounts —
wild, free and strong,
I am Xus the unseen, even mounts heed my song.
Ten is for rebirth, to be bought with Xus' life,
I am Xus the unseen, how can death ever die?

It was a child's rhyme more generally performed to amuse
the very young. My master performed it exceptionally,
drawing it out and making every rhyme poignant and sad,
but the guards had no interest in her art. They wanted, and
expected, something filled with bawdiness and fighting, and
to them being presented with a children's song was an insult.
There was an explosion of noise in the hall. Food and cups
were thrown at my master but she was nimble and easily
dodged the missiles. As I pushed my way along the benches
to the door, my master pulled silly faces at the angry crowd
and jumped around ensuring all attention was on her. If
Queen Adran had not stood and demanded quiet they would
have ripped my master apart.

Or tried to.

"Quiet!" shouted the queen. "You are blessed to witness
a performance by Death's Jester." More shouting. Most loudly
from the rear benches where Adran was not loved. "And as
you all know Death's Jester is allowed to choose its own
dance." More shouting, and she held up her hands for quiet.
"However, as queen I also have tradition on my side, and I
may choose another dance if I am displeased with the first."
She paused, staring out into the quietening room and I
marvelled at how easily she suddenly held the guards, even
the ones who disliked her, in the palm of her hand. "So I
ask you," she said softly, "am I displeased?"

A roar of "Yes!" went up, and it was hard not to admire
how simply she bound these two disparate groups together.

"Very well, Death's Jester. You have displeased my guards

and in doing so you have displeased me. You will give my loyal guards the story of how the first king defeated the three sorcerers."

Another roar went up. This is always a popular story, though it was more suited to travelling mummers than an artist like my master.

Before she had even started, I had left to begin my journey across the walls of the castle.

Chapter 18

My stomach looped and twirled like a black bird in flight as I transferred my weight from the window ledge to fingertips lodged in the brittle mortar of the wall. I had fashioned a climbing device, a piece of wood with nails sticking from it in place of my useless toes, and had lashed it around my malformed foot so tightly it made me gasp with pain every time I found a foothold.

A bitter wind, tinged with the scent of sulphur, was blowing out of the sourlands to batter Castle Maniyadoc and wrap itself around me with icy fingers, before gathering its strength and trying to rip me from the wall. It thrust my hair into my eyes and numbed my hands and feet. Again I had the feeling of the wind as a living thing – malevolent – beating just out of time with my heart and waiting for the moment when I loosened my grip or found a toehold that would crumble before it tried to push me from my roost, high above the courtyard. I was thankful when I entered the lee of the side walls, where I found respite from the wind's grasping currents.

In the courtyard below I watched toys of people I knew march around the water clock and hoped they did not look up. I had decided against the rope and nails. Even with its coating of soot, the rope was still pale, and a quick glance upwards would have given me away, so I climbed the hard way – free hand. Occasionally I found a stone sticking out, probably a support for the scaffolds used to raise the keep, and would hang from it and gather my breath for a while.

On one such rest stop I heard voices – familiar but not clear enough to give names to. The wind distorted the voices by elongating the vowels or turning consonants into hisses that sounded like ghosts, conversing about the secrets only the dead knew.

". . . have had enough . . ."

". . . this . . . or duty . . ."

I tried to pinpoint where they came from. Leaning back to listen.

". . . sick of . . . cruelties . . ."

First they came from one place then another as the wind bounced the sounds around me.

". . . then you doom us all . . ."

And they were gone. All I knew was they had come from within the castle and not below. Had I heard something important or something of no consequence? Plotters talking of assassination or chamber boys talking of broken crockery and mean overseers?

There was no way to tell so I put it aside and continued my climb. Twice I dislodged loose bricks which skittered and clattered down into the courtyard while I hugged the wall, hoping no one too sharp-eyed would look up.

When I reached two floors above our room I started to make my way across the wall, my arms burned with strain as I returned to the capricious arms of the wind, though its determination to see me dashed to the ground had waned a little. I paused at the window of Neander's room. The priest set me on edge and there was definitely something off with him. Not only had he hinted at gathering allies when he had spoken to me but I had found him sneaking around a derelict area of the castle. Whether that made him likely to be the one hiring an assassin I did not know, and he seemed close to Adran. Though, in my experience, a closeness often made someone more likely to want to kill than not. I listened for any sound within and, hearing nothing, thanked Xus the unseen and gently pushed the greased canvas away from the window, letting myself into the welcome warmth of the room. I took a moment to thaw my hands, which had become like claws, in front of Neander's banked fire while wishing I was back in the main hall chucking apple ferment down my gullet until my stomach chose to throw it back up.

Once I had finished feeling sorry for myself I set about my task.

Neander's quarters were full of knick-knacks. A priest is meant to live an austere life, but he clearly cared little for it. Worse, the room was filthy and dust coated everything. He may simply have been slovenly, but he was a clever man and it was as likely he knew a coating of dust would give away a careless intruder.

But I am not careless.

Sewn into my underwear was a garrotte chain, an extremely fine chain with tiny metal teeth cast into it. It had been a present on the day my master had deemed my fourteenth birthday and was one of my most treasured possessions. I did not intend to garrotte anyone with it, and if I had to I would have failed in my mission. Instead I used it as a marker – before I lifted an object I lay the chain around its bottom so I knew exactly where to return it to.

In some ways the dust made my task easier. I could see what had been recently disturbed and avoided anything with more than the lightest coating of dust, knowing it had not been moved for a long time. Once I had checked something dusty over, I took a bottle of false dust, made by sloughing off my own skin with a rough sponge, from my inner pocket and used it to cover anywhere I had disturbed.

From the dust it appeared Neander only ever touched a few of his books and only ever sat in one chair. Paths showed where he walked between his bed, the wardrobe, the fire and his desk. I ran my hand under his bed but left the covers alone as it would be impossible to put them back as they were. I checked under bottles, under cups and anywhere anything of interest could be hidden, but found nothing. Finally I checked his book of names. Mine was the last name written in it, and in the back of the book I found the only interesting thing in Neander's room, though I could not fathom what it meant. Groups of letters, set out in columns: RTK, ATK, DTS, VTSm, HTQC and ZAG.

It looked like there was some pattern but I could not fathom the code. It could be something of religious significance or a shopping list. I memorised the sequence, thinking that maybe my master could make sense of it, then left the room the way I had come in and continued my exploration of the keep's walls. Below me I heard Rufra's voice.

". . . an arrow in my back?"

Then Tomas.

". . . not . . . Hallin. When . . . kill . . . will be . . . to face."

I hoped whatever argument they were having would stop them looking up and at the same time wondered why Tomas hated Rufra so much. A breeze wrapped itself around me just as a stone I was using as a handhold fractured under my weight. I let out a yelp as I clung on to my one remaining handhold.

"What was that?" Rufra's voice from far below as I dangled from the cold stone by an aching arm. The damp seeped through my nightsuit as the throb of tiring muscles seeped into my bones.

"What was what?" Tomas's voice.

"I heard . . . thing."

"Spooked by . . . dark, Rufra?"

Rufra chose not to answer. I could see the pale oval of his face staring up at the walls. He stared for a long time, and my arm was trembling with the effort of holding my weight. Suddenly I wanted to laugh. How terrible would it be if I was to be discovered by my only friend? Eventually, he shook his head and walked away. Then I found myself in the awful position of having to choose speed over care, crabbing across the wall as quickly as I could and hoping my burning muscles wouldn't betray me and twitch or cramp at the wrong time, sending me falling to my death. It felt like it took an age to reach Daana ap Dhyrrin's window. I barely even checked to see if the room was occupied before dragging myself over the stone lip of the windowsill and falling onto his carpeted floor.

As the heat of the room warmed my frozen hands the hot aches hit, and to avoid crying out in pain I had to bite down so hard I thought I would crack my teeth. There was little I could do while I waited for the agony to pass and tears of pain streamed from my eyes. When the burning started to leave my hands it bit into my feet, and my club foot felt like it had been plunged into a fire. I fell to the floor and curled up into a whimpering ball, counting out my-masters until the misery passed.

When I could walk again, I examined the room.

It was far tidier than Neander's, and if a man's room was emblematic of his mind then Daana ap Dhyrrin was the exact opposite of the priest. No dust at all, and his books were stacked neatly. A square decanter of apple liquor and a matching glass were placed on the desk so their corners lined up perfectly with the corner of sthe shining darkwood top. Thankfully, his noisy lizards were with him at the feast. At the first sign of a stranger they would have squawked or spat venom at me.

I was twice as careful in Daana's room as I had been in Neander's – a tidy man likes things just so and is more likely to notice something out of place. I took out my chain garrotte and started going through the books on his desk, though I found nothing except that he had an interest in folklore and a love of old books. I memorised some of the book titles as they were unfamiliar to me.

A sheaf of vellum pages had been laid out on his desk. The top one had Rufra's name on it, and I leafed through them to find they all read the same apart from the names. "I, Rufra ap Vthyr, request the heir, Aydor ap Mennix, be removed from Rider training." Rufra had told me some squires had written to request Aydor's removal, but I was surprised to see there were even a couple of requests from boys I thought of as Aydor's cronies. Not that it mattered. Daana had clearly decided to ignore them and had started to scrape the vellums clean. The word "training" on Rufra's request was already so faded as to be barely readable.

Under the vellum was an elaborate family tree showing the ap Dhyrrin's claim to the throne. There was little doubt that it was stronger than that of the ap Mennix, who ruled currently, but such things mattered little when King Doran had won loyalty with the edge of his blade. It was clear that Daana ap Dhyrrin intended his great-grandson to take the throne at some point in the future. But would he really be so blatant if he had contracted an assassin?

Why did the queen put up with him?

What hold did he have over her?

I resumed searching. In the bin I found some slips of paper that had been scrawled on and ripped up. As I studied them I heard the water clock strike twelve. The feast would be finishing now. I stared at the torn slips of paper, trying to make some sense of them; they appeared to be nothing but angular doodles. Signs of a violent mind maybe but that was hardly a crime in the Tired Lands. I dropped the papers back in the bin. They fluttered through golden, luminescent air. Pain stabbed into my head, needles behind my eyes, and the lines on the paper connected in such a way as to remind me of the signs I had seen in Heamus's room. I squeezed my eyes shut to banish the pain, a sure sign of too much exertion. Then I dipped into the bin and set about making a quick jigsaw of the bits of paper until I saw a definite familiarity, though these symbols did not carry the same sense of revulsion and sat easily in my memory. Surely Doran ap Mennix's right hand would never mix himself up in magic?

I went to the window, readying myself to go out again. The wind had come up and it howled around the keep, making my heart sink. My arms were so tired and my club foot so painful I was not sure I could make it back without falling. I cursed myself for not chancing the rope or at least knocking in some nails. I glanced down, and as if to reinforce my worries the priest of Xus appeared by the water clock in the keep's courtyard. The gibbous moon of his mask was angled straight up at me. Surely an omen.

I took a rag from my pocket and hurriedly wiped as much blacking from my face and my hands as I could. Then I ripped off my climbing aid and, leaning as far out of the window as possible, I dug the nails into the mortar in such a way that it would work its way loose and fall, hopefully long after I was gone, and I could reclaim it later. Then, remembering the guard outside the kennels and how my master had covered her actions by making him appear drunk, I took Daana's decanter and poured out enough liquor to wet my fingers and ran them through my hair. After a deep breath and a quick entreaty to Xus that no guards were posted outside Daana's quarters, I slipped out of the room and into the corridor.

No guards. In my panic I had forgotten they were all in the main hall getting drunk. I made my way as quickly as I could back to my rooms, but when I heard footsteps behind me I started to weave and stumble like a drunk. Not looking where I was going, I walked straight into Heamus.

"Girton, why are you here, boy? And why are you dressed

like— Dead gods!" He laughed as the smell of alcohol hit him. "You have been celebrating, aye?" He laughed again as he held me by my shoulders. I wondered how many innocent lives his big hands had taken as I focused on a tapestry of an old queen on her mount behind him.

"Um . . . lost," I said, swaying. Then I repeated myself. "Lost."

"Ha, you will be a sad one when you ride the cows tomorrow. Nywulf has no pity in him. Let me help you to find your way back, and then I suggest you drink plenty of water."

He escorted me back to my room and because I was with him no one asked any questions or commented on my strange dress. Heamus seemed totally lacking in curiosity, in fact he seemed distracted and did not speak to me again as we walked.

When I slipped into our room my master was staring out of the window. She turned and opened her mouth to speak, but I raised my finger to my lips and pointed with my thumb at the door. We both waited and listened while Heamus thumped away down the corridor.

"Heamus," I said.

"He caught you?"

"No. Ran into him in a corridor." She tipped her head to one side as she often did when she wanted more information. "The climb was harder than I thought. When the wind picked up I did not think I could make it back so I cleaned what blacking I could off me and put alcohol in my hair to play the drunk. I could do nothing about my clothes or lack of shoes."

My master shrugged. "People will expect stupidity of a drunk boy, so it will not be hard to make excuses, if anyone even asks. But for now you should tidy yourself up. The queen wants to see us again."

"Why?"

"To speak to you, I imagine." A lump settled in my stomach. "She is naturally suspicious and sick of hearing the same things from me each night. She probably thinks she can catch you in a lie. Tell her the truth and don't say anything too outlandish, or mention anything connected to the death of Kyril." She nodded knowingly and I felt the same swoop in my stomach at the thought of magic as I had when swinging myself out onto the castle wall.

We ran into the occasional guard, passed out drunk, on our way to Adran's rooms. Celot stood guard outside and inside the queen waited on a carved throne, candlelight shimmered along the golden paint on its arms and back. Behind her stood Aydor, his gaze unfocused as he swayed under the influence of drink. My eye was drawn to the vicious scar his mother had given him.

"When I call my servants," said Adran, "I expect them to come straight away."

"I see no servants," said my master. "Would you like me to find some for you?"

"Stop your insolence," shouted Aydor, but he was too drunk to speak properly, and each *s* came out as sh. Adran glared at him. "Aydor, you have a busy day tomorrow so go and drink some water and get some sleep."

"But—" She cut him off with a sweep of her hand.

"Go!" She transferred her glare from him to me as he staggered out of the room. Once he was gone she leaned forward. "Merela, watch your tongue in front of my son or I'll have it cut out."

"Sorry, Queen Adran. Sometimes I forget we are not the friends we used to be." There was no mistaking the edge in my master's voice.

"Acquaintances, Merela. I seem to remember a merchant's daughter can never be friends with one of the thankful, can she?"

My master looked away. "I understood you had questions

for Girton, Queen Adran. Best ask quickly as he has to ride
out tomorrow and needs his sleep."

"Yes." She smiled at me and turned on her full charm,
inclining her head a little in my direction, and suddenly I
saw what had made a king fall at her feet. "Are you enjoying
your time here, Girton?"

"Yes, my queen," I said, and immediately felt foolish for
my airs and graces and added, "though the beatings get a
little wearing."

"You have picked up Merela's talent for sarcasm." Adran
stood and walked over to me, gently taking my hand in hers,
then she squeezed it so hard I could feel the bones grinding
together. "It is wise to remember, child, that I need your
master, not you." She let go of my hand. "So, boy, who do
you suspect wishes to murder my son?"

"Everyone, Queen Adran," I said and inwardly cringed at
the look on her face. She plainly could not decide whether
I was being sarcastic again. My hand ached. "I only mean
that I seem to do nothing but uncover more motives, rather
than rule people out."

"What do you mean?"

"Well, a good third of the guards—"

"Can be ignored. We know who they are and they are
kept well away from Aydor. Besides, a guard cannot afford
an assassin."

I did not think it politic to mention that my master and
I often worked for free if she thought the cause just. "Well,
then there are the squires."

"Oh?" She raised an eyebrow. "Why would they wish to
harm their future king?"

"Well, they believe he holds them back."

"Explain."

"There . . ." I felt myself wilting under the pressure of
her gaze and cleared my throat with a nervous cough.

"There is a belief that after your son failed to pass his trials for Rider the other squires have been forbidden to advance."

She shook her head and smiled as she returned to her throne. "Foolish boys making excuses. They are embarrassed is all. Aydor was chosen to take the trials first as he is foremost among them. If he could not pass the trials, what point the other boys even trying?" I could not tell whether she was making excuses for her son or if she truly believed what she said. I felt a little sorry for Aydor then, but only a little.

"The Festival Lords were very upset—"

"Politics and business, nothing else. And besides, we knew of the assassin before the Festival Lords arrived."

"Daana ap Dhyrrin has spoken quite openly of—"

She waved a hand, though a look of distaste crossed her face. "I have Daana well in hand, boy. Next."

Silence filled the air of the small room while I thought.

"May I ask a question, Queen Adran?"

"If it is not impertinent, yes."

"Why do you allow Daana ap Dhyrrin to voice treason?"

"Because he is an old man —" she leaned forward "— and it amuses me to hear him rant. He would not have Aydor killed because he believes when I die the common people will flock to Tomas." I nodded. "But before I die, boy, Aydor will be high king, and the common people will not matter. When Aydor is high king, Tomas is welcome to this draughty old castle, and Daana ap Dhyrrin knows it."

"But old men may be impatient," I said, echoing my master's words.

"They may," said Adran, "but Daana ap Dhyrrin has been playing the infirm old man since before I married Doran ap Mennix. I suspect he has a good few years in him yet. He plays a long game. Maybe when Aydor has ascended the throne he will try and have me killed to hurry his plans along, but to kill Aydor now would taint his grandson, and the old man would hate that."

"Neander then, he is an ap Vthyr and—"

"They hate us, that is true. But Neander wants power. He is as committed to seeing Aydor ascend to high king as I am. Forget Neander."

"But I came across him in a disused part of the castle. He was—"

"I know all about Neander's jaunts into the castle for his flock, and you need not worry about them. In fact, I forbid you to go near Neander."

"Forbid?" said my master. "You told me nowhere would be forbidden. And now when we tell you we have suspects you make excuses for them."

"Not excuses," she said, but couldn't hide her discomfort. "I merely do not want you to waste your time on dead ends." She stood and avoided looking my master in the eye. "This is my son's life, Merela. Apply yourself –" she stood behind me, laying a hand on my shoulder "– or I will find a way to motivate you further." A shiver ran through me as Adran walked back towards her throne. She let the silence build before saying casually, "What about that scruffy boy, Girton? What is his name?"

"Which boy?" A coldness settled in my stomach.

"Rufra. You should look very carefully at that boy."

"I cannot imagine Rufra would—"

"Well maybe you should imagine it," she hissed. "That boy has always struck me as untrustworthy, and as you pointed out the ap Vthyr hate us. You should use your closeness to him, boy, to find out what game he plays before I decide you and your master are of no use." She sat back down on her throne of gold-painted pine. "You may leave now, both of you."

We walked in silence back to our room. When we were inside I said in the Whisper-that-Flies-to-the-Ear:

"What was that about, Master?"

"What do you mean?"

"She seemed adamant that we should not look into the people most likely to want to hurt her son. That makes no sense"

"Yes. On both counts."

"But why?"

"Because I suspect she has secrets and we are straying near them. This castle is full of secrets."

"What sort of secrets do you think Adran has that she would risk her son for?"

"Terrible ones, Girton. Most likely she has found who hired the assassin and come to some accord with them. She can be persuasive."

"Then why are we still here? And why did she almost tell us she thought Rufra was to blame."

"Maybe she knows something we don't about Rufra."

"Rufra would not—"

"I don't say he would, but maybe he is not what he seems and now Adran sees us as a convenient way to remove him."

"I—"

"You don't really know him, Girton. A little knowledge of him is all you have, so do as she says for now and stick close to Rufra." She put her hand on my shoulder. "But we will not ignore the others merely to frame your friend. Not if there is another way." I felt her shiver and she removed her hand, wrapping her arms around herself as if she were cold. "I feel like we are in the eye of a storm, Girton. It whirls around us so fast, everything is a blur and we cannot move in any direction for fear of stepping to our deaths."

I could not sleep after her chilling pronouncement, and sleep was what I wanted more than anything. Unpleasant thoughts slid into my mind to war with themselves: the snarling dogs, the lies my master had told me, the terrible feeling those symbols I had found in Heamus's room had caused within me, images of Drusl flouncing off with another squire.

The idea of magic no longer seemed as horrific as it had at first. Was this how it worked its way in? By slowly becoming normal? On the other hand, if those terrible symbols I had seen in Heamus's room were against magic, could it really be so bad?

Had it changed me? Was I a different person?

The sullen anger that had burned inside me ebbed. It was not gone, but I felt foolish about it and recognised it as a childish thing. My master had never done anything but protect me and help me. Her only betrayal was to overestimate my intelligence.

I still could not sleep so went to the window and pulled aside the greased paper to stare out over Festival. Fires burned but they were fewer now. It was late enough for most revellers to have left and movement far below caught my eye. A single torch moved across the courtyard. It was joined by another and then another. Unsure whether this might be important I was about to wake my master when I realised what I was seeing. This was the funeral procession for Kyril.

We always take out our dead in the night. The body is laid out in the house together with the best gifts for Xus the family can afford. Then the family leave and the officiating priest comes with his retainers and his bier and they take the body, and the gifts, away. It is tradition. We pay tribute to Xus the unseen by pretending that our dead simply disappear. Or maybe we do not want to confront the fact that the Tired Lands are so short of resources that even the bodies of the dead have a use. The swillers pay the priests for bodies, and the bodies feed the pigs whose meat keeps us alive.

Death was nothing new to me, but the deaths I had witnessed before had been through the agency of my master or myself and in the name of justice. There had been point and reason to them but this death, this boy who had lain silent and perfect upon the slab? His death served no purpose that I could see.

I did not sleep until very late.

Interlude

This is a dream of what was.

He is thirteen.

Today he will kill his first man.

The land is a painting where the artist has only sickly yellows to daub onto his canvas – a hazy mist of burnt-sienna dust suspended between yellow land and yellow sky.

They have trekked across the eastern sourlands eking out their water and food until they are forced to tap their great mount, Xus's, veins and share the animal's life. They cannot take too much from him and what they have is never enough. Even powered by the mount's great heart he feels light-headed as he stumbles forward. When they leave the sourlands it takes his eyes time to adjust to this new world with its garish, unnaturally bright, colours. The distance to the horizon seems impossibly far and for days after the kill he will smell the sourlands on his clothes, his skin. He will blame his constant nausea on it.

The village is barely worthy of the name. Five houses clustered inside the palisade walls of a longhouse built of timbers and roofed with sods. It squats in the humid air and bored guards in badly kept up leather armour lounge around the gate. Slaves, bent and twisted by hard lives, trudge past through ankle-deep mud as they bring in the harvest from the surrounding fields.

"Friend," says his master to a slave who looks blankly at them as he walks past. All the man's concentration is focused on putting one foot in front of another. He looks impossibly old, he must be in his late twenties, or maybe even thirty. He is missing his front teeth.

"Can't stop," he says dully. The words whistle through his missing teeth. "Work to do."

"Is this Ryneal?" asks his master.

"Aye," he says as he staggers away under his burden of root tubers, "and I would leave while you can."

His master watches the man. "Come, Girton," she says. "We must prepare."

"Yes, Master." He follows, leading Xus along by his rein.

"I have told you of justice, Girton," she says as they come to stop in a copse just beyond the village, "and that justice was blinded by men."

"Yes, Master."

"But I did not tell you why."

"No, Master."

She takes a step forward. "Men blinded her so that they could lead her off the path. Sometimes we must be there to guide her." She puts her finger on his chest. "Tonight you will walk the path with her."

A sudden intake of breath.

"Me?"

Does the wind pick up? Do the trees sigh? Does the world momentarily brighten before cooling and darkening?

"Yes, Girton. You."

"I don't want to." The words tumble from his mouth and leave something in his throat that clogs it up and makes tears start from his eyes. He knows he is letting her down but he's seen her come back from her work: sometimes covered in blood, sometimes bruised, sometimes with a new cut that he will bind and clean and it will become another shining, pale line of damaged flesh on her skin. Even when she comes back unscathed there is always something missing. It is as if some piece of her is gone, leaving glassy, pale, damaged lines behind her eyes. "I don't want to," he says again. She puts her hands on his shoulders. She looks right into his eyes. She looks right into him.

"Good," she says. "I would be worried if you wanted this. Sit with me a while."

They sit, choosing a place where they can see right through the gates and up to the door of the longhouse. They watch. He becomes fascinated by the to and fro of people, the rhythm of a life totally alien to him. He and his master never stop. They are wanderers and when they camp they camp away from people for fear of being found. When they are in towns he is kept close for fear of giving her away. When she strikes they are quick – in and out. He waits outside dark buildings or towering walls with Xus, and then they are fleeing, finding places to hide, usually unpleasant places and often they are there for weeks – in stinking hovels or swamps or worse, the sourlands.

But today he watches people. It would be easy for him to forget this is not his life, easy to fall into the backwards and forwards of these tired people who, even though they are dressed in rags and filth, sometimes laugh. They sometimes smile. They sometimes hold one another. Children play, seemingly careless of the misery that waits for them as adults.

With the strangeness of a dream comes foreknowledge. He can feel what is coming as surely as the children running and giggling through puddles must realise the harshness of the life awaiting them. Unlike them he cannot look away. When he looks up, the clouds make no pretence of reality; they become giant grey daggers reaching down from the sky to rip at the tops of trees tinged with the red of failing day.

Wake me.

"There is a sadness that is more than a harsh life here, Master," he says.

"Yes. Blessed Ryneal uses them cruelly."

"Uses them for what, Master?"

"Whatever he wishes." She stands as if some signal has been given. "Her." His master points as a woman, as stooped as the rest and with a heavy swelling belly, leaves the long-house and walks towards the well.

"Her?" he says. "What about her?"

"She is what is needed. Come with me, Girton." There is something about his master's manner that sends a chill through him despite the humidity of the day. "When I speak to her hang back. Keep your face covered and say nothing."

Please wake me.

His master walks up to the woman. Now he is nearer he can see she is a girl, though her flesh is grey with tiredness and, curiously, her front teeth are also missing. The girl struggles with the handle of the well. No one offers to help her.

"Let me," says his master. "You look like you have worked hard. You must need a drink."

I want to wake up.

Wake me now.

Please wake me now.

The girl looks up, frightened. So obviously and clearly frightened.

It is Blue-Eyes.

How can it be?

The last time he saw her was before the slave market the day his master bought him. She was crying. She was screaming his name as she was dragged off to a wagon and he did nothing to help her. He wants to step forward but he is unable to move and his master has told him he must not.

"The water is not for me; it is for the guards," says Blue-Eyes. "But thank you."

"I am glad to help. Maybe you can help me? I am a player and I was looking for work, but life here seems hard. Is your blessed poor?"

"No." Blue-Eyes' words are hardly audible and her lip has

been split recently. The damaged skin clings to her remaining teeth when she speaks. "He has plenty."

"Then I should introduce myself." She hands the bucket to Blue-Eyes and the girl looks over her shoulder. She leans forward and melds into the silhouette of the well so Girton can no longer see her, only hear her low voice. She is close to tears.

"You have done me a kindness, so let me do one for you in return. Do not enter the longhouse. Take your apprentice, turn away from this place and never come back."

"Thank you for that warning," says my master. "May good fortune come to you."

"I doubt it will," says Blue-Eyes as she walks away with the heavy bucket. Her shadow elongates in the setting sun until it touches his feet and he feels like it is entreating him for help.

His master takes his arm.

"Come, Girton. In an hour the guards will be asleep and you must be ready."

"That was Blue-Eyes," he says. "She was my friend in the slave pens. She was always good to me. She was always smiling."

"She is no longer Blue-Eyes," says his master sadly, and it is as if she shares his pain. "Blessed Ryneal took her happiness with his fists and his appetites. Who you knew is gone." She shakes him. "Blue Eyes is gone, do you understand? But you can free her from this man."

"She begged for my help when they took her," he says. The words are dry in his mouth.

"You were six, untrained and unable to do anything. You were a helpless child." She stares into his eyes. "Now you are not. You cannot change what was but tonight you may at least give her a chance for a future." She places a parchment in his hand together with his stabswords. On the parchment is a truncated circle with the top left quarter missing, the sign of the assassins. Beneath is written, ". . . and the Lords shall care for their people".

"What is this?"

"It is part of the high king's law. We will leave it to remind this blessed's heir that to be blessed is not to be untouchable."

He holds the blades in his hands, and though the calluses on his palms have long ago moulded themselves to the hilts tonight the blades feel alien, like he has never seen them before.

"How will I know who it is?"

"He will reveal himself."

An hour later they slip in past drunk guards slumped at the gates. He is shaking and has built Blessed Ryneal into a monster in his mind – a huge man and a despoiler of all he touches. A creature who shrugs off blade wounds like insect bites.

Time passes too quickly.

His master quietens a group of children huddled in the lee of the wall as they stalk purposefully past. Inside the hall it is almost pitch black and the flickering candles barely light their way, so they squat and concentrate on the exercise of the False Lantern. At the back of the hall is an area curtained off with animal skins. His master points at it.

"Breathe out, Girton," she whispers. "You are the instrument."

He breathes in the words drilled into him. "No room for fear." *Breathe out. Breathe in.* "I am the weapon." He pushes the curtain aside. He walks from one world to another.

Blessed Ryneal is not a monster, only a man, heavily muscled and with a network of scars from battle decorating his naked body. A bed fills the back of the room and he can see figures moving, pulling covers over themselves.

He is shaking with fear as he reaches for the hilts of his blades.

"A boy," says Ryneal. He is gently spoken. "I don't remember asking for another boy." Ryneal walks over to Girton and stares into his face. "Still got your teeth. Guidran knows he's meant to take them out. He's getting either soft or lazy. Still, I can't risk a biter."

Shaking with anger, his hands tighten on the hilts of his blades.

Blue-Eyes.

Ryneal takes the front of his tunic in one hand and starts to draw back his fist.

Everything happens so slowly. It is like the time he got tangled up in pondweed when he was learning to swim and thought Blue Watta had come to take him. It is like drowning.

The tunic bunching around his neck.

The fist reaches full draw.

His clothes are loose.

It is easy to shrug out of them.

The fist comes down.

Into the third iteration, the Maiden's Pass. *She laughs as he gets it wrong again and walks right into her.* One foot around the other so he sways to the side and the fist swishes past his ear. Into the fifth iteration, the Boatgirl's Dip. *She holds his hand and twirls him under her arm.* He grabs Ryneal's forearm with his defence arm and twists it until he hears the crunch of the elbow joint dislocating. Then he's behind Ryneal, stabsword out. He ends with the eighth iteration, the Placing of the Rose. *She bows and takes the pretty flower with a laugh.* His hand is against his partner's neck. Except this time his partner is not his master and his hand holds a blade which is buried in Ryneal's flesh.

No one is laughing.

Blessed Ryneal coughs, then sinks to his knees and falls face first onto the floor. He pushes himself onto his back while one hand grasps weakly at the blade in his neck. Ryneal looks puzzled, stares at him and says, "I didn't ask for a boy." Blood is everywhere. It fills the air with its metallic tang.

A face appears from under the covers of the bed. She looks up. Looks at the body. Looks at him.

Wake me.

"Blue-Eyes," he says. "It's me. It's Club-Foot. I've come to save you."

She shakes her head.

"Who will look after my baby now?" she says. Then she sees the blood and the knife and the screaming starts.

His master is at his elbow telling him they have to leave, and all he can hear is Blue-Eyes screaming, but this time he is the one being dragged away and he is the one calling her name.

And the clouds are like knives in the sky.

This is a dream of what was.

Chapter 19

In the Tired Lands the line between villager and bandit is often drawn by the hunger of children. Conversely, the Tired Lands are a land where the small pleasures of the living – hot food on a cold day, a shared joke, the heft of a well made tool – take on a weight far beyond the understanding of the blessed in their castles and halls.

There is little I like better than the rolling gait of a mount beneath me. Nywulf led us, a yellow and purple Mennix flag flying from a stick bound to his saddle. Behind him came Aydor ap Mennix, holding his father's bonemount, his symbol of war, the skull of a mount festooned with yellow and purple streamers which straggled in the wind as he led his group. Behind them rode Rufra and I. Tomas and his little group were riding as scouts, looking for bandits after the incoming livestock. No doubt they were giving their mounts a real workout rather than trotting along in the dust watching a thousand cows stream into Maniyadoc's gate. The air was full of plaintive lowing and the smell was unbelievable, but it did not upset me. Neither did it matter that I had been given the worst of the bows or that Aydor's cronies took every opportunity they got to snipe and spit at me. None of it mattered because I was riding Xus and so I was happy.

". . . so," said Rufra, "after you told me about the paddles I checked Balance over and, sure enough, bruising on his haunches. I would have missed it had your girlfriend not warned you. You must thank Drusl –" he left a gap in his sentence before leaning in nearer and leering "– whichever way you think best." I attempted to swat him with my whip but he swayed out of reach and, with a laugh, spurred his mount in a circle. "Too slow," he said. "He won't be doing it again now, though I do wish I'd not punched Leiss so hard. I've hurt my knuckles." He flexed his gloved hands and then immediately brightened up. "Do you think Nywulf would let us run? I will take the first chance I get to chase something down. Imby needs a run." He patted his mount on the neck.

He rode Imbalance, a huge black warmount. His other, Balance, was white. Imbalance had got its name as its left antler had only five points where the right had seven. Usually such a thing was a sign of poor quality in a bloodline, but Imbalance was a fine beast, night-black, strongly muscled and with a calm temperament. That and Rufra's obvious love for the beast made me wonder if it was the animal he'd learned to ride on.

"He's a beautiful beast," I said, spitting dust.

"Aye, Bal is a better warmount though – fiercer, more like your Xus."

Xus tossed his head, as if he enjoyed being thought of as fierce, and bared his tusks at a passing rider flying a message flag. A moment later Nywulf brought us to a stop. Rufra manoeuvred his animal around Aydor's group of friends and I followed. As we approached, Nywulf raised his voice.

". . . and I cannot leave them," he shouted.

"Squiremaster," the messenger replied, "I can only give you my message. You are requested to report back to Maniyadoc by Neander, and we have received reports of raiders heading for the village of Calfey."

"And I say I cannot leave the squires alone."

"I am sorry, Squiremaster, but Neander was insistent."

Nywulf pulled on the reins of his mount to face us. "Aydor, this means I must leave you in charge. I will be as quick as

I can, and it is likely that showing your faces at Calfey will be enough to scare off the raiders. If not, then mock charges and bows should do it." He brought his mount up close to Aydor. "You are not to engage with blades and no one is to ride alone, do you understand?" They stared at each other until Aydor chose to squint up into the sky. Nywulf nodded to the rider closest to Aydor. "Celot, stay close to the heir. Do your job." If Celot was excited by the idea of action I could not tell; his face wore the same half-smile that it always wore. Nywulf could have been asking him to pick apples for all the emotion he showed. "Girton, talk with me a moment," said Nywulf, and where Celot's face had barely changed mine must have fallen as Aydor gave me a superior smirk, as if to say, "Stay back, mage-bent, while real warriors do the work."

The other squires set heels to mounts and galloped off towards Calfey, sending panicking cows running and attracting abuse from the cowherds. Nywulf held Xus's bridle and leaned over so he could speak quietly to me. "You're good with that bow, Girton. So hang back and use it if anything happens." Then he locked eyes with me. It was a fierce look and one that worried me as it felt as if he saw right past Girton ap Gwynr and into the boy below. "And watch out for Rufra; he is too trusting though he pretends otherwise." With that he let go of the bridle and slapped Xus on the rear, sending me racing after the other mounts.

There was joy in the speed and the clear air as Xus cut his way through the apple trees. Shadows flashed around me – light, dark, light, dark – and the world was turned into a series of juddering images until I broke out of the apple forest and fields stretched ahead of me for ever and ever. To my right the other squires kicked up a cloud of dust and beyond them I could see a column of smoke that must be Calfey. To my left was Barnew's Wood, where Aydor had been "attacked", and running towards it was a figure being chased by a man carrying a sword. I saw the sparkle of a blade as he lifted it and cut down the figure running before him. On the wind I thought I heard a voice, Aydor's, but I could not tell what he said. A moment later a Rider split off from the group of squires and made towards the swordsman – Rufra on his black mount.

In the back of my mind I heard my master's voice. Many nights we had sat awake by a fire while she had drawn maps with a burned stick and explained what worked in war, how the tactics of battle could be used on the smaller scale of infiltration. How in the end all things were the same: big was small, small was big.

And I saw what was before me for a lie.

Calfey had little of value. Was this a feint to draw us away from the cows while another force hit the herders?

I spurred Xus on towards the main group.

Would Aydor listen to me?

No.

I glanced to my left, the swordsman had entered Barnew's Wood and Rufra was riding hard after him.

Or could this be a trap for one of us?

Sayda Halfhand had gone, but any fool could wield a blade. Could this be a set-up for a move on Aydor?

Why was Rufra riding alone? Had he been ordered to take down the swordsman or was it his own idea? Surely he would never disobey Nywulf?

I heard a roar. The squires, also ignoring Nywulf's orders, charged into the village of Calfey with their swords held high.

What was happening? Was this a raid, albeit a misguided one? Or a feint.

Or a trap for Rufra?

Why would anyone lay a trap for Rufra?

Was it a trap for Aydor?

If Aydor died, then I had no doubt my master and I would soon follow him.

But Barnew's Wood? Was it only coincidence that was where Aydor's ambush had been faked? Adran had hinted that she disliked Rufra. Had the pretend attack on Aydor given his mother ideas? No, she would be more subtle than to just repeat what had happened. Her son however?

Or Tomas?

I reigned Xus in and the warmount screeched in fury, fighting the bit in his eagerness to be part of the action.

Something was wrong.

For a moment I was torn, and then Rufra vanished into the dark space between the trees and a shiver ran through me. I leaned into Xus and with a shout of, "Ha! Xus, ha!" gave him his head. Free to run, he flew towards Barnew's Wood like a bolt from a crossbow. We thundered past the body cut down by the bandit swordsman. It was a boy no older than I was.

At the edge of the wood I pulled Xus to a stop and the mount huffed and pawed the ground in response to my anxiety. Speed or stealth? Everything in me screamed speed but I made myself stop and think.

Breathe out.

No time for this!

Let the assassin work this through, not the boy.

Breathe in.

If it was a trap Rufra was likely to be outnumbered and lumbering in on Xus would only give me away. Then I would have to fight my way to him.

Breathe out.

He'll be dead if you don't act!

Think.

No time!

I slid from Xus's saddle.

"Wait," I told the mount and he bobbed his huge head before lowering it to chew on a bush. Unslinging my bow I half strung an arrow before moving into the undergrowth.

Rufra had ridden up a slim path and the mud had been churned up by his mount's claws. Not far down the path I found the swordsman, dead, his head cracked open by Rufra's sword. After killing him, Rufra must have heard something else as he had continued into the wood, going more slowly, but still at some speed.

I found Imbalance's body fifty steps further on. The animal's neck had been broken by a line of wire stretched across the path, but his strange lopsided antlers had saved Rufra's life. When the mount had struck the line, rather than stopping him abruptly and throwing the antlers back so the Rider was impaled on the tips, it had slewed Imbalance round, throwing Rufra into the undergrowth. I could see where he had rolled into the ferns. From there he had run to the left, going further into the wood. I found a crossbow bolt in Imbalance's side and another buried in a tree.

Further on I found the body of a crossbowyer with her neck opened. I could read the fight in the land. Rufra had hidden behind a tree and waited for her to reload then charged her as she did. A second warrior had been with the crossbowyer, they and Rufra had fought here. From the depth of footprints this fighter was armoured. Another fighter had joined the first and Rufra had fled further into the wood.

I found blood on the leaves of a low-hanging branch and hoped it was not my friend's.

Ten steps later I heard the sound of combat and, keeping low in the undergrowth, hurried towards it.

They fought in a clearing. A huge stone totem of the dead gods had fallen and ripped a hole in the canopy, creating an island of illumination in the dark wood. Bright shafts of light caught dust dancing in the air and glinted off the mismatched armour of six men surrounding another, who used jerky movements of his sword to ward off feigned attacks.

Rufra, definitely Rufra. And he was still alive, though a crossbow bolt stuck out from the plate metal of his right shoulder guard. He didn't look wounded, but the bolt was stopping him raising his longsword. Even if he had been able to lift his arm properly he didn't stand a chance against six.

The clang of metal on metal.

And a death.

A man holding a heavy two-handed mace launched an overhead attack at Rufra. The mace came down towards his head and Rufra danced to the side, dropped his useless longsword and thrust his stabsword into the man's gut, giving it a twist before pulling back. As he fought to push the dying man away another of his attackers dashed in. They were not skilled warriors but they didn't need to be; they had numbers. He brought down a spiked morningstar against Rufra's helm and my friend fell, the fallen statue blocked my view of him. With a roar the morningstar wielder lifted his weapon, ready to bring it down in a killing blow.

I stood.

Raised the bow.

Drew it and let the arrow fly in one motion.

No thought. No conscious aiming.

The arrow took the man through the eye of his elaborate snarling facemask.

The remaining four stood, looking shocked and stupid. I nocked an arrow and advanced on them with the bow at full stretch, snapping my aim from one to the other as quickly as the breath went in and out of my lungs.

"You can't get us all, boy," shouted a man who carried a longsword and stabsword. His voice rang in the still wood, and he dropped the snarling visor on his wide helm. If he thought it would protect him from my arrow he was a fool.

"I can get two of you," I said, sitting on the fallen statue and sliding over it. There was no waver in my voice, no doubt of the threat I posed. "Maybe I'll get three." I returned my aim to the man with his visor down. "You die first." I could see his eyes behind his visor as he watched. Occasionally his glance flicked to his friends as they spread out around me. I walked forward until I was in the centre of the clearing and Rufra lay at my feet. His dented helm had come off and he was still as a corpse. But he breathed.

He breathed.

"Rufra," I hissed and nudged him with my foot. He groaned.

Did his eyes flicker?

The moment I glanced down at my friend the swordsman advanced. I drew the bow the final few fingerbreadths I needed to get the arrow through his armour.

The bow snapped.

"Dead gods," I cursed as the thing jumped out of my hands, stinging my fingertips and leaving them numb.

"You should have run, boy," laughed the swordsman. "Just go. Leave him. We don't expect mage-bent to fight real men."

I could run. My cover would stay intact if I did.

But Rufra was unconscious. He would not see what happened here.

And he was my friend.

I drew my blades.

"If you want him, come and get him."

The warrior shook his head. "Well, you've had your chance, cripple, and you have chosen to be pig food."

I wanted to curse Rufra for falling in the centre of the clearing rather than somewhere more tactically useful. Three of the men were using the traditional long and short sword, one held a large shield and a stabsword. My skills were in close work. I had no doubt that one on one with paired swords I could take any of them. But four on one was a different matter. They could circle me and keep feinting until

I tired. Then, while one distracted me, another would take me from behind. It would only be a matter of time.

Their leader began with a thrust of his longsword. It was an obvious feint as his blade could not reach me. All my instincts said to ignore it as he only tested me but instead I swung wildly, like the novice I was meant to be. He laughed again.

"Not much of a swordsman, are you, boy?"

I lifted my head and tried to appear like a boy faking confidence. "I have trained to wield a blade. I am a squire of Maniyadoc."

"Trained, have you?" His friends chuckled around me. "How long for, an hour?" He feinted again and I swung wildly in return.

"I have had over a week of training at the hands of Squiremaster Nywulf," I said.

"A week?" He laughed and gave a subtle nod at the two swordsmen behind me. "Well, we'd best be careful of you then, eh?"

He feinted again. I did not move this time as I had seen his signal to the men behind me. The two ran in to finish me and I spun on the spot then began to fall, making it look like I stumbled on my club foot. Their swords came up and I turned my fall into the twelfth iteration, the Fool's Tumble. As I fell, I threw my longsword at the man on my right, tangling and cutting his legs. The tumble took me under the blade of the man coming from my left and I came up into a crouch. My extended stabsword hooked under his chain kilt and took the man in the groin, severing the artery. He dropped his blades. I pushed him away and grabbed his stabsword from the ground, turning to send it through the air and into the throat of the second warrior as he untangled himself from my longsword.

The two remaining men did not move as I walked over to retrieve my longsword and then back to Rufra. I stuck the long blade in the ground by my unconscious friend and picked up one of the fallen stabsword belonging to the men I had killed.

"Maybe it was two weeks training with the blade," I said. "You know how time flies when you are doing something you enjoy." Behind me a man wept as his blood pulsed from his body. I lowered my voice and pointed my blade at the leader of the men. "You should run," I said. He knew he should. I had shed Girton ap Gwynr like a wet cloak and there was no concealing how dangerous the assassin, Girton Club-Foot, was.

He rushed me. A foolish move that showed his lack of real skill. He came in trailing his longsword for a big swing and gambling everything on it. As his arm came round I danced with him and was as disappointed as anyone who loved their art could be when confronted with a clumsy partner. *First iteration: the Precise Steps*. One step, two step, and I was within his reach. *Eighth iteration: The Placing of the Rose*. With an upward thrust I drove my blade through the bottom of his jaw and into his brain. Using the remaining momentum of his charge I spun him on the spot and threw his body at the man with the shield who was coming at me from the other side. He did what comes naturally when an object is thrown at you and used his shield to push the body away. Unfortunately for him, the body also hid my actions – *the Speed-that-Defies-the-Eye* – and when he exposed himself I was there. He was unhelmeted and I slashed my blade across his eyes, blinding him.

He screamed. And he kept screaming as I returned to Rufra. My friend's breathing had changed. It seemed faster, almost as if he was frightened. I did not know what that meant though I knew head wounds could be bad. I hoped he was not dying.

I faded out the screaming of the blinded man while I tried to think. I could not help Rufra. I carried no medical supplies and he was too heavy to carry in his armour. Rufra's long-sword lay on the ground and his stabsword was still in his limp hand. It was a terrible weapon, all rusted and nicked. As was the longsword, which was barely bloodied, but the blades gave me an idea. I took his longsword and returned to the blinded man.

"Quiet," I hissed and placed Rufra's blade against the man's throat. "Who sent you?"

"Garim," he choked out. "Dead gods, you have blinded me! How will I feed my children? You have blinded me."

"I said be quiet." I pushed the sword harder against his neck. "Answer my questions if you want to live." He swallowed and nodded. "Who is Garim and why did he want my friend dead?"

"Garim is who leads us. You killed him. As to the rest. I only know someone at the castle paid him. I just do what I'm—"

He knew nothing. I cut his throat before he finished speaking and then made sure Rufra's sword was covered in blood and returned to the man I had shot with my bow. I cut the arrow out of his eye and thrust the blade into the wound. Then placed Rufra's bloodied longsword in my friend's empty hand. If he lived I hoped his head wound would make his memories of the attack hazy. Faced with no other option he would have to believe he had fought off all of his attackers before giving in to unconsciousness.

That done I returned to Xus, mounted and concentrated on becoming Girton ap Gwynr again. As the adrenaline drained from me I realised how dangerous what I had done was. Though it felt as if I had trained for it all my life I had never fought without the knowledge my master was at my back, ready to defend me. And today I had fought five and the killing had been easy. I had been ruthless and it had shocked me, but I had also enjoyed it. I had never really thought of myself as a warrior before, only as an assassin, someone who slunk in silently, avoiding conflict whenever possible. When the shaking started I realised that somewhere, deep inside, I was as shocked by what I had done as the fictional Girton ap Gwynr would have been.

Chapter 20

I threw Xus into a run. Smoke rose above Calfey, and the wind brought with it the whoops of warriors and the screams of the dying. A scruffy mount with short antlers ran past me, dragging the corpse of its rider behind it and leaving a trail of red on the stones of the path. On the far side of the village I saw a group of six raiders being pursued by Tomas and his small squad, whipping their mounts and riding as fast as they could for the village. As the raiders approached Calfey, a volley of arrows brought their front three down and the second rank rode into them, their mounts falling and spilling raiders to the ground. Tomas brought his group to a halt and they dismounted to go about the work of finishing the wounded; they showed no mercy, and I heard them laughing as I drove Xus into the the village.

Calfey was small, only a few dozen houses surrounded by a fence of dried thorn bushes, and as I entered Xus lowered his antlers in response to the presence of death. Bodies lay everywhere, some in armour and some not; men and women ran hither and thither in panic. A child ran past, screaming, and I turned to find the raider he fled from, but instead saw Borniya, his bow drawn and aimed at the child.

As Xus and I came between them he grinned.

"Duck, mage-bent," he shouted and loosed his arrow. I pulled on Xus's rein, bringing him sliding to a stop as the arrow shot over my head. I had to fight to keep my balance in the saddle. At the moment I thought I was safe a mount side-swiped me. If Xus had not moved, swinging about to face the threat with his antlers down and a high-pitched hiss, my leg would have been smashed between the two animals. As it was I fell from his back into the mud. Xus stood at bay above me, trained to protect his rider he would not move. He spat and hissed at Borniya and Hallin as they circled me on their twin black mounts.

"You could have killed me," I said, pulling myself up.

Borniya laughed.

"You're a mage-bent country boy, not a Rider. You fell because that beast is too much for you." Xus let out a low growl as Borniya and Hallin walked their mounts around us.

"A real Rider wouldn't be baiting me when there are raiders to fight."

"They're dealt with, mage-bent," said Borniya. "Now we're just clearing up the dregs." His mount continued to circle and I had to turn to follow him. Hallin rode opposite him, running his thumb along the back of the little knife he was so fond of hurting people with.

"Rufra is hurt," I said.

"Dead?"

"No."

"That's unfortunate." Hallin laughed. Behind them men, women and children were lined up against the lumpy mud and wicker walls of the village hall. Aydor was telling some of his troop to get their bows ready. Tomas stood off to one side, watching.

"You need to help Rufra," I said. "Remember what Nywulf said about us—"

"We have to deal with the traitors first," said Borniya. He pointed at the villagers lined up against the wall. Aydor was driving his mount backwards and forwards shouting, "Treason!" and "Death!" He was a fool with his blood up; the people against the walls were not warriors.

"They are only villagers," I said.

"Villagers who were harbouring raiders."

"They were being attacked by raiders, not harbouring them."

"Or that is what they want us to think," said Borniya. "Maybe it is what you want us to think also? Are you a traitor, Girton ap Gwynr? Dark Ungar knows, the heir would be pleased if you had an accident." Behind him Hallin had put away his knife and was stringing an arrow to his bow. "Maybe you attacked Rufra in the wood?"

"No!"

"Most would believe it. There's something of the yellower in you, you're a bringer of misfortune. Especially to Kyril." I saw in the eyes of these two boys, almost men, an implacable hatred I did not understand. Aydor I understood. He was weak, a bully and eager to throw his weight around because he knew I could not fight back, and in some way he saw my friendship with Rufra as a threat. But these two were different: I was sure they would kill me quite happily, partly to curry favour with Aydor but mostly because they would enjoy it. They were the sort of people my master delighted in ending. I reached for the blades at my hip and Borniya grinned.

"Got a bit of fight in you then, mage-bent?"

"What is happening here?"

The sudden interruption made me jump, and both Borniya and Hallin turned at the shout to see Aydor wheeling his mount and coming face to face with Nwyulf.

"These people are traitors – they attacked us," said Aydor. "The penalty for treason is death."

"Did you announce yourselves?"

"What?"

"Coil the Yellower's piss," hissed Nywulf. "Did you announce yourselves?"

"We carry the bonemount," said Aydor.

Nywulf looked along the line of squires. "You carry the bonemount, Aydor; the rest carry nothing and these villagers are not soldiers, alert to the signs of who is who. One armoured man looks like any other to them. Do you think I told you not to enter the village for my own amusement?"

"Well," began a squire. "Aydor said—"

"Aydor has made a mistake," said Nywulf. "As you are all here, let us discuss tactical failures and . . ." His voice tailed off. "Where is Rufra?" He looked to me but Aydor replied:

"He ran away."

"Like a coward," added Hallin.

"Heir, you ordered—" began Celot, but Aydor cut him off.

"Quiet, fool."

"He's in the wood," I said, pulling myself up into Xus's saddle. "He rode after a swordsman who cut a young boy down. I followed but lost him."

Nywulf went pale and turned to Aydor and his squires. If I had been Aydor I would have been frightened. "Let these people go," said Nywulf in a voice full of barely restrained anger. "You let one of your number ride off alone, Aydor? Did you not hear a word I said about working together?" Even Aydor had the good sense to look ashamed. "You are not fit to command sheep never mind men." Nywulf turned to Celot. "You will take charge, find Rufra and bring him back to me." Celot gave Nywulf a solemn salute and spurred his mount. Nywulf stared at the other squires. "Well? Why are you still here? Follow Celot." They set off at a gallop.

As I was about to join them Nywulf placed his mount in front of mine.

"Does he live?" he asked.

"Sorry?"

"Don't play games. Does Rufra live?" He was staring at me but not at my face; he was looking into my eyes the way a warrior does when he is about to fight. His hand was on his sword hilt. His eyes flicked down to my armour. I glanced down to see a spray of blood, arterial bright, across the many-coloured plates that protected my chest. It became harder to breathe. Air struggled in and out of my chest. Nywulf knew. He knew what I was.

"Rufra is very skilled," I said. "I doubt there was anything in the wood that he could not deal with."

"Then why isn't he here?"

"Few could fight multiple opponents without taking some wound."

Nywulf's knuckles whitened on his blade hilt.

"But he lives?"

I nodded, and then chose my words carefully, unwilling to give anything away.

"The last time I saw him he was alive. No one else was."

Nywulf nodded slowly and when he spoke his voice was as threatening as the clouds that herald the great storms of yearsbirth. "Ride to the castle, Girton. Have the healers be ready and pray that Rufra still lives. For your sake if for nothing else."

I rode Xus as fast as he would go for the castle, sliding off his back and shoving the reins into Drusl's hands when I reached the stable.

"Rufra's hurt," I said, my breath coming in gasps. "I must get to the healers. Then I ran for the keepyard gate shouting for a healer. Minutes later five mounted healers galloped out of the gate with their long grey robes flapping about them. Half an hour later I watched Nywulf ride in followed by the healers and Rufra, slack as baggage, on his saddle. He looked like a child, exhausted after a day's riding, sleeping in the arms of his parent . From the stricken look on Nywulf's face I wondered what his relationship really was with my friend – it was clearly far more than trainer and pupil. More grey-robed healers fell into step behind Nywulf's mount. I was about to follow when a hand stopped me.

"What happened, Girton?"

My master, clothed in the shadow of the gate. She pulled me back into the empty guardroom.

"Raiders attacked Calfey. Rufra chased one into the wood, and it was a trap. I saved him."

"He saw you fight?"

"No. He was unconscious, but I am sure Nywulf knows what I am."

"He said so?"

"Not as such. It was more what he didn't say."

She leaned back against the wall and sighed. "Well, he has said nothing so far, and outside of killing Nywulf – and from the way he moves I am not sure that is something I wish to try – there is little we can do. You said it was a trap?"

"Yes, men waited in the wood. Rufra killed three before he was struck down. I killed the rest, but I left no sign and bloodied Rufra's weapons so he will think he finished them."

She leaned in close to me.

"You should have let him die," she whispered.

"He is my friend."

"If what we are is revealed we become worthless to Adran, and she is ruthless."

"He was unconscious, Master, and a strike to the head can often affect the memory. Besides, the other squires will think he took on seven men alone and prevailed. It will win him respect. Even if he saw me, he'd not be fool enough to throw that away."

"You hope."

"I hope."

She bunched her hands into fists and for a moment I thought she was going to scream at me. Then she unbunched her fists and let out a breath. "What's done is done, Girton. The queen will want to know what happened."

"Her son happened."

"Aydor?"

"Yes, or maybe Tomas. The last attacker told me someone in the castle set this up. It is almost a mirror of the fiction Adran constructed to cover Kyril's death."

"Give me details," she said, and I reeled off an account of the attack and the events leading up to it. "Aydor or Tomas would make sense as no true assassin would do this. Half of Calfey is dead in attempt to accomplish it, and that requires the sort of callousness the blessed excel in." She spat on the floor. "To sacrifice a village to kill one boy. Madness."

"It was not just for Rufra; the raiders must have planned to take cows as well. Tomas intercepted them before they could and they rode back to Calfey."

"They never planned to take cows, Girton. Your friend was the target."

"Why do you say that?"

"Those raiders who headed back to Calfey chased by Tomas. Why would they do that?"

"To collect their fellows."

"Their fellows who attacked a village, presumably as a decoy to draw the squires away from the cows? Why run towards more enemy if you knew they were there?"

"I—"

"Because they thought they were safe to do so, Girton. They thought they would be allowed to escape."

"Why would they think that?"

"Because someone told them it was so."

"Aydor."

"Most likely." She looked at the floor.

"He wanted to kill the remaining villagers, said they were traitors."

"Probably worried there were bandits in among them who may give him away."

My hand went to the blade at my hip. "I will—"

"Do nothing," she said, grabbing my arm. "Nothing, do you understand? Aydor may have been responsible but he may not, Tomas is important too. And what do you think will happen to us if you confront Aydor? Or kill him?"

There was a moment, a passing of time, where the muscles of my arm fought her grip, and then I relaxed and let go of my anger.

"Very well," I said. But I would not look at her, and I could tell it caused her pain.

"If you would do something, Girton, try and find out why Aydor, or Tomas, would want your friend dead so desperately. That may lead us somewhere. And why did Nywulf allow himself to be split from his squires?"

"He was called away, by Neander."

"Neander? But he is Rufra's father – it makes no sense for him to help in such a scheme."

"Unless Rufra is an embarrassment to him, as a celibate priest."

"No. I have heard Neander joke about his lust for women with the queen. He has no shame."

"Master," I hissed, "we should put an end this dynasty now. Aydor is a beast, his mother too. If we do not act there will be a thousand Calfeys across Maniyadoc."

"I cannot do that, Girton."

"Why?"

"Because there are old debts in play here, debts that can never be repaid."

"Debts? What debts?"

"Once, long ago –" her voice was barely audible "– a thankful girl found a rich merchant's daughter on the edge

of death. She dragged her to a healer even though the
merchant's daughter wanted nothing but Xus's touch."

"So?" I said. "You saved Adran once. It does not make
you responsible for her now."

"No, Girton," whispered my master. She stood and lifted
her tunic to show me the twisting, wiry scar that ran across
her belly. "It was Adran that was born thankful, not I." I
did not know what to say, and she did not give me time to
reply. Instead she grabbed my shoulders, spun me round and
pushed me towards the hole where there had once been a
door. "Now go to your friend. Leave me to consider if there
is any way out of this castle which doesn't involve us ending
up in the swillers' yard."

I walked away, but what she had said preyed on me. The
thought of my master being beholden to the queen, and
worse, to hear her speak openly about being young, helpless
and on the point of death sent an almost physical shock
through me. She was strong and she always had been strong.
To find out she had been as weak and fallible as any other
human was to have the rock my world was built on crack
down the centre.

I tried to see Rufra but the healers' servants would not
let me in. They would only tell me that he seemed well and
no permanent damage was done before shooing me away,
saying he needed to rest. At a loss, I let my feet take me
where they would. First I wandered around the castle,
listening while the water clock tolled off half-hours and
hoping that Rufra would leave his room and I could see him.
When it became obvious he would not I slowly made my
way out of the castle. I could not shake an uncomfortable
sick feeling within me that I had made a terrible mistake in
the wood, but what else could I have done?

Eventually, I found myself in the townyard. I could not
get near Festival because of the cows coming into the courtyard, and I swear it was not by design but I found myself

at the stables. I could not tell Drusl why I felt so terrible, but maybe her presence would assuage the dull pain clinging to me.

I heard screaming.

I ran.

Chapter 21

There is a very particular noise a human makes when confronted with unexpected death. A certain constriction of the throat made by the animal buried deep within us when it is forced to confront its own mortality.

It is a sound I know well.

I ran for the stables as fast as my lopsided run allowed, coughing my way through the dust thrown up by cows, my feet sliding on slippery cow shit as I called out Drusl's name. Others were running too. I saw Heamus, his scratched armour jingling as he ran, and although the old Landsman had two good feet to my one he was no match for the speed and strength of youth.

I entered the stables first.

The air was thick with the scents of pepper and honey. Drusl stood in the middle of the clear area between the stalls, rooted to the spot and with her hands over her face like a statue of Adallada mourning her consort, Dallad. About ten paces in front of her lay Leiss, dead. His clothes lay open and an ugly black welt ran along his flesh from shoulder to hip. The walls of the stable block pulsed in time with my heart. Then Drusl was in my arms and pushing her face into the place between my ear and my shoulder. Hot tears ran down my neck.

"He's dead, Girton," she sobbed. "Leiss is dead."

"What happened?" Before she could reply Heamus interrupted. His words barely more than a grey whisper.

"Dead gods in their graves beneath the water, it is the

black whip." Drusl must have felt my body stiffen against her. The black whip was a weapon of sorcerers and at its mention Drusl sobbed harder into my neck. I heard Heamus roaring at the people gathering outside the stable, "Away, all of you! Get away! Someone bring the queen's guard!" The huge doors were shut and we were lit only by the amber sunlight filtering through the panes of crystal set into the roof far above. Gentle arms separated us and then Heamus was stooping so he could look into Drusl's eyes. He took a rag from beneath his armour and gently wiped her face, reminding me of a doting father. He moved strangely slowly. "Drusl," he said, "did you see who did this? If you saw who did this, you must tell me. Did they leave through the back?" He spoke slowly, emphasising each word to break through her shock. "Do you hear my words, girl? You must tell Girton and I what you saw. Did Leiss's attacker leave through the back?"

She nodded slowly and wiped more tears away with her arm. "I was in a stall with Bal, telling it its companion would not return. When I came out, Leiss was shouting at . . . shouting at someone stood at the far end. Near the door to the dung presses. Then he – Leiss, I mean – was dead and the one who did it ran away."

"Did you see his face or was he cowled?" said Heamus.

"Yes," she stuttered, "he was cowled."

"Girton!" shouted Heamus. "Why are you still here? Did you not hear the girl? Leiss's killer went out the back. Follow him, boy!"

"Yes," I said. Then I was running, the door to the tackle room flying open from a hard push. I climbed the dung press to get to the high windows, action clearing my mind.

From the top of the press I could see the sorcerer had chosen a perfect place for his murder. The spilled mount urine from the presses masked any sign of magic, so there was no telltale ring of death to show it had been used.

Outside the window the bales of hay provided a convenient way down. My heart thumped in my chest as I descended. Every time I dropped a level I expected the black whip to reach out and wrap its sharp coils around me. As I neared the ground my heart froze. A cowled figure slipped into one of the many arched doorways cut into the townwall. I had explored the area around the stables in my free time and knew that the inner wall had collapsed and, though it looked like it should be filled with rooms, few of the doorways in this area led anywhere. Most were nothing but short tunnels ending in rubble and fallen blocks. I made my way carefully down the last few bales, all the time keeping the door the sorcerer had gone into in sight. My blades were back in my room and I had nothing more than my eating knife to use as a weapon. However, if I could remain unseen then even a small knife, coupled with the element of surprise, may be enough.

I hugged the outer wall to make my body as flat as I could while I inched towards the doorway in the wall. Every moment I expected the sorcerer to appear and strike me down but I quickly found myself against the lip of shaped stones that framed the doorway.

My breathing seemed impossibly loud and gave me an idea. Silence was usually my ally, but not here. Now my best hope was to make a lot of noise and hope it surprised him enough to stop him doing whatever he did to rip magic out of the land.

I raised my knife and, with a scream, threw myself around the corner. The knife came down. The cowled figure grabbed my wrist with one hand and my throat with the other then, using his hip, threw me to the ground. Before I had time to gather myself I was pinned down and my own knife was at my throat.

"Girton," said my master. I could hear amusement in her voice. "Have you forgotten everything I ever taught you?"

"Master? I did not think it would be you."

"Obviously." She loosened her grip on my throat and sat back on her haunches, offering me my knife. "Now what was that about?"

"Leiss is dead – a line across his body that almost cut him in half." I levered myself up to a sitting position and took the offered knife.

"The black whip."

"Heamus said as much before he sent me off. Drusl said a cowled figure fled through the back of the stables and—"

"And when you saw me, you thought you had caught this sorcerer?"

"Aye."

"Well you were brave, if foolish, to attack." She pulled her cowl off and let her hair free. "Best I make sure no one else makes your mistake."

"Will Heamus call the Landsmen in now? He is honour bound to—"

"Heamus will not say a word," she said quietly. "When a Landsman is too old to carry out his duties he is meant to spill his lifeblood into the sourlands. Heamus should be dead by all rights. They will overlook him as long as he is out of sight, but if they came here he'd be clapped in irons and taken to join the desolate."

"Oh," I said, then added, "but why did he have those things in his drawer?" I suppressed a shudder at the thought of the symbols I had seen in his quarters.

"Maybe they are just to remind him of what he was."

We sat quietly. Talk of magic was making me uncomfortable, which in turn was making me sullen and angry. Leiss's death was a vivid reminder of what dwelt within me. And her.

"Master," I asked quietly, "why are you here and not guarding the queen?"

"Are you suspicious of me, Girton?"

"Never, Master."

"Never say never. You do not know what fate will bring." She sounded terribly sad, and my anger became mixed with guilt. "And to answer your question, Adran gave me the afternoon off. She has locked herself in a room with her son and Neander. Celot guards them." She balled up the material of her cowl. "As to why I am here, first I went to retrieve your climbing foot from the courtyard – I hid it under your bed. Then I came here to tell you so you did not panic when you could not find it, if you thought about looking for it. I thought it likely you were in the stables." She smiled at me and I blushed. "However, as it seems we have had another death, perhaps I should take the opportunity to look around."

"Heamus will think it odd if a jest—"

"No." She dipped into the bag she carried and took from it one of the white masks used by priests' acolytes. "Black robe, white mask. Heamus will accept my presence." She slipped her cowl back on.

"But what if the actual—"

"Don't worry. You go back through the window, and I will go round the front. And Girton?"

"Yes, Master?"

"Be careful of Heamus."

"Heamus? But why? I thought you had decided he was no longer a Landsman."

"Think about it." She stood and wiped dirt from her black trousers.

"He knows about magic?" I said.

"Partly, but more than that. Heamus is trained to fight sorcerers and magic users. Why does he send Girton ap Gwynr, a boy he thinks is barely able to lift a sword without tripping over it, to chase a sorcerer?"

"Oh," I said.

"Oh indeed."

I climbed back up the bales of hay, into the tackle room

and down the giant dung presses. As I opened the door the fragrant atmosphere of the stable wrapped itself around me and the world moved infinitesimally more slowly, giving those within a grace they would not have had otherwise. My master entered swathed in black cloth that moved strangely around her, as if it had its own mind. Rather than an acolyte she had come as a wandering priest of Xus. As I walked to the front of the stable I thought it was amazing how well she aped the priest I had seen around the castle. Her mannerisms, her step — everything about her was the same. I began to speak in the Whisper-That-Flies-to-the-Ear.

"Master—"

She silenced me using a finger on my lips and her body to block me from the sight of those in the main room of the barn. Then she walked away with her head down while I realised, with a feeling like sinking into icy water, how stupid I had been to use magic right in front of an old Landsman. I told myself I hated magic but had used it without thinking. I had a sudden flash of images — blood gibbets and the desolate, the gruesome ends that awaited a magic user.

The air shimmered. My skin became hot. A black sea shivered within.

I threw up. One second I stood, the next I was on my knees, spitting up the contents of my stomach and grimacing at the sour taste of bile.

"Do not worry, boy," said Heamus. He clapped me on the back. "Yours is often the reaction to a great shock such as death. And to a death like this?" He helped me up gently, using my elbow. He seemed to be speaking to me from very far away and I had to fight not to shake him off because his hands dripped with blood — though as soon as I noticed the blood it began to fade away. "Magic is never pleasant to be around," he said and then leaned in close. "Tell no one of this death, Girton," he whispered, his words were blue and icy as they sank into my skin. "We will sort this out ourselves.

Castles have fallen for less and there are those within
Maniyadoc who would use this misfortune for their own
ends." I nodded, looking for all the world like I was shocked
by the death of Leiss when instead I was disorientated by
the way the world around me was throbbing. "Did you find
anything outside the stables?"

"No, Heamus," I said. My voice was no louder than a
breeze and it wound its way around Heamus like a vine. I
glanced at the old Landsman's hands. No blood. Why did I
feel so strange?

"Well, at least you tried, boy."

Behind Heamus my master was crouched over Leiss's body.
She plucked at his wound then stood and walked away,
leaving a slowly fading after-image of a black-clad figure
staring at Heamus from within a mocking mask. I watched
all this through a haze as if the barn were full of woodsmoke.
What was happening? I thought I had almost come to terms
with the idea of magic but now, as my master stared at me
from the door to the pressing room, I felt like I was coming
apart.

Then there was a human warmth. An unexpected touch.
Fingers wormed themselves between mine to clasp my hand.
I turned. Drusl, tear-stained and desperate.

"Leiss did not deserve what happened," she said, her voice
hoarse, her eyes looking into a place past me and the walls
of the stable. "He was not a good man, not really. Nor even
a nice one, as I had believed. But he did not deserve to die
this way." Her misery was utter. It was often the way people
reacted to death, with guilt. To be the one who survives is
its own sort of curse. Her pain was a halo of green and blue.

"Not your fault," I stuttered out, and I wondered how
long it would be before it was me who caused such misery.
The sea within me was shifting again, swelling and growing.
Images filled my mind – it became me who had murdered
Leiss with the black whip and me who killed the land and

the people around me with a wave of my hand. Then I was not thinking any more. Drusl was in my arms, and we were both sobbing: her for the death of a man she had never liked and me for the death of a boy I had never been.

I do not know how long it was before we were separated. Not long, it felt like minutes at most. A slave stood by us. He stood in that patient way slaves do. Happy to stand waiting because it was the nearest he ever had to free time.

"Girton ap Gwynr?" he asked.

I nodded, wiping tears and mucus from my face. Night had crept in. Leiss's body was gone, and the stable torches were being lit by another slave. It all seemed so very normal.

"You are wanted at the castle. Follow me, please, Blessed."

I followed the slave up to and through the castle. Nausea kept rising as the magic I held inside made itself known. I could not shake the feeling I walked through water, not air. We reached the door to the room I shared with my master. I did not want to go in. I had pushed away what I was but events in the stable had brought it back, and the strange woozy feeling had brought anger back with it. What could she say to me? Sorry again? *Leiss flayed open before me.* Sorry that my life had been a lie? That I was a monster just like the creature that had killed Leiss?

But if I did not go in, she would only find me.

My master sat on the bed, her make-up badly removed, leaving streaks of grey where the black and white paint had mixed. She looked as though she was suffering, her flesh dying, and her only wish was for Xus to embrace her.

"Girton," she said. "What happened to you in the barn? You would not answer me or Heamus when we spoke to you. He put it down to young people in love but I am not so sure."

"I . . ." I began and anger twisted within me like cramp. "I saw blood on his hands and smoke in the air. The idea of . . . The thought of . . ." I found I could not finish the sentence. I heard the king's voice in my mind: *Fields and grasslands it was, all of it. In yearsbirth it would be mottled red and blue with flowers and in yearslife it would turn golden with ripening corn.*

"The thought of magic?" she asked.

"Yes."

She stared past me at the wall then ran a hand through her hair.

People left their families and travelled from all over the Tired Lands, so strong was the horror at another sorcerer having risen.

"Sometimes, Girton, those who are particularly gifted –" she paused and gave me a small smile "– are affected by places where powerful magic has recently been performed."

It seemed as though the world took a breath. And then . . . and then the colour was taken from it.

"So I am not just cursed by magic. I am twice cursed to be good at it?"

She sat very still and spoke very quietly.

"Listen to me. It is very important you listen to me now. There are things I thought we would have time for but what is within you rises like a flood. I can feel it. The magic wants to be used."

. . . trees melted. They sucked in their leaves and stalks and branches, leaving only bare trunks pointing at a yellow sky that stretched out as far as I could see.

"You said it was like a tool!" I roared the words. And then she was in front of me, her hand over my mouth.

"Keep your voice down!" she hissed.

He ripped the land apart, ended five thousand lives and created a souring forty miles wide.

"I would be better off dead."

"Never," she said, and for a moment I thought she would hold me to her again but she saw the fire in my eyes and didn't, though maybe she should have. "Never better off dead, Girton. Say that neither in jest nor anger." She sat back on the bed. "Do you remember when you first held a blade and I told you how you must be aware of it at all times or you would cut yourself?" I nodded sullenly. "Well the magic is like that. You must be aware of it and it will fight your awareness." She changed tack. "Think of it like Xus or any strong-willed mount. It seeks to be master until you have shown it you are stronger. It is not clever; it has only force and simple guile."

"Is it the same for all of us?" I asked quietly.

Ten of the men around me died without a sound.

"Some of us," she said. But she did not look at me.

"You?"

"I fought it when I found out."

"Did you hate yourself for it?"

"I already hated myself, Girton, but the magic did not help."

A tear ran down her face and I felt like a cruel boy poking a sick animal with a stick. Still I spoke on.

"Why did you hate yourself?"

"Because I had been foolish." Another tear. "There was a man, a child that died before I could give it life."

"And Adran?"

"I needed someone and she was there. Will it make you hurt less, Girton, if I open these old wounds for you?"

I cut down the Black Sorcerer myself. He was young, terrified. Not only of the death I was bringing but of what he had done.

Like snow, silence settled between us, and like snow, my anger began to thaw.

"No," I said. "It will not."

"You have a great burden, Girton —" she stared into my eyes "— but, if you will let me, I will lend you my strength so it does not break your back." She squeezed my hand and stood. "I will leave you to think," she said, and slid out of the door.

I scraped frustrated tears from my face with the scratchy

wool of my sleeves while wishing fervently I could be someone else. Soured, that was the only way I could describe the way I felt, and the pain was too much. I could not see any escape. I thought of what the king had said about the Black Sorcerer, how terrible he had made him sound and how sure he had been there was only one answer to the problem of magic. My hand found the hilt of my eating blade and at the same moment something fell from the loose sheathe that held my knife. A little bit of paper, and on it was written something that changed everything. It changed it immediately and completely.

Girton
  At ten bells I shall be in the eaves.
  Please come. Please.
  D

When had she put that there? Was it before or after the death of Leiss? I was sure it could only be after, but the day was so mixed up in my mind. She needed me. I had to go, and though I could not tell her the truth, that did not matter. To be with her, to feel her hand in mine would be enough. I knew that if Drusl met me in the eaves and we were together then everything else would cease to matter, just as it had when she held me in the stables. I longed for the silence of the mind that only she could give me.

In the eaves of the castle it was so dark I could not see my own hand in front of my face. I recognised Drusl by the sound of her breathing. Her presence and the darkness and heat numbed my mind. It did not drive away the worry or confusion but made it bearable.

"Drusl," I whispered.

"Girton," she said. I felt her hands touch my shoulders, her lips brush mine. "I want to forget, Girton. I want there to be only you and I in the Tired Lands tonight."

All the heat from the castle's fires collected in the eaves. When she pulled at my buttons and my clothes slid off, the shiver that ran through me was not from the cold. Together, in that dark place, we left behind the trouble and turmoil of the castle and ventured into soft lands neither of us had travelled before.

Chapter 22

I had not expected to sleep but calm descended on me after my time with Drusl. We had parted in a mist of contentment that left me warm in a way I had never been before. It was a warmth that stilled the wine-dark sea inside me. My eventual sleep was deep and dreamless and lasted long past the hour I would usually wake.

I rushed to the squireyard, struggling into my harlequin armour. Thoughts of magic were once again locked behind a door in my mind. When I entered the squireyard something had changed. The two groups, which had previously been so tight, no longer appeared so close.

Rufra stood by the racks of wooden swords with his back to me. A bandage was wrapped around his head and occasionally he rotated the joint of his shoulder as he inspected the swords. When he chose a pair he made some practice swings and thrusts – whatever damage the crossbow bolt had done had clearly been superficial.

Boros approached him.

"Is it true, Rufra?" he said.

"Is what true?" Rufra sounded belligerent, distrustful.

"That you killed seven men single-handed?"

"I doubt it," said Aydor. "He probably had help." He glanced at me.

"It sounds like a fine feat of arms," said Celot guilelessly.

Aydor swatted at him with a glove.

"Be quiet, fool."

"It is if it's true. Is it true, Rufra?" said Boros again, quietly.

Rufra looked at the dirt and drew a line in it with the tip of his wooden longsword.

"Seven died," he said quietly. He flicked a stone away from his feet with the tip of his blade and it skittered across the compacted earth of the squireyard. "Luck played its part, and they were not men well trained for battle. But there were seven and when I woke they were dead and my blades were wet with blood." Then he shot me an unfriendly glance and I knew he had not been unconscious when I killed those men. My feet became leaden and I slowed to a stop.

"I would partner you in sparing, if you will," said Boros. Tomas gave him such a venomous look that if I had been Boros I would have worn my armour day and night from then on. Strangely, Barin gave his twin a similarly vehement glance.

"I would also like to fight with you," said another squire, one of Aydor's, stepping forward.

"And I," said another. I wondered at these boys who were so quick to change their allegiance. Possibly I did them a disservice. Maybe they had always been uncomfortable serving Aydor and Tomas and had only needed an excuse to get away; Rufra's skill and the events in Calfey had provided it. Nywulf watched the boys, his arms crossed and a faint smile on his face. I wanted Rufra to turn them down and say he would spar with me. He should have done. He only had their respect because I had won it for him.

"It seems like you'll be too busy to give me any more training, Rufra." I forced a laugh.

He caught my eye and looked away.

"Yes," he said. Then headed towards the centre of the training ground as if I had ceased to exist.

"Rufra?"

"He has real swordsmen to practise with now," said Boros.

"I don't think you're needed, mage-bent. If he spars with you any more he may get worse rather than better."

I ignored him and chased after Rufra.

"Rufra," I said, grabbing him by his arm, "we are friends. No matter what. You said that."

"I have new friends now," he said. "Friends I can trust." There was no emotion in his voice and it took long seconds for his words, and the fact he was cutting me off, to sink in.

"But we are friends," I said again. I heard a laugh. Someone, Hallin I think, said, "Poor little cripple." I longed to lash out – my arms shook with tension – but this was not an enemy I could fight. I was helpless in the face of Rufra's sudden indifference.

In the back of my mind lurked a shadow that promised it could help.

"I need to practise," said Rufra. He pointed with his stabsword at the straw-filled dummies we used to practise thrusts and swings on. "If it's worth you bothering, the beginner's mannequins are over there." He turned from me. Without even asking for my side and at the first sniff of a change in his fortunes Rufra had dropped me like a bad pear.

"If I am to practise alone," I shouted after him, "I may as well do it somewhere I am welcome." Rufra did not turn but Boros did.

"Good luck finding somewhere, country boy," he shouted and turned away, enveloped in a cloud of laughter. Even Tomas and Aydor smiled at his wit and suddenly there were tears in my eyes. I walked away, my face and hands burning with shame at being so easily used.

Drusl was the only one I could trust.

Betrayal was an entirely new experience for me. I wanted to run to Drusl and lose myself in and with her, as I had the night before, but I knew if I did then everything was likely to come pouring out — who I was, why I was here and how badly Rufra had treated me after I had saved him. Then I would be a betrayer of confidences also. I told myself, with all the haughty pride of hurt youth, that I would not stoop to Rufra's level. I would at least retain my dignity. With nowhere and no one to turn to I did the only thing that was left to me — I returned to our room, removed my armour and I went to find somewhere dark and quiet to feel sorry for myself while thoughts of magic and betrayal whirled in my mind, the distance from cocksure assassin to heartbroken child crossed in a few short steps across the squireyard.

It was twilight before I brought myself under control. Rather than head back to our room and have to look at my master's face I decided to go to Festival. There I would have one drink, despite her warnings. It seemed like a good idea then.

Drink was cheap at Festival. I bought a cup of thick fruit juice that burned my throat as it went down and went straight to my head. A fire breather handed me a cup of drink as she passed, wishing me good cheer and saying that a drink and a smile would free me from Black Ungar's grasp. I had promised myself only a single cup, but her good cheer made me so angry I knocked the drink back in one and made a point of refusing to smile for her. Whatever she had given me made me choke and the fire breather laughed at me, which only increased my irritation. I turned away and almost knocked over a masked woman selling a barley brew, and she would only accept my apology if I bought a drink. Which I did, and drank it because my master had always said I should waste nothing. From then on I barely saw Festival as I walked through it, mumbling and fuming to myself. More drinks seemed to materialise in my hands. Could Rufra sense the magic in me? Is that what made him want to get away? Maybe all the squires could sense it, and that was why they hated me.

I walked through the noise and light, muttering to myself about people of bad faith and the different, and increasingly painful, ways I should kill them. I was so lost in alcohol and thoughts of the pain I would inflict that when the attack came it took me entirely by surprise. An arm shot out of a tent and snaked around my neck. Sober, I would have wriggled away or broken the fingers of whoever grabbed me, but drink had fuddled me. My body had become every bit as clumsy and hopeless as I spent my days pretending it was. The arm dragged me into a tent, a blade was held at my throat.

"I know what you are," hissed a voice. Then I was thrown into a corner of the tent. Rufra stood with his bent and nicked longsword pointed at me. "Don't move, Girton, if that's your name," he said, breath coming quickly. "Don't you move."

"Rufra?" A wave of nausea rolled over me. *He knows exactly what I am!* "Why are you doing this, Rufra?"

"I saw," he said. I tried to sit up and his blade nearly skewered me through the neck. "I said don't move!" he shouted. "I saw what you did. To those men. The ones in the wood. I saw it." His eyes were wild, wet with tears and wide with fear. He repeated his words more quietly. "I saw. You were fast as a Fitchgrass, Girton. I thought we were friends and you lied to me. You used me to try and fit in."

"No, I—" His blade cut into the skin of my neck.

"I believed in you!" he shouted. "Don't lie to me!"

"Yes, then," I said. It felt like the pressure which had been building up inside me for days was suddenly bled away. "I did lie to you, Rufra. But I didn't want to. I had no choice."

"I thought we were friends, Girton, that we had some

common ground, but everything about you is a lie. You let Kyril, Borniya and Hallin beat you. You let Tomas's squires beat you. You even let Aydor beat you. I would have fought Tomas to protect you, and all the time you were better with a blade than anyone I've ever seen."

"Celot may be better than—" I tried to make a joke, but he pushed me backwards with the tip of his sword.

"Assassin." He whispered the word. It was the first time I had ever heard it said without feeling proud. It scorched me. "You're an assassin, aren't you, Girton? It's the only thing that makes sense." The colour in his face fell away. "Are you here to kill me?"

I laughed. I think it surprised him.

"Of course not. If I were here for you, why would I have stopped those men? Do you think an assassin enjoys making work for themselves?"

He frowned. Rufra hated a puzzle he could not solve, hated it. Then he let his blade tip drop and walked to the back of the tent. I started to lever myself up and he spun, his sword coming up again.

"No. I've seen how you move. Stay where you are." I nodded and lowered myself once more. "You are here for Aydor then?" I shook my head. "Then who are you here for?" He cocked his head to one side, but before I could speak he shook his head. "No, don't tell me. It's best I don't know." He took a step forward and put the sword tip at my throat again. "Listen, whatever your name is—"

"My name is Girton."

"Then listen, Girton." He started breathing heavily through his nose, and I wondered if he was going to kill me or burst into tears. "Whether you were pretending to be my friend or not—"

"I was never pretending," I said quietly.

"Be quiet!" he shouted, and the sword dipped again. When he spoke, he spoke softly and it made him seem far more dangerous. It was as if the shadow of the man he would become fell upon him in that tent. A man as honourable as he was ruthless. "You saved my life, Girton, and a life is worth a life." He let go of his battered sword and it clanged to the ground. "I had thought I found a friend in you, but you are just a liar out for yourself like all the rest. For the friendship I thought we had I will let you leave." He pointed at the door flap of the tent and he looked small again, like the fourteen-year-old boy he was. "Go now, and I will tell no one what you are. Leave Maniyadoc."

"I cannot leave." The confrontation had burned the alcohol out of my veins and my words were raw, parched and painful in my throat. "I am here to kill no one and I cannot leave no matter how much you all hate me."

"Why?" His question made it sound like leaving should be simple.

"Because I am here to stop an assassin, not to be one."

"I don't understand."

"The queen thinks someone wants to have Aydor killed. She set me up, caught me, and if I do not succeed in finding out who wishes him dead she will kill me or expose me. Not that it matters which she chooses; exposure is the same as death."

"Festival could hide you. I could talk to them." Emotions warred on his face. Despite his anger he was worried for me.

"It is not only me," I said. "There are others."

"Bring them."

"They would not come. They have given their word, and besides we could not hide in Festival. It is the assassins who do not allow one of their own to live when exposed. They would find us wherever we went."

He stared at me as he worked through what I had said and I could see the same hurt and betrayal in his eyes that I had felt in the training yard. He was concentrating so ferociously I realised that he wanted, as much as I did, to reclaim our friendship.

"You're here to stop a killing?" He studied my face as if searching for some trace of a lie.

"Yes."

Rufra took a step towards me.

"What do your assassin friends think of that?" He watched me, waiting patiently while I stared at the floor, trying to find a reply in the dirt and finding nothing. And though I had been trained that silence was the best option I decided on honesty instead.

"I don't have any friends." I raised my head, so he could read the truth from my eyes. "You are the first friend I have ever had and now even that is ruined."

He blinked, slowly, like a morning lizard before it trills its call.

"You could not tell anyone what you are," he said, sounding out each word as if tasting it, "because the queen made you promise not to?" I nodded. "Made you promise, on pain of death," he added.

"Yes," I said, "on pain of death."

A smile broke over his face. It was as if a wind had risen to blow away all the hurt and puzzlement he felt and I knew a solution had presented itself to him. "Then you did not lie to me, Girton."

"I didn't?"

"No." He smiled. "You really are a hostage. Just like you said."

"But I did lie. My name is not ap Gwynr and I am no fool with a blade"

"No, but you are a hostage. Hiding who you are is part of your hostage conditions . . . so you have acted entirely honourably, and besides —" he shrugged and the echo of something dark returned to his face "— we all have secrets."

Then he brightened. "And as to your skill with a blade? Well, I would not be here to be angry with you without it."

He picked up his sword and then sat by me with his legs slightly apart and the blade tip down in the dirt between them, his hands resting on the hilt. At first the silence between us was uncomfortable, and I could barely believe he would forgive so quickly.

Then he spoke softly:

"Maybe it was two weeks training with the blade." He did a poor impression of my voice and laughed to himself. "You know how time flies when you are doing something you enjoy." He chuckled again. "That was a clever thing to say. I can never think of clever things to say. It made you sound like a hero from the old stories."

"That is because I stole it from the old stories. Gwyfher the bladesmistress says it in the tale of the Angered Maiden."

He looked at me disbelievingly. "You stole it from a child's tale?" He looked so outraged that it struck me as ridiculous. That same hysteria that had bonded us fell upon us again and we could not stop laughing. In moments we were leaning against each other and so helpless with laughter that it hurt. Eventually, our laughter died down and a more comfortable silence fell.

"That is an awful sword," I said, pointing at his blade. "I would have been embarrassed if you had killed me with such a terrible blade."

More laughter, but it did not last as long.

"I'll have you know, Girton ap Whatever-it-might-be, that this sword has a long history of being given to the least popular members of my family, and contributing to their unheroic but convenient deaths."

"My apologies, Blessed ap Vthyr," I said. "I did not realise it was such a storied weapon."

"Aye," he said, suddenly serious. "Sometimes, Girton, I feel like death is always at my shoulder."

"I am."

He laughed again. "Oh, don't make me laugh any more, Girton. My head still aches from yesterday's fight."

"Rufra," I asked gently, "why did you think I may have wanted to kill you? You ran into a trap yesterday so someone clearly wants you dead, but why?"

He turned to me and his thick brows knitted together. "You really don't know? I hope my life never rests on your investigative skills." He idly played the tip of his sword backwards and forwards in the dirt. "The rumour I am Neander's son is just that. When I came here a few knew the truth and spoke of it. They feed the pigs now."

"What secret is so terrible?

"Do you remember me saying that Tomas hated me?"

"Yes."

"Tomas hates me because he is my brother, Girton, my half-brother. I am second in line to the throne, though Adran and Daana ap Dhyrrin have buried the truth under a mountain of fear."

"But Tomas is older than you."

"Aye, by two years. What is kept secret is that Tomas is illegitimate."

I sat straighter. "How can that be?"

"Our father was Dolan ap Dhyrrin, and when he was my age he was sent on an outing to make sure the ap Vthyrs knew their place and were behaving themselves. He met my mother, Acearis Vthyr. They fell in love and they married. My great-grandfather, Daana ap Dhyrrin, was disapproving and had the marriage declared improper. They said it was never consummated and quickly married Father off to someone politically useful, an ap Mennix, but he kept sneaking away. Father had also written a letter swearing he consummated the marriage with my mother and it was legal.

There were witnesses too: my grandfather, my mother, my uncles and our priests."

"That sounds like a crowded bedchamber."

He tried to smile at my joke but it faded from his face.

"They are all dead now. As is my father and his other wife, Tomas's mother. There, now you know my secret. Are you impressed?"

"As a friend? Not really. But as an assassin? Well, I am impressed that you have lived this long."

He laughed, though there was little humour in it.

"But to answer your question – of who would want me dead. Well, first there is my uncle, Suvander, who rules the ap Vthyr. Grandfather is still remembered fondly among the ap Vthyr and my mother was always his favourite. To Uncle Suvander's way of thinking this makes me a threat. But my death would more directly profit Tomas and his great-grandfather as I have a better claim to the throne, and even my existence is a problem for them. Aydor and his mother would also love to see me dead as my claim is as strong as the heir's, stronger in many ways."

"Rufra," I said, turning to him, "how have you survived this long? Honestly?"

"Nywulf," he said simply.

"The squiremaster? But I thought he was an . . . I mean he looks . . ."

"He was a friend to my father when they were young – they trained together here. Nywulf was meant to take over from the old Heartblade but a few weeks after my mother announced she was pregnant Nywulf turned up at our hall. He's followed me around ever since. I don't think he likes me much, if I'm honest. I always seem to let him down." He dug the tip of his sword into the earth. "But I trust him."

"And me?"

His brows came together again, that puzzled expression

that turned an already plain face into something undeniably ugly. "It hurt when I thought you had betrayed me," he said. Again the sword tip carved intricate little nonsense symbols in the dirt. "But I had lied also." More scratching. Then his brows parted and he went from puzzled and ugly to plain old Rufra. "Yes. I don't know why, Girton, but I do trust you." He stood and put out a hand to help pull me up.

"Thank you, Rufra," I said. He seemed much older than me then. Maybe because, though he was a year younger, he was taller than I was. "Your friendship is precious to me."

We left the tent and found Nywulf waiting outside. The squiremaster stared at me for a moment and then gave a shrug. I wondered how much Rufra had told him and touched my neck nervously. My hand came away wet with blood where Rufra's sword had nicked it.

"Here," said Nywulf, and passed me the black scarf he wore. "I want it back tomorrow. And make sure you wash it."

"Yes, Nywulf."

"Did you tell him the truth?" The trainer looked at me.

"Truth?"

"You want me to say it out loud where any may hear?"

"He did, Nywulf," said Rufra.

"You did know then," I said. Nywulf nodded and a shiver ran through me. "And you let him come alone?"

"He generally doesn't tell me when he's going to run off and do something foolish," said Nywulf, staring at Rufra.

"Or brave," said Rufra.

"Often the same thing," the squiremaster growled before turning to me. "He likes to sneak off alone and I have to track him down."

"Nywulf shares very little with me also," said Rufra sullenly.

"For good reason," said Nywulf. "Did you tell him the truth as well?" Rufra nodded. "See, Girton. Boy can't keep a secret to save his life."

"How did you know?" I said quietly.

Nywulf came close enough to me that I could smell the stale sweat on him.

"A skilled man can't hide his skill, and I trained as a Heartblade. You're good, boy, I'll give you that, and if we hadn't been stuck together I may never have picked you up." He leaned in even closer. "And if I hadn't picked up on you I would never have noticed the jester." I looked at the floor, feeling like I had betrayed my master.

"Why did you leave Rufra and I alone if you thought—"

He spoke over me before I could say too much. "I didn't, not at first. I tried to get rid of you."

I had a sudden memory: Captain Dollis, nervous in the wall tavern and wanting a huge amount of money for his information, enough money to start a new life. How he'd approached Nywulf in the alley, his words like a threat – *You should walk away unless you want me to t*—

"The dogs?" I said. "You paid Dollis?"

"Yes," he said simply. There was no a trace of guilt. "After you escaped the dogs, I followed you looking for an opportunity to finish what Dollis didn't. I saw plenty of times you could have tried to kill Rufra and yet you did not. In fact, your friendship with him seemed real." He glanced at Rufra and spoke quietly. "He deserves a friend, needs one." Then he leaned in and grabbed my arm. It hurt but there was no menace in it, just a natural fierceness. "And you saved him in the wood," he said. "I owe you that, and I never forget a debt."

"But you saved me from the attackers in—"

"A small thing, boy, and it only made up for what I did to you in the kennels. Besides, I wanted rid of Dollis. That was why I was following him that night. Man couldn't be trusted to keep his mouth shut." His grip tightened on my arm. "I owe you," he said again, and then walked away.

"I am not sure whether having Nywulf owe me makes my life more or less frightening," I said.

"I have felt like that all my life." Rufra grinned. "Girton, Festival will be gone soon. Let me show you it properly, like I wanted to before."

"I have already seen Festival."

"No, not truly. You have only seen the surface."

"Rufra!" We both turned at the shout.

A Rider approached us, small with the familiar rolling gate of one who spent more time on a mount than off. The Rider's armour was the red and black check of the Festival Lords, but as he came closer I saw the colour had been recently applied and in places I could see purple and green below.

"Cearis?" said Rufra, looking puzzled.

"Aye!" The Rider's lifted his visor and, to my shock, revealed a woman beneath; scarred and rough-skinned from a hard life, but unmistakably female.

Rufra's face lit up.

"Girton, this is my Aunt Cearis. I told you about her – she taught me the bow. Aunt, this is my friend, Girton –" a pause "– Girton ap Gwynr."

The Rider held out her hand. "I am Cearis ap Vthyr and well pleased to meet a friend of Rufra."

As I shook her hand, Rufra spoke:

"Why are you here, Cearis? And why are you wearing Festival colours?"

"My brother, Suvander, becomes less and less enamoured with the old ways every day."

"Uncle has stopped women from riding out?"

She shook her head and her amour creaked.

"Not yet, well, not as of a week ago which is how long the journey here took, but it would not take a tracker to smell his intention in the air. He's finally thrown his lot in with the ap Mennix and is busily adopting all their ways in exchange for a smell of power. Neander has been trying to convince him to unsaddle his women for years, but something has changed recently."

"Changed?"

"Messages from Maniyadoc, repositioning of his Riders and troops and gentle suggestions that I should spend more time in the long hall than on a warmount." I did not need to see her face – though she looked like she had smelt something bad – to feel her disgust. "I am a poor seamstress as you know, Rufra, and rather than risk the ridicule of the ladies I chose to come here and see if Festival would have me." She left a long pause. "Of course, your uncle has never been our most popular leader, has he?"

She left that hanging, and Rufra's eyes shone at what she implied.

"Your troops must miss you," he said quietly.

"Only those that stayed, Blessed" she said equally quietly. What was being said was dangerous, and I felt like I should step away, but Rufra's friendship was only just won back and I would not jeopardise it. "I am fifteen strong, Rufra. We wear Festival colours for convenience but we have sworn to no one, not yet. Your uncle has forty knights but we are better warriors and better Riders, far better, and not all of his forty are loyal to him. Some wait to see the direction of the wind and all still remember your grandfather."

Rufra's step slowed to a stop and for a moment I saw something fierce in his eyes. Then he shook his head.

"Cearis, such talk here will get you a knife in the back," he said sadly. He stepped closer to her and unconsciously I used the Assassin's Ear to listen in. "Even if we took the ap Vthyr lands, Aydor ap Mennix, his mother and the ap Dhyrrin would never stand for me in power, you know that. They would bring everything they had against us. I would need to hold somewhere as strong as Maniyadoc to stand a chance."

"But the Festival Lords—"

"Would stand back and wait. They take sides in Maniyadoc and then every other blessed in the Tired Lands will look upon them with suspicion."

Cearis stared into his eyes and then, with a sad smile, shook her head.

"Wise beyond your years, boy," she said. "Sometimes I see so much of my sister in you it makes me ache." With that she did a curious thing, she lifted her head to expose her throat to him. Then she turned on her heel and walked away.

"What was that she did, Rufra? When she lifted her head?"

"A gesture of respect from a Rider to their blessed, Girton. She was exposing herself to my blade. It's one of the old ways. Now come. Festival awaits." I followed him, risking a surreptitious glance behind me at the ground I had stood on while I listened, but there was no circle of death from my trick. "We should find Drusl too," he added.

"Yes," I said. My heart leaped and all dark thoughts of magic were swept away.

"You," said Rufra, grabbing a passing slave. The boy looked terrified until Rufra produced a coin. "Go to Drusl at the stables. Tell her Girton and Rufra will wait for her by the fire breathers if she wishes to visit Festival."

As we walked through Festival towards the fire breathers I could not help noticing how popular Rufra was among the sellers and performers. In the shadows of the huge tents he became markedly more relaxed, the darting eyes and furrowed brows almost gone. It was like a huge worry had sloughed away, and his step, usually deliberate, was light. If I did not already know how hopeless he was I may have thought he would make a dancer.

"You must have spent a lot of money here, Rufra," I said as a juggler gave him a cheery hello.

"Money? No, what makes you think that?" His dark brows met in the middle, the way they always did when he was puzzled.

"Everyone seems to know you. You are far more popular here than . . ." My words died away. "I do not mean to say you are unpopular, Rufra."

"Yes, you do, Girton, and it is true." He gave me a smile. "But not here. You do not know about the ap Vthyr and Festival?" Before I could answer he shook his head. "Of course you don't. Foolish of me to think you should."

"Then tell me, Rufra."

"Oh, it is common enough knowledge, I suppose. At least it is not suppressed like –" he paused and squinted up into the dying sun "– like some other things are. It is only that the truth is not as simple as people would like to believe. The ap Vthyr were one of the guard clans of Festival." The surprise must have been obvious on my face.

"Were you cast out?"

"Cast out? No. Come, let's get something to drink while we wait for Drusl."

"I think I have had enough alcohol today," I said.

Rufra laughed.

"I thought you were easy to overpower. I was scared you know." He looked away.

"Of me?"

"Aye. You killed five men on your own, Girton. I have never seen the like."

"But you still did it?"

"It was right," he said without looking up. "Follow me." He led me around the fire breathers and we stopped at a stall selling cooled fruit juice. Rufra bought two cups. I noticed that although the stallholder would not take his money Rufra left it on the counter anyway. Then he steered me around the back of a tent and we sat on a bench with a view of the crowd

The fruit juice was cold and both bitter and sweet at the same time. I had never tasted anything like it before. "This is good," I said.

"Aye." He took a sip. "Usually they make it with four parts water but for me and my friends –" he nudged me with his elbow "– they make it half and half. It is better."

"It is." I took another sip, watching Rufra as he rubbed the cup against his lip, deep in thought.

"My grandfather was Arnlath, first blessed of the ap Vthyr," he said quietly. "The blessed of Berrick keep insulted our family, there were deaths. Grandfather chose to leave Festival to exact his revenge."

I waited to see if he would say any more, but he only stared at the ground, pushing the cup against his lip.

"His revenge cost a lot of lives," I said.

"Yes," said Rufra, and took a swig of his drink. "A price was paid for the insult in slaughter and rape by both men and their forces. I don't doubt Arnlath ap Vthyr did terrible things," he said sadly, "but to me he was simply Grandfather."

"You were close?"

"Aye, very. He doted on his daughter and he doted on me. He regretted what he had done as a young man." Rufra looked at the ground. "If he were still alive I would not be here, Girton; I would be blessed of the ap Vthyr instead of my uncle, who is every inch as cruel as Aydor. But Grandfather is not here. He fell down the stairs and broke his neck. A poor end for such a warrior."

Arnlath ap Vthyr did not fall down the stairs. I glanced at Rufra, thinking about how my master and I were never there to see the ripples in the pond caused by the stones we threw.

"Yes," I said, and took another sip of my drink. "A poor

end for such a warrior." We were interrupted before we could talk any more about Rufra's grandfather, something I was very glad of.

"Girton! Rufra!"

We both turned.

"Drusl!" I said.

"I'll get more juice," said Rufra and vanished into the growing darkness. Drusl looked preoccupied, but before I could ask her what was wrong she threw herself into my arms and all my worries melted away.

"I cannot stay long, Girton." She ran a finger along the line of my jaw. "With Leiss gone I have double the work, but I have allowed myself until the water clock strikes nine." Her eyes gleamed with mischief. "Is there somewhere we can be alone," she whispered into my ear.

"I have promised Rufra we will see Festival with him."

"Well —" she kissed my ear "— I am sure that will be nearly as much fun."

As night's hold deepened, the men and women of Festival lit huge torches that made our shadows dance along the muddy ground and filled the air with fragrance. Rufra brought us juice and hot sweet confectioneries on sticks. His face acted like a ticket, and we attended the puppet and theatre shows and laughed and gasped with the crowds. Within the grounds of Festival there seemed to be no boundaries: blessed, living and free thankful were equal. There was even talk that those thankful who had ended up as slaves, if they found the right people, could vanish into Festival and find a new life.

The end of the evening came too soon. Rufra promised to escort Drusl to the stables as it was not far out of his way, while I had to return to the castle. I had hoped to steal some time alone with her, but Rufra was clearly pleased with his chivalrous offer and I did not want to spoil it for him. I kissed Drusl goodbye and could still taste the sweetness of fruit juice on her tongue as I walked through the keepyard gate.

I wished we could have stayed longer but there would be other happy days.

I was sure of it.

Chapter 23

There was no sign of my master in our rooms and as I sat there the gloom threatened to return. If not telling Rufra I was an assassin had hurt him, how would he react when he discovered I had the makings of a sorcerer?

And Drusl? What would she think?

I could not bear to think about it but at the same time could not help myself. I needed to do something, anything.

I remembered the voices I had heard when climbing out to look through the rooms of Neander ap Vthyr and Daana ap Dhyrrin. If I could find that same place on the wall, maybe I could eavesdrop again. It was a slim chance, but at least if I was hanging off the side of Castle Maniyadoc my mind would be far too busy to go round and round in tortuous circles. Sticking my head out of the window made me gasp at the chill bite of the wind, though it was not as gusty as the last time I had climbed, and if I used the rope and nails I should be fine. Quickly I wrapped myself in the nightsuit, blackened my face and hands and strapped on my climbing foot. Then I cut a length of rope and tied it around my waist; the other end I made into a loop and placed my right hand through it. Grabbing a handful of nails I climbed out onto the window ledge.

I transferred my weight to my fingers, and that familiar hollow swooping in my stomach rushed over me as my mind screamed at me for placing my body in such danger. But it was the danger that drove dark thoughts from my mind and painted a grin on my face as a wind out of the sourlands whipped my hair about my face.

Far below, a scum of ice had formed over the pool the water clock sat in and the guards had taken to their room after shutting the courtyard gates. Those who needed to go in or out would have to ask them to open the postern gate, and they saw no need to freeze outside. This was good. It meant that if I found a place where I could hear the voices I could use my knife hilt to bang in a nail without worrying about being heard; then I could hang from it to save my strength. I retraced my path across the wall, keeping alert for the whisper of voices on a breeze which rose and fell but lacked the malevolence of the wind the last time I had done this.

My arms were burning with fatigue as I approached the corner where the inner courtyard wall met the massive stones of the keep and found the protruding stone. It was here I had heard the voices, and I had hoped to wrap the rope around it, but the stone was so corroded the rope slid off. Instead, I took one of the big nails from my belt and pushed it as far into the stonework as I could. Then, using the hilt of my knife, I hammered it once and glanced down. The guards were still inside, no doubt warmed by a brazier. I hit the nail again, then a third and fourth time, before looping my rope over it and, very slowly, letting it take my weight. A slight grinding noise. I lifted myself on my fingers and toes just as the nail fell out of the rotten mortar and fell, each tiny metallic beat of the fall sounding impossibly loud. I waited, heart hammering in my chest, but no one came to investigate. I gave it a minute that seemed to stretch for hours as I counted out my-masters and my muscles complained. Then I hammered in a second nail, and a third into a lower course of mortar just in case. I twisted the rope around the bottom nails and placed the loop over the top one and gingerly let them take my weight.

They held.

I waited, it seemed for an age, as cold seeped through

my nightsuit. At the moment I was about to give up I heard it:

". . . not what I agreed to . . ."

Then another voice, lower, reduced to sounds no more sensible than the hiss of leather against leather.

"No! . . . id not leave . . . sma . . . more cruelty . . ."

That voice. I knew it, but by the time the wind had tumbled it around the keep's inner walls it had lost its familiarity.

". . . cannot continue . . . not after . . . iess . . . poor boy . . ."

Poor boy? What poor boy? And what could not continue?

". . . other ways . . . manage the gift . . ."

I knew that voice.

Then the other roared,

"You are wrong and you are wicked! I cannot let it continue!"

I heard a door slam, and it came to me.

Heamus! It was Heamus. I unlooped the rope and was making my way back to our window when I heard a door open far below. I froze as Heamus strode across the courtyard. He was fully armoured and wore blades at his hip. He was no careless guard and despite his age I felt sure if I moved he would somehow sense me. What had he meant? The gift? The boy?

Heamus hammered on the postern gate and a guard came out.

"None to leave. Queen's orders," said the guard.

"Let me out. I must go to the stables."

"Queen says none can leave after—"

"Open it," shouted Heamus and he pulled out his stabsword. "You know who I am."

The guard stared at him for a moment then shrugged.

"Ain'tn't no need for blades, Heamus." He opened the postern door to let the old Landsman out. Once he was gone,

I heard the guard say under his breath, "Mardy yellower," before he returned to the gatehouse. Then, quickly as I dared, I made my way back to our room. Boy? The Gift? And Heamus was going to the stables. Drusl was in the stables! Was the boy Leiss? Did Heamus suspect Drusl of having something to do with Leiss's death? But how? Why?

What if he hurt her?

I pulled myself in through the window and found my master standing with her back against the door in her full jester's suit, a blade in her hand.

"Girton," she said. "What are you doing? I thought you were an intruder."

"No time," I said, gasping for breath as fiery pain ripped through my hands and feet. I fell to my knees. "Heamus. Going to the stables," I hissed. "Drusl."

"What?"

"Armed. Something about Leiss?" Pain was stealing my strength. "Please, Master. Drusl may be in danger."

"But, Girton, we will not be allowed out."

I searched my mind for what to do.

"Fire, Master! I could start a fire in the keep and it would distract the guards on the gate. Then you could use the windlass to open the main doors."

"Girton –" she knelt in front of me "– slow down. Think. A fire big enough to distract the guards would likely bring half the castle running, and the windlass is heavy. I'd barely have any strength left to help you after turning it alone." She stared into my eyes "Breathe, Girton. Out and in. Calm yourself and think. We don't climb a wall where there is a staircase without good reason. Think. Simple is always better."

I took a moment. Breathed. Each second seemed a minute, each breath brought the danger to Drusl closer.

"The letter the queen gave me, to leave for Festival, we can. . ."

"She dated it. And her instructions were specific, I can forge her handwriting but it will take me— "

"Daana ap Dhyrrin," I said.

"What of him?"

"He defended me in front of Queen Adran when she questioned me about Kyril. He either wants my friendship or wants to ensure Neander doesn't have it, I'm not sure which, but he may help."

"And that helps us how?"

"I could tell him I want to visit my girlfriend in secret. The best lies contain truth – right, Master?"

"Aye. But you wait here, clean the blacking from your face and hands and put on your armour," said my master. "You are shaken and he will sense that. I will go to him for you."

"What if he says no?"

"Then we will think of something else." And then she was gone. The pain of climbing ebbed as I struggled into my armour, and when she returned she carried a letter from Daana ap Dhyrrin allowing us to leave.

"That was easier than I expected," she said. At first she had to help me limp along the corridors of Castle Maniyadoc but walking helped bring the feeling back into my hands and feet. Then we ran. As we left the keep I glanced back over my shoulder and, just for a moment, thought I saw a figure at the lit window of Daana ap Dhyrrin's window, watching as we ran for the gate. I banged on the door of the guardroom. The guards were in no hurry and I hammered on the door again. The guard who eventually answered seemed annoyed and puzzled to see us, a squire and Death's Jester rushing through the night demanding he open his doors and dragging him away from his warm brazier, but let us through.

We skirted Festival, which was full of light and noise, and ran as fast as we could for the dark stables. Even armoured and with my club foot I outran my master, or maybe, judging Drusl my business, she let me go ahead.

I skidded to a stop at the open stable doors. The sun had dipped below the walls and flickering torches lit the interior in gold and red. Light caught the antlers of the mounts, their heads swayed restlessly, as if they were aware something was wrong and antlers threw a forest of needle shadows over the walls. At the edge of the torchlight I was held, as if the dome of light were some impassable barrier – I saw a mountbiter, tiny as a jewel, float through the air, the high whine of its wings pulsing in my ear as it flew into the stable, but I could not follow. My body refused to listen to instruction. I willed my legs to move but they would not. I begged my mouth to open but I made no sound. Instead I was forced to stand and watch, a mute, helpless audience to a tragedy.

Heamus stood in front of Xus's stall, too intent on what he was saying to notice me. He spoke gently, using the same voice one would use on a frightened animal.

"There is no time for this, no time. Come." Something was said in return, something so quiet all I could make out was fear in the voice. Heamus shook his head. "No, not that, never that again." A muffled reply. The air in the stable felt like it had thickened, as if it wished to stop me hearing what was said. I could hear no words, discern no meaning; only that terrible fear came through, and the mounts picked up on it, starting to hiss and cough. "You must forget him, forget this place, forget it all. It is no longer safe for any of you." A shuddering through the stable, as if a wave of sadness passed along it, blowing around loose straw and slamming shutters. Xus remained almost entirely still, except for his great head, which swayed as if he were hypnotised. The other mounts began to rear and strike out. The thunder of clawed feet beating against wooden stalls filled the stable, the forest of antler shadows on the walls twisted and bucked as if caught in strong winds.

Then Heamus raised his voice. Breaking the spell. His shout brought a crushing, heavy silence down on the stable that stilled the mounts, deadened all feeling. Heamus's voice was the only sound. The stable around him became a blur. He became the focus.

"Dead gods' sake, girl, will you come out!" His hand went to the blade at his waist – not, I think, because he wished to use it, but because it was a habitual gesture when he lost his temper.

A scream.

Everything changed, moved.

The air bowed and became a great lens, thick as honey and filled with the scent of spices. It spoke out with a deep voice, like the paralysing bark of an impossibly huge dog. The stall which housed Xus seemed to breathe in and Heamus raised his arms in a futile attempt to shield himself. A woman screamed, as if giving birth and dying at the same time, and Xus, my beautiful, powerful Xus, crumpled as if he were made of wet paper, his massive body shrinking, muscle falling away until his bones became stark against his skin and he was dragged down by his own weight. Darkness exploded from the stall. A plug of ink-black air throwing itself against the Landsman, peeling back his armour, shedding spears of black like water crashing against rock. It slammed Heamus back against the door of the empty stall behind him and he screamed as his bones were shattered along with the wood.

The darkness vanished as quickly as it had come. The moment felt like a dream, but the smashed door and Heamus's broken body showed it to be all too real, horrifically real. The front of the Landsman's armour and the flesh of his face had been flensed from him. After hitting the stall door he had fallen forward, dead, his face turned towards me and his wet red skull grinned mockingly from his bent helmet.

"No!" The word that came from within Xus's stall was a howl of anguish. It sounded as if all the pain and worry I had felt over the past days was bundled up into one forlorn, sour syllable, and though I knew what I would find I still refused to accept it. Slowly, dreading and knowing what I would see, I advanced on Xus's stall through hazy air and over ground which felt like it was made of sponge. Each step brought me closer, each pace brought me nearer to knowing that, in my life, there were to be no surprise escapes, no happy endings. There was only one explanation for what I had seen and heard.

"Drusl," I said.

She stood with her hands held away from her body as if they were animals that would bite her. Her eyes were wide with horror at what she had done. Next to her was Xus. The once-mighty mount had fallen to his knees, his muzzle prematurely greyed and his fur hanging loosely from a starved and skeletal body. The animal looked a thousand years old. How could this be him? He was strong. He had carried me across the land with the wind whipping my hair. Xus was indomitable, the only thing stronger and more constant than my master. His warmth had sheltered me through long nights, his fur had been my comforter, and the smell of him was the nearest thing I had ever known to home. Mounts could live for hundreds of years; mounts should live for hundreds of years.

But Xus would not; he was broken. Breath wheezed in and out of his lungs in painful gasps. The great antlers he had always been so proud of were now too heavy for his head and had pulled it to the floor, tilting it to one side and painfully twisting his scrawny neck. Saliva ran from his mouth, around gums that had receded from black and rotten teeth, to pool on the floor of the stable. His small black eyes were empty of life, the great spirit that had animated him horribly, permanently reduced.

"Xus," I said.

"I'm sorry," said Drusl. "I'm sorry." She looked to Xus

and then to me but whether she saw me or not I do not know. Her gaze was far away and then it focused, returned to her shaking hands, regarding them as if they were covered in blood only she could see. I started forward. A firm hand on my shoulder stopped me.

"No, Girton," said my master. "It is too dangerous for you."

"He wanted to hurt me; they all wanted to hurt me." Drusl lifted her hands and stared at them with wide brown eyes. I think she could see nothing else. Another long breath struggled in and out of Xus's lungs. My heart broke within my breast.

"All?" said my master softly. "Kyril and Leiss? They wanted to hurt you too?"

"Yes," the word barely audible. "I never wanted to hurt them but they wouldn't go away. They wouldn't. I only wanted to make them go away."

"Stress and hurt are often the triggers that wake us, girl," said my master softly, taking a step towards her.

Drusl seemed to see us for the first time, and her face twisted into a grimace. The floor and walls started to sweat.

"I didn't want it. They cut power into me. I didn't want it."

"Who did this?"

"I won't give up the other girls. It isn't their fault."

"What you are is no one's fault, Drusl," said my master. I watched, rooted to the spot like a tree. "But someone woke your power with pain, Drusl, on purpose? Is that what you mean when you say they cut it into you?"

She nodded slowly then fell to her knees and stretched out a hand as if to touch Xus before jerking it back in horror at the sight of him. "Xus," she said, "poor Xus." She turned from the mount to my master. "They said the symbols would stop me hurting anyone."

Gossamer flakes of ash hung in the air around us as I watched, unable to think or move.

"It was a lie," said my master. "They sought to control you but have only twisted you; they have taught you no control at all."

My words came then – desperate ill-thought-out words planted in the sour ground of desperation, not reality.

"We can help you escape," I said.

"Oh Girton." Drusl gave me a small, shy, smile. "I knew you'd want to help." She held out a hand towards me, then looked at the dying Xus and her smile fell away. She turned back to my master, the small hope I had seen in her eyes dying. "But he doesn't understand, does he? There is no escape from this, is there, wise mother?"

The old woman stares at his master, and a tear tracks down her face, flowing along the banks of her many wrinkles.

My master's face was set like stone and if I could have found my voice I would have begged her not to speak.

"No, daughter," she said. "There is no escape." Drusl bowed her head, and her hands fell to her side. She took a deep shuddering breath and then raised her head.

"I love you, Girton. What I am doesn't change that." She tilted her head to one side. "It's not all bad. I saved you from the dogs, slowed them for you."

"That was you?"

She nodded.

"It was worth it for that at least."

"Drusl," I said. My voice died in my throat.

She watched her left hand as she ran it through Xus's coat. His fur came away at her touch, falling to the floor to lie against his barely moving side. The mount's breathing had slowed until it was hardly discernible. "I love Xus too." A tear ran down her face. "I never meant to hurt him; I never thought I would hurt him." She stared at the dying mount and then raised her face to me. "You love him."

I nodded. "And you."

"No one will find out about you, Girton. Don't worry."

"You knew?"

"Of course." She looked puzzled and then smiled. "You didn't? It makes me love you more." She met my eye, something steely in her gaze. "Remember our happy times together, Girton, and take this gift from me." She reached into her tunic and drew out a small knife, the type used to pare the hard claws of a mount. "Don't forget me, Girton," she said in a whisper. Then, with a final smile, she brought the knife up and it flashed in the torchlight as she opened her neck. A jet of arterial blood sprayed out over the dying Xus. It seemed to slow, to bend and twist, becoming elastic and wrapping itself around the dying animal.

It feels like a dream.

I scream, I think.

The blood, so red, floods my memory. My master holding me tight. I fight her. She stops me running to Drusl. Blood flows, sprays and turns.

"This is what she wants, Girton. This is what she wants."

"No."

I struggle. I kick. I cry.

"This is what is best."

"She's dying."

I struggle. I kick. I cry.

"Nothing can stop that now. Let her blood flow as she wills it."

This is not a dream.

Drusl slumped forward, and I folded into my master's arms, crying "No" again and again. I felt the movement of life around me. What had been contained and bound by Drusl's blood was freed and sought its source, binding itself to the great animal lying before me. I felt the walls of his fluttering heart thicken and strengthen. I felt his huge lungs fill with air and begin to work like blacksmith's bellows. Colour crept across his fur, changing it from grey back to brown and white, and it thickened as though he moulted his summer coat and grew his winter one all in seconds. The muscles of his neck twisted and knitted themselves back to strength, and his heavy head with its huge spread of antlers rose. He struggled, clawed feet slipping on the bloody ground, but only for a moment, and then, with a shrill cry of triumph, he lifted himself and stood over us, huffing and hissing, shivers passing along his flanks.

And at the same time Xus was standing, breathing, living, my mind was working, seeing pictures. Making sense of what I had seen – what I had missed.

"Others." I said the word quietly into my master's chest. "She said there were others." I heard a voice I could not quite place. I saw a priest in a place he should not be, heard a woman crying in the distance. I saw groups of letters in the back of the book of names and they burned across my mind with new meaning. I raised my head, looking into my master's face. "Drusl in the stable," I whispered it to myself as if to test the truth I found in the words. Columns of letters span in my mind, twisted around themselves. One particular grouping shining especially brightly. "DTS," I said. "Drusl, the stable."

"What?" said my master as I untangled myself from her arms.

"The priest Neander did this."

"What do you mean?"

I stood.

"She spoke of others. The letters in Neander's book. They were names and places. DTS, Drusl, the stable."

"Girton, you cannot be sure."

"But I am."

I walked away from her as guards swarmed through the stable doors.

"Get out of my way," I said and drew my blades. They lowered their pikes, but I would not be stopped.

I could not be stopped.

The world changed.

I fell into a new existence. My vision became a series of glowing lines drawn on black. The stable, the guards, their weapons, all became unreal – simplified. Only I was real, only I existed. Beyond the paper-thin veneer of reality I could sense a roiling, a black fire fuelled by life. All I had to do was reach through and the fire below would be mine. I could cast away the guards, the stable block, the rotten castle that housed it and every blessed who used others like tools. I could do it all with a thought and a flick of my mind.

It would be a pleasure.

"I am sorry, Girton. But I cannot let you do this now."

A whisper from another world.

A cool hand against my neck.

A darkness all-enveloping.

Interruption

This is
         a dream?

He swims.

Swims after her

Swims through a sea above the land. Through water blue
as flame, red as hot liquid, green as life. Pellucid water clear
as duty and as thick and murky as choices. Animals swim
around him. Shoals of mounts dart through the water
between waving fronds of seaweed that reach up into the
black sky to become the pillars supporting it. Herds of fish
run across the land and far away the sourings sing sewage
and the throne of the hedgelord, Blue Watta, rises.

He swims after her.

The water passing through his lungs is as sweet as
sorrow: it tastes of fear and spite. It is the warmth of a
hand offered in unexpected friendship. It is the drowning
steel of a knife blade through the gullet. Currents pull him
through the doors and windows of a ruined castle and the
decayed faces of people he-may-but-may-not-know scream
a welcome at him. The dizzying spin of a whirlpool drags
him through a hedging's door, shrieking and joyful into
the depths.

He swims after her.

Beneath him his mount supports him, and it is a marvel-
lous creation of mechanical scales, as intricate and perfect
as a water clock. It writhes and twists through the water
with all the striking grace of death. Its antlers are gilded for

war. Its saddle is as supple as love. Its eyes are scars that can see through time. In the distance is death and in the foreground is death and in the mid ground is death and in the roof of the stars is death and in the floor of the ocean is death. Xus the unseen laughs at him from where he hides between the shining cracks of his mind.

He swims after her.

Beneath him are the dead gods with their throats slit, imposing bodies piled carelessly upon one another, flesh of alabaster, ebony, azure, ruby and sand. Skin as soft as refracted light within a diamond, faces as achingly beautiful as they are terrifying. A pair of eyes, heavily browed and puzzled, stare out of an ugly face. "Why?" He does not know why or what or who. He feels judged and judgemental. He feels guilty and proud. The bodies of dead gods writhe together in a fertile frenzy, slit throats moan in ecstasy, bodies grow scars. Their forgotten children, the hedgings, shout for attention from below a wall of transubstantial flesh.

He swims after her: ghosts in the water

She is a reminder.

He is a creature of the land. He should walk on two legs. His mounts are furred and his fish swim. This is not real and the water he breathes is as lethal as any ligature. His memory is a memory of life that dooms him to a watery death as surely as it steals away the magnificence of the seascape around him.

He chokes.

She goes where he cannot follow.

A noose constricts around his neck.

The pain is a knife in his eye. It is his heart being cut out. The strange world fades. Little by little it becomes more mundane until it is gone and he stands alone in an amphitheatre. Below there is a play on. Merela Karn fights off a thousand little men armed with tiny daggers, and when she is finally overwhelmed blades rise and fall like bloody metronomes.

a dream

Is this?

Chapter 24

I lost three days to grief and shock.

The first day I cannot remember at all.

The second was a haze. A mist of sweat, pain, twisted blankets and mental recriminations. Should have saved her. Could have saved her. I should have saved her.

How? How could you have saved her.

Merela Karn should have saved her. Cleverest person I've ever met. Best fighter, greatest assassin. Wasn't she? Wasn't she? She could have done it, should have done it. She could have disguised her, hidden Heamus's body away . . .

How? The guards were on us almost immediately.

Somehow! She should have done it somehow. Instead she practically talked Drusl into suicide.

Drusl. Oh Drusl. The pain is sharp like Conwy steel cutting into my breast. My master, how could she? How could she do that? Let Drusl die. She just let her die. Let her die. How could she let her die. Kill her.

My master killed her. Talked her into death.

What else could she do?

Something!

She could have done something. She should have done something. Instead she talked the woman I loved into death.

Did she?

Yes!

"Thank you for your kindness, daughter."

Drusl said there was no way out. She knew there was no way out.

She was right.

No.

She was right.

No, she wasn't!

Should have saved her. Could have saved her. I should have saved her.

How?

And round and round and round it went in a circle of tears and anger.

On the third day I faced the truth, met my master and woke to a new world.

It was not the world I had walked through before. It was a world dulled. My colours were the washed-out colours of a land beneath sky the grey of threatening storms. I heard sound as though I stood in a landscape covered in deadening snow, the highs and lows absorbed by ice. Somewhere, far away, a piper played but I could no longer hear the melody, only noise. When I ate the food which had been left out for me it was even more tasteless than usual.

There had been no escape for Drusl. Three times she'd killed when threatened and each time she had used more power. It had never been under her control. If it had been under her control she would never have harmed Xus. Never.

And I'd touched the magic in a way I never had before.

At the thought of magic my mind started to slide away on a sheen of silver, sword-blade bright. I pulled it back.

I'd felt the magic in the stable that day in a different way. I had felt its power, its terrifying power, and I knew the truth of it was just as my master had said. It wanted to be used. It desired to be used, and its voice was a slick, an oily membrane that spread across the mind it touched. It promised so much: pleasure, power, safety.

Revenge.

Whatever you wanted was within it. "I can give you that," it said, though it had no voice. It was more subtle than that.

It was as if the magic were a dark bird that settled on your
desires and its weight pushed them to the forefront of your
mind.

"I can give you that."

I felt the pull again but it was dulled, like everything else.
The only thing that was sharp and focused was the pain in
my chest.

"Drusl."

"I'm sorry, Girton." My master's first words as she entered
the room that evening. She had shed her Death's Jester
make-up and motley. Instead she wore a plain leather jerkin
and skirts as she strode across our room and opened the box
at the end of the bed to remove our packs and drop them
on the floor. She sat on the bed. I moved my legs so I was
not touching her and she looked like I had driven a blade
into her side, but I could not take the action back. "I am
sorry," she said. "I had no other option. We had no option.
And . . ." Her voice tailed away.

"I understand," I said quietly. Her hand inched across the
sweaty blanket towards my own, as if she unconsciously
desired my touch. I moved my hand away. "Understanding
is not forgiveness, Master." I looked away from her with
tears in my eyes. I could feel what I was doing, feel how I
was thrusting my own pain into my master's heart. It showed
as new grey in her hair and new lines etched onto her face
– *silvered lines in her eyes.*

"I understand too," she said.

"We are leaving?" I nodded at our bags.

"Yes. You do not have to stay with me, but . . ."

"But?"

"What you were about to do in the stable . . ."

"You mean destroy the castle?" I said dully. "Bring it all
down around their blessed ears?"

"The power within you," she said, "it was like nothing I
have felt before."

"I didn't want to hurt you."

"But you would have, Girton. You would have hurt everyone." Her voice dropped so low I could barely hear her. "And that is not who you are, so I have cut you," she said, staring at the floor.

"Cut me?"

She nodded, and without looking at me her hand came up, moving aside my jerkin so I could see a shape incised into the flesh above my heart, a knotted tangle of lines and whorls that would not stay still in my mind. As soon as I knew it was there it started to hurt as if it was eating into my flesh.

"It is like the symbols I found in Heamus's rooms."

"I am sorry. It was the only way to hold the power at bay."

I think she expected me to explode with anger. Instead I pulled my shirt across to hide the cuts. "Good," I said.

She smiled sadly, shaking her head.

"It won't last, Girton. The magic wants to be used."

"I know."

"It will find a way around."

"I know," I said. My voice sounded as dead as Drusl. "That's what she meant when she said there was no escape, wasn't it?"

"Yes. But it is different for you, Girton. You have learned control, and together we can make sure that you don't . . ." Her voice faded again.

"Destroy the land?"

She wouldn't look at me.

"You would never—"

"I nearly did," I snapped. "It wants to be used, that's what you just said. You should kill me. If you don't then I will. You've seen the sourlands, the people starving. We cannot afford another sorcerer. I cannot bear to be responsible for more—"

"No!" She grabbed my shoulders, shaking me. "Never say that! Never think it!"

"I see no other way, Master!" It seemed such an obvious way out. A way to safeguard the land and to end the terrible pain within me. She stared at me and her mouth moved, but no words came out. She bit on her lip as she held my gaze.

"You were right about Neander," dry words. "He escaped the castle along with a number of young girls, the 'others' Drusl spoke of. In his quarters was found a letter from Rufra requesting the death of Aydor."

Suddenly I felt something apart from my own pain.

"That cannot be," I said.

"It was."

"But Rufra would not—"

"It seems he did, and tomorrow they will burn him alive as a traitor. But I must leave, and you intend to die so . . ." She shrugged and stood.

"Rufra is a good man, far better than any blessed or king we have come across."

"Good men do not become kings."

"Then what does become of them?"

"They die, Girton." She would not meet my eye. "They die, and usually they die so that bad men may remain kings."

"Rufra should not die just because . . ." There were no words. I closed my eyes to try and banish the room and the castle and my master but only succeeded in conjuring up images of Rufra on the pyre – my friend screaming in agony on a fool's throne, the wood seasoned and dried so it burned cleanly and the smoke did not suffocate him, his clothes daubed with oil so they caught the flame. He would die hard, and I could feel the currents of magic roiling and turning far below me, distant but full of possibility. I felt like a thirsty man on a mountain, reaching for the line of the sea on the horizon in an effort to wet his hand.

A letter.

I opened my eyes.

"Master, did you see the letter?"

"Only for a moment."

"'I, Rufra ap Vthyr, request the heir, Aydor ap Mennix, be removed,'" I said. My master stared hard at me.

"You knew about this, Girton?"

"No."

"But that is what the letter said."

"Daana ap Dhyrrin," I said. "Dark Ungar curse him, he saw an opportunity and he took it." I tried to rise from the bed but my master stopped me by placing her hand on my chest.

"Explain yourself. What does Daana ap Dhyrrin have to do with this? What have you been hiding from me?"

"Nothing," I said. Rage started to build within me. Rage at the people in the castle and the way they twisted the lives of others to suit themselves, rage with my master for getting us mixed up in this and rage with myself for not seeing the danger sooner. "When I broke into his room there was a pile of vellum on his desk. I thought it was nothing, only requests from the squires to have Aydor removed from the squireyard. Rufra's was on top. Daana had been scraping it – I thought to clean the vellum for reuse – but it wasn't. It was to make it look like he wanted the heir dead."

"Why would he want to make it look like Rufra was responsible?"

"Because Rufra is next in line to the throne."

"Rufra?" She looked surprised, and I realised I had not had the opportunity to tell her of Rufra's lineage.

"Rufra and Tomas share a father in Dolan ap Dhyrrin, Daana's grandson. When Tomas was born, Dolan ap Dhyrrin was already married to Rufra's mother, Acearis Vthyr."

My master stared at me as if I had torn back a curtain mid-act to reveal how a trick was done.

"So Tomas is a bastard who cannot inherit? Well, now we

know what Adran holds over Daana," said my master to herself, "but what does he hold over her?"

"Rufra must be innocent, Master, he must be."

She stood, paced. "You may be right. There is something far darker than simple murder and politics here, Girton. This business with Heamus, Neander and Drusl? Magic? It feels like the tip of a blade pointed at the heart of the Tired Lands. We have missed something. How did Neander know to leave? How did Daana ap Dhyrrin know when to place the letter in his room? It must have been done between Neander leaving and his quarters being searched. Hardly any time."

"Did you mention Heamus when you asked Daana for authorisation to leave?"

"Aye, but only said we worried about him."

"But if he knew what Heamus and Neander were doing . . . ?" I said. 'I saw symbols in Daana ap Dhyrrin's bin that resembled the Landsman's Leash. He must have been preparing protections in case he needed them." My master considered what I had said before shaking her head.

Did I catch a gleam in her eye?

"It is not our problem, Girton." She turned away. "Adran has told us to go."

"But Rufra will die."

"We cannot solve this before dawn tomorrow, Girton. We have had our time here and found nothing. Events have only happened to us. And besides, you have given up."

"Master, please, let us at least free Rufra."

"Why should I care?" she hissed, tears in her eyes. "Why should I put myself in danger for your wishes if you only plan to kill yourself afterwards?"

For a moment I was lost for words. Then I realised my despair had passed, replaced by something new.

"I want to live. And I want revenge, Master, revenge for Drusl."

"We are assassins, Girton; revenge is not our trade." She

said this quietly and before I could get angry she spoke again: "Adran has given us a chance to leave alive and we must take it. But —" she held up her hand before I could shout at her "— I think we can free Rufra. I can give you that at least, I think. If you will promise to live."

She sat again, and this time I did not move my leg though she did not seem to notice. Her warmth seeped into my cold and painful clubbed foot.

"Thank you, Master."

"The Landsmen have been sent for. They will scour this place, and if anyone else was involved in Drusl's death they will find them. They will make them pay."

She held my gaze. It was the moment I changed from child to adult. She lied to me and I knew she lied. A few weeks before it would never have occurred to me that she may lie as I had a child's total belief in my guardian. A few days ago her lie would have made me angry, but no longer. She lied to me and I understood it. I understood it from the tear held in her eye, the lines in her face and the grey streaks in her hair. The Landsmen would no doubt find a scapegoat. It would be no one important. They would come and favours would be exchanged and everything would return to how it was before — only the names may change. I had once believed we were the hand of justice, but now I knew us for what we were — pinpricks on the back of a great beast that careened forward heedless of what it destroyed. We could prick it a million times and it would barely notice.

My master was tired.

I was tired.

"Very well. Let us free Rufra and be gone."

She gave me a small smile, more an acknowledgement of our shared impotence than anything else.

"Thank you. Now pack. Adran has made it clear that if we are not gone before the water clock strikes for the midnight signing sermon she will tell everyone we are here.

A king cannot countenance assassins in his castle, even if he is dying. I would rather not leave with the castle's guards on our heels."

"But the king already knows we are here," I said.

My master stiffened, and then stared into the air as if it contained secrets only she could see.

"He does. You are right. In my worry for you I had forgotten that." She tipped her head back and let out a long breath then ran a hand through her hair. "Girton, tell me exactly what was said and done between you and the king."

"I was on one of the towers," I said, puzzled by her reaction, "and he told me he was familiar with the ap Gwynrs and knew they had only daughters, so I must be his assassin."

"Those exact words?"

"Yes, he said, 'So you must be my assassin,' then he raised his head to offer me his throat. I was about to tell him I wasn't there for him when—"

"Girton!" She sat me up, holding me by the tops of my arms and smiling her feral, dangerous smile. "Why didn't you tell me this when it happened? He was not offering you his throat. That was a salute – subject to king or king to subject." She stared at me, her gaze boring into me as if she expected some reaction. "Don't you see, Girton? It changes everything."

"It does?" She talked over me, no longer listening and the tiredness that had seemed to be all but overwhelming her a moment ago had fled.

"There are times, Girton," she said. "Times, moments when everything may change." Her grip loosened but she did not let go. "You said your friend Rufra would be a good king. Are you sure?" I didn't understand what she saw. I didn't know what to say. "Are you sure?" She shook me.

"Yes. I am sure."

She nodded and a gleam appeared in her eye that I had not seen for long on long. She let go of me and hopped off the bed to pace up and down the room. "Very well. Remember what Adran said? 'We work with what we have.' How many Riders did you say Rufra has at Festival?"

"Fifteen," I said. "The woman Cearis said she had fifteen good Riders."

"Fifteen." She brought her hand up to her mouth, pushing the knuckle of a finger against her lips. "Fifteen good Riders, Girton. It is not many, but if the stables are taken no one else will have cavalry, and it might be enough you know. That may do it, yes. Go now, Girton. Free Rufra from the dungeons and get him to Festival. Tell him to ready his Riders."

"Why?"

"To take his throne of course. Why else?" She picked up her blades and strapped them to her waist.

"With only fifteen knights? But Master—"

"Tonight the castle will be thrown into disarray." She cinched buckles tight. "Rufra will never have a better chance. They want to burn him on a fool's throne? Well, we will do what we can to put him on a real one. Do you still have the letter Adran wrote allowing you to leave?" I nodded and handed it over; she sat by the window and began to scrape at the ink with a knife as she spoke. "Find some slave's clothes. By the time you have done that I will have altered the date, wording and authority on this to allow a slave carrying a message to pass through the gates. No one looks at slaves. Once you have Rufra away, tell Adran that this business is not over yet and if she values her son's life she will meet me in the king's chamber. You must get Adran, without Aydor, to the king's chamber by —" she pushed her head out of the window so she could see the water clock "— ten o'clock. That should be enough time."

"And what then, Master?"

She pulled her head back into the room and turned to

me. Her eyes shone, and she smiled her assassin's smile, more a showing of teeth than anything else.

"Then we shall do what you wanted to do in the stables and what I have dreamed about most of my life, though I expect it to cost us ours." She took out her stabsword and checked the keenness of the edge. "Tonight, Girton, you and I shall bring this entire castle tumbling down around our ears."

Chapter 25

Castle Maniyadoc's dungeons had two entrances. One was within the keep and the other led in from the outside – so those who were to be executed or had been tortured didn't trail their misery, blood or both through the keep. The inner stairway was well guarded and designed to be defended – a tight spiralling staircase that could be held by a single guard – and as I was known to be a friend of Rufra I knew I had little chance of getting past the guards without an alarm being raised. The outer door, however, was rarely guarded as it was garlanded with thick chains, heavy locks and, after all, who breaks into a dungeon?

I wore no armour as this would arouse suspicion, and all I carried to defend myself was my Conwy stabsword and my eating knife. I itched for the comfortable weight of a second blade at my hip, but my master had taken my longsword with her, saying it would serve me well later.

I felt alive.

The courtyard was quiet; only faraway shouts and calls from those enjoying themselves at Festival echoed around the shadowy landscape. A movement in the darkness below the wall caught my eye, a figure trying to keep hidden. He was not being obvious about it, no hugging the walls or moving at a crouch, but his walk was too casual for a man just strolling, although there was a familiar, taut, anger in every step the figure took.

Nywulf.

He was being followed: two people, a man and woman both dressed as slaves and utilising the same blindness to the doings of slaves that I intended Rufra take advantage of. They were good. They did not stay close to Nywulf and changed who watched him frequently. I melted into the shadows and reached for the Simple Invisibility, but where it should be I found a rock face as dark and pitted as the keepyard wall. The sigil incised into my chest throbbed and squirmed as if my chest were infested with worms. I put the sensation out of my mind and hugged the wall, keeping low and thanking my master for the nightsuit she had made me. Without shoes and with the hood pulled down I was skilled enough to remain practically invisible, even without magic. For a moment I thought about taking down the watchers – it would not be difficult – but then I put that thought aside. I would have to hide the bodies, and if they were expected to report to someone then who knew how long I would have before they would be missed? Besides, they watched Nywulf not me, and that could be used to my advantage. I easily outpaced the squiremaster and his watchers then waited behind one of the wedge-shaped buttresses of the wall. I hissed his name as he walked past.

He sauntered to a stop within a short distance of me as if he were a man having second thoughts about something. Now he was nearer I could see the bulge of weapons underneath his jerkin, more than one man would usually carry.

"Girton," he said slowly. "I did not expect you to be here but I should not be surprised." His hand went to the hilt of his blade. "Have you come for Rufra?"

"Yes," I said. His hand tightened around the blade hilt at his hip.

"You must be angry," he said, "about what happened to the girl. I understand that. But Rufra was not with Neander;

he had nothing to do with the death of Drusl, no matter what you may hear."

A stab in my heart at Drusl's name.

"I know Rufra isn't responsible," I said. "I'm here to free him."

"As am I. You would be a welcome help."

"You are being followed, Nywulf."

"I know," he said. "Two of them."

"They'll bring the guards before you can free Rufra."

"I am no amateur, boy." His knuckles whitened around the hilt of his weapon. "Besides, you could easily take care of my watchers for me. I have a key to the dungeon and, in truth, I don't expect that Rufra or I will make it past the keepyard, but it's better that the boy die with a blade in his hand than on the fire." He breathed heavily, like a bull about to charge. "I'll not let them burn him," he said. I remembered what Rufra had said about his awful sword and how it was given to those destined to die.

"He need not die at all." Nywulf turned his head towards me, only a fraction, something barely noticeable, but I felt his scrutiny of me double. "Lead your shadows away, Nywulf," I whispered. "Drop the key there and lead them away. I have a forged letter and clothes which will get Rufra through the postern door and keepyard gate as a slave. I will free him and send him to Festival. Trust me. There is a Rider at Festival called Cearis—"

"Cearis is here?" Now his concentration on me was almost a physical thing, like it pushed against my skin.

"Aye, with her Riders, and she says they will follow Rufra. Tell them to be ready. Bring any others you can find."

"Be ready for what?"

"I don't know yet. Not exactly. But an opportunity will present itself and you must make sure Rufra is ready to act."

Nywulf stared up at the slow dance of the stars.

"I'm a fighting man," he said, his voice rough as newly cut planks. "I'm not fitted out for this sort of skulking in the shadows." He glanced at me "You promise you'll get Rufra out safe? Promise he'll get a fighting chance?"

"I can only promise I will do my best."

He turned to look at me, gave me a quick smile and ran a hand over his bald head.

"If you'd said anything else I'd have known you for a liar and killed you here." He stared up at the castle, swore and turned to walk away.

"Nywulf,' I whispered. He slowed. "Take the stables. My master said that you must take the stables."

He gave a small nod and walked away from me with the air of a man who had changed his mind. Where he had stood a key shone in the dirt. I counted out a hundred my-masters and heard Nywulf talk to the guards, be let out, then the postern door shut behind him. Fifteen my-masters later the door opened and closed again. I waited without moving for another fifty my-masters to see if I picked up any movement in my peripheral vision, but there was nothing. Nywulf had taken his shadows with him.

Now Rufra's life depended solely on me.

Nywulf's key opened the huge locks and the chains fell away. When I lifted the bar from across the door it seemed so loud I thought the whole castle must hear. I waited, first tracking the movements of the guards at the massive gate until I was sure they had heard nothing. Then I pressed my ear against the door to make sure I was not heard by anyone inside. If there was a crossbowyer behind the door then my attempt to free Rufra ended here.

The door inched open at my touch. The heavy wood was bound with iron hinges that creaked loudly as I slipped in and shut it behind me. It seemed impossible I was not heard. I crouched, holding my breath and waiting in the dark for my eyes to adjust and for someone to investigate the noise, but no one came and I breathed again. In front of me a staircase curved away, and torchlight from below created an arc of warm light against the stone. Within the light was the shadow of a helmed head – a guard further down the stair.

I remained still, listening.

Voices echoed up the stairs. Three male, one female, and they were taunting Rufra. I heard snatches of laughter and cruel words, talk of fire and the pain it caused. At first they spoke in such a way they could pretend it was an innocent conversation, but it was obviously enacted entirely to cause pain to a fourteen-year-old boy.

"Nah, Forig. I reckon they stay alive for at least half an hour on a fool's throne."

"Could be – remember Banil? He were twitching and screaming for 'is mother for a good hour."

"Aye, wonder who you scream for if you don't have a mother? Hey, traitor! You ain't got a mother. Who you gon scream to help you when you burn?"

The anger within suddenly had a target. These people were hurting my friend, delighting in it, and I would kill them for that. No turning back. No doubt. No room to get this wrong.

Down a step. *Breathe out*.

Fear made my hands shake. Fear of facing the guards in the dungeon. Fear of failing and leaving my friend to burn.

Down a step. *No time for fear*.

The back of a guard's head just visible around the tight turn of the staircase. He takes off his helmet and scratches his head. He has a scar high on his pate that shows pink and tight against his dandruff-filled hair. A crossbow dangles at his side. Beyond him is the dungeon.

Down a step. *Breathe in*.

In front of the guard is a large room with a wide corridor

between walls that run with damp. Inset in the walls are thick wooden doors. The same cells my master and I had been kept in. Where is Rufra? Is he hurt? Have they beaten him? What if he can't walk? Sometimes they blind traitors . . .

Down a step. *No room for fear.*

I see him. They have opened his door the better to taunt him.

Down a step. *Breathe out.*

He is chained to the back wall of his cell. His clothes are filthy. He stares at the dirty straw of the floor. Around the dungeon burn torches and in the fireplace a piglet roasts while the guards laugh about how good it smells and ask Rufra if he likes it, if he wants some roasted flesh.

Down a step. *Breathe in.*

I slide out my stabsword. The Conwy steel shines in the dim light, so different to the rough black iron of the eating knife in my left hand.

Down a step. *I am the instrument.*

I had always imagined myself as the sharp shining blade created for, and excelling in, my purpose. But without access to the tricks I had taken for granted I felt more like the blunt, dark eating knife.

Down a step. *Breathe out.*

I can see all four guards. The man with his back to me.
Breathe in

Two men at the table, eating.
I am the weapon.

The woman by the far door.
Breathe out.

She sees me.
I am the weapon.

I am the weapon.

My stabsword flashes out and the Conwy steel goes through the spine of the man with his back to me. He's dead before he knows I'm there. The woman by the door turns to raise the alarm and I throw my eating knife. It cuts through the air and catches her in the side of the neck. She tumbles backwards in a cascade of crashing armour. The two at the table stand and draw their blades. They come at me instead of trying to raise the alarm. I meet them.

First iteration: the Precise Steps. Into the third iteration, the Maiden's Pass. I go under a blade, and my Conwy steel darts out, through the eye and into the brain. *Fourteenth iteration: the Carter's Surprise.* I spin hand over foot across the table and land behind the last guard. He turns, slashing at me with his blade. *Sixth iteration, a Meeting of Hands.* I block the downward swing of his longsword. *Fourth iteration: the Surprised Suitor.* I jump back out of reach of the follow-up swing of his stabsword. *Second iteration,* the Quicksteps. Forward, forward, forward, pushing my opponent back and forcing him into a defensive posture. *Eighth iteration: the Placing of the Rose.* My blade up through his mouth and into his brain.

Rufra watches, open-mouthed.

"Girton?"

"Yes."

"You came for me?"

"Yes."

His eyes widen. There is fear there. Fear of me.

"I had nothing to do with Drusl's death. I swear I would never—"

"I know," I checked the dead guards for keys. Found them and unlocked Rufra's shackles. "Quickly, Rufra. Put these on." I threw the slave's clothes I had under my jerkin at him then went to look through the inside door to make sure no one had heard the brief struggle.

"Slave's clothes?" said Rufra.

"Yes."

"But I am not a slave."

"You are someone who wants to escape." He looked sceptical. "Look, Rufra. How many slaves are there in the castle?"

"I don't know. I've never thought about it."

"Exactly, Rufra. No one thinks about slaves; we barely even see them. Keep your eyes down and press yourself against the wall if anyone approaches. Get to Festival as quickly as you can."

"Festival? I doubt they will give me sanctuary, not while they are in the castle grounds." He pulled the slave jerkin over his head and then stared at me, his eyes wide. He looked frightened and young.

"This is not about sanctuary, Rufra."

His face screwed up in puzzlement.

"Not about—"

"Rufra, we do not have time for questions. Get dressed before someone comes."

"How will I get past the guards on the keepyard gate?"

"Here." I gave him the letter. "That was given to me by the queen and everything about it is real but a few words and the date. Nywulf is waiting for you with Cearis and her Riders. Be ready to act."

"Act?" He pulled on the slave's trousers and I dragged him out of the cell, pushing him towards the stairs.

"Yes, act. Arm up and be ready to act. Now go."

"But Girton," he said, "what about you?"

"I will be . . ." I tried to smile, remembering how my master had said we would most likely be going to our deaths. "I will be fine, but I have to go back into the castle."

I think he heard it in my voice, the belief that I would not be fine at all.

"I . . ."

"Go, Rufra," I shouted. "Nywulf waits."

He nodded and would have thanked me but his eyes were filling with tears and I think he was worried his voice would betray him. Then he glanced down at the body of the guard at the bottom of the stairs and nodded at me. I retrieved my eating blade and cleaned the cheap black iron on the guard's kilt, realising that whether I was the dull black knife or the shining Conwy blade it made no difference.

Both killed equally well.

Chapter 26

I changed my clothes and wiped what blood I could see from my skin then went to find Queen Adran. She was in conference with her son, Borniya, Hallin and Celot.

"Merela's boy," she said. "I see you are back on your feet. Shouldn't you be gone by now? I doubt the Landsmen will look kindly on the lover of a sorcerer."

"Mage-bent in more ways than one, eh?" added Hallin. Aydor laughed and his mother gave him a withering glance.

"Well?" she said. "Why are you here, boy?"

"Queen Adran," I said, and imagined crushing Aydor's throat with my bare hands, "my master requests your presence."

"She does?" Adran smoothed down the material of her jerkin. "And why would that be?"

"She thinks Rufra is innocent and there is another who wants Aydor's death, yet to be uncovered."

Aydor laughed.

"Quiet." His mother cut him off with a slash of her hand. "Unequivocal proof was found for Rufra and Neander's guilt. You and your master have done your work, so I suggest you both leave before the king finds out about your presence in his castle."

I opened my mouth, wanting to tell her the king knew about me but stilled my tongue. Whatever my master had planned may require surprise and so I would give away as little as possible.

"I only know my master is waiting for you in the king's room, Queen Adran."

"What?" Shock polluted her hauteur with harsh lines. When she spoke again she spoke quietly, her voice an urgent hiss. "Why is she there?"

"She has asked both you and Daana ap Dhyrrin to meet her there. I am afraid I do not know why, Queen Adran. As you said, I am only her boy." She glared at me and then leaned in close to Aydor and his friends, whispering something that Aydor clearly didn't want to hear and pointing at the door. Aydor's eyes widened and his hand went to the hilt of his blade before she hissed at him to get control of himself. He nodded, touching the scar on his face as he did. Behind him Hallin smiled and Borniya glared at me, nodding to himself.

"I'll see you two later," Aydor said sullenly to Borniya and Hallin as they pushed past me. Aydor's gaze settled on me and there was nothing but hate there. "Celot, you follow me," he added harshly. As he left he made sure to bang into me with his shoulder.

"Well, boy," said Adran, "are you going to lead me to my husband's chambers or simply stand there gawping at me?"

"I am sorry, Queen Adran." I turned to lead her through the castle as if I were a simple servant. As we walked it was like an invisible force travelled before us, pushing everyone – thankful, living or blessed – out of our way and back against the walls. Our small procession moved through a corridor of men and women with their eyes cast down until we arrived on the royal floor.

"You're a poor thing, aren't you?" said Adran. I ignored her. "I suppose the mage-bent get few chances at love, and Drusl, well, she was a pretty girl. If you like that washed-out scrawny look." I wondered how the queen of Maniyadoc even knew who her stable girl was; I could not imagine her setting foot in the stables. "Girton, the crippled assassin's apprentice, falls in love with a stable girl and she turns out to be an abomination. It is almost like one of those terrible stories Merela is so fond of."

I walked on with my hands balled into fists until she stopped me with a gentle touch to my shoulder and turned me so I looked into her face.

"Merela Karn will bring you only misery, Girton. That is her fate in life. It is what she brings to those she loves and who love her in turn." She stared down at me with a distant sort of pity, the type someone has when they hear another's pet has died. "I could use you. An intelligent boy with a talent for weapons could go a long way in my court. Women would want you, Girton, despite your foot." She took a step closer. She smelled of citrus and spices.

"Why are you offering me this?"

"I think Merela may be about to make a mistake." Her eyes flashed to the blade at my hip. "She and I were close once. We dreamed about changing the Tired Lands, making it a better place. I am near to being a power, a real power. Think about all the good I could do then, boy. You could stop your master making a mistake." She licked her lips and I wondered whether she meant a word she said.

"The Tired Lands is a cruel place," I said.

"Yes, and you have experienced more than your fair share of cruelty. Dragged around to kill, never having any friends of your own age. All these things that others take for granted have been denied you because of Merela's crusade."

"Crusade?"

She leaned in close, the smell of her perfume almost overwhelming as she stared into my eyes.

"She has never even told you, has she?"

"Told me what?"

"She lost a child, family, to a cruel man, Girton. And that is a wrong that can never be put right, so she seeks to right it for others. She is blind to all else."

"We strike on the order of the Open Circle," I said, my mouth dry.

"When it suits her," said Adran. "Merela does what she

wants, Girton. She uses people mercilessly for her own ends."

"As do you, Queen Adran. After all, the Tired Lands are cruel, are they not?"

She almost smiled and I wondered whether she thought I was taken in by her sudden offer of friendship.

"I could change that for you, Girton."

"Would you free Rufra If I stopped this 'mistake' happening?"

The almost-smile fell away.

"Someone has to be guilty, Girton; it is the way of things." She placed a hand on my shoulder. "You will make other friends — with my patronage even Aydor will come round to you."

One, my master.

Two, my master.

"They will be waiting for us," I said.

The queen nodded at me and her face became cold. "Well, let us hurry then. But you would do well to remember that some mistakes you do not get to live to regret."

We walked on in silence and as we approached the king's room our footfalls were joined by those of two guards. I glanced back to see Adran do the same, and when she turned back to me a smile played around her mouth.

The king's chamber was a huge room made claustrophobic by the stink of sickness. Doran ap Mennix lay in a massive four-poster bed of expensive slow-growing darkwood. He was propped up by mounds of pillows and had thick blankets tucked in around his chin, which made him appear nothing more than a thinly bearded head, the skin tinged with yellow and lined with pain. Breath stole in and out of his mouth as if it felt guilty for keeping the man alive but despite this his eyes remained bright and aware as they darted around the room, taking in all the players who had come to his stage.

My master leaned against the wall to my left, and by the opposite wall stood Daana ap Dhyrrin with four guards, each with a dab of red paint on their armour. Queen Adran went to stand by the head of the bed. The king ignored her. When his gaze settled on me he smiled, though it was a weak thing, more a twitch of the corners of his mouth.

"Why are you bothering my husband on his deathbed, Merela?" said Adran. "You should be leaving, along with your charge." She gestured at me as I went to stand by my master. The king's gaze followed me.

"Aye, but you gave me a job to do." The king's eyes flicked to my master.

"And it is done." To Adran.

"What job is this," said Daana ap Dhyrrin querulously, "and who is this woman, Queen Adran?"

"You will have seen her as the Death's Jester who came with Girton." She nodded in my direction. "They came here to find out if we had a traitor in our midst who wanted the heir dead."

"And we did," said Daana. "Tomorrow Rufra ap Vthyr will burn for his treason."

"Exactly," said Adran, "so why we are here I do not know. We should leave our beloved king in peace." She started to turn in a rustle of stiff brocaded trousers.

No," said the king. It was barely a whisper but it stopped everyone in the room dead.

"No?" said Adran. "But, my king, you are ill. We cannot—"

"I think our king means that Rufra is not a traitor," said my master.

The king's head moved, an almost infinitesimal nod.

"Be quiet," said Adran, "or our king will find out more than you wish him to know."

"The king already knows, Adran."

"Knows what?" said Daana.

The queen turned to him.

"She is Merela Karn, an assassin. The boy is her apprentice."

Daana ap Dhyrrin's rheumy eyes widened, and the guards either side of him lowered their pikes.

"You brought an assassin into the castle?" said Daana.

"To catch a assassin, use an assassin, Daana," said the queen. "And she has ended the threat."

"Then why do we waste our time here?" said the old man.

"Because I have not caught who hired your killer," said my master. "Not yet."

As they spoke the king's eyes flicked from one player to another and I was sure I saw the hint of a smile on his weathered face.

"Then please tell us," said the queen. "If it is not Rufra, a boy who expressed his wishes plainly in a letter, then who is our traitor?"

"Are," said my master. After a brief, stunned, silence, Adran started to laugh. It was not a false laugh, more a relieved one. I swallowed hard. I had been so sure my master had realised some particular truth that I had missed. But if that was it then her dart had not flown home.

"Are you suggesting, Merela, that I wanted to have my own son assassinated?" She laughed again. "Your time in the wilderness has addled your wits. I should have had you killed the moment you entered the castle."

"You misunderstand, Adran," said my master, and I let out the breath I had been holding. "I do not say you wanted your son dead; in fact, I know you have high hopes for him. I said that you were a traitor."

"Traitor to who?" said Adran. She took a step towards my master. The king watched with bright eyes and there was no mistaking his smile. The stink of sickness thickened in the room.

"To your king, to the high king, to the entire Tired Lands."

Adran laughed again . . . but was she a little less sure of herself?

"You talk madness. Guards!" She turned to the man and woman she had brought with her, "Arrest this woman and the boy. If they wish to ally themselves with the traitor, Rufra ap Vthyr, they can join him on the pyre."

The guards started forward but a word from the king stopped them in their tracks.

"No."

Adran looked from them, to me, to Daana ap Dhyrrin and then to the dying king.

"Guards," he whispered, "leave us a while. I want to hear what this assassin has to say." The few words seemed to steal all the energy from him. He let his head fall back against the pillow and in the time it took the guards to leave I do not think he breathed at all, though that small smile still played about his lips.

"So be it, Merela," said Queen Adran with a shrug. "Tell me of this madness that has possessed you. Expose your foolishness to us all."

My master pushed herself away from the wall. The yellow and purple tapestry behind her rippled. "Very well. Neander was training sorcerers together with Heamus. We are all agreed on that?"

"And Rufra was helping them," added Daana ap Dhyrrin.

"No." My master shook her head. "Not Rufra, though I am sure you would love us to think that. But we shall come to you later." She gave Daana ap Dhyrrin a brief smile. "Heamus was going out into the Tired Lands and using his Landsman skills to find those who showed some promise of magic and bringing them here. We know about Drusl, but Girton saw a list and there were others. No doubt they either left with Neander or they have gone to feed the pigs."

"We know this," said Adran.

"But I did not understand why Heamus would do such a thing."

"He held a grudge against our king," said Daana ap Dhyrrin, "over a serving girl. The heart can be a cruel master." Shock on the king's face at that? If so it was fleeting. There and gone, briefly considered and cast away as beneath him.

"Oh the heart can be. It is," said my master. "And as he knew how much King Doran hated magic, revenge may well have been the leash that drew Heamus into the plot, but Heamus did not strike me as cruel. If anything he struck me and Girton, who knew him better, as a kind man. Albeit one haunted by guilt."

"Not so kind if the stripes and scars on Drusl's back were to be believed," said Adran. I dug my nails into my palms.

"No. Not if he was the one who did that, but I truly believe Heamus was trying to make up for his past cruelties. Girton heard arguments between Heamus and Neander. Maybe Heamus was told bringing those gifted here would give them a chance at a good life as well as provide him with some small measure of revenge and redemption. Maybe he believed he was to watch over them and ensure they never hurt anyone. Truthfully, I do not know how he was persuaded to take part and I doubt we will ever find out."

"But Merela," said Adran softly, as if she were talking to a child, "if he was misled by Neander, why would he carry on once he realised?"

"Because once he had started it was too late, Adran. Once he had helped Neander he was caught. What could he do then? Who could he go to? The king?" Doran ap Mennix gave a soft shake of his head, his eyes steely hard. "And imagine what the Landsmen would do to him if they found out he had been protecting sorcerers. It's a mercy he died when he did." A nod from the king.

"All I see so far, Merela, is proof that Rufra and his father were working together."

"But they weren't, Adran. They weren't. And we all know that Neander was not Rufra's father." Was there a twitch of worry in Adran's smile then? And a mirror of it on Daana ap Dhyrrin's lined face? A widening of the king's eyes?

"Do we know that?" she said.

"Yes. Rufra is a threat to you, your son and also to Daana ap Dhyrrin's ambitions for his great-grandson. You may believe Rufra is guilty but Daana certainly knows different."

"What do you mean?"

"The squires wanted your son removed from training so they could progress as Riders. Daana had them put in written requests." The king's gaze was fixed on the old man. "I sent Girton into your rooms, Daana, and he saw them. What did Rufra's letter say, Girton?"

"It said, 'I, Rufra ap Vthyr, request the heir, Aydor ap Mennix, be removed from Rider training.' The other letters read the same but were signed by different squires. Rufra's request was on top, and someone had started to scrape off the the words 'from Rider training'." Adran shot a furious look at Daana ap Dhyrrin.

"You tried to have my son killed to set up Rufra?"

My master smiled. "He didn't try to have your son killed, Adran, but he did try to set up Rufra. He probably came up with the idea when the king's Heartblade was killed and he realised an assassin had been employed. By placing blame on Rufra, he removes a threat to his favourite grandson and ensures you let your guard down for the real assassin to move in. All his problems are solved in one sweep and his hands are never dirtied. When I asked him for leave to exit the castle he saw his opportunity. He must have seen Heamus leave and made the connection. Fitchgrass knows, the man made enough noise."

"And how, mistress assassin," said Daana ap Dhyrrin, "would I know what Heamus storming out the castle meant?"

"I was just getting to that, Daana," she said. "It seemed

very strange to me that you were so open about your ambitions for your grandson. Unless, of course, you knew something that made you feel like you were safe." She turned away from Daana. "Queen Adran, how are your negotiations going with the high king regarding marrying Aydor to his sister?"

"I don't see that's any of your business," she said. "Ambition is not treason."

"No, it is not. But it is no secret that the marriage is unlikely. The high king is not the type to be blinded by your beauty and do as you wish. No doubt he sees your ambition and has no wish to invite a scorpion into his castle." A soundless laugh from the king. "So, knowing that, you have made other arrangements."

Adran glowered. "I don't know what you mean." The king was staring at Adran now, his gaze unswerving.

"When I explained to Girton about the high king's family and why I thought a marriage unlikely, he asked if you were going to start a war. I thought the idea ridiculous because you could never scrape together enough troops." Queen Adran blinked, looked to her husband, looked away. "But it wasn't ridiculous, was it? You didn't think you'd need an army. Daana ap Dhyrrin knew what you were doing –" Doran was nodding now, his head moving slowly up and down as my master spoke "– which is how he knew that Heamus storming out to the stables meant Neander may soon be running for his life. And it's also why Daana ap Dhyrrin was not frightened of you. He knew Neander and Heamus were training sorcerers –" she smiled at the queen "– and he knew they were doing it for you and your son. He could expose you so you daren't move against him."

"I'd be a fool to use sorcerers," snapped Adran.

"Oh you would. The Landsmen would bring everything they had against you. Maybe you thought the threat would be enough. And Daana ap Dhyrrin didn't stop you because he couldn't lose. You get what you want? He gets Castle Maniyadoc for Tomas. Something goes wrong with your scheme? You are disgraced, and he gets Castle Maniyadoc for Tomas. I expect you pushed Neander and Heamus to give you sorcerers quickly. You have never been patient. So Neander used increasingly brutal methods. It was probably falling apart well before Drusl killed Kyril. Heamus had no stomach for Neander's methods, and his sorcerers, as poor Drusl showed, were increasingly unstable. When we started looking for the assassin we started to get too near to your secret—"

"This is all nonsense," said Adran, but she could not look at her husband who stared intently at her from his deathbed. "Why would I invite you here if I was planning such treason?"

"You invited me here," said my master quietly, "because you thought our past meant I could be manipulated and because, though you have many terrible and ruthless qualities, Adran Mennix, you do love your son. In your own way."

"I think the strain has broken you, Merela," said Adran. Did she sound frightened? "You cannot expect me to believe Rufra innocent when all you have is a fairy story concocted from fancies and wishful thinking."

"This woman sounds desperate, Queen Adran," said Daana ap Dhyrrin. "Maybe she wants to ingratiate herself with the Landsmen in the hope they will overlook the fact she is an assassin?"

"Possibly," said Adran, "though I doubt anyone would believe the word of an assassin. As long as we stand together, Daana, we have nothing to worry about."

"These 'fancies', as you call them, were necessary so you would understand who really wants your son dead." My master's tone was ice, and her fingers flicked out signs telling me to stand close to her.

The king's head slowly turned so he could look at my master, and his mouth opened slightly, his tongue wet his lips.

"And just who is it that wants Aydor dead?" sneered Adran. "I see no one else here." She sounded smug.

"Look harder, Adran." My master stared past Adran at the bed.

"The king?" Adran's face went white. The king coughed. His cough became a laugh and then a cough again. He forced a smile onto his face though pain wracked him and drool ran down one side of his chin. Adran took a step back to stand next to her husband's head and placed a hand on the bed. "Doran?" Her hand scrabbled at the blankets looking for the king's hand, but she could not find it. He simply stared at her. She turned from him, back to face my master. "You lie, Merela. You are a bitter, beaten woman trying to cause trouble. My husband hates assassins."

"Not as much as he hates sorcerers and poisoners." The king continued to watch, the only life left in his eyes, which sparkled, as if in amusement.

"No," said Adran.

My master carried on speaking, using a pointing finger to stab out her words – she was relentless.

"Nothing made any sense here. Such a web of lies and deceit. Aye, it is the same as all castles, but it was not until Girton told me twice that the king recognised him as an assassin that everything came together in my mind. Do you know what he said to Girton, Adran?" The queen sank down until she was sitting on the bed. "He said, 'make it quick', and he raised his head to bare his throat. Girton thought the king believed we had come for him – natural enough as we all know you are poisoning him. Girton didn't know the king was saluting him and asking him to make sure his target didn't suffer. The king would only do that if he expected an assassin. And he would only expect an assassin to present themselves to him if he had requested one." She lowered her voice to a harsh whisper. "He knew what you were doing, Adran. He knew."

The king did not move, could not for all I knew, but his eyes were constantly shifting spots of light as he watched the people in the room play out their drama.

"No," said Adran in a much softer whisper than my master's. She turned to the king. "Doran, he is our son."

"Magic," said King Doran ap Mennix in his weak rasping voice, "is an abomination. It cannot be allowed back into the land. There could be no worse betrayal, Adran."

"But it was for Aydor, Doran – all of it. If you had asked I would have stopped. You should have told me. I would have stopped."

"No," said Doran, "you would not. You lie even now. You know no other way."

Something ignited in Adran's eyes then, a fierce anger.

"It was for our son, Doran!" she shrieked. "Our son!"

"He's weak, Adran, not fit to rule. And to use magic? So much pain you have caused me." He narrowed his eyes and a thin line of blood-flecked spittle ran from the corner of his taut mouth. "I wanted you to watch your son die, Adran. I wanted you to hurt and then I wanted to watch you die in despair. Just like I am." He started to laugh but it become a cough. Droplets of blood hung like dew in his beard

Adran stared at her husband, her face frozen as if an artist had drawn the worst possible version of her; a woman haggard, old and bitter. Then she drew on some well of inner strength and her face hardened, her lips became a thin white line.

"All this relies on the king being alive to vouch for you, Merela." She stood. "Without him you have nothing." She drew a long slim dagger from her jerkin. "And my husband will be dead well before any Landsmen get here."

"I have a letter signed by the king." My master tapped

her jerkin and her other hand flickered out, "Be ready". "I will leave it with the Festival Lords and instruct them to give it to the Landsmen when they arrive." A flicker of a smile crossed the king's face and I wondered whether it was really magic he hated, or his wife. "You are over, Adran. You are finished, and so is Aydor."

Adran glanced over at Daana ap Dhyrrin who nodded slowly.

"She is right, Adran, I am afraid," he said, "and you will bring us all down with you."

"Do not listen to this assassin, Daana," said the queen. "There is a way out of this for all of us."

"Yes, of course. You are right, my queen. There is always a way out." Daana ap Dhyrrin reached back into his elaborate headdress, like an old man about to scratch his head in thought. Then his hand flashed forward. A throwing knife cut a glittery path across the room and buried itself in the throat of Queen Adran Mennix. She slumped to the floor, a look of surprise on her face as she began to drown in her own blood. Her eyes searched for help. First she looked to my master but found no pity there. Then she looked to me for help she was already far beyond. Lastly she reached out a bloodied hand towards the king but his face was stone as he watched the light go out of her eyes.

Daana ap Dhyrrin smiled as he watched the queen die. Then he raised his voice. It was far louder than I expected of a man so old.

"Help!" he shouted. "Assassin! Assassin! The queen is dead! Assassin!"

I drew my blade to silence him, but my master grabbed my arm.

"Forget him, Girton," she said. "Now we run."

Chapter 27

My master pushed back the tapestry; behind it were our weapons. She took her stabswords as I grabbed my Conwy longblade. Then she pushed me towards the door and I kicked it open. Daana ap Dhyrrin continued shouting, "Assassins!" while he advanced on the king with a blade. I spun, ready to help the king but my master pulled me from the room.

"Doran ap Mennix knows he's finished no matter what. At least this way is quicker than the poison. Come!" She grabbed me by my shoulder. "Kill anyone who tries to stop us. We have no friends here."

I'd expected the guards that had been sent out of the king's room to be waiting for us. Instead I was greeted by the clash of arms. Adran's two guards were fighting two of Daana's guards; the other two were vanishing down the corner stairs, shouting, "It has begun, it has begun!" Forgetting I was meant to be escaping the castle, I watched the soldiers lay into each other with pikes. For a moment I was hypnotised by the struggle and then my master was dragging me away.

"What is happening, Master?"

"You know how nervous the guards have been? This castle is full of spies, Girton. Behind the timidity of the blessed is a hotbed of paranoia and factions. Two hours ago I made sure four guards loyal to Daana ap Dhyrrin were found with their throats slit." She grinned her feral grin. "Such a move is close to a declaration of war. This place has been a wildfire waiting to happen since the moment we got here and we have set the spark. Now we must hope not to get caught up in the ensuing blaze."

We rounded a corner and four guards, all with red paint splashed on their arms, rushed at us with their pikes held low. With a flick of her wrists my master sent two sleek throwing daggers spinning out to take the front two guards in the throat, then slid to a stop, coming down on one knee as I followed up with my longsword. The two guards following jerked their pikes aside to avoid skewering their stricken comrades and I slashed my sword across at throat height, cutting them both down.

The deaths of the four guards had taken less than a second.

At the first stair we came to there was a thick scrum of guards with red splashes trying to stop another group coming up.

"Back," said my master before the guards noticed us. "We head for the other corner stair, though I imagine that will be guarded too."

"What about the main staircase?"

"Will be the most heavily guarded of all."

"We could go down the outer wall."

"Not in this wind, and both factions will have archers and crossbowyers watching the walls."

"Then we fight and die here," I said.

"No. Never give up, Girton. Not until the last drop of blood has run from your body." She grabbed my sleeve. "Come on."

We ran back the way we had come and straight into another small group of guards. They were ill prepared for us. I cut the first down before she had the chance to draw her blade. The second raised a sword and I ran forward, barrelling into him with my shoulder and knocking him off balance. As we fell I forced my dagger in beneath his armpit, hearing his heart burst in a pained gasp, feeling it in the rush of hot blood over my hand. Beside me my master dodged a sideways slash and darted in, her blade opening the neck of one attacker, who fell, clasping at a wound that would not be staunched. With a backwards slash she brought down her second attacker.

And then misfortune caught us.

There are moments in a fight when no amount of skill can save you, and this was one. A crossbowyer stood further down the corridor, his weapon loaded and aimed at my master, his eyes wide with fear. The second my master saw him she threw a knife and leaped out the way of his bolt. Had he aimed true all would have been fine, but in his fear he had turned to run at the same time he loosed the bolt from his crossbow and it went wide. Instead of leaping out of danger my master leaped into it. The bolt took her in the thigh at the same time her knife took the crossbowyer in the back of the neck

"Dead gods!" Her leg gave way under her.

"Master!"

"Help me up, Girton."

I pulled her up taking her weight on my shoulder. I heard voices – more guards coming towards us.

"We're lost," she said.

"No." I glanced behind, expecting soldiers to appear around the corner. Instead, down the corridor, I saw the priest of Xus, clothed in black robes and with a face eternally locked into a half sneer/half smile. He was bent over the corpse of the crossbowyer. I froze. He straightened up and raised his head, exposing a milk-white throat to me, then pushed aside a tapestry and vanished behind it.

"Come on, Master."

I pulled her down the corridor and behind the tapestry was a door – a secret passage. I caught a glimpse of a black robe vanishing into the darkness ahead of us and followed, letting the tapestry fall back into place behind me and plunging us into a darkness so complete I could not see my own hand in front of my face.

"Shh," said my master. I could hear water dripping and something scraping rhythmically against stone. Faint voices raised in anger, though they seemed to be a long way off, and somewhere in front of us the pitter-patter of footsteps.

My master's warm hand found mine.

"Well done, Girton," she gasped. "I did not even know this passage was here."

I was about to say something about the priest of Xus but realised my master had not seen him, even though she had been looking straight at him.

"Are you badly hurt?" I asked.

"No." She spoke through pain-gritted teeth. "The bolt passed through, but I am bleeding freely." I heard the ripping of material and then a gasp as she pulled a tourniquet tight around her leg. "I should be able to walk now, Girton. You lead."

I followed the sound of the priest of Xus's steps.

"Stairs," I said as my foot probed the ground before me. "Careful, Master, they are damp and slippery." We moved down and along, always following the footsteps, which skittered away in front of me. Occasionally the priest would stop to allow us to catch up, and sometimes I heard strange and inhuman laughter – though it sounded like it came from very far away.

"Hedgings, master."

"Stories for children, Girton. Keep moving."

Round and round we went, feeling our way along damp walls and down slimy stairways. These tunnels felt different to the ones Adran had taken us through to see Kyril's body: older, so old it was almost like we travelled through another world. When I finally opened a door back into the keep a blinding light flooded the tight space between the walls, and though it felt like we had walked a long way, I realised we had only gone down two floors.

We crept along a corridor until we found two guards wearing yellow and purple tabards identifying them as loyal to the ap Mennix line. They were on edge, jittery, but all their attention was focused on the door to the stairway in front of them.

"Tomas's lot going to come up or down the stairs, Girron?" said the guard on the left. Despite her wound my master still managed to be utterly silent as we limped towards the two guards.

"Whichever way they comes, we'll not let 'em any further."

I slid my blade from its scabbard.

"What if they win?"

"They won't. Some o' ours been sent to take the stables. Who has the mounts wins the fight, everyone knows that."

The one called Girron, tall for a Tired Lands man, turned – only a little but it was enough – and he saw us. He barely had time to shout. As he brought round his pike to face us in the narrow corridor he tangled himself up in his friend. I lunged, my Conwy blade cutting through his leather armour and the flesh beneath, silencing him in one swift move. At the same same my master slashed her blade across the throat of the second guard, who fell, coughing as she bled out.

Come, Girton," said my master, reaching for the door to the stairs. "It may be clear further down now."

"No, Master." Down the corridor the priest of Xus pulled aside another tapestry and vanished behind it. "This way," I said, pulling her after me and into more tunnels, more darkness, slimy walls and crumbling stairs. We went round and round, listening to men and women fighting and dying for Aydor and Tomas. Sometimes, as we made our way through the tunnels, I had the oddest sensation we were surrounded by huge crowds of people, it was not unlike the dizzying claustrophobia I had felt at Festival. But this time I had not been drinking and when I put my hand out it met only cold and empty air.

We left the black tunnels and this time there was no shadowy mocking figure waiting for us, only the sound of war and the bite of the air, cold and thick with mist. The passages had led us outside the walls of the keep and we had exited near where I had entered the dungeons. There were bodies scattered around and shadowy figures half hidden in the mist. I saw Aydor, with Celot by his side. He had gathered some troops and arrayed them across the court-yard, their shields locked into a wall bristling with spears and pikes. Opposite them, Tomas, his squires and guards, all with red material tied around their arms. Both sides were working themselves up into a frenzy, beating swords and pikeshafts against shields to attract their fellows. More guards ran from the keep, pulling on armour as they rounded the water clock. The castle was like a disturbed lizard hive, disgorging defenders to the beat of the shields. Aydor had the bigger of the two forces and had placed his shield wall across the courtyard to stop Tomas getting to the gatehouse and from there to the stables. Behind them the great gates were shut.

"Stay in the shadows, Girton. We can't fight them all." I nodded, glad she wanted to avoid a fight. My master was in no state for combat and my muscles were burning with fatigue. "We need to get out. Our best option is to get to Festival, claim sanctuary."

"The gate is shut."

"I am wounded, not blinded, Girton."

"You have a plan, Master?"

"No, I didn't expect we would live this long." She let out a hiss of pain, and I glanced at her leg. It was awash with blood. She pulled on the tourniquet around her thigh, tight-ening it. "We must open the gate. Rufra will need it open for his Riders."

With a shout of "Huh!" Aydor's guards beat their swords and pikes against their shields in unison and took a step forward. Tomas's troops gave an answering shout and advanced. Insults began to fly across the narrowing gap between them. From the windows above arrows began to fall, but there were not many and in the mist and the darkness they were poorly aimed. We hugged the wall as we worked our way around the two sides, they were too intent on each other to notice us. When we neared the towers that flanked the gate my master switched to sign language.

"Guard me while I work the windlass."

We skirted the tower, keeping low, and found two guards in the windlass room watching the shield walls from a small window and exchanging bets on who would win. We cut them down before they knew we were there. My master put her back against the windlass that opened the gate and took two deep breaths, stealing herself for the pain.

"Master, I should do that."

"No," she grunted as she pushed against the windlass. "When the gates start to open, troops will come." The windlass started to turn. "My leg will hamper me in a fight."

"At least let me help." I started towards her, the chains of the windlass shaking and rattling as they began to move.

"No! Take up that bow." She nodded at the weapon lying on the floor. "Give those who will come reason to stay back."

I picked up the bow, glanced around the gatehouse.

"Master, there are no arrows."

She grunted again, and now the windlass started to turn more easily.

"Then . . . Girton . . . get ready . . . to . . . fight."

I stood guard at the door as the gates inched open. Behind me my master sweated and hissed in agony as she turned the windlass. The two lines of troops were so preoccupied with each other that we had the gates half open before a shout went up.

"The gatehouse!"

Aydor's wall turned their heads and Tomas took advantage

of the distraction to charge his troops forward. The sound of metal on metal as the two lines met crashed through air which quickly filled with the sounds of grunting, screaming and shouting as the troops set about each other.

"The gates!" Aydor shouted. "It is the cripple." He pointed his blade at me then at some men in the rear of his line. "You and you and you! Kill him! Ten bits for his head."

Five guards broke away from the rear of Aydor's line as the gates crept further open. I drew my longsword and stabsword. The guards ran toward me, four armed with pikes and their captain with a sword.

I readied myself. These were not bandits like those I had faced in the wood. These were real soldiers, and out in the open their pikes were an excellent weapon. The captain ran at me but all he saw was a mage-bent child and he was overconfident, leaving behind the men who would have protected him. He grinned as if he already had his coin and held his longsword high for a downward slash. As his blade came down, I simply stepped forward and dropped to one knee with my stabsword held out. In his eagerness to kill me he impaled himself on my blade.

"No," he said quietly. "That is not right." I pulled my stabsword loose and he fell to his knees, staring up at me. His mouth moved without making a sound as his strength drained out onto the cobbles. It had not been a killing blow so I slit his throat. I did not want to worry about him at my back while I faced the guards following him. On his back he had a quiver with four arrows in it and I took them, picking up the bow and stringing an arrow. The pikers slowed in their approach, stopped and took a moment to organise themselves, hunkering down behind their shields. I loosed an arrow which stuck in a shield as the four advanced on me. Armoured I would have stood a fair chance, but I was unarmoured; even a glancing blow from one of their pikes would end me. I strung another arrow and backed away, switching where I aimed the bow from guard to guard. Quickly, I fired my remaining three arrows. One found a chink in the shields and a woman fell screaming. Then the hard grip of my master was around my arm.

"The gate is open. Run." I dropped the bow and we ran as best we could. Within twenty paces the mist had concealed the gatehouse and the guards who had followed us, though I did not doubt they were still there.

"Rufra will be at the stables," I said. "He will come. He will protect us."

"No, Festival, Girton. We head for Festival."

I was about to argue when we were sent sprawling in the mud. I had tripped over a corpse. The dead man had the red rag of Tomas, and further on we found a second corpse, this without a rag. The ground underfoot was churned up by the feet of guards, and in between the footprints I found the tracks of mounts. I could not tell how many.

"Everyone wants to control the stables," said my master. "Who has the mounts, wins the fight.'

"This looks like a lot of troops," I said, staring at the ground. "Rufra may need our help."

"We are tired and hurt, Girton. We need help, we are in no position to give it. Head for Festival." I stared at her. She was tired. Blood ran down her leg and stained her skirts.

"Very well." I slung my master's arm over my shoulder and she had found a pike which she used as a crutch. We moved as quickly as we could. Out in the mist I heard guards shouting to each other. They were looking for us, and I heard far more than four of them now. Above the shouts rose the sounds of battle. The cloudy air was alive with the sound of suffering and death.

We slipped and slid forward. As well as her wound, my master was fatigued from days of staying alert to watch Aydor and Adran, and the sheer physical effort of turning the giant windlass. As we moved through the misty darkness her legs kept going from underneath her. The sounds of fighting were swallowed by the mist and we struggled on through an eerie quiet. In the darkness I saw the flickering torches that marked the entrance to Festival.

"Master, we are here."

"Stop!"

The voice came out of the night, we staggered to a halt.

"Sanctuary," shouted my master, but her voice was weak. She spat and tried again, this time louder. "Sanctuary! We request sanctuary at Festival."

"Tomorrow," came the reply. "Festival shows no favours or sides. While the fighting continues our doors stay shut."

"But that is not the way—" began my master. The unseen gatekeeper interrupted:

"Blame your queen, she changed the rules."

"Adran is dead," said my master. "And we are not her subjects and so not safe out here."

"Our gates are closed," came the voice again.

"No!" I took a step forward, my blades coming out of their sheaths. "She is hurt. We need—"

I heard the twang of a crossbow and a bolt buried itself into the mud by my foot.

"Next one is in your throat," came out of the mist.

I felt my master's hand on my arm.

"Come, Girton. There is no help for us here."

"Then we try for the stables." I put her arm over my shoulders. "Rufra will help."

"Rufra will have enough to think on, if he lives," she said. "He will not care about us."

"He will come," I said, and we headed out into the night.

Gradually, as we moved through the night, my master transferred more and more of her weight onto me.

"Don't stop, Master," I said. "We need to keep going. Rufra will take the stables and ride on the castle. He will come."

"If he lives," she gasped. "Both Aydor and Tomas have sent troops . . ."

"He will come."

We stumbled on, slipping as much as walking in the freezing mud. Out in the mist I heard more voices echoing around us, searching. My master dropped the pike she had been using to walk with and fell. I slid to a stop, trying to pull her up.

"I am done, Girton. Run." She took her blades from their scabbards and pushed herself up to a kneeling position. "They will find us. It is only a matter of time. I will buy you as much time as I can when they do."

"No." I pulled her up. "Listen, Master." She cocked her head to better hear the voices in the mist. "They are moving away from us, I am sure of it."

"Girton . . ."

"And Rufra will come."

"You cannot be—"

"He will come!"

She stared at me, long and hard, then nodded, too tired to argue and, knowing I would not leave her, she put her blades away and struggled up. I picked up the pike, put it in her hands then glanced over my shoulder into the mist. We forced ourselves on. Somewhere in front of us I thought I heard fighting.

"Girton," said my master. She was near to finished – I could hear it in her voice – and I was not much better. "Listen to me, Girton . . ."

"Look!" I pointed into the mist. Mounted figures were approaching. "Rufra!" We staggered on a few steps. "It is Rufra, Master."

"There are only two mounts," she said.

The Riders approaching from the mist were armoured for war, holding shields and lances. Razor-sharp gilding glinted on their mount's antlers.

"Rufra has sent them for us!" I shouted. The knights put down their visors, lowered their lances.

"Girton, that isn't Rufra."

"But—"

"It isn't Rufra!" she shouted in my face

The mounts screamed as their Riders put in the spur. Then they charged forward, heads coming down to impale us on the points of their antlers. I tried to run and pull my master with me.

'No," she shouted, gripping tightly onto my arm, holding me still against all good sense while my mind screamed, Run!

The two mounts raced towards us, growing until they filled my vision and the sound of their galloping feet filled my ears. I was sure my master intended us to die together on their antlers and I closed my eyes. Then she shouted, "Now!" From somewhere she mustered up the energy to shove me out of the way. *Fourteenth iteration* – cartwheeling out of the path of the rampaging mounts. I slipped in the mud as I landed, falling to all fours. The moment I had my feet under me I heard my master shout.

"Girton! Pike!" I turned. My master threw me the weapon and I plucked it from the air. Then, to try and draw the Riders away from my master, I ran as fast as I could away from her until I heard galloping feet behind me. A glance back. Dead gods! Only one followed. I counted the animal's footsteps as it gained, trying to feel the rhythm of its run. *Duh-duh-duhduh, duh-duh-duhduh, duh-duh-duhduh*. When it was near enough to gore me I clasped the staff of the pike tight and dropped, rolling under the animal's feet, hoping the Rider wasn't well trained enough to change his animal's gait and trample me – he wasn't. I heard him swear as I rolled under the galloping mount unscathed and came to my feet behind him with the pike extended. The mount screamed as its Rider pulled hard on the rein and it skidded to a halt on its haunches. To my left, almost lost in the mist, my master was limping in a tight circle, making it hard for the other Rider to get at her, but it was a desperate move and she was tiring quickly. Both Riders rode black mounts and I knew they must be Borniya and Hallin, though I had no idea which of them I faced. My attacker came round again, this time keeping his mount's head low to stop me going under his animal. He spurred the mount on and I brought the pike down. The animal started to sweep its head back and forth to knock the weapon away. As it closed on me I dived to the side, throwing the pike between the mount's legs. With an audible crack and a scream of agony, the animal and Rider went down in a tangle of broken legs and broken wood. Had I been lucky, the fall would have killed the Rider but I was not. He dragged himself to his feet and, taking the shield from his back, unhooked a warhammer from his belt. He used his weapon to kill the screaming mount before turning to me and lifting his visor to reveal a misshapen face. Borniya, which meant the Rider trying to skewer my master must be Hallin.

"We were disturbed in Calfey, mage-bent, but this time I'm going to kill you. I swear it." He hefted his warhammer and brought his shield round in front of him.

"I didn't kill your friend Kyril, Borniya."

"I don't really care." He grinned at me.

I attacked first, my long sword flickering out. I expected him to take the blow on his shield but he danced back out of my reach and I stumbled forward two paces before catching myself. My breath came in great gasps.

"You've had a long day." He let the shield slip from his arm and drew his stabsword. "You're tired, mage-bent." He lunged at me with the stabsword, and I jumped back, sliding in the mud and fighting to keep my balance. Ordinarily I would have walked over Borniya, but he was fully armoured and fresh to the fight where exhaustion had robbed me of my skill and the pattern cut into my chest stopped me using any assassin tricks.

"If you're expecting your friend Rufra to save you then I'm sorry. He ran into a little surprise in the stables. I don't think he'll be coming." He feigned coming forward and I staggered backwards again. Making him laugh. "Oh dear, mage-bent, oh dear."

Out of the corner of my eye, I saw my master fall – Hallin's mount sweeping its head backwards and forwards, catching my master a glancing blow that sent her stumbling away to fall in the mud. While I was distracted, Borniya attacked. He brought his stabsword down and I brought my blades up – *sixth iteration* – to block his attack. He'd been waiting for me to block and followed the blow from his stabsword with a blow from his warhammer. I tried to move but wasn't quick enough, and the longsword was ripped from my hand by the impact. Before he could follow up I lunged with my stabsword, aiming for his eye. He was quick to dodge but the blade still scored his cheek. It wasn't a killing blow, but it was enough to make him back off a little. He wiped at the blood running down his face then stared at the stain on his gauntlet.

"Hallin!" he shouted. "Kill the woman quickly. I don't want you to miss out on killing the cripple."

"Am I too much for you, Borniya?" I said. He licked his lips where blood running from his cheek had stained them red. "Are you scared of me?"

I threw myself at Borniya. It was the last thing he expected and the last thing I should have done. I hit him hard, pushing us both down into the freezing mud, but he was armoured and physically bigger than me. I tried to bring my knee up into his groin, but the rods of iron laced into his kilt protected him. I tried to find the edge of his armour with the point of my stabsword, scraping the tip across the metal squares

He stank of old sweat.

Borniya grabbed my hand, slamming it into the ground until I could no longer hold the blade. I had been stupid to go in close with him. Bit by bit his greater strength and weight started to tell. He rolled me away from my blade and, grunting like pigs in the mud, we continued to struggle and roll until we were stopped by the warm corpse of his mount.

My left arm was trapped against the dead animal. I tried landing punches with my right but only bruised my knuckles on his armour, while Borniya's punches left me gasping. He tried to get his hand round my throat I broke his grip, once, twice, three times. He delivered three quick rabbit punches into my side with a gauntleted hand, stealing the wind from me. His strength was too much. His hands locked around my throat and this time I could not loosen them.

"This," he hissed, thumbs pushing down on my windpipe, "is much more satisfying . . ." The edges of my vision began to darken. I stretched my right arm out, searching for a rock, a stick, anything to use as a weapon. ". . . way to . . ." My fingers hit wood, closed around it. ". . . kill you." With the last vestige of my strength I swung the piece of wood, seeing a flash of metal in the moment before I shoved the spiked end of the broken pike into the vulnerable area of his armour under the arm. His eyes widened. I pushed harder. His grip loosened. "No," he said. He leaned forward, drool spilling from his mouth onto my face. "No," he said again. Then he went limp, falling dead onto the stomach of his mount.

Gasping, and with every muscle aching, I pulled the pike loose and used it to to help me stand. Further out in the mist Hallin, armed with sword and shield, was advancing on my master as she stumbled away from him, doubled over in pain.

"Hallin." The word came out of my mouth as barely more than a whisper and I had to gather my strength before shouting again. "Hallin!" He turned. "Borniya is dead. I killed him. Now face me. Unless you are only brave enough to kill my servant?" He stopped, turned in my direction. It was drilled into squires not to leave a live enemy behind you, but I had to distract him from my master. "Are you a coward, Hallin?" I felt my legs begin to buckle and clasped the pike staff harder. "I think you are a coward."

Hallin took a step towards me.

"I am not a coward."

"Prove it."

He came towards me at a jog, his shield up. He slowed and came to a stop when he saw the body of Borniya, and for a moment I thought I stood a chance. You really are a coward, I thought. You are afraid. Then my world spun, faded, and when it came back into focus I was on one knee, only the broken pike keeping me upright. Hallin smiled.

We both knew I was done.

"Aydor will reward me well for your head, cripple." He walked forward, swinging his blade.

I had nothing left.

Nothing.

"You!"

The shout filled the mist. Hallin's sword stopped mid-swing.

"You! Face me! Face me now!" Out of the mist strode a warrior in a blessed's armour, all silvered and sleek. His visor was down and he held a blade in each hand. I did not know the armour, or the device of the golden flying lizard emblazoned across it, but there was no mistaking the voice.

Rufra.

Rufra had come. He had come alone, but he had come.

"So —" Hallin spat on the ground "— the filthy ap Vthyr has come to die with his mage-bent friend." Rufra didn't answer, only lifted his longsword and pointed it at Hallin as he marched forward. "I'll kill you, ap Vthyr," said Hallin, "and then I'll kill your pet cripple."

"No," shouted Rufra.

"Oh, I think so. I'll kill the cripple slowly. Slice him up.

You know all about that, eh? You begged me to stop when I cut you; you think your friend will beg as well, eh? Think he'll cry like a child when the knife bites?"

Rufra threw himself into an attack, roaring as he brought his blade down in a heavy overhead swing. Hallin brought up his shield and Rufra rained blows on it. He punctuated each blow with a word. "No!" The first blow staggered Hallin. "You!" The second forced him back. "Will!" The third pushed him to his knees. "Not!" He landed the fourth blow so hard his blade broke in two.

Hallin reacted immediately, pushing Rufra back with his splintered shield and swinging with his longsword. Rufra dodged the blade and attacked again. I knew Rufra was a skilled swordsman but he showed none of his skill here. His attack was all fury, a withering hail of blows with his stabsword and broken longsword. He made no attempt to defend himself; he only attacked, forcing Hallin to react to him and giving him no room to counter. Pace by pace he pushed Hallin back until, with a vicious swipe of his stabsword, he broke Hallin's guard. Rufra followed up with a blow of such strength his broken longsword punched through the chest piece of Hallin's armour. Then he pulled the dying Hallin close to him, shoving the broken sword further up into the squire's body. He gave the blade a final twist and I heard Rufra's voice, a harsh whisper:

"I will not let you hurt my friend."

Rufra stepped back, pulling the blade from Hallin's corpse and letting the body fall. He lifted the broken and blood-covered blade that was meant to secure his death, stared at it, then threw it to one side in disgust before hurrying towards me, lifting his visor as he approached.

"Rufra," I said. There was so much more I wanted to say but the words would not come.

"Let me help you." He put my arm over his shoulder, taking my weight and helping me stand.

"My master," I said, pointing to where she had fallen. He nodded and helped me limp over to where she lay face down. As we approached she pushed herself over with a painful grunt.

"Master, are you—"

"The beast's blow broke a few ribs, wrenched my arm." She winced. "I've had worse." I helped her to sit up and she looked at Rufra. "You are alone?"

"I am with my friend," he said, glancing at me. Then he pointed into the mist, "And we are not alone any more." The shades of Riders were slowly solidifying. At their head they carried a bonemount, the skull of a mount which carried the authority of a Tired Lands king. I recognised the skull amid the fluttering streamers tied to it: one antler was shorter than the other, which meant it was Imbalance, Rufra's mount killed in Barnew's Wood. I do not know whether it was exhaustion or something other, but as they appeared these Riders seemed something more than human: taller, thinner, their mounts barely making a sound as though they trod on air, not filthy mud. Both mounts and Riders appeared to glow. If you had told me at that moment that the gods had returned to life, I would have believed you.

"The stables are ours now," said Nywulf, and the moment was gone. Before me were twenty Riders in scratched armour. Some still bore the remnants of Festival colours; others wore the armour they had used in the squireyard. Every one of them had a golden flying lizard painted on their armour, some done crudely, some beautifully but the insignia left no question of their allegiance. These were Rufra's Riders.

Nywulf had brought Rufra's pure white mount, Balance. He let go of the mount's reins.

"We'll take the castle next if you'd be good enough not to run off again."

Rufra smiled and gave me a shrug.

"Will you fight with us, Girton?" said Rufra.

I wanted to, more than anything. My eyes darted to my master, small and hurt, trying to force herself to her feet. "I . . ."

Rufra followed my gaze and bowed his head, then gently placed his gauntleted hand on my arm.

"I understand." He squeezed my arm and turned, putting one foot in Balance's stirrup.

"Wait!" I called. He turned, raising a quizzical eyebrow. "Wait, only a moment." By now his Riders surrounded us. I could feel their impatience in the air and hear it in the growling and hissing of their mounts. I found what I was looking for quickly, shining in the mud: my blades. I limped over and retrieved them. "Take my blades, Rufra." I placed them in his hands. "You seem to have lost yours. You will need a good blade."

He grinned, then noticed the wording on the longsword where the binding had fallen away during the fighting.

"Conwy? Girton, these are a king's weapons."

"And you are a king," I said. We locked stares for a second, then he looked away and nodded before turning back to me. He placed the Conwy stabsword in my hand.

"Keep this," he said, his voice coming close to breaking as he closed my fingers around the hilt. "And know where you find its twin, you find a brother." Then he pulled himself up into Balance's saddle, unable to look at me.

Rufra bent forward in his saddle with his head enveloped in the smoky clouds of his breath and he took two long deep lungfuls of air, as if filling himself with courage for the task to come. Then he stood in his stirrups, lofted his Conwy blade and pulled on his mount's rein so it turned in a tight circle that allowed him to look each of the mounted men and women around him in the eye. You would not have known he was only fourteen. He seemed to age five years and the nervousness and melancholy that had followed him in the squireyard was replaced by a ferocious smile.

"Today," shouted Rufra," a king will be made in that castle." He pointed his blade at Maniyadoc. "If you will take up a sword for the dream of a fair land and a good king, then I say . . ." He pulled the rein harder, and Balance screamed and reared. The light of Festival's fires flashed from his Conwy blade. "I say," he shouted again, "raise the bonemount and follow me! Raise the bonemount! Follow me now!" Then he slammed down his visor and the air filled with the thunder of heavy cavalry as he rode out to make his name famous.

King Rufra ap Vthyr

My brother.

My friend.

Epilogue

You will, of course, know a version of what happened next. Rufra stormed the castle and, if you believe common gossip, it was he who murdered Queen Adran and King Doran ap Mennix, though I swear it was not so.

My master and I left the lands of Maniyadoc, running from the ghosts of assassins we never saw but felt sure were always there. We would return, and when we did I found out a curious thing that makes me shiver whenever I think of that looming black castle. I spoke to a man who had been a slave. He was old, blind and free by then but what he told me had the ring of truth. He said that Maniyadoc had never had a priest of Xus.

That ancient castle is where I started along the road to adulthood and it would draw me back again and again, no matter what I wished. My name would never appear in the history books; I would never sit for a portrait and my actions would be known to only a few. Nonetheless, those actions would change the Tired Lands for ever.

Whether that was for good or ill? Well, I am still unsure.

I am old now, and when I look at the times I lived through – knowing what was to come for myself, my master and for Rufra – I ask myself, could I have acted any differently?

The answer?

Though I wish I could have saved Drusl, and fading memories of her face and a night spent together in the warm dark are all I have left of her. Though I know the strife and pain I would be put through. Though I know the price that would be paid in death, sorrow and betrayal. It is still always no. The Tired Lands are cruel, and much blood was spilt but, for a while, the tiredness was banished from Maniyadoc. It was a wonderful time – though far too short – and I am proud of the part I played in it.

When I think of Rufra ap Vthyr, I always think of him as young and full of hope, at that moment when I had given him his famous Conwy blade – his mount rearing, his shining sword aloft and his face alight with the thought of action.

We would meet again of course. And death, as it always was, would be the dog snapping at my heels.

So ends the first confession of the murderer, Girton Club-Foot.

Acknowledgements

Writing, though it's done alone, is not actually a very lonely business and I'm indebted to so many people that a comprehensive list would be longer than the book itself – so if you read through this list and think "I can't believe he forgot me!" then a) you probably know me well enough to work out it's rubbishness on my part and b) let me know; I'll put you in the next one.

So, on with it. First off, thanks to my agent, Ed "The Wilson" Wilson of Johnson and Alcock, for taking this (and me) on and letting me just write while he did all the boring stuff. You're a gent, Ed, and a pleasure to deal with. Thanks to everyone at Orbit and my editor, Jenni Hill, for helping me focus the thing down into something people will (hopefully) want to read and for not being scary and definitely not a miserabilist (it was always going to appear somewhere). I also owe a debt of gratitude to Rob Dinsdale whose advice on a previous project went, in no small way, to setting me up for this one. Micheala and Stephen Deas who gave me a leg up when it was much needed. As did Simon Spanton whose quiet and timely advice is, and has always been, welcome. And Mathilda Imlah, a long chat with whom about an entirely different book ended up being the genesis of *Age of Assassins*.

Then there's the people who read various versions and offered their ádvice and opinion on what worked and what didn't, so Fiona Pollard, Matt Broom (much goodminton, never badminton), Marcy Hindson, Aidan Williamson, Dylan

Godfrey, Alasdair Stuart and Dr Richard Clegg, thank you for your time, your positiveness and your patience with my constant questions.

Television and Radio's Dr Katherine Lewis, DOCTOR Simon Trafford, Dr Kate Vigurs and Dr Christopher Heath whose knowledge of history and willingness to chat about it provided much grist to the mill and actual bits of history for me to maul (all maulings are my own). You are all lovely, but you know that.

Then there's the people who have been such a help/ hindrance (I'm looking at you, Twitter) in many and various wonderful ways: Richard Palmer (have you actually read it yet?) Bernardo Velasquez, Maureen Kincaid-Speller, Jonathan McCalmont, Paul C. Smith, Eric Edwards, Tomoe Hill, Paul Watson, Gary Quinn, Lyndon Marquis, Sam Diegutis, Tom Parker, Hookland's very own David Southwell, (the award-winning) Ian "Spaceship" Sales, Rhys Wilcox, KT Davies, Helen Murphy, The Famous Author Susi Holliday, Kev McVeigh and Clare Bowey (for distracting my wife from my indolence). And all the others who keep me distracted on Twitter, it's much appreciated; I only wish I had more room here.

Jane, Deborah, Dr Linda Juby and all the staff at Bradford Royal Infirmary for doing a stirling job in keeping me alive to write things and, well, the entire NHS in doing a stirling job full stop.

Jason Arnopp, Scott K. Andrews, Kit Power, Andrew Freudenberg and Nazia Khatun for making my first ever con such a hilarious experience (thankyou xtra).

Music has always played a huge part in in everything I do and of particular effect on *Age of Assassins* were: The Afghan Whigs, Fields of the Nephilim/The Nefilim, Jay Munly, Slim Cessna's Auto Club, Reverend Glasseye, Black Moth, Purson and Blood Ceremony.

A whole host of authors have kept me going through the years and their work has fed back into everything I do so if you're reading this and have enjoyed the book you could do worse than look at any of the following: Richard Adams, Hilaire Belloc, Iain M. Banks, Agatha Christie, James Lee Burke, Alan Dean Foster, Robert Crais, John Connolly, Bernard Cornwell, Steve Mosby, Susanna Clarke, C. J. Sansom, Marlon James, William Hope-Hodgson and Patrick O'Brian.

Di and Bob Dark for letting your glorious daughter marry someone who didn't exactly have a real job at the time. Or any job. Their glorious daughter, Lindy, for always encouraging me to do this and never being anything but wonderful. Our son, Rook, who is a constant source of joy and amusement. My brother, John, for being my brother. Lastly, Mum and Dad, for always being there and instilling a love of words and a healthy curiosity in me. I guess that worked out.

And of course you, gentle reader. I hope you have enjoyed spending time with Girton as much as I have.

Oh, and, Mikko I-told-you-so Sovijarvi. Yes, yes, you did tell me so. And you were right. Don't get smug. No one likes a smug Finn.

Look out for

BLOOD OF ASSASSINS

Book Two of the Wounded Kingdom

by

RJ Barker

The assassin, Girton Club-Foot, is tired. After five long years away, hiding in the guise of a mercenary, Girton and his master have returned to Maniyadoc and the Long Tides in hope of finding sanctuary in the court of King Rufra.

But there is to be no rest, and death, as always, dogs Girton's heals. The place he knew no longer exists. War rages across Maniyadoc, intrigue creates sinister shadows in which true intentions are hidden and distrust is everywhere. Girton finds himself hurrying to uncover a plot to murder Rufra on what should be the day of the king's greatest victory. But while Girton is faced with threats from outside, he can't help wondering if his greatest enemy hides beneath his own skin.

orbit

www.orbitbooks.net

extras

orbit

www.orbitbooks.net

extras

about the author

RJ Barker lives in Leeds with his wife, son and a collection of questionable taxidermy, odd art, scary music and more books than they have room for. He grew up reading whatever he could get his hands on, and has always been 'that one with the book in his pocket'. Having played in a rock band before deciding he was a rubbish musician, RJ returned to his first love, fiction, to find he is rather better at that. As well as his debut epic fantasy novel, *Age of Assassins*, RJ has written short stories and historical scripts which have been performed across the country. He has the sort of flowing locks any cavalier would be proud of.

Find out more about RJ Barker and other Orbit authors by registering for the free monthly newsletter at www.orbitbooks.net.

interview

When did you first start writing? Have you always wanted to be an author?

I first started just after leaving school but was drawn away by guitars and loud music and spent a lot of time imagining I was going to be a rock star. Sadly, my almost complete lack of musical talent turned out to be more of a handicap than I'd imagined (fancy that, eh?) so I ended up not becoming a rock star, though I did have a tremendous amount of fun, which is what really matters. Then I sort of drifted back to what I'd always loved most – books and words – and the idea of doing something with them that I'd put aside in favour of a bass guitar. That was about thirteen years ago.

But, well, that leads neatly into the next question. . .

It's really refreshing to see a protagonist with a disability, what was your inspiration for Girton Club-foot?

Me! I was in the inspiration. At least six of the thirteen years were spent being really, really ill and nearly dying and all that other very boring stuff chronic illness involves. I have Crohn's disease and one of the symptoms is chronic joint pain. This can vary between being an annoying ache and being barely able to walk, but – and in this I am like most ill or disabled people – I just get on to the best of my ability. Girton is a (very) exaggerated version of this. He is not his disability; it is only a part of him. He does not let it stop or define him.

Can you tell us a little bit about your writing process?
Sit, write. Eat lots of crisps. I don't really have a process; it's just a thing I do. That I am always doing. Or thinking about doing. Or dreaming about doing.

What was the most challenging thing about writing this novel?
Copy-editing. I am, by nature, quite chaotic in everything I do and detail isn't one of my strengths. Having to sit and consider e v e r y s i n g l e co m m a was a new experence for me and really quite hard. In fact I may have gone slightly mad and did at one point dream a giant semi-colon was chasing me through our house.

Though, I must stress, it was also enjoyable, because new stuff is always good. I may have done the odd thing that, possibly, might be seen as idiosyncratic in the text, but now I know why and I have *really* thought about it. First-person writing, for me, is a journey through someone else's head and the copy-edit was about deciding on Girton's voice, which maybe isn't something you would worry about as much in a third-person piece of writing.

So, if the way I have written this book annoys you, you can rest assured that it was entirely deliberate on my part. You're welcome.

In the novel, Girton and his master have a unique and distinctive fighting style. Where did the idea for this come from?
I fenced for a bit, until illness forced me to give it up because

it became too painful to hold the sword, and that's in there. I wanted to bring in dance in as well, the idea that the assassins evolved from dancers. And pain management, the breathing techniques and idea of "becoming" something are a way of coping with pain – though for Girton this sort of "meditative" idea is applied to fear.

As to the rest, not entirely sure. I think it's come partly from a desire to produce a narrative effect as much as to produce a fighting style. I wanted the idea that Girton isn't really thinking about it. When he's in full flow (which you don't really see very much of in this book) I wanted the text to give you the idea he's reacting on a very instinctual level. The mix of italics and tenses in this passage:

> *First iteration: the Precise Steps.* Into the third iteration, the Maiden's Pass. I go under a blade, and my Conwy steel darts out, through the eye and into the brain. *Fourteenth iteration: the Carter's Surprise.* I spin hand over foot across the table and land behind the last guard. He turns, slashing at me with his blade. *Sixth iteration, a Meeting of Hands.* I block the downward swing of his longsword.

You get the moment. In the italics he's not consciously thinking. You get the starting point, *the Precise Steps*, then he thinks about the next move, the Maiden's Pass, that's conscious. And the move works and then he locks into it, into the muscle memory. It kind of, to me, slows the action and gives you this sense of flow, of a dancer linking together a set of moves that are second nature to them. In the book, Girton loses this: he's put into an unfamiliar situation and it unsettles him; he has to not be everything he is. And then he has to find it again and you get that gradual rebuilding of his skills as he comes to terms with this new world he's been pushed into.

Of course, I may just be being very pretentious. But that's the thought behind it anyway.

What do you think are the essential elements of epic storytelling?

I have no idea. I genuinely thought I'd written a whodunnit with a bit of swordfighting and magic in it.

Many fantasy writers have been influenced by myths and folklore from different cultural heritages. Is this something that resonates with you?

Yes, although it's mostly English folklore and some of the very early beliefs from Sumaria and the fertile crescent that's influenced me. There's also some bits of Austin Osman Spare and Crowley bobbing about.

I was especially interested in woods and land as a child and this came into being (and at quite a late date) as the hedgings. I did a piece of writing for a site called Minor Literatures with an artist called Paul Watson, who uses a lot of masks to play with the idea of spirits, and it definitely started something turning. Also, I'm fascinated by David Southwell's *Hookland Guide* which is an invented history of an England that could just have been.

And antlers. I've always had a bit of a thing about antlers. But who doesn't?

Do you have a favourite scene in *Age of Assassins*? If so, why?

Yeah, a couple. Scene-wise it's probably when he gives Rufra his sword. It's never said, but all the way through Girton is quite lonely, really, and then you have this final confirmation of the friendship he's longed for – they both have – in a physical gift. And of course, swords have always been powerful mythic symbols. But, and this is cheating as it's not really a scene, I also really like Girton's gradual realisation that his master is a person in her own right, as fragile and flawed as anyone else, not a superhero.

And Xus, the mount. I love Xus the mount.

When you aren't writing, what do you like to do in your spare time?
Read. Daydream. Play games. Do family stuff (my son and I are currently working our way through *Star Wars: Rebels*). Search antique shops for particularly weird taxidermy with my wife. Buy extravagant clothes. Play badminton really badly.

Are you mainly a fantasy reader, or are there other genres that you're partial to?
I have read a lot of fantasy but don't tend to at the moment. Partly because I'm writing it and have a terror of unconsciously ripping people off and partly because I think if you're coming to a party you should probably bring something, so I try and read more in other genres. I've always been a huge crime fan and I love history (Queen Adran came out of research on Margaret of Anjou I was doing for something else) and SF. To be honest, I'll read anything but have a rather Dirk Gently approach and base my reading on what I've randomly come across rather than any particular allegiance to a genre. (And that, dear reader, is how I once ended up reading *Flowers in the Attic* by V. C. Andrews, so you don't have to.)

Actually, it's not been asked, but I'd say music is just as big an influence on what and how I write as books are.

Without giving too much away, can you tell us a bit about what can we expect from the next novel in the series?
To save the king, kill the king.

That was cryptic wasn't it?

I suspect Orbit might want a bit more of hook.

Okay. More murder. Girton, in full flow, the opportunity to see mounts in action. More antlers. Big battles, betrayal, intrigue and redemption.

if you enjoyed
AGE OF ASSASSINS

look out for

SKYBORN

by

David Dalglish

*The last remnants of humanity live on six islands floating high
above the Endless Ocean, fighting a brutal civil war in the skies.
The Seraphim, elite soldiers trained for aerial combat, battle one
another while wielding elements of ice, fire and lightening.*

*The lives of their parents claimed in combat, twins Kael and
Breanna Skyborn enter the Seraphim Academy to follow in
their footsteps. They will learn to harness the elements as
weapons and fight at break-neck speeds while soaring high
above the waters. But they must learn quickly, for a nearby
island has set its hungry eyes on their home. When the invasion
comes, the twins must don their wings and ready their blades to
save those they love from annihilation.*

PROLOGUE

Breanna Skyborn sat at the edge of her world, watching the clouds drift beneath her dangling feet.

"Bree?"

Kael's voice sounded obscenely loud in the twilight quiet. She turned to see her twin brother standing at the stone barricade that marked the end of the road.

"Over here," she said.

The barricade reached up to Kael's waist, and after a moment's hesitation, he climbed over, leaving behind smoothly worn cobbles for short grass and soft dirt. Beyond the barricade, there was nothing else. No buildings. No streets. No homes. Just a stretch of unused earth, and then beyond that . . . the edge. It was for that reason Bree loved it, and her brother hated it.

"We're not allowed to be this close," he said as he approached, each step smaller than the last. "If Aunt Bethy saw . . ."

"Aunt Bethy won't come within twenty feet of the barricade and you know it."

Wind blew against her, and she pulled her dark hair back from her face as she smirked at her brother. His pale skin had taken on a golden hue from the fading sunlight, the wind teasing his much shorter hair. The gust made him stop, and she worried he'd decide to leave her there.

"You're not afraid, are you?" she asked.

That was enough to push him on. Kael joined her at the edge of their island. When he sat, he sat cross-legged, and unlike her, he did not let his legs dangle off the side.

"Just for a little while," he said. "We should be home when the battle starts."

Bree turned away, and she peered over the edge of the island. Below, lazily floating along, were dozens of puffy clouds painted orange by the setting sun. Through their gaps she saw the tumultuous Endless Ocean, its movement only hinted at by the faintest of dark lines. Again the wind blew, and she pretended that she rode upon it, flying just like her parents.

"So why are we out here?" Kael asked, interrupting the silence.

"I was hoping to see the stars."

"Is that it? We're just here to waste our time?"

Bree glared at him.

"You've seen the drawings in Teacher Gruden's books. The stars are beautiful. I was hoping that out here, away from the lanterns, maybe I could see one or two before . . ."

She fell silent. Kael let out a sigh.

"Is that really why you're out here?"

It wasn't, not fully, but she didn't feel comfortable discussing the other reason. Hours ago their mother and father had sat them down beside the fire of their home. They'd each worn the black uniforms of their island of Weshern, swords dangling from their hips, the silver wings attached to their harnesses polished to a shine.

The island of Galen won't back down, so we have no choice, their father had said. *We've agreed to a battle come the midnight fire. This will be the last, I promise. After this, they won't have the heart for another.*

"It is," Bree said, wishing her half lie were more convincing. She looked to their right, where the sun was slipping beneath the horizon. Nightfall wouldn't be long now. Kael shifted uncomfortably, and she saw him glancing behind them, as if convinced they'd be caught despite being in a secluded corner of their small town of Lowville.

"Fine," he said. "I'll stay with you, but if we get in trouble, this was all your idea."

"It usually is," she said, smiling at him.

Kael settled back, sliding a bit farther away from the edge. Together they watched the sun slowly set. In its glow, they caught glimpses of two figures flying through the twilight haze, their mechanical wings shimmering gold as they hovered above a great stretch of green farmland. The men wore red robes along with their wings, easily identifying them as theotechs of Center.

"Why are they here?" Kael asked when he spotted them.

"They're here to oversee the battle," Bree answered. She'd spent countless nights on her father's lap, asking him questions. What was it like to fly? Was he ever scared when they fought? Did he think she might become a member of the Seraphim like they were? Bree knew the two theotechs would bless the battle, ensure everyone followed the agreed-upon rules, and then mark the surrender of the loser. Then would come the vultures, the lowest-ranking members of the theotechs, to reclaim the treasured technology from the fallen.

The mention of the coming battle put Kael on edge, and he fell silent as he looked to the sunset. Bree couldn't blame him for his nervousness. She felt it, too, and that was the reason she couldn't stay home, cooped up, unable to witness the battle or know if her mother and father lived or died. No, she had to be out there. She had to have something to occupy her mind.

They said nothing as the sun neared the end of its descent. As the strength of its rays weakened, she turned her attention to the east, where the sky had faded to a deep shade of purple. The coming darkness unsettled Bree. Since the day she was born, it had come and gone, but it was rare for her to watch it. She much preferred to be at home next to the hearth, listening to her father tell Seraphim stories, or their mother reading Kael ancient tales of knights and angels. Watching the nightly shadow only made her feel . . . imprisoned.

It began where the light was at its absolute weakest, an inky black line on the horizon that grew like a cloud. Slowly it crawled, thick as smoke and wide as the horizon itself. The darkness swept over the sky, hiding its many colors. More and more it covered, an unceasing march matched by the sun's fall. When it reached to the faintly visible moon, it too vanished, the pale crescent tucked away, to be hidden until the following night. Silently the twins watched as the rolling darkness passed high above their heads, blotting out everything, encasing the world in its deep shadow.

Bree turned her attention to the setting sun, which looked as if it fled in fear of the darkness complete.

"It'll be right there," she said, pointing. "In the moment after the sun sets and before the darkness reaches it."

Most of the sky was gone now, and so far away from the lanterns, the two sat in a darkness so complete it was frightening. The shadow clouds continued rolling, blotting out the field of stars that the ancient drawing books made look so beautiful, so majestic and grand. But just as she'd hoped, there was a gap in the time it took the sun to vanish beyond the horizon and for the rolling shadow to reach it, and she watched with growing anticipation. She'd seen only one star before, the North Star, which shone so brightly that not even the sun could always blot it out. But the other stars, the great field . . . would they appear in the deepening purple?

Kael saw it before she did, and he quickly pointed. In the sliver of violet space the star winked into existence, a little drop of light between the horizon and the shadows crashing down on it like a wave. Bree saw it, and she smiled at the sight.

"Imagine not one but thousands," Bree said as the dark clouds swallowed the star, pitching the entire city into utter darkness so deep she could not see her brother beside her.

"A field spanning the entire sky, lighting up the night in their glow . . ."

Bree felt Kael take her hand, and she squeezed it tight. Neither dared move while so close to the edge and lacking sight. Perfectly still, they waited. It would only be a matter of time.

It started as a faint flicker of red across the eastern horizon. Slowly it grew, spreading, strengthening. Just like the shadows, so too did the fire roll across the sky, setting ablaze the inky clouds that covered the crown of the world. It burned without consuming, only shifting and twisting. It took thirty minutes, but eventually all of the sky raged with midnight fire, bathing the land in red. It'd last until daybreak, when the sun would rise, the fire would die, and the smoky remnants would hover over the morning sky until fading away.

A horn sounded from a watchtower farther within their home island of Weshern. The blast set Bree's heart to hammering.

"They're starting," she whispered.

Both turned to face the field where the two theotechs hovered. The horn sounded thrice more, and come the final call, the forces of Weshern arrived. They sailed above the field in *V* formations, their silver wings shimmering, powered by the light element that granted all Seraphim mastery over the skies. Hundreds of men and women, dressed in black pants and jackets, armed with fire, lightning, ice, and stone that they wielded with the gauntlets of their ancient technology. Despite her fear, Bree felt an intense longing to be up there with them, fighting for the pride and safety of her home. Sadly, it'd be five years before she and her brother turned sixteen and could attempt to join.

"Bree . . ."

She turned her head, saw her brother staring off into the open sky beyond the edge of their island. Flying in similar *V* formations, gold wings glimmering, red jackets seemingly

aflame from the light of the midnight fire, came the Seraphim
of Galen. The two armies raced toward each other, and Bree
knew they'd meet just above the fallow field, where the
theotechs waited.

Bree pushed herself away from the edge of the island and
rose to her feet, her brother doing likewise.

"They'll be fine," she said, watching the Weshern Seraphim
fly in perfect formation. She wondered which of those black
and silver shapes was her mother, and which her father.
"You'll see. No one's better than they are."

Kael stood beside her, eyes on the sky, arms locked at his
sides. Bree reached for his hand, held it as the armies neared
one another.

"It'll be over quick," she whispered. "Father says it always
is."

Dark shapes shot in both directions through the space
between the armies, large chunks of stone meant to screen
attacks as well as protect against retaliation. They crashed
into one another, and as the sound reached Bree's ears, the
battle suddenly erupted into bewildering chaos. The Seraphim
formations danced about one another, lightning flashing amid
them in constant barrages. Enormous blasts of fire accompanied them, difficult to see with the sky itself aflame. Blue
lances of ice, colored purple from the midnight hue, shot in
rapid bursts, cutting down combatants with ease. The sounds
of battle were so powerful, so near, Bree could feel them in
her bones.

"How?" Kael wondered aloud, and if he weren't so close
she wouldn't have heard him over the cacophony. "How can
anyone survive through that?"

Boulders of stone slammed into the fallow field beneath,
carving out long grooves of earth before coming to a stop.
Bree flinched at the impact of each one. How did one survive?
She didn't know, but somehow they did, the Seraphim of
both islands weaving amid the carnage with movements so

fluid and beautiful they mirrored that of dancers. Not all, though. Lightning tore through chests, lances of ice with sharp tips punctured flesh and metal alike, and no armor could protect against the fire that washed over their bodies. Each Seraph who fell wearing a black jacket made Bree silently beg it wasn't one of her parents. She didn't care if that was selfish or not. She just wanted them safe. She wanted them to survive the overwhelming onslaught that left her mind baffled by how to take it all in.

The elements lessened, the initial devastating barrage becoming more precise, more controlled. Bree saw that several combatants were out of elements completely and forced to draw their blades. The battle had gradually spread farther and farther out, taking them beyond the grand field and closer to the edge of town where Bree and Kael stood. Not far above their heads, two Seraphim circled in a dance, one fleeing, one chasing. They both had their twin blades drawn. Bree watched, entranced, eyes wide as the circle tightened and the combatants whisked by each other again and again, slender blades swiping for exposed flesh.

It was the Galen Seraph who made the first mistake. Bree saw him fail to dodge in time, saw the tip of the sword slice across his stomach. The body fell, careening wildly just before making impact with the ground. The sound was a bloodcurdling screech of metal and snapping bone. Bree's attention turned to the larger battle, and she saw that more had been forced to draw their blades. The number of remaining Seraphim was shockingly few, yet they fought on. "No one's surrendering," Kael said, and she could hear the fear threatening to overtake him completely. "Bree, you said it'd be quick. You said it'd be quick!"

The area of battle was spreading out of control. Galen Seraphim scattered in all directions, loose formations of two to three people. The Weshern Seraphim chased, and despite nearing town, they still released their elements. Bree screamed as a pair streaked above their heads, the thrum of their wings nearly deafening. A boulder failed to connect with the fleeing Seraphim, and it blasted through the side of a home with a thundering blast.

"Let's go!" Bree screamed, grabbing Kael's hand and dashing toward the barricade. More Seraphim were approaching, seemingly the entire Galen forces. They wanted to be over the town, Bree realized. They wanted to make Weshern's people hesitate to fight with so many nearby. As the twins climbed over the stone barricade, the sounds of battle erupting all about them, it was clear their Seraphim would have no such hesitation. Lightning flashed above Bree's head, and she cried out in surprise. She ducked, stumbled, lost her grip on her brother's hand. He stopped, shouted her name, and then the ice lance struck the cobbles ahead of them. It shattered into shards, and Kael dove to the ground as they flew in all directions.

"Kael," Bree said as she scrambled to her feet. "Kael!"

"I'm fine," he said, pushing himself to his hands and knees. When he looked to her, he was bleeding from several cuts across his face and neck. "I'm fine, now hurry!"

The red light of the midnight fire cast its hue across everything, convincing Bree she'd lost herself in a nightmare and awoken in one of the circles of Hell. Kael pulled her along, leading her toward Aunt Bethy's house, where they were supposed to have stayed during the battle, waiting like good children for their parents to return. Hand in hand they ran, the air above filled with screams, echoes of thunder, and the deep hum of the Seraphims' wings.

They turned a corner, saw two Seraphs flying straight at them from farther down the street. Fire burst from the chaser's gauntlet. It bathed over the other, sending her crashing to the ground. Kael dove aside as Bree froze, her legs locked in place from terror. The body came to a halt mere feet away from her, silver wings mangled and broken. Her black jacket bore the blue sword of Weshern on her shoulder, and Bree shuddered at the sight of the woman's horrible burns. High above, the Galen Seraph flew on, seeking new prey.

"Bree!" her brother shouted, pulling her attention away. He'd wedged himself in the tight space between two houses, and she joined him there in hiding.

"We have to get back," Bree insisted. "We can't stay here."

"Yes, we can," Kael said, hunkering deeper into the alley. "I'm not going out there, Bree. I'm not."

Bree glanced back out of the narrow alley. With the battle raging above the town, Aunt Bethy would be terrified by their absence. They were already going to be in trouble for not coming in like they were supposed to in the first place. To hide now, afraid, until it all ended?

"I'm going," she said. "Are you coming with me or not?"

Another blast of thunder above. Kael shook his head.

"No," he said. His eyes widened when he realized she was serious about going. "Bree, don't leave me here. Don't leave me!"

"I can't stay," Bree said, the mantra overwhelming her every thought. "I can't stay, Kael, I can't stay!"

She dashed back into the street, racing toward Aunt Bethy's house. As strongly as Kael wanted to remain hiding, Bree wanted to return to their aunt's home. She wanted to be inside, in a safe place with family. Let him be a coward. She'd be brave. She'd be strong.

A boulder crashed through the rooftop of a home to her right then blasted out the front wall. Bree screamed, and she realized she wasn't brave at all. She was frightened out of her mind. Fighting back tears, she turned down Picker Street, where both they and their aunt lived. Five houses down was her aunt's home, and Bree's heart took a sudden leap. Her legs moved as fast as they could carry her.

There she was. Her mother was safe, she was alive, she was . . . She was bleeding. Her hand clutched her stomach, and Bree saw with horrible clarity the red gash her fingers failed to seal. She lay on her back, her silver wings pressed against the door to Aunt Bethy's home, a dazed look on her face. Beneath her was a pool of her own blood.

"Bree," her mother said. Her voice was wet, strained. Tears trickled from her brown eyes. "Bree, what are you . . . what are you doing out here?"

Bree didn't know how to answer. She fell to her knees, felt her pants slicken from the blood. She reached out a trembling hand, wanting so badly to hold her mother, but feared what any contact might do.

"It's all right," her mother said, and she smiled despite her obvious pain. "Bree, it's all right. It's . . ."

Her lips grew still. She breathed in pain no more. Her hand fell limp, holding back her sliced stomach no longer. Bree touched her shoulder, shook her once.

"Mom," she said, tears rolling down her cheeks. "Mom, no, Mom, please!"

She buried her face against her mother's chest, shrieking out in wordless agony. She didn't want to see any more, to hear any more. Bree wrapped her arms around her mother's neck, clutching her tightly, not caring about the blood that seeped into her clothes. She just wanted one more embrace before the vultures came to reclaim her wings. She wanted to pretend her mother was alive and well, holding her, loving her, kissing her forehead before flying away for another day of training and drills.

Not this corpse. Not this lifeless thing.

A hand touched her shoulder. Bree pulled back, expecting to see her brother, but instead it was a tall Weshern Seraph. Blood smeared his fine black coat. To her surprise, the surrounding neighborhood was quiet, the battle seemingly over.

"Was she your mother?" the man asked. Bree could barely see his face through the shadows cast by the midnight fire. She sniffled, then nodded.

"Then you must be Breanna. I—I don't know how else to tell you this. It's about your father."

His words were a dagger to an already punctured heart. It couldn't be. The world couldn't be that cruel.

"No," she whispered. "No, that can't be right."

The Seraph swallowed hard.

"Breanna, I'm sorry."

Bree leapt to her feet, and she flung herself at the man, screaming at the top of her lungs.

"No, it can't. Not both, we can't lose them both, we can't . . . we can't . . ."

She broke, collapsing at his feet, her tears falling upon his black boots. She beat the stone cobbles until she bled, beat them as she screamed, beat them as, high above, the midnight fire burned like an unrelenting pyre for the dead.